MORTUARY MANSION

Richard Johnson

Matchstick Literary
1-888-306-8885
orders@matchliterary.com

~ *Chapter One* ~

A CHANGE OF RESIDENCE

If only I had known what problems were awaiting my wife and me, I would never have agreed to buy that dismal, and depressing old house. First impressions have always been important to me, and I should have acted upon the sense of melancholy and morbid gloom that overcame me when I first set my eyes on that place. I agreed to buy the house to please my wife Elaine who was bound and determined to have her way. Looking back in time, it seems so very long ago, but in reality, it began but a few short months ago.

A sequence of disturbing discoveries and other upsetting events had their beginnings on an early Sunday morning last spring when I had finished with my breakfast, laid my morning newspaper aside, and gazed out the kitchen window. I watched as a bank of snow-white clouds went skidding across the azure-blue sky almost as if they were racing with one another. That would have been a great day for me to enjoy some much-needed rest, but unfortunately, that was not what Elaine had in mind for me.

Another busy week at the office had left me fatigued, and finishing up the yard work yesterday had physically almost done me in. I felt I deserved some time for myself; however, Elaine's plans for me did not include my lounging around the house that morning. I would have loved to have gone back to bed and pulled the covers over my head and taken another forty more winks of sleep, but instead, I decided that I had better get myself moving or there would be no peace around the house this day. When my darling wife Elaine makes up her mind to do something, it seems there is just no possibility of swaying her!

For the past several months, Elaine had practically been driving me crazy about our finding another house for us to buy. Ever since our two boys grew up and got married, Elaine had been after me to buy an older home in the suburbs. Luckily for me, she had been willing to scout along with a real estate agent while previewing a variety of older and larger houses which saved me the trouble. Finally, when I found myself in a weak moment, I had promised Elaine that I would accompany her to look at a Victorian mansion Elaine had seen and liked. For the life of me, I just could not possibly imagine that she would ever be happy living in an old house after having lived for many years in a modern home with practically every comfort and convenience possible. The upkeep of an older house like Elaine was dead set on us buying, could probably bankrupt us, and if nothing else, my Sunday cookouts would come to an end for me to keep up with the house and the yard work.

Before I delve any deeper into this story, I want first to introduce myself to the reader. My name is Rick Braden, and I am a forty-eight-year-old accountant who has been employed by the Raymond Bennett Engineering Company since I completed college. It is not a particularly exciting job, but the pay is good, and it has provided steady employment for me since I began working there.

My wife Elaine is working part-time as a sales clerk in a woman's high-fashion apparel shop at a nearby shopping mall. Soon after our two boys left home and went off on their own, Elaine insisted on going to work. She told me it was not for the money, but it was more to keep herself busily involved. She further told me that she was lonely during the daytime hours with our boys no longer at home and while I was at my office. I did not like the idea of her working, but with it only being a part-time position, it did not seem to present any problem for either of us.

Elaine and I have enjoyed a loving relationship with a happy and contented marriage for more than 25 years. Thankfully, we both like many of the same things, such as music, reading books, playing bridge with friends, and watching our favorite television shows in the evenings. While Elaine was in college, she studied architecture and interior design, but she never got to pursue either of those fields after she graduated because she and I were married within a week of her graduation.

We have been blessed with two fine boys who have both completed their higher educations, and Elaine and I are very proud of that fact because it was not always easy for us financially, but we still managed. We often have the two of them along with their wives, visit our house for Sunday dinners; that is, except for this weekend.

Ronald, who is our oldest boy, is an accountant like I am. He and his wife Paula have a four-year-old son named Henry. Our youngest son Glenn is pursuing his career as a graphic designer, working for a major advertising agency in Bradenton. He and his wife Martha have no children yet, but they hope to change that situation sometime soon.

At our family weekend social gatherings, we often cook outside in our backyard whenever weather permits us to do so; otherwise, my wife Elaine will do all of the cooking in her kitchen. I like our outdoor cookouts the best because that is when I get to demonstrate my culinary skills while using our new barbecue grill with its electric spit. I thought I would be cooking baby back-ribs this Sunday, so I made it a point to buy two racks of them at my favorite butcher shop located close to my office.

The plan for our outdoor barbeque had been set by us for more than weeks, but this morning before our breakfast Elaine had me agree to look at a prospective property instead of our cookout. Elaine's house hunt had been going on for so long that it was finally beginning to get her down, so I did not want to disappoint her by refusing to go with her to look at a house which she seemed quite excited over.

"It's just perfect!" That was Elaine's highly excited description of the place after she arrived home a couple of days ago after having seen it with her Realtor? "I promise you that you will like it as much as I do, Rick!" Elaine said a bit breathlessly. "We have an appointment on Sunday morning for the two of us to take a look at it along with the real estate agent." I was hooked! There was nothing I could have done other than to agree with Elaine and go with the two ladies and check out the property.

I suppose I am nothing more than a creature of habit, at least that is what Elaine often tells me. The appointment for us to see the house would be disruptive to my regular weekend plans, and that did not make me any too happy. It seemed that Elaine had also taken it upon herself to call our boys and tell them not to come on Sunday. If the truth is known, they were probably happy about the change in those plans because I sometimes think their wives have had enough of our weekend cookout routine. Elaine has been having a hard time adjusting to the change in her life from being a full-time mother, but one would think she would be used to it by this time since both boys were away at college before they were married.

When Sunday morning rolled around, I was just finishing the last gulp of my warm coffee when the doorbell chimed. It was the real estate agent, and she was right on time. Elaine introduced her to me as we locked the door to the house behind us. Pat Driscoll was a middle-aged, rather plump woman, with long, bleached-blonde hair. Under her arm she carried a thick book of real estate listings, and I could clearly see a number of page markers sticking out of it. I moaned to myself as I wondered how many other houses she planned to show us in addition to the one Elaine was so set on seeing again. After Elaine and I got comfortably settled into the back seat of Mrs. Driscoll's late model, Lincoln Town Car, we were on our way.

"May I ask where we are going?" I asked casually.

"Forest Oak," Mrs. Driscoll replied.

"I think that suburb is located pretty far from the Bradenton business district where I work," I said.

Before Mrs. Driscoll responded to my comment, Elaine took my hand in hers, gave it a soft squeeze and said affectionately "It's not all that far from your office Rick, and the house and lot looks to be just perfect for us. You'll see when we get there, and I'm guessing you'll love it! It has a large back yard with huge oak trees, so it will be an ideal setting for your usual Sunday afternoon cookouts." Immediately after having said that Elaine ended further conversation with me and she turned her head toward the window on her side of the car. I was a bit agitated by her dismissing the subject in that manner, and by abruptly cutting short any further comments from me.

"I guess that's all you care to say about it now, Elaine, but maybe later we can talk about it again."

Elaine again made it clear to me she wanted no further conversation on that subject as she again turned her head toward the car's window.

I had known for a long time that Elaine was interested in our buying an older house like the one we were heading to because she wanted a place she could completely renovate. Since she graduated from college, Elaine never had the opportunity to use any of her college training or decorating skills, and now that our children are raised and living on their own, this would be her last opportunity to fulfil that desire. It was something she'd talked about to me for the past twenty-five years. In spite of my own misgivings about, I knew I would go along with her program, but only to a reasonable degree.

I had no intention of stretching our funds beyond our ability to keep up our savings program for my retirement since I had less than sixteen remaining years to work until I planned to retire. The passing years have taught me that time flies by pretty darn fast, and because of that, I knew that we must look ahead and be prepared. Elaine and I had thoroughly talked about that aspect of our future when we discussed our buying another house, and at that time Elaine had been in total agreement with me. Since the marketing value of our present property had appreciated beyond our expectations, we hoped to be able to make this house exchange almost a lateral move for us financially. Of course, the greatest expense that would be facing us would be the cost of remodeling and redecorating an older house. After 25 years of use in our present home, most of our original furniture is ready to be replaced with brand-new, more modern-styled furniture. I was fast becoming a bit worried that Elaine's extensive remodeling plans might not fit neatly into our budget.

There was another troubling thought that began to nag at me as we drove along toward our destination. That was the idea of our moving into an older suburb like Forest Oak. The residential area where we have lived for all of the years since we were married is a relatively young development, and everything that we may need or want is within a large shopping center within easy walking distance from our house. For the last few years, Elaine has been working part-time there in a woman's fashion shop. With those disturbing kinds of thoughts occupying my mind, I decided to pose the question to Elaine.

"Of all the lovely suburbs for us to choose from, Elaine, why would we want to settle for a home in Forest Oak? That community is the same today as it was a hundred or more years ago, and to my knowledge, there is not even a shopping mall anywhere within its limits. We will have to travel all the way back to Bradenton to do our shopping. The only entertainment that is available in Forest Oak that I know of is a small movie house which probably shows nothing but old westerns on Saturday nights. I suppose even the television reception will be bad, and we will be forced to buy one of those giant, directional TV dishes for the roof or a post in our front yard. And, not that it is at all important to me, Elaine, but you know that you will have to give up your part-time job at the mall. Have you thought about any of those things I just mentioned to you?"

I had purposely asked Elaine those questions because I finally realized that I should have taken the time and the energy to go with her during her house hunts, rather than having relegated that job entirely to her. If I had done that, perhaps I would not now be heading to Forest Oak to decide upon our buying an old house located in a turn of the eighteenth century town.

"Which one of your questions do you want me to answer first, Rick?" Elaine asked in a voice tinged with sarcasm.

"Oh, forget about it!" I said. "We can discuss some of those things after we have seen the house." I mumbled those words under my breath with a feeling of impending defeat.

The drive from our house to Forest Oak took us about an hour or so and rather than head there directly toward the center of the town, Mrs. Driscoll decided to drive the scenic route through the countryside. During our drive, I half-listened as Elaine and Mrs. Driscoll chatted about a lot of meaningless trivia, while outside of the car the sunshine bathed the landscape in a silvery hue as we breezed steadily along. On both sides of the tarmac, I could spot farmers working their newly-plowed fields, while everywhere I glimpsed groups of cows grazing in the shade under the trees. At one point along the way, I saw a shiny black stallion freely galloping across an open field of lush, green grass. I supposed that people who are raised in the big city would eventually become used to that kind of lifestyle, and for Elaine's sake I would try to be a little more positive about my attitude, but I would still think very carefully before agreeing to buy an old mansion in an aged Victorian suburb like Forest Oak.

While we were slowly driving through the small, downtown section of the city of Forest Oak, I was surprised to see that their movie theater had been turned into a VFW hall. Farther along near the corner of the main intersection, was a newly opened Hookway Drug Store with a bright Grand Opening banner still hanging across the front windows. The many pickup trucks in town were all parked diagonally in front of a quaint little business area with a sign on one building that read Belamy's Family Restaurant. I imagined that the breakfast counter would be lined up with farmers who worked their fields nearby. I could almost visualize them dressed in their blue denim bib overalls, with their red-and-white polka-dot hankies sticking from their hip pockets. I have always known that farmers are friendly people, but I worried that I could never be able to fit into this lifestyle comfortably, and that thought was very disquieting to me. Elaine looked at me and seemed to sense my uneasy feelings because at that moment she took my hand in hers and gave it a firm, reassuring squeeze.

Upon our leaving the business center of the town, we drove along a grassy embankment alongside a railroad right-of-way. Before our arrival at the rail crossing, the gates started to close, bells began clanging, and red signals were flashing. Mrs. Driscoll slowed her car down to a complete stop, and we sat and waited there while we looked out at the beautiful and serene countryside.

In less than a minute or two, we watched as a big, Diesel locomotive pulling a long string of boxcars, appeared down the track from out of the distance. Almost as soon as the train appeared in front of us it passed us by with its haul of boxcars. We then watched as it lurched its way down the track until it finally faded off somewhere in the distance.

As soon as the railroad crossing gates lifted, Mrs. Driscoll drove her car very slowly and carefully over the rough set of tracks, and we continued on our way. Within several more minutes, we entered an attractive paving-stone, lane. Along each side of its grassy parkways was a row of stately oak trees.

"What a picturesque setting!" I said to Elaine as I reached over to her and took her hand in mine. As we continued slowly driving, I noticed several very large, wooden mansions built in the style that had been popular in the mid-to-late 1800s. That was at a time when there was plenty of cheap lumber available to build houses, and the cost of labor to construct them was rather low. The cost of heating those large homes was also not a deciding factor in those days when coal was plentiful and cheap. I cringed when I thought about the expense of heating and cooling a home of that size today.

The mansions along both sides of Cobblestone Lane were set well back from the street, and they were framed by oak trees that shaded the neatly-groomed lawns. At the entryway to several driveways, I could see brightly-painted, iron horse-hitch relics from the bygone days when horses and carriages were fashionable, and a time before automobiles replaced them. A few of the properties had separate buildings behind them, and I guessed they had probably been servant quarters, or possibly fancy horse barns. Most of them had long since been converted to garages to house the owners' automobiles.

It was quite easy for me to visualize a team of horses hooked up to a fashionable carriage, or a lone horse pulling a spindly surrey prancing along. With a bit more imagination, I could almost hear them galloping over the street in front of us. What a perfectly quaint setting this is, I thought. It's no wonder that Elaine likes it here so very much. It's certainly much different from the area where we now live with the tiny residential lots, asphalt streets, small driveways, and much smaller and more modern, homes.

"What you both are now looking at once was the Gold Coast Section of Forest Oak," Pat Driscoll said to me and Elaine over her shoulder. Her comment immediately disturbed my previous train of thought as she pointed a well-manicured finger toward a very large and ugly, brownstone mansion on our right. "That place was where Governor Augustus Weedan was born--in that house right there."

"Which of our governors are you speaking of," I asked never having heard that name before, "and what year might that have been, Mrs. Driscoll?"

"Oh, from what little I read about it, he lived in this part of town late into the last century, about 1882 or 1883 or so. His father Thomas Weedan built the house. There were quite a few prominent families who owned homes in this neighborhood over the years. Forest Oak's Historical Society has an entire section that contains some interesting old photographs, as well as a variety of other information about members of those families. It may well be worth your time to stop in there and read about them sometime. That's if you have an interest in Forest Oak's local history."

"We may decide to do just that, Mrs. Driscoll," I answered in a disinterested manner.

In a matter of minutes, Mrs. Driscoll brought her car to a stop in front of a large, red brick house half-hidden in a high-fenced lot heavily overgrown with a maze of thick shrubs, and several mature oak trees. The six-foot-high wrought-iron, spear-topped fence was crawling with vines which obscured part of the house from our view. Looking up through the side glass of the car's window, I could see the dark, multicolored slate roof tiles that capped the building, and an octagonal turret that made up the third level of the house. From the top of its main roof, I could see several tall, red brick chimneys jutting upwards toward the sky. At the back of the yard was a horse barn with three bays, which I guessed were now used to store cars. While looking at the property, I could not help but think that the house and its setting were a somewhat disturbing sight right out of an old spook movie, and I felt a chill ran all the way through me at that very moment!

"Well! What do you think? Isn't it a lovely house?" Mrs. Driscoll asked as she half-turned in her seat to look at my reaction.

Before I could respond to her, Elaine answered for me.

"It has terrific possibilities, Pat, but I would not exactly call it a darling house, not at this time anyway. If Rick and I decide to buy it, you can tell me that sometime next year after we finish renovating both the interior and exterior. The yard is also a mess, but Rick is very handy with gardening, and he could change it into something of a botanical garden."

"Are you serious about our buying this place, Elaine?" I asked in an incredulous voice as I turned and looked at her. "If the interior of the house is only half as bad as the outside, I can tell you right now that I hate it!" I had no sooner spoken those unkind words to Elaine when I regretted it.

Elaine pushed herself closer toward me in the car's seat with a wounded look on her face as she spoke. "Please, Rick, I am asking you not to jump to any conclusions until you have seen inside of the house. I know it will take a lot of hard work to get the outside in shape, but that's what I want you and me to do. As for the yard, I am sure our boys will be more than willing to help you with whatever needs to be done. You will also be quite surprised at what a good cleaning and a fresh coat of paint will do to spruce up the exterior of the main building and the garage to make them bright and cheerful again."

"All right! All right!" I responded feeling somewhat defeated. "I am willing to keep an open mind on the matter. I would like us now to get out of the car and check the house inside." I opened my side of the car just as Pat Driscoll got out, and the three of us walked over to the yard's entry gate, which was locked with a heavy chain and a padlock. Pat pulled a key from her purse, opened the lock and then removed the chain. As she pushed the iron gate open, it made a loud squeaking sound which caused the three of us to laugh, and that helped to ease the tension that had been building up between Elaine and me since my first sight of the house.

Proceeding directly to the steps leading to the front porch landing, we approached a double set of ornate leaded-glass doors. Centered in each door was a coat of arms made of various sized pieces of colored leaded glass. Inside each was a prancing gray stallion wearing a silver knight's helmet with a black feather on top. The horses were covered with a black cloak with a gold dagger pointing downward. Under each stallion was a white scroll with the name Burns in bright golden letters.

According to Mrs. Driscoll, Burns was the man who had built the house back in the year 1886. She then said she didn't have more to tell us about the previous owner, saying she knew only that much because it was part of the real estate background in the county recorder's office at the time she did the title search.

After retrieving a key from her purse, Mrs. Driscoll opened one of the front doors for us to go inside. The first thing that captured our attention as we entered was a large staircase about twenty feet in front of us. It curved much like that of a cornucopia which seemed to draw us toward the dark shadows of its upper reaches. A deep and dark purple carpeting began at the bottom, the stairway and wound its way upward to a higher level. Directly overhead in the foyer, hung a heavily-tarnished, antique brass chandelier with a dozen or more candelabrum-styled lights.

The entryway's floor was of a greenish looking gray slate, terminating where the carpeting of the stairway began. On either side of the foyer stood tall, oak curio cabinets with leaded-glass doors. Both were empty except for a thin layer of gray dust which blanketed the shelves. I was guessing the thick moldings along the ceilings, door frames, and mantels would all need to be stripped and revarnished because the near-black varnish was checkered with age making the room very dark and unappealing. As I stood there surveying the scene, I mentally tabulated all the work and cost in just this small part of the house acceptable for me, while I winced at the thought of what the rest of it would require us to have to spend.

Within a minute or two, Pat Driscoll's voice broke the silence. "Since Elaine's been here before, Mr. Braden, I think it would be a good idea to have her escort you thru the building. I will wait for you two in the living room if you don't mind. Now, if either of you has any questions at all, please give me a holler."

"Thanks, Pat!" Elaine said as she took my hand in hers and slowly began to lead me through a long, narrow hallway. After a negative comment to Elaine about the condition of the peeling and faded wallpaper, I followed closely behind her like an obedient little puppy dog as we entered the first room. Inside was what appeared to be a sitting room with a stone fireplace which covered almost one of the walls. I was surprised to see that a few of the old, dusty furnishings remained in the room. "I thought this place was empty, I said to Elaine."

"Oh, most of the furniture in the house has already been disposed of," Elaine quickly responded. "There are only a few rooms like this one where the previous owners left some things. Anyway, most of it is not worth saving-- just as you can see, Rick. However, they did leave a few pieces which appear to still be in reasonably good shape, and I have plans to have them refinished. Doing that would be a lot cheaper for us than buying everything new, and they would also fit well into this setting. You'll see!"

Stopping in my tracks, I spoke to Elaine in an elevated voice. "Do you mean to tell me that you plan to redecorate this place just as it was done originally, Elaine? You know that I dislike antique furniture. I think you are pushing me a little too far, Elaine. I am more than willing to go along with you to please you whenever I can, but there is a limit to my indulgence."

"I didn't say that, Rick!" Elaine responded in her familiar, wounded voice. "I only said that there are a few pieces of furniture I may want to save and have restored. If we decide to buy this place, I plan on doing the house entirely over in contemporary styling. That is what you always told me you liked best, and I know how important your comfort is to you and I respect that, now let's go on with our tour of the house," Elaine said rather forcefully.

As we continued looking through the house, I was reminded of the absolute dreariness and bleakness everywhere inside. Each room we entered seemed to be darker and gloomier than the last. By the time we finished with the five bedrooms on the second level, we were both tired and ready for a breather. We were lucky to find an old and dilapidated couch in a back hallway for us to sit on while we rested ourselves. Looking around the room, I began to shake my head in bewilderment because I could not possibly imagine what had possessed Elaine to want us to buy this disaster of a house. After another minute or two of thought, I decided to ask Elaine that very question.

"Do you seriously believe you can turn this old place into a warm and happy home for us Elaine?" I made it a point to speak very softly and very deliberately since I wanted her to also understand about my many nagging doubts about our buying the old house, and her plans to completely renovate it inside. "Positively!" Elaine immediately responded with absolute conviction in her voice.

Not wanting to get involved in an argument with her at this time, I decided to drop the subject. I would take it up with her later after we return home. Besides, I was not anxious to get into a row with Elaine in front of Pat Driscoll.

"Would you like to look upstairs at the attic now?" Elaine asked as she pulled herself up from the couch. "That big turret room on the third level commands a view of practically the entire area. I have already come up with some great ideas for that room."

"I do not think so," I answered with a heavy sigh, "but I would like to check out the roof and the foundation for possible water leaks. I will also like to take a look at the heating plant. By the way, is there a central air-conditioning system in the house, and have you already asked Pat Driscoll about those important questions?" My questions to Elaine were with a note of sarcasm.

"There's a new air-conditioning system," Rick, Elaine answered. "It is supposed to have been installed in recent years. Anyway, that is according to what Pat told me during my first visit here."

Leaving the first level of the house, the two of us went down the stairs into the cellar, which to my utter amazement, was clean and dry. In contrast, the back half of the basement is cluttered up with a pile of cartons stacked against one wall, along with an assortment of other seemingly useless things. The original coal-burning furnace is now an efficient gas-fired boiler, and the water heater looked to be new. It was clear to us that the electrical service fuse box and the house wiring had also been recently installed. "Someone has spent a good deal of money on these things," I remarked. "Thank God for small favors because if we had to replace any of those things, the whole deal would be off, as far as I am concerned," I said as I looked at Elaine.

"Does that mean, Rick, that you like the place?"

"To tell you the truth, Elaine, I hate the house, but I know what wonders you will do to it to turn it into a showplace. Still, I want you to be confident it is what you want, and then I will go along with your plan for us to make an offer to buy it." With that, I then pulled her tightly against me and planted a kiss on top of her hair.

"Oh, Rick, I have such great ideas for this house which you will see, and most of it without spending too much money," Elaine quickly exclaimed. "The most significant expense is going to be remodeling the kitchen because there isn't a thing in there that we can save."

"I am still having a lot of misgivings about this property," I said, "and I can see us spending an awful lot of money and hard work to get everything into an acceptable shape. That kitchen, as you just said, will positively need to be gutted to the bare walls. We will also have to buy all new cabinets, floor coverings, and major appliances, and those things take a lot of money. The remodeling is entirely your department, Elaine, but whatever we do, we will have to carefully budget our funds so that we do not get ourselves into a financial jam."

"I am sure I can do a lot of the outside work that might be needed, that is, with some help from our two boys whenever they are available."

"Our purchase of the property still depends on our being able to strike a deal for the price of the house. What did Mrs. Driscoll say the seller was asking for the place?"

"Pat told me that the seller was hoping to get $230,000 for it, but I think we can get it for about $215,000. What do you think our offer for it should be, Rick?"

"I think we should make an offer of only $205,000 and see if the seller accepts it. If the seller does not, we can always make them a higher offer, but once we do that, there is no turning back. I hope you understand?"

"Yes, Rick, I understand, and that's what I would like us to do. Please let's get back to Pat to tell her of our decision. I want to get it done as soon as possible. I would hate for us to lose the house to someone else because we delay a decision to buy it."

Immediately after our telling Pat Driscoll of our decision to buy the house, we accompanied her to her office in Bradenton, where we made a formal offer which Elaine and I both signed. Our present home was not currently listed for sale, and we need that money to buy the house in Forest Oak. We then signed the agreement with Pat making our offer to buy the new house contingent on the sale of our present home. Having signed all the necessary papers, I handed Pat Driscoll my check for $20,000 which covered the earnest money.

Upon our leaving the real estate office, Pat drove us back to our house where we said our goodbyes at the curb. Just before she drove away, Pat promised us that she would contact us the moment she got a decision from the seller.

Because it was now rather late in the afternoon, we decided to enjoy an early dinner at our favorite Italian restaurant named Papa Luigi's. It is a place where we would often stop for a bite to eat when Elaine felt like getting away from her cooking meals at home. For a change, we ordered a bottle of Italian Chianti wine with our food. After we poured the dark, red wine into our glasses, we clinked them together to make a toast to our new house venture. I cannot remember when I last saw Elaine looking so excited and so happy about anything.

I did not mention it to her, but I had a very disquieting feeling in my stomach--a feeling that just would not go away, and the feeling was not from the wine we drank with our meals, it was something I had left with me from that old house, and I hoped that we had not made a terrible mistake by our offer to buy it.

While we were sitting in our quiet booth at the restaurant, I now had a lot of second thoughts about our decision to buy the house. Well, the offer was rather low, and it was also coupled with a contingency agreement. That fact alone might discourage the seller from accepting our offer. I found myself hoping that the offer we had made would be rejected. One thing was for sure if he made a higher counteroffer from our offer of the $205,000. That would kill the deal as far as I was personally concerned. If that displeased Elaine, then I guess she would just have to learn to live with it.

~ *Chapter Two* ~

MOVING IN

Our low-bid-offer to buy the house in Forest Oak, along with the contingency agreement had been accepted by the seller, and it was just short of a month later when things began to come together for us. We were lucky because our Realtor found a buyer for our house in Bradenton who was willing to pay our full asking price for the property. We then set a firm closing date for both of the properties, arranged for the money transfers, and for the coinciding date of occupancies. Those events made it possible for Elaine to begin ordering all the new appliances for our kitchen, and also for her to hire teams of workmen to start working on some of the more immediate renovations. Their first order of business would be demolishing the old and ugly outdated kitchen. By the time those projects would be underway, we expected we would be into the warmer spring weather.

Pat Driscoll told us that the seller of our new property was a businessman from California by the name of Clayton Matthews, and he was the previous owner's grandnephew. It seemed that Mathews had inherited the house from his Grand Uncle, a man by the name of Sedgwick Burns. It was a little disconcerting for us to learn at the closing, that the house we had bought had been empty for more than eight years after the owner had mysteriously disappeared and he had not been seen or heard from since. We were reassured by the Realty Office that during that time the property had remained vacant and had been well cared for by a very reputable property management company. For those years, the same management company arranged to have extensive electrical work done, central air conditioning installed, a new fifty-gallon automatic water heater installed, and an efficient gas furnace converted from the old coal burner. As it happened, those were the prime improvements that had stimulated me to agree to buy the property.

The explanation for the long vacancy of the property was that Sedgwick Burns had disappeared without a single trace, and after the passage of seven years the court had declared Burns dead. His Grandnephew, Clayton Matthews, who was Burns' only living blood relative was the heir to the estate. Mr. Matthews resided in San Francisco, and he was the one who had decided to complete all of the needed improvements to the house and then to put it on the market to sell.

Most of the furnishings of any value that had been left within the house had already been removed and sold by Matthews. At the time of the real estate closing of the property, Elaine and I were told that we could either keep or dispose of anything that was still left inside the house and in the garage. The furniture I had seen during my first visit there was convincing to me that nothing that had been left there was worth keeping, but it seemed that Elaine had her own ideas about what was to be done with a few of those things.

On a warm Saturday afternoon several weeks later, and just before our scheduled occupancy of the house in Forest Oak, we were again driven there by our real estate agent Pat Driscoll. It was only my second time to visit the property, but Elaine had been back a few times in the past when she had measured every wall, ceiling, and window in anticipation of her starting her renovation project. Our visit this time was to have Elaine decide upon which pieces of the remaining furniture in the house she wanted to keep and have refinished, and what things we would be disposing of in the city dump. As things later turned out, there were only three pieces of the old furniture Elaine felt was worth our while to consider.

Once we decided upon those few of the remaining pieces of the furniture to be restored, Elaine and I went about carefully examining the house from the attic to the cellar. I was impressed with the third-level turret room with its tall windows commanding a 300-degree view of the surrounding neighborhood. With the use of my often active imagination, I could visualize it being turned into a bright and sunny office for Elaine and me, but that was not going to happen because Elaine had other plans for that room, it would become an observatory, and she even decided she would buy a large telescope so we could watch the stars and the moon on clear nights. It took a further bit of thought by me before I warmed up to her idea, and when I did, I offered to buy some colorful astronomical charts to be pinned on the inside wall for us to study the stars in the night sky.

The spacious attic was something else again for us to deal with. That dark and dusty depositary was cluttered with a few old pieces of baby furniture, a wicker baby carriage, several old steamer trunks, stacks of dusty old books, and a wide variety of other seemingly useless things. The entire back quarter of the attic was made almost inaccessible by the sheer volume of cardboard cartons that were stacked up into a high mound against one wall. The room appeared to be the collection of more than a hundred years or more of occupancy by very frugal people, causing it to become their receptacle for everything that was no longer useful but was thought by the owners to be too good to throw away. I told Elaine I would like all of it out of there and hauled to the county dump, but she insisted on my leaving it untouched, at least for the time being. She reasoned there could be some undiscovered treasures hidden there, things which would be ideal for her decorating use. As soon as we move into the house and get things on the inside organized, she had plans to go through those things. That was okay with me because I knew I would have more pressing problems to attend to. In particular, I wanted to get the back and side yards of the property into some fair shape for our first Sunday outdoor cookout.

The morning of our move to the new house, a large furniture van arrived before eight. We had already disposed of most of our old furniture from our home in Bradenton a week before that the move, a few pieces went to our boys, some were sold at a garage sale, and the rest of it we donated to The Salvation Army. There were not too many large pieces left to load in the moving van, but over the years we had managed to accumulate a sizeable number of personal items and clothing which filled several dozen cardboard cartons. Both of our boys and their spouses were there to lend us a helping hand during the packing and loading of everything. By noontime, the truck was loaded and was now on its way to our new residence in Forest Oak.

Since Glenn nor Ron had yet seen the new house, they had followed Elaine and me there in Glenn's station wagon. When we pulled our car into the driveway on Cobblestone Lane, I quickly glanced into the rear-view mirror to see that my boys were still following behind us. The furniture van had already been backed up to the front porch, and the movers had already started unloading our things from the back of it. Both front doors were wide open and several of the furniture loaders were there awaiting Elaine's instructions for placement of the furniture and our cartons of personal effects inside the house. At the time we packed the boxes, we numbered each one of them so it would make Elaine's job a lot easier later. All she would have to do is refer to her list describing the contents of each carton by its outside number. She is a talented lady, my wife.

Taking advantage of our temporary uselessness to the project, Glenn, Ron and I walked around to the back of the house where we visually examined the landscaping. It occurred to me that the boys just wanted to look the house over to determine if we had made a sound decision when we bought it. After having rounded the north end of the building, we stopped to survey the side yard. Ron stopped and stood there with his legs wide apart and with his hands on his hips. He was looking up at the top of the house with a very sad look on his face.

"My God, Dad!" Ron said to me, "Do you mean to tell us that this house is an improvement over your other one?"

Even before I could answer him, he continued.

"The building is much too big for the two of you, and it will take a fortune to fix it up and another fortune just to keep it up. I cannot possibly imagine why you let Mother talk you into buying it. What do you think, about it Glenn?"

Looking a bit embarrassed at Ron's remarks, Glenn hesitated for a second or two before answering him.

"It is not all that bad, Ron. The place is a bit too large--as you just pointed out about its upkeep, but it's built well, and the neighborhood is beautiful. I especially like the large oak trees around the backyard, and that three-car garage is excellent. The only problem is that you have only one car, Dad. Are you planning to buy another car for Mom, and maybe later get a boat to fill that third stall? Now that's an idea I like a lot he said with a grin and a chuckle."

"Come on boys!" I heard myself say, "I realize it is not a very attractive place at the moment, but that will all be changed after we get your mother's inside projects completed. I also have a few great ideas of my own regarding the exterior of the building and the garden. For one thing, I will tear out some of the old lilac shrubs and use that space for flower gardens in the front of the house and along the driveway. Using a few gallons of bright exterior paint here and there, and a lot of elbow grease, you will never know this place when we get through with it. I am also hoping that you two boys will be lending me a hand whenever you can find the time."

"You know you can depend on us, Dad," Glenn said as he looked at Ron who nodded his head in agreement.

Having completed our quick tour of the yard and the garage, we entered the house through the open front door. We had to dodge one of the movers who was carrying a heavy end-table which he had braced on top of his head. For the next hour or so, my sons and I walked through the house, and while we examined each of the rooms as we made our comments, both pro-and-con. Each of my sons, like myself, had some serious doubts about their mother's ability to tackle such a colossal renovation to the interior of the house, but knowing my wife Elaine I felt she was fully capable of it. "Well, boys," I said with a slightly loud sigh, "this ancient piece of property is ours now, and the fact of the matter is that we will all have to learn to live with it!"

Ron and Glenn both were wild about the turret room, and each of them had his own idea of what it should be used for. Glenn thought it would be just perfect as an artist's studio because of the large windows that considerably brightened the room, while Ron thought that a better idea would be turning it into a computer room. After I told them about their mother's plan to turn it into an observatory, they both thought that idea was the best possible one for it.

When we arrived in the attic, Glenn was fascinated by all the junk that was stored up there, and he asked if he could help his mother sort through it when the time came. I told him that she would surely welcome any help he could give her. Looking at the heaped-up mountain of cartons, Glenn was all for opening up a few of them just to see what they might contain. I could not begin to imagine what was packed inside those cartons, but this was certainly not the time to find that out, so I hustled the boys back downstairs.

Both Ron and Glenn were intrigued because all five of the bedrooms had native-stone, wood-burning fireplaces, some with marble mantles and firebrick hearths. Neither of the boys was keen about the fact that none of the bedrooms had a closet. In place of closets, each room had a large oak wardrobe cabinet with double doors, and was lined with sweet-smelling cedar. All of the bedroom ceilings were ten feet tall and surrounded by thick, darkly varnished oak crown moldings, which only added to the overall gloominess of each room. Elaine told me that she planned to have all the bedrooms painted the same color as the ceilings, which would be white. She felt that would do a lot to brighten up those dark and dreary rooms. I certainly hoped so because they were now much too gloomy for my liking.

My sons were wild about the mahogany-paneled den just-off the first level hallway, with its extra-large, wood burning fireplace that practically covered one entire wall. They marveled at its heavy, rough-hewn mantle that would provide a convenient ledge for me to display my collection of colorful German beer mugs. Not having had a place to show them at our other house, I kept them stored for years inside cardboard boxes in our basement storage room. A spot centered directly over the fireplace would be reserved for a beautifully stuffed and mounted head with horns of a mountain goat. It is a treasured trophy I had acquired from the early days before either of my sons was born and before I gave up hunting. I felt happy that I would finally be able to impress my friends with one of my long-past accomplishments. I was willing to allow Elaine to dictate the decorating of every other room in the house, but I wanted this den to stay pretty much as it was, and I would not stand for Elaine's making any changes to it before first consulting with me.

After the furniture movers had everything brought inside the house and placed according to Elaine's instructions, they bid their goodbyes and they left. We then thought this would be the proper time for us to order our dinner because we were all just about famished. I had Glenn drive to a nearby Kentucky Fried Chicken outlet and pick up a large bucket of chicken, mashed potatoes, coleslaw and a couple of quarts of soda pop.

Because our newly purchased kitchen table and chairs had not yet been delivered to us from the furniture store, we sat down in the middle of the kitchen floor where we balanced our paper plates of food on our laps. It was just like having a family picnic when our boys were young, except for our eating on the floor instead of on grass. In spite of our discomfort, we were all having a good time while relating tales and events from our past. It was as though we were back together again as a complete family, and Elaine and I loved every single minute of it.

Just before it got dark, Elaine and I said goodbye to our two sons, and we left the house with them for us to enjoy the cool evening air. We then watched from the side door as Glenn backed his car out of our driveway and then slowly drove away. Once they were out of sight, I quickly picked Elaine up in my arms and carried her across the threshold into our not-so-new home. Elaine was a mite heavier than the last time I did that, and I nearly dropped her.

Within the following week, our new furniture arrived from the store, and this time it took two large vans to make the delivery. By early afternoon, Elaine and I had everything arranged in its proper place. Although nothing had yet been done to redecorate the rooms, just the addition of the bright new furniture improved the looks of the house considerably, and I soon began to unwind a bit from the underlying tension that I had felt since we bought the house. I thought I could even get to like the place if I was given enough time. Little did I know then what problems and other difficulties were there waiting us. How could I have possibly known any of it?

~*Chapter Three* ~

MEETING DAVE FARRELL

By the end of the first week in our house, we were inundated with a large group of workmen who were anxiously ready to get the job started. They were there in response to Elaine's frantic telephone calls to start the ball rolling! She was, of course, referring to the start of the substantial renovating project which would include almost the entire inside of the first level of the house, but the kitchen in particular.

The first of the men inside began feverishly tearing out everything inside the kitchen, starting with the double-drain sink, and the huge cast-iron stove. It took four husky men to carry that monstrous cookstove out of the house and into the back of their waiting truck. After they rested a bit, they attacked the ceiling and base moldings, walls, paneling, the lighting fixtures, and everything else, right down to the original dried-out, wooden lathing in the walls. I saw a terrible mess of plaster dust and wood splinters everywhere, and the sounds of their destruction could be heard in every corner of the house, and even as far as into the middle of the street.

While the workmen were busily doing their jobs, Elaine was somewhere in another room happily engaged in reviewing and updating her drawings and blueprints for her new kitchen. She was anxious for the appliances to be ordered and delivered by the time the kitchen mess was completed and cleaned up. As I walked into the room and peeked over her shoulder, I saw that Elaine was busily sketching a large gas stove with a fancy smoke bonnet. Some weeks before our moving in, she had decided on most of the appliances; things like the kitchen cabinets and base cabinets she liked. Appearing to be deep in concentration, she took no notice of me standing close behind her.

"How is your schedule coming along, Elaine?" I asked as I continued to scan her drawings. She apparently was unaware of me standing so close behind her, and I surprised her which caused her to jump and swivel around to face me with an angry face.

"My God Rick!" She responded in a loud annoyed voice. "The next time you come up behind me like that, please be thoughtful enough to announce yourself. You scared me half out of my wits!"

"I am very sorry! I said. I thought you heard me when I came into the room, but with all that racket that is going on in the kitchen, it is a wonder either one of us can even think around here. I tried finding some place in the house where I could get some quiet place where I could think, but it just was not possible. I even spent some time in the upstairs turret room hoping it was far enough away to escape the noise, but it also was not. By the way, Elaine, how much longer do you anticipate it will take the workmen to finish ripping out everything in the kitchen?"

With a look of distress still etched in her face, Elaine said, "the foreman told me that they should be finished with it sometime after five o'clock this afternoon. The kitchen cabinets are supposed to be delivered here later, and they will temporarily be stacked in the dining room, and they will have to stay there until they are ready to be installed. The cabinet men are to be here the first thing tomorrow morning, but as luck would have it, the counter tops won't be ready for another day or two. The delay had something to do with the laminating of the Formica, and that means that the cabinet installers will have to come back again to complete the job after the counter top's are finally delivered."

"Nothing ever goes as planned, you know that, Elaine. The only thing that bothers me is all the noise and confusion we have to tolerate in the meantime."

Quickly dismissing me with a shrug of her shoulders, Elaine went back to whatever it was she was doing and I promptly left the room.

Because Elaine has been unable to use the kitchen to prepare food for any of our meals, we continued to eat out for most of them. That afternoon we thought we would try our luck at Belamy's Family Restaurant, located in the business area of Forest Oak. I had noticed it sometime back when we were on our way to see the house with the Realtor for the first time.

After leaving the house and having taken a short drive to the center of town, the two of us arrived at the restaurant where I parked my car in the lot and we walked around to the front door. I remembered thinking that the clientele would probably all be farmers, but was I ever wrong about that! There were a few farmers there, but the bulk of the customers appeared to be office workers, businessmen, and families.

We placed our food orders from the menu with our waitress, and later, after we had sampled the food they had served us, I knew then why Beamy's was so popular. The place was clean, the prices were reasonable, and the food was quite delicious. In my mind, I realized that it was a place we would often be visiting.

Having finished our most enjoyable meals, we left the restaurant and went directly back to our house where we could still hear the loud tearing and ripping sounds emanating from within the building. Just as I pulled my car into our driveway, I saw one of our neighbors standing in his backyard looking our way. He had a garden hose in his hands with which he was watering a big bed of peonies next to our fence. As we stepped from the car, he looked our way and smiled and spoke to us. "Hello there! Nice day, isn't it folks?"

Before I could answer him, Elaine chimed in. "How do you do? Those are very lovely flowers you have there. Do you mind if I take a closer look at them?"

Walking over to the fence, I extended my hand through the iron rods while I shook his wet hand. "My name is Rick Braden, I said, and this lovely lady standing next to me is my wife, Elaine." With a warm and beaming smile, Elaine held out her hand.

"Welcome to our neighborhood, folks!" He said "I'm sorry about the wet handshakes. By the way, my name is Dave Farrell, and may I ask what's going on inside there?" He asked as he pointed an index finger toward our house. "It sounds like all heck has been let loose there. I saw a couple of trucks loading up a bunch of stuff, so I guessed that you've been doing some major remodeling."

"That's correct! Mr. Farrell," I said. "Elaine is having the entire inside of the house done over in a twentieth-century motif. I do not know if you have ever been inside our home, but it was like a throwback to the eighteen-eighties." As I spoke, I glanced at Elaine who appeared uncomfortable over my last comment.

In an impatient voice, Elaine said, "Do you gentlemen mind if I leave you now? I have to check on the workmen to see how things are progressing in my kitchen. Maybe we can talk again a little later this afternoon after things calm down inside."

"She's a pretty lady--your wife," Farrell remarked as we both watched Elaine leave and head for the side entrance to the house. "My better half is inside watching a soaper on TV. I think this fence is getting in my way here. How about you coming around to my side of it and we'll have a beer and get better acquainted? I don't feel like doing any more watering today, and besides, the weatherman is talking about a shower possibly moving in sometime later this afternoon."

Dave popped open the lids on two cans of beer, and then our friendly neighbor opened up a couple of folding patio chairs and we sat there facing each other in his yard in the shade of his garage. After taking a long drink of his beer, Dave asked me a question.

"Did you ever get to meet the seller of your house before you bought it? I'm referring to that Matthews fellow. I can tell you that he spent a lot of his time hanging around here last fall. I also remember that he was having a lot of things hauled out of the house and loaded into furniture vans. From what I could see, they should have been heading those trucks directly to the county dump. I briefly talked to him about that, and he told me that the furniture in the trucks was being taken to an antique shop in Bradenton. From the looks of the things in the trucks, it all looked like a bunch of old, worn-out and dusty furniture. But what do I know?"

"No, Mr. Farrell, I have to say that I never had the pleasure of meeting that fellow Matthews you just mentioned. Our attorney dealt directly with his attorney over the business of our buying the house. About the only thing we know about him is that he had inherited the property from his Granduncle, a man by the name of Sedgwick Burns. At the time of the closing of the property, the only thing we were told about Mister Burns was that he had disappeared many years ago."

"That's just about the same things that Matthews fellow had told me," Farrell said. "I mean about his having inherited the house. Of course, that was when he was still hanging around the property." With that comment, Farrell quickly popped the lid of another can of beer and then immediately took a fast gulp of it. Care for another can he offered as he pressed it toward me.

"No thanks, Mr. Farrell, I am still drinking the one in my hand, and one beer before my dinner is my limit. May I ask you a question? Just what kind of man was that Mister Burns? Since he had been your next door neighbor, I suppose that you got to know him reasonably well."

"Well, my wife and I have been living here in this same house for many years, but I can honestly tell you that I barely spoke two words to that man in all that time. He wasn't a bit friendly, but that might have had something to do with his profession, he was a mortician. I suppose you already know about that, and from what I'd been told by Hector Bates, whose another neighbor of ours, Burns had lived in that house since he was born somewhere around 1915 or 1916. By the way, would you please call me Dave? Calling me Mr. Farrell makes me feel a lot older than I am. Would you also mind if I call you Rick? I hate formality, don't you?"

"That is entirely okay with me, Mister Far . . ., ah, Dave! You said that Burns was a mortician and that he lived here since around 1916 or so. Did he tell you that, about his being a mortician, I mean?"

"Oh, no! In all the time I've lived in this house, that's got to be going onto twenty-five years now, he never bothered with me. He was an unfriendly and reclusive old coot! In fact, there isn't a person in this neighborhood who could ever get close to that man. It was a rarity even to see him because he spent most of his time at his funeral parlor or locked up inside there." He then pointed his beer can in the direction of my house. "All I ever knew about him was what I'd heard through neighborhood gossip, and there was plenty of that because he was such a creepy and mysterious character. But in all honesty, Rick, I wasn't too keen becoming friendly with a man who makes his living off of dead people. In my mind, he must be a little weird to begin with; otherwise, he wouldn't be doing that kind of work."

"Well, Dave, I suppose someone has to do it--taking care of the dead, I mean. Personally, I would not have the stomach for it myself. Did you ever see him out in his yard cutting his grass, pruning his trees, or anything else like that? Did the man ever have a backyard barbecue or a party of any kind?"

"Never!" That was his quick and forceful response to my question. "All of his landscaping and other yard work had been looked after by his gardener, and besides that, Burns had no one who would come to his party even if he gave one." As he talked about the man, his face screwed up into a snarl. It was apparent to me that Dave Farrell never had any particular liking for his next-door neighbor, Sedgwick Burns.

"Did he own a car? With that three-car garage, he must have owned at least one vehicle."

"Yes. Before he disappeared, Burns had cars in all three of those stalls. One of them was a beautiful antique Cord roadster that he'd kept hidden inside under a tarp. I saw him pull it out of his garage one day, and he was very sportily dressed, which was something very unusual for him.

"Any time I'd ever seen him before that day he was wearing a black, pin-striped suit, which is apparently the uniform of an undertaker. However, that particular time when I saw him he looked entirely different. I just happened to be sitting out here in my yard that afternoon when I watched what he was doing. Burns had on a red-and-white checked cap, and he was wearing a bright red jacket, along with white pants and black patent-leather shoes. The effect of his outfit was terrific, just like he was back in time to the Gay Nineties. The only thing I thought was missing from his outfit was a pair of gray spats. With his flaming red hair, his red beard, and his ridiculous waxed mustache, Burns looked like a throwback in time.

"As I'm thinking about that car now, it was the last time I saw that beautiful Cord convertible in his garage. Burns must have sold it soon after that. Anyway, he had another car which he used most of the time. It was a big, black meat wagon that became the talk of our neighborhood. I can tell you that every time I saw him drive that vehicle into or out of his garage, I felt a cold chill run up my spine."

"What kind of a car was that?" I asked somewhat louder than I had intended, and as if I had not heard what he had said. "By any chance, Dave, are you talking about a hearse?"

"That's what it was, a big, black hearse, and he kept it in his garage even after he gave up the funeral business. As I said earlier, he had been a mortician, but he retired some time before he disappeared. From what I'd heard from others around our neighborhood, undertaking the dead was the Burns family's profession for more than a hundred years, and they did most of their business in and around Forest Oak. Burns Mortuary buried everyone who was anyone, it seems. Say, Rick, that's a bit comical what I just said, don't you think? It's a jingle they could have used for Burns business. It still gives me the shivers just talking about it. And to think I had to live next door to a reclusive, old mortician who drove around town in a large, black hearse."

I did not mean to do it, but after Dave made those last statements to me, and when I saw the serious look on his face, I began to laugh aloud. When I regained my composure, I apologized to him. It was not just his words and his look, but also the way he said it that had caused me to laugh. He was talking just like a little kid who was afraid of the boogie man.

"I suppose his grandnephew Clayton Matthews kept the hearse," I said in a fast attempt to change the subject.

"No, Matthews didn't keep it. Another neighbor told me that he sold the limousine to one of the local funeral homes. Sometime later when I saw Mathews in his yard, I asked him about it by telling him I'd noticed it was missing from the garage. Matthews said to me that he had no use for it since he wasn't in the mortuary business. Burns' third car was a 1966 Ford sedan, and it was in stark contrast to the other two he owned. That Ford was so rusty it's a wonder to me it didn't fall apart in his driveway. It was a joke seeing him drive that piece of junk around this nice neighborhood. That Ford was a real clunker, and many of the mornings I'd hear him cranking away on it trying to get its engine started. I could tell that it was a problem with the timing chain, but I wasn't about to tell him that. He was such a sour, old pickle I wouldn't waste my valuable time telling him anything. I suspect that Clayton Matthews may have had his Ford junked when he couldn't find anyone crazy enough to buy it."

"I thought you told me that Burns drove the hearse," I said, sounding a bit confused. "Now I am getting the impression that his Ford was his everyday car, or Am I wrong about that?"

"No, you're right! That old Cadillac limousine was an excellent running car. It would start at the first click of the starter, and it ran smooth and quiet. I'm a rather good mechanic, and I'm aware of these things, but he used the hearse only in the evenings. Come to think of it, after Burns retired it was unusual to see that car out of the garage in the sunlight.

"As for that antique Cord, it was a wonderful-show car, and I saw it up close only one other time. That was when Burns pulled it into his yard and turned the hose on it to wash it. I remember it was a nifty cream-colored convertible coupe with side-mounted spare tires and great looking wire wheels. Because I liked it so much, Rick, I would almost have been willing to mortgage my house to be able to own that car for myself, but instead, I had to settle for my old Dodge Dart.

"From where I stood in my yard, I watched Burns from behind my rose trellis, and I could easily see the crazy Burns family's emblem, or crest, on the driver's side door. You know, those two prancing stallions and the down-thrust daggers. Once while discussing that car with Matthews, I asked him what those things represented, and he told me it was the family coat of arms, and it had something to do with the Burns' strength of conviction which was depicted by the two prancing stallions. The down-thrust dagger, he told me, represented death, but I never could understand why. Can you imagine someone using a family crest with that kind of a ghoulish theme? If you don't mind, Rick, I'd like us now to change our discussion back to Burns' car. What a beautiful classic automobile that Cord was, and what do you think something like that would be worth on the market?"

"I do not have even the vaguest idea about that, but it has to be a lot of money. There were not too many of those built, and I believe they were all custom-made cars. I seem to remember that they were created in Auburn, Indiana. That car was a lot too rich for my blood, whatever it might now be worth, Dave."

"The embalming and burial business must have paid him very well for him to be able to afford a vehicle like that, Dave remarked. Maybe you and I are in the wrong racket, Rick. By the way, what is it you do for a living, may I ask?"

"I am an accountant, and I work in an office in Bradenton's downtown business section. I have been with the same company ever since I left college."

"Well, I'm just a simple automobile mechanic," Dave said "with my own auto repair shop in town which keeps me somewhat active most of the time."

We continued talking for the next half-hour or so, but by then Dave had turned our conversation away from Sedgwick Burns. I had the feeling that he was a bit peeved at me for having laughed at his story earlier, and he may have felt a little foolish for having expressed his childish fears to me.

Just before I left his yard, his wife, Shirley came out of their house to meet me. She was a rather attractive, middle-aged woman with a winning smile. I had the feeling that she was the one who wore the pants in the family because when she told Dave it was time to eat so you had better get washed up, he instantly replied, "Yes Dear!" When our introductions were out of the way, he invited me to stop over, along with Elaine, and get acquainted. I promised her that we would do that as soon as Elaine and I had a free moment.

Upon my returning to the house, I found Elaine standing in the kitchen surveying the results of the day's destruction. The workmen had already left in their heavily loaded truck and were now on their way to the county dump. While I was visiting with our neighbor Dave, I saw them go in a big white cloud of plaster dust chasing behind their truck as they drove away. Elaine had a look on her face of intense concentration, and she took no notice of me as I walked up to her and asked, How is your project shaping up, Elaine? "Do you think this kitchen work will be completed before the snow flies?" I was trying to inject some light humor into the conversation, but I could tell from the look on her face that it was not a bit appreciated.

"There's a lot more plastering that needs to be done in the kitchen than I had bargained for," was her quick answer. "The plasterer should be here after the cabinet installers are through with their work tomorrow."

"I would think he should be here before the cabinets are installed?" I said.

"That's right!" Elaine shot back rather curtly and with a hard look at me. "I told you that I had not anticipated that much plastering, therefore, my dear husband, I suppose I goofed!"

"What does that mean? I asked wondering why she quickly became so irritated with me over my innocent remark."

"What it means is just as I said! I am only human, and being human I make mistakes sometimes--just like you often do! But my anger will not get the job done, so I have to call the cabinet man and tell him to delay the installation for a couple of days. It will take that long for the walls to be plastered and more time for it to properly dry."

With the realization that Elaine was feeling the pressure of the job, and because I was not wanting to antagonize her further, I spoke very softly. "It is a shame that it worked out that way, Honey, but a few more days will not upset the apple cart too much. Besides, we have found ourselves an excellent restaurant where we can eat our meals until this project is done." With that, I hastily turned and left the room.

As soon as I had seated myself comfortably in my recliner in the living room, I picked up the evening newspaper. About the time I was halfway through the sports page, I heard our front doorbell chime. It was the man from the millwork shop delivering the new kitchen cabinets. Two men carried them into the house from their truck, and in about twenty minutes they had everything neatly stacked inside. When they brought each piece into the house, Elaine carefully examined it for any scratches or damage that might have occurred while in shipping, and then she checked it off her list. When Elaine was satisfied that everything was in good order, she signed the bill of lading, and they left.

Upon my returning to my recliner in the living room to finish reading the newspaper, I was just about to sit again when Elaine came into the room and plopped herself down on a lounge chair opposite from me.

"What do you think of our next door neighbor?" Elaine asked unexpectedly. I sensed she was feeling a little guilty for having jumped on me in the kitchen earlier, but before I could answer her, she said, "Did you get to meet his wife? I had hoped that we might make a friendly visit over there, but then I got all wrapped up in my kitchen project."

Dropping my newspaper onto my lap, I answered her. "Dave seems to be amiable enough, but Dave has got a negative hang up over the guy who used to own this house by the name of Sedgwick Burns. Apparently, Burns was a bachelor and a recluse. He was also a mortician by profession. As a matter of interest, Dave told me that Burns was from a long line of morticians, and those things did not set too well with him. Also, he said to me that Burns drove around town in a large black, hearse--which was something that did not set too well with anyone else in the neighborhood."

As I spoke, I carefully watched the expression on Elaine's face as it turned from one of casual interest to an immediate look of distress.

"As for Mrs. Farrell," I continued, "I met Shirley briefly when she stepped out into their yard. She seemed rather nice. The last thing she said to me as I was leaving was to be sure to stop back with you for a visit. Maybe we can slip over there for a little while after we have eaten our dinner. Are you in the mood for doing that, Elaine?"

"I don't think so, Rick. I am feeling somewhat tired and a bit irritable, and I still have a call to make to postpone the cabinet installation. So as you can imagine, I am in no mood to trade small talk with any of our neighbors today. Maybe I will feel more like doing it tomorrow."

"I am quite sure they are not expecting us tonight anyway," I said in a weary voice. "Where do you want to go for dinner? I suppose that you are not anxious to try eating at Belamy's again."

"Belamy's is okay with me," Elaine said, "although I feel that I cannot handle a full meal again tonight. I still have a few leftover pieces of the chicken in the refrigerator I have been picking at some of it. Would you like some of it?"

"No thank you! I do not want to eat anything that may spoil my dinner. You still have not told me what you think about Burns being a mortician and the fact that he drove around town in a funeral car."

"That is very upsetting to me Rick," Elaine quickly remarked, "and frankly, I do not care to talk about it. If I thought for one minute that any part of this house was used for that purpose, I would not want to stay here. You know how squeamish I am on that subject."

"He did not conduct his business from this house," Elaine, I responded rather forcefully. "He only kept his hearse in the garage. So please do not get yourself all worked up over it. I am sorry now that I even mentioned it to you, and I would not have even talked about it except our neighbor told me about it. You still have your telephoning to do, and I have my newspaper to read." As Elaine got up from her chair to leave the room, I asked, "What time do you want us to go out for dinner?"

"I am not a bit hungry," was her reply. "I've changed my mind about eating, and I am just not in the mood to go out. You can have the rest of the cold chicken I told you about; otherwise, you can call and have a pizza delivered." With that, she walked out of the room. I could say she was not in a perfect mood, and I was not about to look for an argument with her. I now found myself in a quandary over my earlier misguided remarks about the previous owner of our house. As sure as the sun sets in the morning, we will both be bombarded by our neighbors with grim stories about Sedgwick Burns. Everyone, it seems, loves to speculate about reclusive people, mainly when one is a mortician who had disappeared under mysterious circumstances. My offhanded remarks to Elaine had already developed into an unhappy turn of events that neither of us had wanted to happen. I could only hope that it would not create such a problem for us that it would affect our relationship while living in our new home.

Unsettling thoughts and fears of the unknown began to creep into my mind. Perhaps I had already said too much to be able to remedy it. I think we should have been told a bit more about the background history of the house, and about its previous owner from the real estate agency. If I had been a bit more interested in what was going on, I would not have relied so heavily on our attorney, and I would not be commiserating over those things now. God, I only hoped that our buying this old house with its upsetting family history had not been a terrible mistake for us to have made.

~ *Chapter Four* ~

THE FIRST DISCOVERY

A few days after the kitchen cabinets had been delivered to the house, the missing plaster in the kitchen had been dried and replaced, and the cabinets were finally installed. Elaine had been acting much like a caged lion clawing the bars of her cage while waiting for that much-delayed job to be completed. Thinking back, I realized that she had been very nervous and irritable ever since I told her about my conversation with our next-door neighbor. I wished that I had never said to her that Burns had been in the undertaking business. I should have known from the past that bringing up subjects of that nature would be extremely upsetting to Elaine, and after seeing how it affected her, I avoided talking about it again.

It was sometime later that day when I saw Dave Farrell, and I asked him to please refrain from mentioning anything negative to Elaine about our house and its former owner or his profession as an undertaker. He was a bit surprised at my request until I told him about Elaine's upsetting reaction to the information which he had conveyed to me. He merely chuckled, but he promised to comply with my wishes and avoid that subject in front of Elaine. He also said that he would caution his wife Shirley about talking about it as well. By

Dave readily agreeing to do as I requested of him, it seemed to help relieve some of my anxiety.

A short time after I left work on the following afternoon and arrived at my home, I changed into my work clothes and went out into the yard to prune some of the honeysuckle bushes at the side of the house. I happened to see Dave Farrell standing by his car in front of his garage, and I hollered over to him.

"Hello, Dave. If you are thinking about washing your car, the radio says there is no rain predicted until the weekend."

"The weather man's crazy," Dave responded as he looked in my direction. "It won't rain until Monday because that's when we'll both have to be back at work. Come on over when you're through with whatever it is you're doing, and we'll empty a can of beer or two."

"That's fine Dave, but this time I am bringing a cold six-pack along with me when I come. I bought it primarily for you because I know it's your brand." "Are you kidding me, Rick? Any brand of beer at all is my brand," he answered with a laugh.

My hedges and other bushes had not been touched since the yard maintenance man had last trimmed them, and that was sometime before we had occupied the house. Once Elaine and I moved in, I inherited the job of taking care of the yard, as well as the maintenance of the exterior of the house. While I was busily clipping the bushes, I noticed that the paint trim around the windows at the back end of the building would soon need repainting, and the putty around some of the window panes also had to be replaced since it had become cracked and dry with age. I made a mental note of those projects that are necessary to be done and thought I would start on them as soon as the hotter weather cooled off.

After I finished with the pruning job, I walked over to Dave's yard with the cold six-pack of beer I had bought earlier to give to him. We would talk about the weather and about sports and I would have a beer or two with him. For one reason or other, he seemed to be all wound up with excitement.

"What's going on, Dave?" I asked.

"I'll begin my three-week vacation next month, and Shirley and I have agreed to take a trip to Las Vegas this year. I just cannot wait to get away from here and park myself in front of one of those crap tables. I have a hunch I'll be lucky for a change."

"Have you and Shirley been there before?" I asked as I popped open the tab on a can of beer and passed it over to him. "It's been more than five years since we visited Vegas, and my luck was unusually bad that time so we came home broke," Dave said with a scowl. "This year it's going to be different because I can feel it in my bones. Not to change the subject, Rick, but have you had a chance to go through your cellar or your attic yet?"

"Why do you ask me that, Dave? Is there something there I should know about?"

"No, no! It's just that I was always coming up missing with things from my yard and my garage when that old skinflint Burns was still living next door. I always had an idea that he was the one who was responsible for those things missing from my yard." "And Just what kinds of things might you be talking about, Dave?"

"Well, to begin with, there was a new spade I'd bought a week earlier, a big roll of canvas that I'd bought to make a cover for my porch glider, a pitchfork, several buckets, some clothesline, and one of my best hoses. There were a lot of other things that had become lost as well, but over the years my memory has dulled a bit. Every time one of those items turned up missing, I would park myself next to my fence and crane my neck looking for it in Burns' yard, but I never saw a thing of mine there. I have a habit of burning my initials into everything I own, and that way it could identify my property if I ever saw it again. I picked up that habit because those neighbors where I used to live were always borrowing my tools but never returning them to me.

"Anyway, the reason I always suspected Burns was behind the thefts is that he used to roam around his property at night after everyone was asleep. I'm a very light sleeper, and at night I keep my bedroom window open in the window that faces your house. I'd often hear his shoes crunching on the gravel at the side of his driveway. Just before that, I usually hear his hearse being driven into his garage and the doors slamming shut. Oh, he was out there all right, and for my money, he was the culprit who stole all those things that belonged to me. I wasn't the only one in the neighborhood who came up with missing items either. If you get a chance, Rick, you should talk to Hector Bates. Hector is your neighbor to the north of you. He told me he also lost a lot of his stuff from his yard when Burns lived there. In fact, he can tell you stories about Burns that would curl your eyelashes."

When Dave finally finished with his highly opinionated conversation, he tilted his can of beer to his lips for a swallow. He then watched me closely to gauge the effect over what he had just said had on me. I was a little rattled by his disclosures, but I tried not to show it.

"During the eight years or more this property had been vacant," I asked. "Did you ever take the opportunity to look around the house to see if your missing things were there?"

"No! The house and garage were locked up tight, and the property management guy wouldn't even let me inside the yard. He was a miserable old crab, and it was very apparent to me that he didn't like me very much. Later on, when that Matthews fellow was staying here, I was going to ask his permission to look for my things, but I figured it would make him angry if I hinted that his granduncle was a common thief. I even thought about telling him that I had only let him use those missing garden tools and that they had my initials burned into them for identification. Somehow, I never got up enough nerve to do it."

"I suppose you were happy when you eventually saw the house for sale signs go up in front of Burns' house."

"Both Shirley and I were as happy as can be about that! It wasn't any fun for us living next door to an empty house for all those years. I'd have to say that the place was always well cared for by the property management people. Sometimes a house becomes empty, and the place turns into a vandalized hulk in short order, but thankfully that never happened here. This neighborhood wouldn't tolerate that kind of situation because we all have too darn much invested in our properties. All one has to do is to take a look at the houses and the yards around here to know we are people who have a strong sense of pride in ownership. We're not like some of those inner-city neighborhoods that look much like garbage pits."

"Had you and Shirley ever wondered, along with the rest of the neighbors, what possibly could have happened to your longtime neighbor Sedgwick Burns?"

"He disappeared, Rick!"

"Yes, but did that strange disappearance of his not seem odd to you? What I mean is, one day the man is living here in his big house next door to you, and then no one ever sees him again. Had you ever wondered what happened to him?"

"There was a heck of an investigation which began soon after he was found to be missing. Several police investigators talked to Shirley and me, and to almost everyone else in the neighborhood. Within a day or so after that, I saw the investigators carrying out a lot of file boxes from the Burns house and loading them into their car. We thought that Burns might have been involved in some IRS fraud and that they were looking at all of his financial records, but as far as we ever know, nothing ever came of it. We even watched the daily newspapers looking to read something about it, but there was never anything written about it that I read. Nothing that is, until we finally read a small article in one of the newspapers that mentioned Burns was missing.

"All of that had occurred about eight years ago. We were all a little surprised, our neighbors and Shirley and me, when we suddenly saw that for-sale sign get posted in front of Burns' house. At first, I thought he'd finally surfaced somewhere, and the house was being offered for sale by him through a relative. Hector Bates told me later that it was Burns' grandnephew; a man named Clayton Matthews who'd put the place on the market, and that Matthews was Burns' only remaining relative and his heir. Hector also said that after seven years had passed, Burns was officially declared dead and his will and his property had been probated. I didn't know about that law, and anyway, this wasn't the first time that Burns had disappeared. I even told one of the police investigators about that when he came around here asking questions."

"What do you mean about his missing some time before?" I asked pressing forward to be sure to hear what he was about to tell me.

"Well, it had to be more than ten or eleven years ago when it first happened. I hadn't seen the old buzzard for almost six months, and then one evening when I was working in my garage, I heard that old tin-can Ford of his start cranking its starter. Although I didn't bother looking out from my garage door, I knew it had to be Burns. I wasn't interested in ruining my day by casting my eyes in his direction, so I never went over to the fence to talk to him about where he was during all that time he was away. Anyway, it was none of my business.

"One day during Burns' first absence, I casually asked our mailman if Burns' mail was still being delivered to the house, and he told me that it was. Apparently, the reason it wasn't piling up outside the front door was that it was delivered into a mail slot right next to the door. At that time, I even had thoughts that maybe he had died, and his dead body was lying inside the house on the floor. Sometime after that, I peeked inside his garage through the side window, and I saw the Ford that he usually drove was missing from its stall. That's when I knew he was still alive out there somewhere and still kicking."

"Did you ever consider that maybe Burns was on an extended vacation during that time he was thought to be missing?"

"A vacation for six months! Not on your life!" He quickly responded. "I can assure you that Burns was too darn cheap to ever spend a dime for a vacation, even a short one. All that man ever knew was his mortuary business, his house, and his three cars. By the way, Rick, did Burns have money problems, or wouldn't you know that? What I mean is, was there a significant mortgage still left to pay on the house when you bought it from Matthews?"

"I thought I had told you that before, Dave. I never knew a thing about the man's personal life or his finances. My real estate deal was handled entirely by my lawyer, and he told me nothing about the seller other than his name. At the closing, all I was required to do was endorse and initial a sheaf of legal papers, which, I am ashamed to admit, I never read very carefully. So if Burns had a mortgage on the place, I never knew about it. I also had no idea that he was in the undertaking business. I also did not know anything about what you have just told me about his disappearances. Anyway, Dave, it occurs to me that some people just want to cash out when they get into their retirement years, and they decide that they want to have a little fun before they die. That may be just what Burns did. It would not be a surprise to learn that he has been lollygagging in the sunshine down in Miami or in Bermuda ever since he has been missing, but who can say?" "Maybe you're right, Rick," Dave responded, "but in my opinion, that man wasn't the kind of person to enjoy anything except his solitude. I don't believe he ever smiled or laughed or had a happy moment in his entire life--not as far as I had ever seen. The only time I saw a pleasant expression on his face was the time I watched him washing that beautiful Cord automobile in his driveway, and that was more an expression of greed and not one of happiness or joy. In all the years I've lived here, I had never seen a visitor arrive at his house and stay for longer than an hour or so. Come to think of it, I'd never heard a radio or a TV being played there, or any other happy sounds coming from the direction of that house. The other day it was the noise from the workmen who were ripping everything out your kitchen that had to be the first sound of life from that house in all the time I have been living here. Talk about an unhappy and morbid character, it seemed to me that my neighbor Sedgwick Burns took away all the prizes."

"The first time that you and I talked, Dave, I thought you told me that Burns had been retired?"

"That's right, I did tell you that because as it happens, he was retired. What's the point you're trying to make, Rick?"

"The point is just this, if he was indeed retired from his funeral business, why was he always leaving his house in the evenings and driving his big hearse? You told me that he had another car, the old

Ford, which he also used. Oh, he also had the antique Cord, but that was not a car to be casually driven by a man like Burns, not according to your negative description of him." Dave looked squarely at me with a bewildered look frozen on his face. "God! I never thought about that. Maybe I was wrong, and he wasn't retired. On the other hand, he might have been using his big car as a conveyance for livery purposes." With a shrug of his shoulders, Dave picked up another can of beer, quickly snapped it open, and then took a very deep swallow.

"At night?" I asked loudly and in a skeptical voice.

Dave did not answer my last question. He just seemed to stare blankly at me. When he finally seemed to have regained his composure, he continued. "Could it be possible that the old gent had a girlfriend?" After saying that, his face screwed up into a big grin, and his hearty laughter broke the serious mood completely. "Who in the world would have wanted anything to do with that ancient, tight-fisted, old fossil?"

I quickly realized that there would be no further conversation with Dave worth anything this day, so it was now my cue to go home and face the music with Elaine. When I left the house earlier today, I told her that I would be back in about ten minutes, and that was more than an hour ago. Hopefully, she would be so involved with her renovating projects that she would not have even noticed that I was gone for so long.

When I entered the kitchen, I was surprised to see that all the wall cabinets had been hung and only the base cabinets had to be positioned and bolted down. Since the counter tops were not yet delivered, we would need to have our dinner out again. Darn it! I could hardly wait until this project is completed so we could sit down to one of Elaine's home-cooked meals. I was hungry since I had eaten only a couple pieces of leftover pizza for my early lunch. I also had a couple of cans of beer while I visited with Dave, but I was not about to mention that to Elaine. Why should I be asking myself for trouble?

"Hi Honey!" I said as I embraced Elaine with a light squeeze. "How is it coming along with your project?"

"Take a look for yourself," she responded.

"Wow!" That was my only word I could think to describe what I saw? "I have to say, Elaine, that those wall cabinets look great, and they will look even better after the counters are installed. There is nothing like a new kitchen to brighten up an old house. What time do you think they will be finishing here so we can go out somewhere to eat our evening meal?"

Elaine reached out to put her arms around my waist as she pulled me against her. "It looks like it will take them about an hour to bolt down the cabinets, and it may take another hour or more to finish putting all the workmen's tools away and get their mess cleaned up. So, are you telling me that you're hungry? Well, I am a bit surprised at that because when I looked through the kitchen window a little while ago, I saw you and Dave guzzling down your cans of beer. By the way, Rick, what of any interest did he have to talk about?"

"We were just reviewing the sports scene and gassing about politics." I lied. "When do you think you will want to go over there with me and meet Dave's wife named Shirley? Dave asked me about it again."

"Maybe I'll be able to get away for an hour or so tomorrow because it looks like the counter tops will not be ready for another day or two. I am getting very anxious to have this project completed so I can get back to doing my cooking around this place. I'm getting a little tired of our meals being eaten from carry-outs, and from fast-food restaurants."

"You and me both!" I answered. "I can hardly wait to be sitting down at our table with a platter of your extra-delicious spaghetti and meatballs. If I have to eat fried chicken or pizza one more time, I swear to you I will throw up! As I said that, I stuck my finger part way into my throat in a mock gesture of retching." Elaine laughed as she quickly shoved me away from her and said, "Amuse yourself for a little while, and I'll be along with you shortly."

I finally had some additional time to myself, so I thought I would go down into the cellar and locate the instruction handbooks for the furnace and the water heater. When we closed on the purchase of the house, the seller's attorney gave us everything except those two books, and I wanted to read them to learn how to maintain all that new equipment. I certainly knew how essential it was for to check out the furnace and make sure that it's in good working order before the winter months arrive.

On entering the cellar, I started my search for the manuals in the back storeroom which had once been a coal bin, but it had been converted for storage after the new gas furnace had been installed. Apparently, that had been done sometime within the last eight years. Piled up against the back wall in that room were many hastily stacked cardboard cartons and just what they contained was anyone's guess. I had seen them there earlier when the boys and I checked out the cellar, but I never took the time to inspect them to see what they might contain because I had assumed it was just some more useless trash items that we would eventually have to dispose of. Several of the cartons were bound with twine, so I used my pocket knife to cut the bindings from one box and then opened the flaps I saw six, one-gallon sized bottles of some liquid. Removing one of the bottles, I was startled when I quickly scanned its label which read: Egyptian Chemical Company, Aromatic Embalming Fluid. Unexpectedly, I flinched and almost dropped the bottle from my hand and onto the concrete floor. When I had finally regained my composure, I quickly placed the bottle back into the carton and shoved it to one side. After opening a half a dozen more cartons of that size, weight, and shape, I was satisfied they all contained the same product, so I then carefully interlocked the carton's before I placed them back in a pile.

I did not want Elaine to know what I had found in our cellar because the implication of that find would only serve to get her more nervous and anxious than she already was. I knew she would immediately assume that some of the embalming processes for the previous owner's funeral parlor had been performed right there in our cellar. That would be ridiculous for her to think that way, yet, I did not want to chance her learning anything about it and then jumping to her own conclusions.

While I was in the process of inspecting those cartons from within the pile, I ran across a wooden crate which required the assistance of a pinch bar to open. It contained some kind of mortician's device and a book of instructions packed along with it. The instruction book explained the process of using the device to extract blood from a corpse. Ugh! I quickly closed the lid of the crate and then pressed it tightly shut.

I was profoundly shaken-up by my findings, not for myself so much, but because of what Elaine might think about them. Above it all, I was more than ever convinced that I had to hide the morbid discoveries from her prying eyes. If she had the slightest inkling that the house had been used in any operation whatsoever of Burns' funeral business, including just the storage of excess embalming chemicals and paraphernalia, she would not want to stay in this house for a single night. As it was, I was so disturbed knowing about it, I doubted that I would be able to get a minute of sleep myself tonight.

Because of those disturbing items I had discovered stacked up in our cellar, I made up my mind that as soon as I got to my office in the morning, I would arrange a conference with our Real Estate Agent Pat Driscoll. I would then throw all of this intrigue right into her lap. However; after giving it a lot more thought, I decided not to do that since Elaine might hear about it from Pat, and I had to be very careful not to let that happen. Just how I would be able to keep Elaine from finding out about that disturbing discovery in our cellar was something I had not yet figured out, but I definitely would be working hard on the problem to resolve it.

~ *Chapter Five* ~

DISPOSING OF UNWANTED ITEMS

Two days had passed since I made the discovery of the cartons of embalming chemicals and the mortician's appliance stacked up in the storage room of our cellar. I never said a word about it to Elaine, and I had no intention of ever doing so. Still, with Elaine's rather extensive upstairs remodeling going on in full swing, she was likely to run across those things by accident. Elaine was always looking for empty cartons for one reason or another, and she might have remembered seeing those cartons in the cellar. In fact, I was sure of it since I now recognize that she mentioned them to me more than a week or so ago. What if she decided to scrounge around looking for an empty carton for some need of hers? The shock of her discovering about those chemicals would be disastrous for her, and she would insist that we sell the house. I could not allow that to happen because Elaine and I did not need that kind of disappointment or trouble at this point in our lives.

I knew, with absolute certainty, that I would have to dispose of those cartons, and would have to get it done in secret and in a big hurry. If I could figure out a way to get Elaine away from the house for a few hours, maybe I could enlist the help of Dave Farrell to help me get that job done. On second thought, it would be better do it myself because Dave loves to talk. With the things that are inside those cartons and that disturbing bloodletting apparatus I found there, it would probably be too much for Dave to keep it to himself. With Dave's knowing about it, chances are it would not take very long until the whole neighborhood would be buzzing with all kinds of rumors and innuendos about what might have gone on in our house during the time Burns was living there. Surely, Elaine would hear about it from Dave, or from his wife Shirley, or even from some stranger at the local supermarket. No! I would have to manage the disposal of those things without his help. I could ask my two boys to help me because there are an awful lot of heavy cartons down in our cellar to be removed, and I was not in the best physical condition to lift and carry them all by myself. Removing those things from our cellar would be, at the very least, a two-man job.

Both Ron and Glenn are well aware of just how sensitive their mother is, and they also both know how to keep their mouths closed if I ask them to. I would have to tell them about her latest reaction when she heard about the previous owner's profession of being a mortician. My recent distressing discovery of that embalming fluid in the cellar could push their mother entirely over the edge if she learns about it.

It was not until the Saturday morning a few days after my disturbing discovery in the cellar when a thought hit me almost like a thunderbolt. That thought was about how I might get Elaine away from our house for a couple of hours by arranging to have a family barbeque cookout--much like one of those we often used to have at our other home. Tomorrow is Sunday, and we had already waited much too long for an old-fashioned barbecue and family get-together in our side yard. Anyway, the interior of our house is still in such utter disorder that it could be the perfect solution to my problem over having to dispose of those disgusting things from our cellar.

By mentally reviewing the solution to the problem, it somehow gave me a small sense of relief after having a bit of difficulty sleeping at night. Since the day I first discovered those items in our cellar, I not only had trouble sleeping, but I also had been feeling quite edgy and irritable. I continually worried about Elaine finding them and her jumping to immediate conclusions about why they were in our cellar in the first place. That was also a question that kept rolling through my mind, just why in the devil were they there? While I thought it could be possible they had been placed there in temporary storage, the question I keep asking myself was why a private home's cellar is selected for them to be kept? I also wondered why Burns' grandnephew did not have them removed at a time ahead of putting the property up for sale. That would have been the correct thing for him to have done.

Sedgwick Burns may have been on the weird side, according to what Dave Farrell had told me, but the man certainly had no need to store those chemicals in his cellar to perform embalming procedures inside his own house. The man had owned a modern funeral parlor equipped to do that kind of work. More than likely, the cellar of his house probably was just a temporary and convenient place to store some of his overflow stock, and it had been left here and forgotten about after he suddenly disappeared. None of that seemed to be something for me to be unduly concerned over. Elaine, on the other hand, would be thinking the chemicals were being used for embalming dead bodies down in our cellar, or even inside the house itself. For my peace of mind, I did my best to dispel my concerns over those items being where they were in our cellar, but I had little success in doing so.

I was not able to put my barbeque plan into motion until later that Saturday afternoon when I found an opportunity to talk to Elaine about my idea of having a Sunday family cookout. At first, she was not too keen on the idea of arranging it with the family on such a short notice. She also felt that since our house is in such an uproar, Sunday would be a good day for her to get the house into some manageable order.

Tomorrow will be the only day that the construction crews will not be here, Elaine reasoned, and she wanted the place to be in perfect order before her daughters-in-law got to see it again. I very firmly told her I was getting pretty darn weary of the whole scene, and that we both deserved a bit of fun and relaxation for a change. I then reminded her it had been a long time since we had seen the boys and their spouses, not to mention our little grandson. Apparently, that remark did it! We would have our family gathering after all, and it would be just as I planned for it. Something good finally seemed to be working in my favor for a change.

Since Elaine was still busily involved with her renovation project, she asked me to extend the invitations by telephoning our boys and their spouses. Frankly, that was precisely what I had in my mind to do anyway. Using the upstairs telephone so Elaine could not overhear my conversations, I called Glenn's house first.

Glen's wife Martha answered the phone after three rings.

"Hello, Braden residence, may I ask who's calling?" Martha asked.

"Hello, Martha! This is your father-in-law calling. How have you and Glenn been doing these last few days?"

"Oh. Hello, Dad. We're both doing just fine and dandy. How's Ma doing?"

"She's quite well, but you know your mother-in-law. She is up to her shoulders in her house remodeling project, and it has not been very much fun around here for either of us. These past weeks have been much more than we had ever bargained for, but we are thankful it will not be too much longer before the worst of it will be completed, at least I hope so. Is Glenn there anywhere where I can speak to him?"

"He's standing right next to me. Do you want to talk to him?" "Yes, I would Like to speak to him, if you do not mind."

After a short silence on the other end of the line, Glenn answered. "Hello, Dad! What's cooking? How's Mom?"

"Your mother is just fine, but she is almost totally involved in her remodeling project--just as you would expect of her. It seems that she is finally doing some of the things that she always wanted to do, but never had the opportunity to do it until now. It is something that she has thought about ever since she finished her interior designing studies at college. Anyway, how would you and Martha like to come over tomorrow morning for a good old-fashioned barbeque cookout--just like the ones we used to have at the other house? Your mother and I are darn weary of the routine around here, and besides, we miss you all a lot. How about it, Son, do you possibly think you two can make it?"

"That sounds good to me, Dad, and anyway, Martha's anxious to see just what the house looks like since some of the renovations have been moving ahead. Mom attempted to describe it to her on the phone a few days ago, but you know how that goes. Wait for just a second, Dad, while I run it by her. After a momentary silence, Glenn came back on the line. No problem Dad, we'll be there, and what time do you want us to come, and what can we bring along with us for the table?"

"Your mother and I will be expecting the two of you early, say about eight in the morning would be okay, and all you have to bring with you is a six-pack of whatever brand of beer that you like. The reason that I am asking you to bring your own beer is because you do not seem to like my brand of beer. Oh, before I forget, Glenn, can you toss some of your work clothes into the trunk of your car? There are several cartons that I want to remove from our cellar, and they are just too darn heavy for me to lift all by myself because my back seems to be suffering from some of the beginnings of old age lately. Your brother Ron will also be there to help, or at least I hope he will. I still have to call him and ask if he can make it along with his family. Do you know if he's home today?"

"Your guess is as good as mine, Dad. Do you want me to call him for you and ask if they're planning to come to the barbecue?" "If you take care of that detail for me, I will certainly appreciate it, Glen, but also tell him about the work clothes because I will need his help as well as yours. I also think it will be a good idea for you to let me know sometime today if Ron and his family are going to make it tomorrow so your mother can prepare enough food for the cookout tomorrow."

"Okay, Dad, We'll be talking to you later. Be sure to say hello to Mom from the two of us. Good Bye."

"Just wait one second before you hang up, Glenn! There is another thing I want you to do for me, and I want you to stress this to Ron when you talk to him. If either of you takes time to talk to your mother later today or tomorrow, I prefer that you do not tell her about the work clothes that I asked you two to bring with you. I do not want her to know that I asked you two to help me move those things out of the cellar, and do not ask me why now, I will fill you both in on all the details when I see you tomorrow morning. Please do not say anything about any of this to your wives as well because they may comment about it to your mother. Is that understood, Glenn?"

"Why all the mystery Dad? Just what is it you want us to help move? Could it possibly be a dead body you found hidden in your cellar?" The next thing I heard was his laughter.

"Just trust me on this, Son. I promise you that I will tell you all about it when I see you and your brother, and then you will both fully understand what all the mystery is about. Goodbye, Glenn."

"Goodbye, Dad."

Hanging up the telephone, I immediately began thinking about a way to get Elaine out of the house for a couple of hours after the boys arrive on Sunday. Maybe I could talk her into taking the girls and Little Henry into town for some reason or another. I would have to plant a suggestion in her mind about something that could possibly interest all of them. I still have a little time before Sunday to give that idea a lot of hard thought. I also had to think of a place for us to dispose of those cartons from our cellar with their disturbing contents.

For the remainder of that day, I was kept busy helping Elaine with various projects around the house. Now that her kitchen part of the project was finally nearing completion, she wanted all of her cooking utensils and dishes removed from their shipping cartons and thoroughly washed, which was what we did in the laundry tubs in the cellar. During the time we were down there, I worried that she might go poking around and run across those cartons of the embalming chemicals stacked up in the storage room, but she never went anywhere near there. When we completed washing and drying all the dishes, we next inventoried her canned goods which we then placed on shelves inside her new kitchen pantry. By the time we finished with everything, we were both tired out and ready to go to bed. I was just about to climb into the shower when Elaine reminded me that I still had to buy the food for our cookout. Ah, I said to myself, that is just the excuse I was looking for to get her out of the house in the morning! I would have Elaine and the girls do the shopping for the food right after we finish with our breakfast. Getting them to do that should be an easy task because they all loved to go shopping, even if it was just to do grocery shopping.

In response to Elaine's current request for me to go out to the store, I exaggerated a tired and weary look and said, "I am just too darn tired to get dressed and take care of that tonight, Elaine. After the workout you put me through today, can this possibly be put off until morning?"

"I guess so," she answered, "but you had better take care of doing that right after we finish with our morning coffee. I am expecting them all to arrive here at eight in the morning, and I would like to have the food cooked and on the table before one-thirty or two in the afternoon. That way we can all sit down and have a very friendly card game after we finish eating."

On Sunday morning, the alarm clock woke me at seven o'clock, disrupting a deeply troubled dream. For several minutes I laid there in my bed reviewing in my mind that frightening dream, or, I should call it a nightmare. It seemed that I was lying on my back on a cold metal table with a bright light shining down on me. The light was so intense it bathed my eyelids in a fiery red glow. As I slowly opened my eyes, I could see a heavily bearded man standing directly over me. He was wearing a pair of black, horn-rimmed glasses with powerful lens magnification that enlarged his eyeballs to the size of two pale-blue billiard balls. His red-bearded face was heavily flushed and sweaty, and I could see drops of sweat dripping off of his wrinkled forehead and the tip of his nose as he bent over me. When I was just about to scream, he lifted his hand above my face, and I saw that he was holding a long, thin tube--it was a probe, and he was just about to jab it into my neck. As he began pressing the instrument closer to my neck, I tried to scream but I could not because I was in a state of complete paralysis and unable to do anything at all about it. I then felt a sharp pain as the probe grazed my neck which immediately woke up from my nightmare. For several minutes, I laid in my bed dripping wet with sweat, and my entire body was shaking. It took me several long minutes before I was able to bring myself out of that upsetting nightmare and for me to arrive back into the real world.

Elaine and I had just finished drinking our cups of hot tea that Sunday morning when I heard a car coming into our driveway. I quickly looked out the window and saw that it was Glenn and Martha, then I Glanced at the wall clock and noticed that they had arrived a little early. Just as they began to climb out of their car, I saw Ron's car turn into the driveway and park next to Glenn's station wagon. After it was parked, Ron, Paula, and Henry got out and walked over to greet Glenn and Martha. I watched from the corner window as the two brothers shook hands and sparred around in a joking manner. Those are two fine boys, I thought. I am a happy man to have such sons as Ron and Glenn, and for me to have married such a helpful and devoted woman like my dear wife, Elaine.

Having finished with their brief visit in the driveway, they all started toward the side door of the house. I saw that Glenn had a six-pack of beer in his hand, and Ron was carrying a brown bag under his arm. Just as they approached the entrance door, they made a detour to the side end of the house, where I could see Glenn pointing to the turret room high up on the roof, and all their eyes turned upward in that direction. Undoubtedly, Glenn was telling the girls about Elaine's plan to turn it into an observatory. I could easily see the approving looks on all their faces. A minute later, they walked deeper into the backyard where I lost sight of them.

Within several minutes, I heard the sound of the front door chime, but Elaine reached the door before I could get to it and she let them all into the house. When we had finished with our greetings, Elaine invited them to look at our not-quite-completed, kitchen.

As I stood there quietly in the kitchen, I listened to their many compliments over the work Elaine had done, and I then realized that I also should have been a lot more complimentary to her about her project than I had been.

"The only major improvement that has not yet been completed in this room as you all can all plainly see," Elaine said, "is the flooring. According to my schedule, that project should be done next Wednesday when the floor will be finished in an off-white vinyl with a slightly embossed finish. It will not be overpowering because I don't want it to clash with the wallpaper that I've picked out for the room. After that, we are planning to start in the living room, and that place will also be a big job, but nothing at all like the kitchen project had turned out to be."

Leading us all out of the kitchen and into the dining room, which was still a mess, Elaine went on to describe what plans she had for that room. While approaching the living room, we had to dodge a bunch of boxes and other construction type items just to enter the center of the room. The walls had all been stripped of their original dark and drab wallpaper, which now openly exposed the original plaster which had evolved into a dirty looking mustard color. After Elaine had given us a brief description of her plans for that room, we moved to the next part of the house. I thought it was just the right time for the boys and me to break away from them so that I could fill them in on all the critical details of my plan for what I had found in our cellar.

"Pardon me, Honey," I said to Elaine just as she was about to speak, "do you mind if the boys and I take a breather for a while? They have both seen most of the place before, and they will have some more time to go through the house again later."

Without looking at me, Elaine said, "The three of you go right ahead, the girls and I will not be too much longer anyway. But do not stray very far away because we will be having a breakfast of oatmeal, coffee, and the pecan coffee cake Ron and Paula brought for us. I know that's not much, but we don't want to spoil the delicious lunch of baby barbeque ribs we will be having later this afternoon."

Leaving the ladies and Henry, I motioned the boys to follow me down the stairs and into the cellar. When we arrived, I cautioned Ron and Glenn to please use your soft voices when you are talking because I did not want any loud responses from them that might be heard by the ladies upstairs. As I did that, I saw a questioning look pass from Ron to Glenn, who merely shrugged his shoulders.

"Dad, what's up?" Ron asked with a quizzical look. "What is it you found here that's got you so concerned and worked up, and also what's inside all those cartons stacked up there? Glenn told me that there were only a few cartons you had to be removed, but there appears to be quite a pile of them."

"Please be patient for just a minute more while I explain it all to you. Did you both remember to bring your work clothes with you? I hope neither of you said anything about those clothes to your wives. Did you?" I looked squarely at both of them as I asked that.

They both responded at the same time, "No, Dad!"

"All right," I said, "I am now going to show you why it is so important that your mother does not know what was left here in this cellar and is stacked up here. If your mother knew, or if she finds out about it, we may as well put this house right back on the market and try to sell it. With all the work your mother has already put into her remodeling project, it will surely break her heart. Not only that, but it will cause us a very substantial financial loss. At our ages it would not be something we will be able to recover from easily. So you see, this is a serious situation, and I want you both to understand that. Now if you are both quite ready, I will show you what is in those cartons."

Picking up a box closest to me, I opened its flaps and carefully removed one of the bottles which I then handed to Glenn. Ron quickly moved closer to read its label along with him. I could immediately hear a low whistle emanate from Ron.

"My God! It's formaldehyde or embalming fluid! What the heck is all of that funeral home stuff doing stacked down here in your cellar, Dad?"

"Keep your voices down!" I again cautioned both of them. "I do not want your mother to hear us and come down here to see what is going on. You can hear sounds through these old, wooden floors like they are made of paper."

"I'm sorry Dad. What's this all about?" Ron then asked.

"I do not want to talk about it down here where we may be overheard or interrupted, so after I show you a few more things, we will go out to the garage and I will fill you both in on what I know about it." I then reached for the wooden crate which contained the bloodletting device and I opened its lid. As they peered inside and quickly scanned the label, I could see a look of shock and disbelief on their faces. Closing the crate and the carton, I shoved them back toward the wall and turned to leave the storeroom. Both boys followed closely behind me as we left the cellar, then exiting the house, we headed outside toward the garage.

Upon our reaching the front of the garage, I pulled up three of our old kitchen chairs which I had earlier stacked just inside one of the doors, and the three of us sat facing each another. It took me about twenty minutes to tell them what Dave Farrell had said to me about Burns having been a mortician and the story about his disappearance. Once more I stressed the adverse effect my remark about the previous owner's profession had on their mother, and after a bit of speculation on their part, we all agreed that we had no other choice but to remove those cartons before she had a chance to discover them. I again cautioned them not to breathe a word of any of this to their wives; otherwise, it could leak back to their mother. They both agreed that not discussing anything about it to their spouses was probably the wise thing for them to do.

When we left the garage and returned to the house, we found that the ladies and young Henry were all seated at the table in the dining room. "We were just about to call you," Elaine said as she looked up from the table when we entered the room. "Let's just eat our breakfast now, and then you had better get to the supermarket and pick up those groceries we need, Rick. I am anxious to get the potato salad started, and Martha promised to help me in the kitchen while Paula looks after Henry." I could hear the impatience in her voice as she awaited my response.

"Would you mind terribly, Elaine," I said, "if I do not go this morning to do the shopping? The boys and I have a few things we want to look at in the attic, and I would much appreciate it if you and the girls would go. You can stop off at that new supermarket downtown, and while you are there, you can buy Henry a fun toy from his Grandpa and Grandma. How about it, Elaine, are you all willing to do this for me?"

Turning her eyes toward Paula and Martha, Elaine asked, "what do you girls think we should do? Shall we give your father-in-law a little time to be alone with his two sons this morning? Are you in favor of doing some shopping even if it is only to our local supermarket?"

"Fine with me," Martha said.

"The same with me," Paula chimed in happily.

"Then, let's all finish up our breakfast and get ready to leave," Elaine said as she sliced the coffee cake into a dozen or more small wedges and began passing them around the table to us.

As soon as the ladies and Henry left the house in Paula's car, Ron, Glenn, and I quickly changed into our work clothes and went down into the cellar. We had already decided that the easiest way for us to remove the cartons was to hand them out through the no-longer-used coal access door. Because we found it was rusted tightly shut, it took several blows from a hammer and the use of a wedge to get it open.

Since Paula had taken Ron's car, it left Glenn's station wagon and my sedan available to load all of those cartons. There were so many boxes for us to remove from the cellar that I was a little concerned that we would not be able to fit all of them into the two cars. Because my car was smaller than Glenn's station wagon, we loaded his car first. The cartons filled both the back seat and the large cargo area at the rear. By the time we brought out the last of the boxes from the cellar, we were just barely able to squeeze them into the back seat of my car.

The three of us were rather tired after our workout, and Glenn suggested we should stop somewhere to rest and have a cup of coffee. I immediately put the squash on that idea because I wanted to have the load dropped off somewhere, and then have us back home again before the ladies returned from their shopping trip. We would also have to clean up and change back into our street clothes before their arrival.

While we were trying to decide where we would take those things and dump them, Ron came up with the bright idea that we could drop them off at a local funeral parlor. "It seems such a shame, he said, to throw them into the dump when they appear to be brand-new items." After we kicked this idea around for a minute or two, we agreed that it probably was the best solution to our problem.

Having checked to be sure that we had everything fully loaded into both vehicles, we then quickly left the house and began driving toward the downtown area while praying that we did not see the ladies on their return trip from the market. That seemed rather unlikely though because Elaine usually took a fair amount of time when doing her shopping. I was riding in the driver's seat of my car next to Ron, while Glenn was following behind us in his station wagon. We were just a few miles away from my house, when Ron, who had been watching intently, spotted a funeral parlor. As I swung my car into its parking lot, I glanced into the rear-view mirror to be sure that Glenn was still behind us. After we parked both cars in the lot, Ron volunteered to go inside and talk to the funeral director. His idea was for him to ask if he wanted the things we had brought with us in our cars.

Within several minutes from Ron's entering the building before we saw him come out the side door of the parlor accompanied by a tall, slender, middle-aged man. The neatly dressed man was wearing a sharp looking black pinstripe suit. After the brief introductions were over, the man asked to see what we were offering him. Opening up one of the cartons containing the embalming fluid, I showed him one of the bottles. I also told him that there was a new mortician's device packed inside the crate that he could also have.

As the man viewed the cartons of embalming fluid and the contents of the crate, he listened to what I had to say about them, and his expression remained unchanged. I explained to him that I wanted no money for them and that I only wanted to get rid of those things. When he asked how I had acquired them, I told him the truth, they had left in my house by its previous owner whose name was Sedgwick Burns. His bland expression changed instantly while stifling an audible gasp upon hearing that name, then he said he had no need for those items, and that we should probably take all of them directly to the county dump if we did not want them. Then, turning on his heel he quickly walked away from us and entered the side door of his mortuary and went inside. My sons and I were stunned by his unexpected actions, and for several minutes we just stood there in the parking lot looking at the building. Finally, not knowing what to say about his entirely strange reaction, we climbed back into our vehicles and headed both cars straight toward the county dump.

Within a short driving time, we had reached the entrance to the dump where I paid the attendant his fee for both cars and we drove them to the disposal site. Within several more minutes, we unloaded everything from both vehicles and leaving them next to a massive pile of trash and mixed garbage.

Glancing into the rearview mirror as we drove away from the dump site, we saw the attendant open one of the cartons and then watched as he removed one of the bottles from it. I hoped he did not think it was something alcoholic to drink, and I cringed at the thought of it. Ron gave me a sideways look and then laughed loudly.

"What a day this is starting out to be, Dad," Ron said. "It's a day I would like to write down in my memoirs."

"If we hurry, we may get back to the house before the girls return from their shopping trip," I said. "I hope your brother is capable of keeping up with us," I remarked somewhat jokingly as I applied more pressure on the gas pedal.

As it turned out for us, we were lucky because we beat the ladies back to our house by about twenty minutes. That gave the three of us the needed time to clean ourselves up in the basement wash tubs and change back into our street clothes.

Our barbecue that Sunday afternoon turned out to be a big success for our family, and what happened earlier that day, our disposal of the embalming fluid, remained a secret between my two sons and me for quite some time.

~ *Chapter Six* ~

THE SECOND DISCOVERY

Once Elaine's kitchen remodeling had reached the final stages of completion, several other aspects of her project got started. The direction now was toward restoring all the woodwork trim and the hardwood floors from the top to the bottom of the house. That work mainly would consist of stripping the old, darkened varnish, doing extensive sanding and staining, and finally revarnishing all the wood with a durable, light varnish. That particular facet of the project was going to be a messy job and would require quite a bit of time. Although Elaine was not happy with the small double-hung windows in most of the house, Elaine was not willing to replace any of them because she was determined to preserve the original outside appearance of the building I was happy she felt that way since I knew the cost of replacing windows would be a lot more than our budget could handle. In a short time, the expenses connected with the project were mounting up and they were beginning to trouble me.

All week long the work crew had been sanding and refinishing the woodwork surrounding the ceiling moldings, the inside doors and window frames, and the wardrobe cabinets. The job foreman told Elaine that he hoped to finish that work before they would start stripping all the floor base moldings, and lastly the hardwood floors. Workers began in the foyer and they were now busily working in the living room. Another crew of wood finishers was sanding wainscoting alongside the stairs and second floor hallways. There were also several squeaky stairs which needed to be tightened, along with replacement of all the carpet treads and pads all the way up the central stairway's third level. Finally, high-quality carpeting would be replacing all of the old floor coverings in the Landings and hallways.

I was elated when the workmen uncovered beautiful parquet flooring that long ago had been covered over by the old carpeting in the downstairs den. When it is refinished, I guessed it would look great, and I had already laid my claim to that room as my private office. I cautioned Elaine not to make any other changes in that room without consulting with me first since that is the one room in the house that I wanted to be able to have some input over. I was happy when Elaine agreed to my wishes, although it was evident to me that she made that decision reluctantly.

By the time the project was into the middle of the summer months, we had just about reached the halfway point of renovating the interior of the house, and to my dismay, there had already been some significant cost overruns in most areas. I warned Elaine that she might have to reconsider some of her more costly remodeling plans, but she assured me that the final figure would end up close to her original estimate. "I am an accountant," I told her adamantly, "and if you can do that, I would like to learn how." "Well, I suppose I will just have to save on the window treatments after everything else is completed," Elaine responded in an irritated manner. From the twenty-five years, I have been married to her, I knew that Elaine always disliked hearing uncomfortable facts that she did not agree with.

"Do you mean to tell me that the window treatments will account for that much of the cost of the entire project?" I asked incredulously. Somehow I found that not to be even possible.

"The window treatments which I've already selected for every single window inside the house will cost us somewhere close to a quarter of the renovation's total cost," was her matter-of-fact reply. Because Elaine did not want to talk to me further on the subject, she hurriedly left the room in somewhat of a huff. Her parting excuse for her exit was she had to make a fast check on the progress of the sanding and staining of the main hallway.

Because I was feeling a state of growing agitation over Elaine's attitude, I decided to get out of the house for a while and try to cool down and relax my thoughts. As I stepped out the side door to the yard, I was loudly greeted by Dave Farrell who was in his yard knocking a golf ball around.

"How are things going over there at your place, Rick?" Dave asked. "Lately it sounds rather as if you're getting things under control inside because it's been so quiet." Leaning his putter against a nearby tree, he walked over to the fence close where I stood.

"Why are you so glum looking, Pal?" Dave asked with honest concern. "Is all that activity inside your place finally getting to you?"

"I would have to say yes, Dave, it is getting to be old stuff," I responded, "and we are only about halfway through the blasted project. I had no idea when we started this thing just how long it would take to complete it, or just how much it would end up costing us. If I had also known what our house has turned into with everything piled everywhere; we could have stayed in a hotel room until the project is finished, I said sullenly."

"I can understand that feeling, Rick, but just think how nice it's going to be for you two when it's all finished. By the way, do you know that I've never once seen the interior of your house? Is there any chance of my taking a quick peek inside there now? I've always wondered about the way that old hermit Burns had lived. Was the place clean when you moved in there?"

I was a little taken back at his last question, but I tried not to show that I was a bit annoyed over what he had said. Because I had visited with Dave several times, I had become aware of his nosey personality, and I also knew he had a direct manner of speaking.

"It is not a good time, Dave. There is a pack of workmen inside sanding and refinishing every piece of hardwood in sight, and it is in a state of chaos everywhere. Elaine is still up to her eyeballs in work, and that is why I came out here in the yard. I needed a breath of fresh air and a little space away from it all." "Yeah, I know what you mean! My Shirley isn't much fun to be around when she's got her mind all cluttered up with problems. Women are like that you know. Say, Rick, I saw you and your two sons loading carloads of boxes a couple of sundays ago. What the heck was that all about? Did that Matthews fellow leave a ton of his old garbage inside there for you to have to dispose of?"

I had the immediate feeling that Dave was probing me for information, and it was just to satisfy his nosey curiosity. When my sons and I moved those cartons of embalming fluid from the cellar, I never thought that Dave might be watching us from his yard. I had no intention of telling him the truth because I knew where that could lead to. I quickly realized that I would have to fabricate a little white lie to appease him. It seemed to me that I was beginning to become quite good at lying to everyone over the damn old house.

"Oh, it was nothing more than a lot of old newspapers and magazines that were left stacked up in boxes down in our cellar. Burns must have been busy reading that media to have accumulated so much of that kind of stuff, some of which dated back to the tail end of the war years. My sons and I hauled it all to the county dump to get rid of it." I carefully watched his face as I spoke, and it seemed apparent to me that he had bought the lie. "I'd have to say that Sedgwick Burns was a collector," Dave said. "I'll bet he never tossed out a thing in all the years he lived there. On garbage and trash pickup days there was usually very little of anything at the curb in front of his house for the weekly pickup. Now that I think about it, I never saw him do any shopping at our local supermarket. He must have eaten all of his meals out, yet I never saw him eating in any of our local restaurants." Almost as an afterthought, Dave asked, "Was there a refrigerator in the house when you bought it, Rick?"

"No, there was not," I responded. "The refrigerator had been removed earlier, but there was a huge cast-iron stove that must have weighed at least a ton or more. We soon had the workmen dispose of that monster."

"Yeah, Shirley and I saw that thing being carried out by four husky guys. Not to change the subject, Rick, but have you had an opportunity to look around your property for any of those missing things of mine that I'd previously asked you about?"

"What are those things, Dave?" I asked feeling a bit baffled at his question.

"I'm asking about my missing gardening tools and some other things of mine that turned up missing when Burns lived here. You know, the items I branded with my initials, the tarp, the buckets, and the spade. I told you some time ago that they were missing, and that I'd always suspected Burns had taken them."

"Oh, those things!" I said as I finally realized what he was talking about.

"No," I said, "I have not seen anything like you described anywhere around my house. To tell you the truth, with all that has been going on inside there, I have not had any time to look for them. I also have not peeked into that loft over our garage to see what treasures might still be stored up there. I can see several windows that are so opaque from years of dirt and grime I doubt they allow any light to illuminate the loft. Say, Dave, would you mind holding the ladder for me while I poke my nose up there through the ceiling's trapdoor? I am curious about how much storage space there is since I may need it to store our lawn furniture and a few other things before the cold weather sets in on us on us."

"I'll be more than happy to oblige you, Rick, but why don't you just go up into the loft using the inside stairway?"

"What stairway might you be talking about?"

"I'm talking about the inside stairway at the north end of your garage, Dave said. There's a door that goes to a narrow staircase leading up to the loft. I happened to hear about it one time when I was visiting your neighbor to the north of your house whose name is Hector Bates. Have you met him yet?"

"No, I answered," and I then I waited for more information from Dave about the stairway.

"Well, I seem to recall it was several years ago and, Hector and I were sitting in his backyard having a beer or two while we were solving some of the problems of the world. I just happened to glance over in the direction of Burns' garage, and that's when I saw the door there. In all the times I'd visited with Hector in the past, I'd never noticed it, so I asked him what was behind it. He told me it was an enclosed stairway that led up to the garage's loft. He also said that he occasionally saw Burns carrying boxes and other things in and out through that door. Apparently, Burns stored a variety of items upstairs in the loft. I even remember that Hector once described an incident that happened one evening just before dark. He said he walked closer to the fence to try to get a better look at what they brought up the stairs, and just as he got to the fence, Old Man Burns came down those stairs with another man. He said that when Burns saw him standing there next to the fence, he gave him a hard look that could kill. Hector immediately turned his back to the two of them and returned to his lawn chair. Don't you think that's a rather strange story, Rick?"

"Yes, strange," I said. "I guess that stairway is the easiest way to get up there all right, and I hate to say it to you, Dave, but I never noticed that there was a door on that north end of my garage."

"Would you mind if I go with you and take a closer look for myself?" Dave asked.

"I would not mind at all. Come on over. I can use the company."

When Dave joined me next at the garage, I realized that the reason I had never noticed that door before was it was made of the same siding material as the rest of the building, and it had no trim to set it off. When we approached the door, I grasped its rusty handle firmly and gave it a hard yank. It would not budge! It appeared to be tightly locked, so I pulled a set of house keys from my pocket, and I began trying each of them in the lock, but none of them fit. Now, just what in the heck do we do? I asked as I looked at Dave.

"I guess you'll just have to use your ladder and go up there through the overhead trapdoor, just as you had already thought of doing." That was Dave's simple solution to my problem.

That was just what I had already decided I would do, but I wondered why I had not been given a key to that door when we attended the meeting at the realty office during the house closing. I had assumed that we were given the keys that fit the locks to every door on the property. Could it be possible there are other locked doors I will find? I hope that would not be the case!

After having opened one of the overhead garage doors, Dave followed me inside and helped me lift the heavy wooden ladder from its wall hooks. Having visually located the trapdoor in the ceiling, we positioned the ladder against the side wall, and I climbed the rungs to the top while Dave held the ladder firmly at the bottom. I had considerable difficulty opening the trapdoor because it so snugly fit, but I finally popped it open by hitting it upward a few times with the palm of my hand. As the door dropped inside to the floor of the loft, a thin cloud of gray dust descended on top of me. After I had wiped the earth from my eyes and cleared my throat, I climbed a few more rungs up the ladder and poked my head into the loft. The odor of dry rot, mildew, and dust immediately invaded my nostrils, and the warm, foul air nearly took my breath away. I gazed ahead as far as I could into the semi-darkness of the room, and it took me a few seconds before my eyes were able to adjust to the dim light. I was stunned to see that the area closest to me was piled high with cardboard cartons appearing to be similar to those the boys and I had hauled out of the cellar. Could it be that this was more of the same kind of merchandise? I sincerely hoped not! I could not believe that I might have to face the ordeal again of disposing of more of that embalming fluid.

I stood on the ladder for several minutes more while I continued gazing toward the back of the dark loft. Finally, when it was apparent that Dave's curiosity could stand it no longer, I heard him shout from below.

"What is it you're seeing, Rick? Are any of my things there, or can't you see inside well enough to determine that?"

Without answering him, I started back down the ladder, and after I had descended only a few rungs, I reached up and pulled the trap door shut. Again a shower of dust and dirt engulfed me causing me to gag and cough. Upon entering the bottom of the ladder, I brushed myself off as I looked at Dave standing there staring hard at me while still awaiting my response to his question.

"It was too dark up there in the loft for me to see very well, Dave. About the only things I was able to see were stacks of magazines, some pieces of old office furniture, and a row of metal filing cabinets. I guess I will have to go up here sometime later with a flashlight or an extension cord. The loft is also full of scary looking spider webs, and I am not dressed for climbing around in the dirt and dust. Maybe I will do that sometime later this afternoon after I change into my work clothes."

I could not help noticing Dave's disappointment over my comments. I was thinking he was hoping that all of his missing items would be hidden up there in that loft. I had to change my clothes, as I said to Dave, and come back later, but this time I will be alone when I examine the contents of the loft. One thing that I did not want was to have Dave looking over my shoulder when I did that because I had a good idea about what was inside those cardboard cartons.

As things developed, I was not able to get back to the garage until after Elaine and I had finished our dinner because she had me working with her upstairs in the turret room where we spent most of that afternoon peeling the ugly old wallpaper from the walls using an electric steamer and hand scrapers. By the time we finished that dirty and tiring project, it was time for us to clean up, get dressed, and have our evening meal. We were both so fatigued because of our hard labor, I suggested that we drive to Belamy's Restaurant. Elaine was not in favor of that much food, so we settled for a couple of Whoppers with French fries we ordered from a nearby Burger King.

We immediately returned home after we finished our meal and I changed back into my work clothes and located a long extension cord and a trouble light to take with me to the garage. As I left the house, I watched for Dave because I did not want him to see what I was up to. I had told him I would be returning to the garage in the afternoon, and since it was now in the evening, I felt reasonably sure he would not spot me. I was guessing that Dave was probably comfortably seated in front of his television set while half asleep with a can of beer in his hand. That is what he said he and Shirley did every night after they finished their evening meal.

Upon my entering the garage, I slowly opened the overhead door while being careful not to make any noise that Dave might hear. The ladder was still against the wall where it had been left earlier. I located an electrical outlet, plugged the end of the extension cord into it, and played it out as I slowly climbed up the rungs of the ladder. Upon reaching the ceiling, I pushed the trapdoor open with one hand while I held the trouble light with the other as the door dropped inside with a dull thud. I held my breath until the dust down settled because I dared not cough loudly and alert Dave who just might hear it.

When the foul air had cleared enough for me to breathe freely again, I flipped the light switch and poked my head into the loft. With the light brightly illuminating the area, I could see strange lacy shadows which had been created by those spider webs that seemed to be just about everywhere. Along one side were the cardboard cartons I had seen earlier, and they were arranged in a neat row three levels high. When I examined one of them in the light, I realized they were somewhat different from those my boys and I had removed from my cellar, these cartons were more rectangular, while the others were square. I could not read the printing on the sides of the boxes because the labels were so discolored. I had to get a better look inside one of them to see what they contained. But before I did that, I wanted to search the rest of the loft.

I next held the light high over my head because I wanted to get a better view of what might be lying in the dark shadows at the back end of the room. At one end I could see many things covered with a thick layer of gray dust, they appeared to be pieces of old, wooden office furniture including a large desk, several file cabinets, chairs, and the like. Peering deeper inside the loft, I spotted a row of newer looking metal filing cabinets with something like large hat boxes stacked on top. Beyond the file cabinets, I could distinguish something that appeared to be something lying on the floor that was rather large and dark. I Removed one of the boxes from the top of a file cabinet, and after I opened it I found it to be a record storage box filled with old yellowed papers and documents. Carefully, I set that box to one side, then proceeded to remove several more of the boxes to enable me to see what was lying on the floor behind the cabinets. Holding my light ahead and forward through the opening, I saw that whatever it was there lying there was covered with a tarp, and as much as I did not want to examine it further, my curiosity got the best of me. With a bit of difficulty I was able to climb over the top of the file cabinet and hook the trouble light onto an overhead rafter. Taking a firm grip on one corner of the tarp, I slowly and carefully pulled it toward me. I was taking it slowly because I did not want to stir a lot of dust into the air.

Good Lord! I gasped loudly, I could not believe what it was that I was looking at. Right there in front of my eyes stood a neat row of dark and highly-varnished, wooden coffins, and each of them had a heavily tarnished brass nameplate affixed to its cover.

It took several minutes for me to collect my senses after that shock, When I was finally able to regain my senses again, I quickly unhooked the electrical cord from the overhead rafter, and carefully directed the trouble light ahead of me. I then climbed back over the file cabinet as fast as I could. After taking a few seconds to catch my breath, I sat down on a dusty office chair and allowed my heart to return to a near-normal beat. This situation is getting entirely out of hand. What is the heck kind of place this, anyway? I said aloud. I then began to wonder what other shocking surprises might be in this loft, or possibly still hidden somewhere else within the property.

Before I left the loft, I opened one of the cardboard cartons, and just as I had suspected, it contained more bottles of embalming fluid similar to those we had removed from the cellar. After thinking about the implications and the magnitude of this latest discovery, I realized I had to do something drastic to bring an end to it. Leaving the loft through the trapdoor I closed it tightly behind me, and before I left the garage, I moved the ladder away from where it was standing beneath the trapdoor, and with some effort, I replaced it on its wall hooks.

After I returned to the house, I went down to the cellar to wash my hands and face, using the laundry tubs and some of Elaine's heavy-duty laundry detergent. I did not want Elaine to see me before I got cleaned up, or she would ask a lot of questions of me for which I was not prepared to answer. I did not want to have to explain my recent activities to her either because I did not want to have to lie to her again. I decided that tomorrow I would try to learn some badly-needed answers. I also had to learn a lot more about the mysterious and eccentric Sedgwick Burns, and about those upsetting and disgusting items that had been popping up on the property.

~ *Chapter Seven* ~

MEETING HECTOR BATES

Everything my neighbor Dave Farrell had previously told me about Sedgwick Burns was interesting to me, but I felt there was a lot more of his foolish fancy than there was fact in his stories. Because of his apparent personal dislike for Burns, I became reasonably sure that he tended to exaggerate many of the things he had told me. I also felt that Dave probably was jumping to conclusions over the missing items from his yard, such as the garden tools he accused Burns of stealing. If the truth was known, Dave probably had lent those missing things of his to some of the neighbors, and just forgot which of them had borrowed them from him. And as for Burns and his late-night carousing, some people are just night people who never seem to accomplish anything during the daytime, so they do their jobs late in the evenings. It is possible Burns was just that kind of a man.

Although the items that I found, the embalming fluids and the caskets, were shocking to me, they were not that illegal to store in a home, as far as I knew anyway. After all, Burns had worked for many years as a mortician. He also owned his own funeral business, and his family had been in that line of work for practically a century. It would stand to reason they had produced a lot of worn-out tools of the trade, along with outdated items such as those old and unsaleable coffins and chemicals of no further value to him. Being a frugal individual, he probably hoarded them in the house and garage loft rather than having thrown them away. From the looks of the house's attic, the storeroom in the cellar, and the loft in the garage, it is possible that my conclusions may be correct. After several minutes of this kind of mind-probing, I was beginning to realize I was allowing my fears and prejudices to influence my better judgment about everything. Dave Farrell's negative comments to me, most definitely, helped to sway me along in that direction.

There was some doubt in my mind that Sedgwick Burns was, or is, depending on whether he is still alive or not, a strange and eccentric character. If even only half of the things I had been told about him by Dave were true, Burns could be a prime subject for a behavioral study. I suppose living by himself for so many years had served to intensify his peculiarities. His having to deal with dead bodies and bereaved people through the years, probably did not help matters very much either. Well, I also knew that some people take on the burdens of those whom they have contact with, and as far as I was concerned, for me that is reason enough to seek out happy and contented souls and try my best to live an upbeat and happy lifestyle.

I decided to get out of the house for a little while and visit a neighbor by the name of Hector Bates. Mr. Bates lives in the house next door to me and I want to introduce myself to him. According to what Dave Farrell told me, Hector knew a lot more about what had happened in the Burns' house over the years than anyone else in the neighborhood. The only problem, as I saw it, was that Bates could be just as prejudiced against Burns as Dave is, perhaps even more so. Nevertheless, I wanted to get his opinion of Burns for what little it might be worth to me.

I had intended to visit next door and introduce myself to Hector Bates ever since we moved into our house, but for one reason or another I had never gotten around to doing it. I would use that as my excuse to talk to him today. It seemed rather funny though; I had not set eyes on that man from the day we moved here. Anyway,

I will go over there right now and ring his doorbell and see if he is up to a visit from me.

When I arrived at Hector Bates' front door, I pressed the doorbell and waited. For almost a full minute there was no response, so I pushed the button a second time and waited. Again there was no response. The man is not at home, I said aloud. Maybe I should come back later this evening and try again. I was just about to leave when I saw the door open a crack and I could see a pair of tired looking eyes peeking out at me. "Hello there," I said as I looked into those eyes. "I'm your neighbor from the house next door, and I thought I would stop over and introduce myself to you, Mr. Bates."

The door opened a bit wider, and a small, slender, gray-haired old man, wearing a pair of thick spectacles, stepped out onto the front porch to face me. Taking a few seconds to adjust his pale blue eyes to the bright outside light, he then extended a delicate hand to me for a handshake.

"How do you do?" He said in volume and tone that was somewhat more than a whisper. "You look unfamiliar to me. Did I hear you say that you're my neighbor?" As he spoke, he half-cocked his ear toward me to better understand my answer. Apparently, Hector Bates had a hearing problem because I could see a black hearing-aid sticking in his left ear.

Leaning closer to Bates, I spoke in a louder voice. "My name is Rick Braden, Mister Bates, and I am your new neighbor to the south of your house. I bought the old Burns residence earlier this year. You are Hector Bates, are you not? Dave Farrell told me about you, Sir, and I am ashamed to tell you that I have been living next door to you for a few months now, but this is the first opportunity I have had to visit your House and introduce myself to you. Please forgive me for the long delay, Sir." I could immediately see his face soften into a smile as I spoke, and his tired old eyes seemed to have taken on the hint of a smile.

"That's entirely all right, young man, and, yes, I am Hector Bates. I know you've been busy next door because I can hear all the noise of construction that's been going on there. Won't you please step inside and take a seat in my parlor? It gets very lonely for me in this big old place all by myself, and I always welcome some company." As he spoke, he reached out and took my elbow and gently guided me inside through the front door.

As soon as we were both comfortably seated in the living room, he asked me if I would like a cup of hot tea. I was just about to say no to him when he said it was his tea time and he would fix a cup for each of us. With that, he left the room and slowly headed toward his kitchen.

Sitting there in my chair, I casually glanced around the room. The decor was very old looking and somewhat run-down. In that regard, it was much like our house had been before we began making the much-needed changes to it. Everything in the parlor was very old-fashioned and quite drab, with thick base moldings and matching crown moldings twelve-feet across the ceiling. The room had a rather formal and ornate fireplace which was faced with an olive-colored ceramic tile. I began to think both this house and our house next door could have been built by the same contractor sometime back in the 1880s. At least a dozen old framed photographs were strung side-by-side across the mantle. On the far wall from where I stood were three fairly large, oval-shaped tintypes. One was of a couple who were dressed in turn-of-the-century wedding clothes. To the left of that one was a photograph of a man in a dark suit wearing a high celluloid collar and a cravat. On the right of that was a photo of a heavyset woman with a huge hairdo and an ostrich feather sticking out of her hat. I was looking that way as Hector Bates returned from his kitchen with a tray in his hands.

The two of us sat quietly facing each other while sipping our cups of tea and munching on oatmeal cookies. For the next half hour, we chatted about everything but what was really on my mind, which was Sedgwick Burns and that house Elaine and I had bought next door. Finally, I decided it was time to get right to the heart of my visit, and I leaned forward in my chair as I spoke.

"May I ask you, Mister Bates, what was your impression of your neighbor Sedgwick Burns? Do you mind telling me that? Although

I bought his house from his estate, I have yet to see a photograph of him. I have also heard a few unflattering remarks about him from our neighbor Dave Farrell."

Before he answered my question, he reached into his breast pocket and pulled out a well-worn looking and tobacco-stained Meerschaum pipe which he immediately clamped between his teeth. I watched and waited for him to fill the pipe's bowl with smoking tobacco and then strike a match and light it, but he merely continued to bite down on it.

Hector saw me watching him intently, and he said, "Nope, I don't get to smoke it anymore. My doctor says I can't, so I just use it much like a pacifier. The darned old thing seems to calm my nerves, but I surely do hanker to light one of my favorite mixes every now and then.

"Now, young man, let me give it some thought for a second or two about your question before I answer it for you. I want you to know that I have lived here in this old house for more than forty years, and I have known Sedgwick Burns for that long. I'm a bit reluctant to say this to you, but during those years I never once had an opportunity to talk to him in a neighborly way like you and I are now doing. In fact, I've never had any occasion to speak to him outside a business conversation. Despite the fact we'd lived next door to each other, he never one time spoke a word to me over the back fence. As for a few of our business conversations, he and his staff handled the funeral arrangements for both of my parents, and later on for my dear wife Alma, after they had all passed away." Recalling their deaths seemed to evoke an immediate look of sadness in the old man, and I noticed a few small tears appear in the corners of his eyes.

"From what you have just told me, Mr. Bates, it seems that you did not know much about the man at all, I said."

"Oh, you are dead wrong about that, young man, I knew that man very well indeed. Just because he and I never were friendly or talked together, or never have had any other social contact, didn't mean that I wasn't aware of a lot of things that went on over there at his house before his disappearance." With that, he pulled his pipe from between his teeth and used it by pointing the stem of it in the direction my house.

"My neighbor Dave Farrell has told me a lot about things that he had seen while he was looking over his fence, Mr. Bates, but some of those things seem somewhat hard for me to believe, I remarked."

"What might that be for instance?" Bates shot back at me.

"Well, for one thing, Dave told me that he suspected Burns had stolen several items from his yard, like a shovel, a pick, and other gardening tools."

"That's the gospel!" Bates responded. "Half of everything I had in the way of garden tools was stolen or removed from my backyard or from my outside shed, and for my money, it was Sedgwick Burns who was responsible for it."

"Did you ever see him take anything from your yard, Mr. Bates?"

"Well, no! Not exactly, that is. But Dave Farrell told me about Burns habit of wandering around on his property at night, and he certainly had the opportunity to do it. I think he was one of those kleptomaniacs you sometimes read about in the newspapers. You know, someone who can't stop himself from taking other people's property. It's very possible!"

"I imagine it is possible all right," I said, "but I would not want to accuse the man without seeing him stealing something. I guess if any of those missing things ever turn up there on the property that would prove it?"

"That sure would do it!" Bates responded.

"Did anything of yours ever turn up over there?" I asked.

"Not to my knowledge," he responded.

"Dave Farrell said that you told him you had seen Burns and another man hauling things down from his garage loft. Did you ever wonder what he was hauling in and out of that place?"

"No, I didn't have to wonder about that because I knew what he was hauling since I once watched Burns and another man carry in a big pile of cardboard cartons of some kind. Another time, I saw Burns and that same man bringing a used coffin up those narrow stairs to the loft. That old tightwad Burns wouldn't let go of a thing; in fact, there was never much in his trash cans for the weekly garbage pickups either. Dave Farrell and I always wondered about that. We couldn't understand what that man ate to keep himself alive since neither of us ever saw a bag of groceries going into his house. Just talking about Sedgwick Burns still gives me the willies."

"That seems very strange to me about them carrying a used coffin up to the loft, I said, because after giving some thought to what you just said, Mr. Bates, I have never heard of a used coffin. I always thought that once it was occupied by a dead body, the coffin was buried in the ground, and that would be the last time you would see it again."

Bates did not respond to my statement as he continued to sit there across from me with his pale blue eyes staring at me through his thick spectacles. Finally, he slowly got up from his chair and said, "I never thought about that. Maybe it was just an old sample from his display room. Well, it's getting kind of late, and at my age bedtime arrives before it gets dark."

Soon after Hector Bates and I said our farewells, I returned to my house and slid into my comfortable recliner chair in front of the TV. Although one of my favorite shows had just started, I could not concentrate on the program because my mind was busily reviewing some of my conversation with Hector Bates. I did not learn much about Sedgwick Burns that I had not already heard from Dave Farrell. Not much that is, except that Bates, like Farrell, was making the same accusations about Burns being a common thief. He also offered up some new information about Burns and another man moving a coffin into the loft. I wondered just why Bates never told Dave Farrell about his witnessing that coffin incident. Perhaps it happened sometime after he and Farrell had an earlier conversation.

Having given it some more thought, it began to occur to me there might be two places where I might be able to get some reliable information about Sedgwick Burns. That would be from Burns himself, which was not very likely because no one seems to know where he is, or perhaps from the person who took over his funeral parlor after Burns retired. I did not know who the name of that person who owned the business now, but I was certain it would be in the telephone directory. After all, how many Burns Mortuaries are there around here?

After scouting out the telephone directory from under a pile of magazines in the dining room, I turned to the section in the directory listing Funeral Parlors, Mortuaries, and Crematories, and there it was, Burns Funeral Home, Since 1887. I quickly wrote the telephone number and the address on the back of one of my business cards, and then tucked it neatly inside my wallet. The first thing I thought that I would do after I finish work in my office tomorrow afternoon, is to drive to the Burns Funeral Home and try to get some answers from the present owner of the establishment. I glanced up from my chair just as Elaine entered the room. She had a glass of milk in one hand and a slice of pecan coffee cake in the other. "Where have you been, Rick?" Elaine asked. "I was calling you because I thought you might like a late snack while the two of us watch our favorite show. It's been on for only a few minutes, so you didn't miss much."

"I stopped over to the house next door, and I finally met our neighbor to the north," I said as I pointed my finger in that direction.

"Oh, what's he like? I seem to recall you telling me that his name is Bates, Hector Bates."

"Yes, that is right, Elaine, his name is Hector Bates," I answered, "and he is a sweet old gentleman and a widower. He even poured me a cup of hot tea, and we sat in his parlor and visited for a short time just like a couple of old ladies drinking the tea and munching on cookies while we talked.'

"I had heard he lost his wife a long time ago. Shirley spoke about him the other afternoon when I talked with her in the yard while she was hanging her clothes on the line."

"Did she have much to say about anything else?" I asked, wondering if Shirley had told Elaine any of that other nonsense that upset Elaine so badly when I made the mistake of telling her about it.

"Only that the entire Burns family was in the burial business, but you had already told me that. She also said he was a queer duck who never associated with anyone in the neighborhood, but I suppose being in the business he was in, it was hard for him to make friends with living people." She laughed a bit nervously as she said it. "Tomorrow's another busy workday, Honey, Elaine said, and I think it's time the two of us retire for the evening."

~ *Chapter Eight* ~

MEETING BLAKE CRANSHAW

My day which I spent in the office at work went just as smoothly as it usually did, with a cost analysis report I prepared, and some bills that needed to be reviewed and paid. Other than those relatively routine projects, there was nothing else for me to do that was particularly pressing. When it was near my quitting time, I took the business card from my wallet with the Burns Funeral Home's telephone number on it and I made a hurried call. After having heard three rings, someone picked up the phone on the other end of the line and said, "Burns." It was the only word spoken by a throaty female voice, so after my waiting a few seconds, I said, "May I have the name of your director, and will you please connect me to him?"

"Our Director's name is Blake Cranshaw," she said. "Please hold the line, and I'll put you right through to his office." After another short pause a male voice answered, "Blake Cranshaw, speaking, how may I help you?"

"Perhaps you can help me, Mr. Cranshaw. My name is Rick Braden, and you do not know me, but if it is at all possible, I would very much like to stop by your office sometime later today and talk to you."

"Is your inquiry about funeral arrangements he asked in a soft consoling voice?"

"No, it is nothing like that, it is . . ."

As I was about to continue with my explanation, he cut me short and said, "Then it must be something else you that have in mind, perhaps our prearrangement plan. I'll be more than happy to talk with you about that, Mr. Braden."

"I am sorry, Mr. Cranshaw, but apparently, you have entirely the wrong idea about what I want to talk to you about, it has nothing whatsoever to do with your funeral services, my call to you has more to do with your ex partner Sedgwick Burns."

At the very mention of Burns' name, I detected a slight gasp followed by several seconds of silence before he spoke again. "Sedgwick Burns, did you say? Are you a policeman, Mr. Braden? I believe I've already given the police department all the information that I can about that man."

"No, I am not a policeman. I am the man who bought Mr. Burns' house in Forest Oak earlier this spring."

"Oh, that's who you are," he said in a relieved voice. "And just what is it that you want to discuss with me?"

"It is not something that I prefer to go into over the telephone. Is it convenient for me to come to your office, at say 5:30 this evening and tell you all about it? It is essential to me, and I feel that you can be very helpful in dealing with my problem."

After another short pause, Cranshaw said, "I suppose that will be all right. Five-Thirty you said? That should work out within my schedule. I'll see you then, Mr. Braden. Do you know the address?"

"Yes, I have your address, and thank you very much. I will see you here at 5:30."

At a quarter to five that afternoon, I left my office and located my car among the two dozen cars parked in the company's parking lot. Having turned the key in the ignition and starting the car, I quickly pulled it out of the lot and into the flow of homebound traffic. I was anxious to try to get ahead of some of the heavier traffic that clogs the streets at the business section's quitting time. Since I was heading toward the north end of town, the streets in that area would be even more crowded than those I usually drove through at this hour. I mentally calculated my driving time and hoped to arrive there just about as I had planned. I have always been proud of the fact that punctuality is one of my strongest attributes, and Elaine has often said to me that she can set her watch by me.

The time on my dashboard clock told me it was 5:25 when I drove my car into the parking lot of the Burns Funeral Home. It was an attractive one-story building with an impressive front lawn, and the building was bordered with a patchwork of bright flowers and a score of beautifully-matched and well-pruned maple trees. The name BURNS appeared on a sign in highly distinctive, raised, gold lettering centered in the lawn at the front of the building. The asphalt parking lot looked like it could accommodate more than a hundred or more cars, and I could see there were at least fifty vehicles currently parked there.

While I sat in my car for a minute of two, I surveyed the property through my car's windows, I could not believe that this impressive looking business had previously been co-owned and operated by the likes of Sedgwick Burns, the strange skinflint I had heard so many unkind and negative comments about. The building looked to be expensively built and well-maintained. Of course, my expectations of the business were definitely influenced by Dave's remarks, and later by Hector's negative description of the former owner. I briefly thought about it, and realized that I should not have allowed their ridiculous tales to get to me like they had done. Now that I was parked in front of the business, I felt like a darn fool, but my appointment was set so I had no choice but to keep it.

Climbing out of my car, I quickly glanced at my watch and verified that I was right on time, so I made a fast walk to the front door and went inside the building. After proceeding halfway through the foyer, I saw a signboard announcing the various chapels with names like Sundown Parlor, Meditation Parlor, Eventide Parlor, and Twilight Parlor. Lingering around a large sitting area was a smattering of people, and most of them were wearing dark clothes and had somber looks on their faces. Little groups of three and four people were sitting or standing at various points in the Sundown Parlor, and everyone was talking in subdued voices. The sickly sweet fragrance of mixed flowers permeated the air; it was an unearthly scent which I have always associated with wakes and funerals.

I was just about to look around for the door to the director's office when an elderly, well-dressed man approached me. He placed a hand on my shoulder and offered his other hand to me for a handshake. As we shook hands he said, "You must be Bill Polarmo."

"No, I answered, I am sorry, Sir, but you have the wrong person. My name is Rick Braden, and I am here to see Blake Cranshaw, who is the funeral director. I have an appointment with him."

"Oh, I'm so very sorry, Mr. Braden," he responded with an embarrassed look. I thought you were someone else. Mr. Cranshaw's office is at the far end of this corridor to the right," he said then turned and walked around the corner into the Eventide Parlor, where I saw printed on a small placard at its entryway was the name: Able M. Polarmo.

As I proceeded along the corridor toward Cranshaw's office, I heard the sound of someone crying, so I stopped at the doorway and looked inside the Twilight Parlor. On the billboard was the name John P. Williams Sr. Several people were standing before an open coffin at the front of the room, and a very old looking white-haired woman dressed all in black was standing at the head of the open casket. She had her right hand pressed inside the casket where she apparently held the dead hand of the corpse. The woman was softly crying, and a younger man was trying his best to console her. I felt a sense of deep sadness as I watched the woman, whom I assumed was the widow of the deceased, and the young man whom I guessed was her son.

A minute or two after I arrived at the open door to Blake Cranshaw's office, I saw him sitting behind a large mahogany desk, and he was filling out some kind of document. He briefly stopped what he was doing and glanced up at me, then looked at a notepad on his desk and said, "You're right on time, Mr. Braden. Please have a seat and I'll be with you in just a few minutes. I have to finish this paperwork for an interment set for tomorrow morning. If I don't have it ready, they won't allow the burial. I'm sure you understand."

Taking the chair closest to Cranshaw's desk, I sat down and crossed my legs while I waited for him to complete what he was doing. I was surprised that he did not shake hands with me and introduce himself formally because I thought the people in this kind of business tended to be very formal and overly courteous. Well, he already knew that I was not a client of his, and it may be that he did not care what I thought, but it was a mistake for him to take that attitude because I would someday need his services. Still, I hoped that day would not occur until sometime in the far-distant future.

I continued waiting while I watched Mr. Cranshaw closely as his pen glided smoothly over the document in front of him. He appeared to be so deeply engrossed with his writing; he seemed to be unaware of my observing what he was doing. Nattily dressed in the traditional dark clothes of a funeral director, Cranshaw had the somber appearance of his profession. I guessed his age to be about the same as mine--late forties to early fifties. His hair was lightly peppered with gray with a receding hairline, and he was wearing a pair of black, horn-rimmed bifocals which kept slipping over his nose as he bent forward in his chair to write. I thought he had the look of a bank clerk, or a college professor, or an undertaker. When Mr. Cranshaw finally completed his writing task, he swivelled his chair around to squarely face me, and he quickly stood up and extended his hand to me as he spoke, "I'm sorry to have kept you waiting, but some things are so timely they can't be set aside. I hope you understand."

"I certainly do, I said, I completely understand your situation. I am a businessman myself, and at times I also have very tight schedules to keep."

"Now, what is it that's on your mind, Mr. Braden?" Cranshaw asked as he retook his seat and then removed his glasses and placed them inside the desk drawer. "Just what is it I can do for you?" "What

I have to talk to you about concerns Sedgwick Burns," I said as I awaited some kind of negative response from him. There was none. His appraising eyes remained calm and steady.

"What is it that you want to discuss with me concerning Sedgwick Burns?"{ Cranshaw asked while now sounding a bit impatient.

"I think it is best that I immediately state my problem and then hope you can fill me in on the missing details so that I can finally enjoy some peace of mind." When I looked into Cranshaw's eyes, I could see the slightest hint of distress, and I continued with my answer. "My wife and I bought the Burns' house in Forest Oak a couple of months ago, and we moved into it immediately after we sold our home in Bradenton. Since that time we have been heavily involved in a significant renovation covering the entire interior of the house because it was outdated and in need of repairs."

"Please go on with it," Cranshaw said, "let me hear the rest of it." I could still hear the impatience in his voice but now there was also some interest as well.

"My troubles with the house began for me a short time ago while I was moving some things around in the cellar of the house, I ran across a large number of cardboard cartons containing one-gallon bottles of embalming fluid. There was also a wooden crate containing a kind of bloodletting device, or whatever it is you call those contraptions." Again I watched his eyes--and this time they revealed some instant discomfort.

"Continue on with it, please, Mr. Braden, what else is there?"

"Well, you may not believe this, Mr. Cranshaw, but yesterday I ran across six, very old-looking and highly-varnished wooden coffins stored in the loft over my garage. They had been covered over with a dusty tarp, and when I pulled the tarp back to see what it was covering, there they were, all six of them lying next to each other on the floor. The discovery practically shocked the life out of me! In addition, I found a large number of cartons there containing embalming fluid--much like those I had earlier found in our cellar."

"What did you do with all those things after you found them?" he asked. Now Cranshaw was showing some real distress as well as discomfort.

"The cartons of embalming fluid and that other apparatus which I found in my cellar earlier were all removed from my cellar and taken to the county dump. My two sons and I took care of that within a few days of my discovery. Those boxes of the same product which I found yesterday are still up in the garage loft, along with those six old looking coffins. Now, Mr. Cranshaw, that is the reason I am here is to try to get some advice from you about what I should do with those coffins and the rest of that stuff in my garage loft."

"Why did you do that?" Cranshaw asked.

"Why did I come to you for answers?" I was a bit confused by his question to me.

"No, what I mean to ask is, for what purpose did you dispose of those cartons of embalming fluid and that other item you had found earlier in your cellar?"

"Well, If you knew my wife Elaine, Mr. Cranshaw, you would have the answer to your question. She is extremely sensitive and squeamish about those kinds of things, and I had to get them out of the house before she found them. Believe me, if she had even the slightest idea concerning those coffins that are stored in our garage loft she would not stay one night in our house. I still have to dispose of them, and I have to do it fast before she learns about them. I have made a point of not telling anyone, other than my two sons, about my earlier discovery in our cellar, and they know nothing at all about what I found in the garage's loft yesterday. I do not want that information getting back to my wife under any circumstances. But how to do it is my problem, and that is why I need your advice."

"I'm finally beginning to understand the difficulties you've found yourself in, Mr. Braden," Cranshaw responded. "Are there any other things of that type you came across in your house that I should know about?"

"There may be other things in the garage's loft, but I have not yet been able to examine the contents of that space very thoroughly.

When I ran across those coffins, I was out of the loft almost like a shot out of a canon."

"So, you're telling me that the coffins and the cartons of embalming fluid are your problem, and possibly some other yet to be uncovered items? Is that about the total of it, Mr. Braden?" "Not quite," I answered. "I found, in addition to those coffins and the embalming fluid, a large number of storage boxes containing old files, along with several file cabinets filled with documents. I am guessing they are probably records from his, ah, your funeral business. It is my understanding that you and Mr. Burns were partners at some time in the past. I did take the time to have a quick look inside a couple of the boxes and cabinet drawers, and that is just what they all looked like to me, old looking records connected to your past funeral business."

"What exactly is it that you want me to do?" Cranshaw asked.

"I need to have those items removed from my premises, and while I am here, I would like to get some more information about Sedgwick Burns, the man who had owned the house my wife Elaine and I bought."

Cranshaw took a few seconds to mull the situation over in his mind, and while doing so, he straightened himself in his chair and opened a desk drawer from which he removed a pack of cigarettes. When I declined a cigarette which he offered to me, he lit his cigarette with a lighter, and he then leaned back in the chair. While he dragged deeply on the cigarette, he spoke firmly and deliberately, his eyes pinned to mine as he spoke.

"I can probably help you to handle the removal of those items from your property, Mr. Braden; however, I'll first have to go to your house and inspect those things you just talked to me about. Those old files, for instance, are probably just what you've already thought them to be, old and outdated records of our business with no current value to me. If that's the case, you'll have to arrange to dispose of those things yourself. The county dump is probably the best place for them to end up. As for the coffins and the embalming fluid, I'll take any of it which is in a condition to be removed"

"Just what do you mean, Mr. Cranshaw, by using the words condition to be removed?" I asked, feeling somewhat confused by Cranshaw's last statement to me.

Hesitating momentarily before answering me, he then said, "What I mean by that is that the coffins in your loft are all empty of corpses."

"Good, God!" I loudly blurted out. "Are you really serious?" "I'm as serious as death," Cranshaw responded. "Now, are there any other things on your property that I'm to take, and what might you be expecting for them?"

Not knowing exactly what he meant, I did not immediately answer him.

Sensing my misunderstanding, he then asked. "What, if anything, are you expecting me to pay you for any of those things?"

"Not a dime! I quickly responded to him. I will just be happy to get them out of my house and off my property. What possible use would any of it be to me? As it was, I had offered that first load of stuff found in my cellar for free to a funeral parlor over on Fourth Street in Forest Oak, but the man quickly turned it down. In fact, the gentleman became very upset when I mentioned Sedgwick Burns' name, and that is another one of the reasons I wanted to know more about him. So far, the only information I have been able to gather about Burns was from a couple of my neighbors, and according to the two of them, he was a particularly revolting man."

"Why is that?" Cranshaw asked.

"Well, it is reasonably apparent to me that they both intensely disliked Sedgwick Burns, so those feelings could influence anything they may have told me about the man."

"I see your point, Mr. Cranshaw said, but I thought you told me that no one other than your two sons and you knew about those things you found in your cellar. How many more people have you told? Did you discuss those things you'd found with those neighbors of yours you've just mentioned?"

"Positively not! I did not," I said firmly, "and except for my two sons and that funeral director on Fourth Street, no one else knows anything about it. Wait a minute; I have forgotten to tell you about my other neighbor, Hector Bates. He told me he had seen Burns and another man carrying a coffin into the garage loft several years ago. As far as I know, he never mentioned it to anyone else before he told me about it. Besides, Bates is a very old man who keeps to himself pretty much, and I doubt that he will ever mention it again. Anyway, the only reason he told me about it was that I was questioning him about Burns."

"That's good," Cranshaw said. "Let's just hope you're right about that because the fewer people who know about this, the better it will be for the two of us."

"Why is it so important that we keep it quiet?"

"Because the things that you have stored inside your house, Mr. Braden, are most probably there illegally. I know that you don't have any personal responsibility for them being there, but it could still create a lot of difficulties for you and your wife, and also for me. Your wife, for instance, will hear about it, and you have already told me how that information would negatively affect her. Once I fill you in with more information about Sedgwick Burns, I'm confident you'll better understand my reasons for keeping these discoveries highly confidential. Now, I'm sorry but I have a service to supervise, and I'm now running a bit late. Is it possible for you to come back here later this evening, let's say about eight and we can then conclude our discussion?"

"I will be here, Mister Cranshaw, and thank you for your time and your patience with me."

"Goodbye, Mr. Braden. I'll look for you to be back here in my office again at eight."

After leaving Cranshaw's office, I stopped briefly at the Twilight Parlor, and I glanced inside. Everyone was gone from the room except the corpse. All I could see was the tip of his nose from the side of the white satin fringe of his casket. "Goodnight Mister Williams," I said softly. "I hope God will guide your destiny from here."

~*Chapter Nine* ~

A QUESTION OF ETHICS

Our evening meal was over, and Elaine wanted me to take a ride with her to the hardware store to buy some curtain rod brackets for the kitchen windows. I had to think of some excuse not to go with her because I had that eight o'clock appointment with Blake Cranshaw at his funeral parlor. She knew nothing of what had been going on, so I had to lie to her to be able to keep that engagement, and I hated having to do that. When I was late getting home today, I told her I had tire trouble, and she believed me. I felt like a rotten heel at the dinner table, and then it began to dawn on me that one lie leads to another lie and that lie to yet another. I started to wonder when it would all end.

Just as we were about ready to leave the house, I told Elaine that I had just remembered that I had a report to finish and had left it on my desk at the office. That meant I would have to drive there, retrieve it, and bring it home to work on it. A much better idea, I suggested, than my going with you to the hardware store is for me to take care of that critical business I had forgotten about. I would finish the report at my office since I have all the documents available there to work there.

Elaine offered to go with me and wait for me to complete it, and we could then stop at the hardware store on our way home. It took a lot of effort for me to talk her out of our doing that. I hoped she would not misconstrue my actions and think maybe I had a lady friend I was meeting on the sly. I was very much aware of how risky my telling her a lie was because it could undermine Elaine's faith and trust in me.

I arrived five minutes earlier than my appointment with Blake Cranshaw at the Burns Funeral Home. It was at 7:55 P.M., and when I pulled my car into the parking lot, I saw there now was less a dozen cars that were parked there. Entering the front door of the building, I noted a lot fewer people standing around in the various parlors than I had seen earlier, and as I passed the Eventide Parlor, it was dark and the signboard that had been in front earlier had been removed. That must have been the interment Cranshaw was preparing papers for when I was there earlier. I then proceeded straight down the corridor toward Cranshaw's office, and when I passed the doorway to the Twilight Parlor, I glanced inside. A few people were seated at the front of the room chatting, and the old woman I had noticed earlier was standing at the casket and crying softly while she was still holding Mr. Williams' dead hand.

Upon my arrival at the door to Cranshaw's office, I found he was not there. Checking my watch, I saw that it was now precisely eight o'clock. While I stood in front of his door, I looked down the corridor in the direction of the main sitting room. At that very moment, I saw him come out of one of the side parlors, and when he spotted me in front of his office door, he began a fast walk in my direction. Extending his hand for a handshake, he said, Sorry to keep you waiting, I had some last minute details to take care of. Please come into my office and have a seat and we'll continue with our earlier discussion.

Once we were inside, Cranshaw turned his attention toward a file cabinet and removed several documents, and after a fast glance, at them he placed them into his valise which he then closed and snapped shut. When we were both comfortably seated at his desk, he lit a cigarette and leaned back in his chair.

"It's been quite a day for me because this kind of business tends to be very demanding," Cranshaw said. "A twelve-hour day is an average for us, but that isn't what you came here this evening to hear from me, Mr. Braden, so let's get right down to business," he said as he turned his chair to face me. He studied my face carefully for several seconds and then hesitated for another second or two more before deciding to begin talking to me.

"Burns!" Cranshaw loudly emphasized that name. "That was a name in this town and in this business to be respected, and it still is. Before I discuss the character of Mr. Sedgwick Burns to you, I want to tell you something of the Burns' family. You had indicated to me earlier that you know practically nothing about him other than some unfriendly gossip you'd picked up from a couple of your neighbors. I'll start telling you about him from the beginning, but before I do, I want you to tell me if you'll have the time to hear the story in its entirety since it may take a while. I also must warn you that some of the things I'm going to reveal could be quite shocking to you, and because of that, I have to rely on your utmost discretion to guard the confidentiality of some of those highly personal things I am about to talk to you about."

"I understand what you are saying to me, Mr. Cranshaw," I responded, "and I will implicitly comply with your wishes. As far as time is concerned, please take as much time to tell it you feel is necessary," I answered while feeling a bit puzzled by his remarks. "That's fine," Blake responded. "To begin with, I'll have to go a long way back in time to the year 1867, or the same year a man by the name of Solomon arrived in this country from a little town in Germany. He was an immigrant, whose family name at that time wasn't Burns, it was Burnstein. Like so many others who emigrated here from the old world and were starting businesses in America, he quickly discovered that his name tended to be a liability to him, and he shortened his family name from Burnstein to Burns.

"In the beginning, Solomon Burns wasn't in the funeral business, Solomon Burns was a merchant, a fish merchant to be precise. That was what his family had done in Germany for many years, and that was the trade with which he was most familiar. In fact, selling fish at a little market he had opened near the New York waterfront, was the way he and his family were able to survive for the first fifteen years or so of their arrival in this country. It was an honest profession, if not too glamorous.

"While he was working in his trade, he met and married a young Hungarian girl by the name of Hettie Ginsberg. Her father was a grocer, and her mother was a seamstress. In the course of that marriage, they had three children whom they named Aaron, Sylvia, and Sedgwick. Aaron was the first son born, and he was the child most favored by his father.

Over the years as the Burns family grew, so did the family owned fish business. As a young boy, Aaron worked in the family's fish market where his father taught him the trade--just as his father had trained his son in Germany. In time, the business prospered, and the family was able to save a little money. When Aaron was about Fifteen years old, Solomon made plans to open a second fish store and have Aaron manage it for the family.

"One early spring day, Aaron was alone in his father's fish store when two men walked into the store and pulled out a gun and immediately demanded that Aaron turn over the store's cash receipts to them. Aaron wasn't about to give them his father's money as they demanded of him, so he put up an argument and the robbers immediately shot him in his face and took what they wanted from the cash box.

"Later that day Solomon almost went insane with grief when he found his oldest son lying dead on the floor in the fish store. As soon as he was able to cope with his deep sorrow over the death of his son, he made arrangements for Aaron's burial. He and his wife Hettie took the body to a local mortuary to prepare for a one-day wake before his son's burial.

"When the robber shot Aaron, the bullet passed through one of his eyes and exited through the left side of his head, leaving gaping holes and disfigurement on both sides of his head and face. When a few of Burns' family members arrived early at the mortuary for the wake, they were shocked when they saw the condition of the body because the mortician hadn't done anything to mask the terrible damage to Aaron's face. Solomon exploded in a terrible rage and threatened to thrash the mortician within an inch of his life. When he finally calmed down, Solomon insisted that he be allowed to do that which the mortician failed to do, which was to make Aaron look presentable for his final viewing.

"Using the facilities of the parlor and some softened candle wax, Solomon did a masterful job of reconstruction of his dead son's face and head. He did such a good job, in fact, no one who later attended the service was aware of the extent of the damage that had occurred to Aaron as a result of the shooting.

"Soon after his beloved son was buried, Solomon decided to close the second fish store and use that money to open a mortuary. At forty-five years old, he was starting a brand-new profession with nothing more backing him than sheer determination and guts. He vowed that he would never allow what happened to his son's body to happen to anyone who used the services of Burns Mortuary, which was the name he had printed on the bright tin sign he hung at the front of his new establishment."

Ending the conversation for a moment or two, Cranshaw lit another cigarette and then exhaled a big puff of blue-white smoke into the room. After a puff or two, he said, "I hope I'm not boring you, but I feel that this somewhat detailed background information is quite essential to enable you to fully understand the family, and especially the mind of my ex-partner, and the past-owner of your house, Mr. Sedgwick Burns."

"It is not in the least bit boring to me, Mr. Cranshaw because I am finding everything you are telling me to be extremely interesting. You also seem to have the details down so well I am truly amazed.

How is it you know all these intimate things that you are telling me about Burns' early years with his family?"

"I'm an excellent listener," Blake answered, "and my ex-partner Sedgwick Burns was a good talker. Most people who knew the man couldn't get the time of day out of him, but I occasionally knew how to draw him out of his shell. His most significant weakness was his family, and he was fiercely proud of their accomplishments in the field of mortuary science, especially in the very delicate area of cosmetic body reconstruction.

"Sedgwick Burns and I worked together in the funeral business for nearly sixteen years before we severed our partnership and he left. Over the course of those many years, we had many highly detailed conversations about body preservation and reconstruction. Sedgwick had studied dozens of books detailing the processes used by ancient Egyptians to mummify the dead. Sedgwick told me that he'd reviewed those books to try and duplicate some of their successes. Sedgwick was an intelligent man who said to me that he'd also read extensively about the use of hypnotism because he felt that it might be a way for doctors to relieve the pain and suffering of patients who were in the last stages of dying painfully. He claimed he'd gotten that idea while reading a story by Edgar Allen Poe called The Story of Mister Valdimar."

"I'm quite familiar with that gruesome Poe story," I responded.

"Well, now I'll get back to what I was saying. Let me see. Oh, yes, Solomon Burns and his remaining son Sedgwick Burns, who would have been the father of the man who had previously owned your house. Anyway, Solomon Burns decided that running a mortuary was a lot better business than running a fish store. He reasoned that all people die, while only some of the people eat fish; therefore, everyone was a potential customer of his new business. I would have to say that it was an avaricious attitude to say the very least.

"Since young Sedgwick was only about twelve years old at that time, he was much too young to work with his father in the new family venture, so he continued helping his mother and his sister at the fish store. He did odd jobs and made deliveries of fish to their customers, but he was never allowed to visit the family's mortuary because his father felt that the sight of dead bodies would be harmful to a child that young.

"One dark and rainy day, Sedgwick made a fish delivery within the same block where this father's mortuary was located, and he decided to stop in the business and pay a surprise visit to his father. Unlike the fish market, which was the dominant topic of discussion during their evening suppers, his father would never talk about his other business. Each time Sedgwick attempted to question him about it, he was told that it would be explained to him when he was older and could better understand it. That remark had only further served to stimulate his son's burning curiosity.

"Upon young Sedgwick's arrival at the mortuary, the boy opened the door and went inside the front of the building. Not finding his father there, he walked into the back room looking for him. His father had his back turned while he was engaged in preparing a body which was lying on a table, and Solomon didn't see the boy come into the room. As Sedgwick approached him, Solomon turned around and saw his son staring at the naked corpse of an old man lying there. The boy was standing wide-eyed and rigid with shock, and he looked like he was about to faint. It seemed that Sedgwick had no idea what his father was doing to that dead man, or why he was doing it. All kinds of dark thoughts flashed through young Sedgwick's mind and he began to cry. Solomon quickly hustled him out of the room and into the front of the shop where he tried to calm the boy down.

"When Sedgwick appeared to have recovered from his trauma, he was chastised for being there, which was a place he was never supposed to visit. Sedgwick was then firmly told by his father that his job was at the fish market helping his mother and his sister with the chores, and he was never to come to that place again. Sedgwick then asked his father what he was doing to the body in the back room, and he was told that it was being prepared for viewing by the family. When he pleaded for his father to explain that further to him, His father finally decided that it was apparently the time for him to discuss the nature of the mortuary business with his son.

"Soon after that disturbing incident with his son, Solomon softened his attitude and allowed the boy to visit the mortuary from time to time. Eventually, Solomon accepted his son's being involved, and the boy was told the true nature of the business and the inevitability of death without incurring any apparent adverse psychological effects, so his father began allowing Sedgwick to assist him in preparing the bodies. It seemed to Solomon that the boy had a natural instinct for the business, and he soon learned all that his father could teach him. Before long, young Sedgwick was developing many new ideas for the reconstruction of damaged faces and skulls. He became successful through his use of things like wax, plaster, rubber, and a few of the more modern compounds that were made available in those early days.

"The name Burns soon began to earn a wide reputation within the county where it was becoming synonymous in the mortuary business with professionalism and concern for the feelings of the bereaved. Solomon Burns' business was built on the caring attitude of himself and his son Sedgwick, along with their almost unique ability to make the departed look as natural in death as they had looked in life. That was the springboard to their success, and it began to make them their fortune."

"It indeed is a most interesting story you are telling me, I said, and I must say that I am truly amazed at the amount of detail you have retained from listening to your old partner's stories. You are both a good listener and a great storyteller, Mr. Cranshaw." I was genuinely pleased and impressed with Blake Cranshaw for giving me so much of his time to relate everything to me.

"Would you care for something to drink?" Cranshaw asked. "I have a bottle of good, imported Scotch in the cabinet here that's twelve years old." He then pointed his finger toward a file cabinet in one corner of his office.

"No, thank you," I said, "I make it a point not to drink alcohol of any kind when I have to drive but thank you for your kind offer."

"Then, if you don't mind, Mr. Braden, I'll pour one for myself," he said as he got up and walked over to the cabinet where he removed the bottle. After he poured out half a glass of the amber liquid, Cranshaw again sat down behind his desk while he took a swig of the scotch before he continued telling his story.

"The Burns' family fortune, as I had previously said, was made through the caring nature and the foresight of two men, namely Solomon Burns and his young son Sedgwick Burns. After Solomon Burns passed on, Sedgwick took over the operation of the family mortuary business. In the meantime, his mother and his sister Sylvia continued operating the little fish market on the New York waterfront. Solomon made that decision just like his father before him, who never wanted either of the women of the family to become involved in the mortuary business. They both felt it was depressing and morbid and it was best left to the men of the family who could better handle it.

"A bachelor until the age of forty-two, Sedgwick finally met and married the widow of one of his clients by the name of Bernadette Matthews. The marriage was a total surprise to Sedgwick's friends because he was an Orthodox Jew, while Bernadette Matthews was a practicing Catholic. Back then, those kinds of things just were not done. As a result of that nuptial union, many of Sedgwick's close Jewish friends shunned him. He also lost most of his orthodox Jewish patrons business as a result of it. "Bernadette Matthews was a few years younger than Sedgwick, and she was still capable of bearing a child. Never having had any children with her first husband, she was anxious to have a child before it was too late for her to conceive. Three years after they were marriage, a son, Sedgwick Burns Jr. was born. It was a delightful time for them, and the parents planned a lavish party to celebrate the happy event. Sedgwick's rabbi refused to attend the affair unless Sedgwick promised to raise the boy in the Jewish faith. Pleading with his wife, Sedgwick was eventually able to get her to agree to it. It turned out to be a joyous occasion for Sedgwick when most of his friends who had previously avoided him attended the party. There was little doubt that Sedgwick's rabbi had played a decisive part in that happy outcome.

"In the years that followed, young Sedgwick Junior was brought into the family's mortuary business to learn the trade. He worked odd jobs at the funeral parlor in the evenings and on weekends while he also attended primary school. Early on, young Sedgwick never liked the mortuary business, and he vowed that he would get out of it as soon as possible. After graduating from high school with high honors, he left for a medical school planning to become a doctor, which was something that very much pleased his mother. His father, on the other hand, was disappointed because he had expected his son to join with him in the family business right after his high school graduation. His thinking was that someday his son would take it over--just as he had done many years earlier after his father Solomon died.

"After three long and grueling years of hard work and study as a student at the medical school, Sedgwick flunked out, and he eventually accepted the fact that he was not cut out to be a doctor. Returning home to live with his parents, he half-heartedly went back into the family business, which was something that made his father happy. Sedgwick worked in the business under his father's guidance for many years right up until the time of his father Sedgwick Seniors death.

"When Sedgwick Burns Senior died suddenly of a heart attack in the year 1947, his son Sedgwick Junior had almost entirely taken over the management of the business, which by that time had grown to six mortuaries--later called funeral parlors. During the ensuing years, and mostly through his gross mismanagement, Sedgwick bankrupted all but one of the parlors, which was the one in Forest Oak, where in later years I went into partnership with Sedgwick Burns Jr. If I had only known what kind of person Sedgwick Burns really was, I would never have formed a partnership with him. Still, In spite of his business failures, the name Burns always commanded respect and admiration in our field. When I first met Sedgwick, I had just received my diploma making me a mortician, and I was awed by the man. I was his junior partner for several years, and he taught me quite a bit about the details of his business. Having attended three years at medical school, he knew much more about human anatomy than I had ever learned during the years of my training as a mortician, or later on as a funeral director. Much of the knowledge I'd gained from understudying Sedgwick was extremely helpful to me in the course of my work. It was after I saw him do something repugnant that I began to lose my respect for the man." Quite unexpectedly, Cranshaw quit talking when he lit a cigarette and then seemed to stare off somewhere in the distance. I immediately guessed that he was waiting for me to question him about his last statement. After he took a deep drag on his cigarette and then expelled a cloud of blue smoke into the air, and after he swallowed another fast gulp of his Scotch drink. I took advantage

of the pause to ask him what I knew that he wanted to hear me ask. "May I ask what it was it that you saw him do?"

Speaking in a highly confidential manner, Cranshaw answered me in such a low voice that I was almost too faint for me to hear. "I saw him steal a ring off the finger of one of our dead clients." After making that statement, Cranshaw remained silent for several seconds as he watched to see what effect his words had on me. It was apparent to me that he was able to see the look of shock that had quickly flashed into my eyes.

"You saw him do that?" I heard myself say to him a bit too loud. "What did you do about it?" I asked.

"Nothing!" That was his unacceptably abbreviated answer to my question.

"Why was that?" I asked because I was utterly surprised that he would have allowed such a thing to pass in that manner. " "Because at that time I had thought that it might have been an isolated incident. I guessed that Burns probably been overcome by a moment of uncontrollable temptation, and I expected that he would put the ring back in the woman's casket later. He never did!" "How do you know that for sure?" I asked.

"Because I checked the coffin sometime later to see if it was there, and that was just before it was loaded into the hearse and sent to the cemetery for burial. I did that at a time when Sedgwick wasn't watching me, but I can positively tell you that the ring was still missing when the coffin was buried. The only reason the client's family was unaware of it missing on the woman's finger in the coffin, was that they had already paid their last respects to the departed woman and the coffin had been closed and locked. It was only one of many other occurrences like that one which I was later to discover.

"Several months after that incident, I was looking around Sedgwick's office for an organ tape I wanted to use for one of our services, and I ran across a shoe box. It was in one of his bottom cabinet drawers hidden under some old files. When I opened the lid of the box, I discovered it was crammed full of rings, tie tacks, broaches, earrings, and other assorted pieces of jewelry. All those items had been left with the bodies, along with instructions from the families to bury them with the deceased. Most of the jewelry in that box had little intrinsic value, and the families wanted those things entombed with their loved ones only as a show of sentimentality. I also found several watches in the box, and they also were of relatively little value. I was so shocked by that discovery I could barely talk. I knew that this pilfering was done by a man who owned many beautiful pieces of jewelry and several expensive watches. It seemed evident to me he did not need to do what he was doing, but at that time I knew nothing about his massive debts to the gamblers.

"Later that same day after the services were over, I confronted him in his office, and we had a terrible row. As a result of it, I was ordered by him to leave the premises immediately, so I left the chapel that night in a disturbed state of utter disgust and fear. I couldn't believe that a man of Sedgwick Burns' stature could stoop to anything as low as grave robbery--for that's exactly what he had been doing. I knew that he'd be charged with a serious crime if I reported it to the police, and I wasn't anxious for the bad publicity that would inevitably follow. I worried that if his actions ever leaked out, it could very well destroy our funeral business. On the other hand, what he was doing was against everything that I believed in, and I felt I had to do something about it, but the question before me was what precisely I could do?

"Early the following morning when I returned to my office in the funeral parlor, I continued conducting myself and the business just as I usually did while purposely avoiding another confrontation with Burns. However, sometime later in the afternoon, I had a brief encounter with Burns when he unexpectedly stopped into my office to apologize to me for having ordered me out of the parlor the previous evening, saying he was upset and he didn't know what he was doing. After that, he left, and I had no further contact with him during the rest of that day.

"That night while I was in my bed, I tossed and turned as I wrestled with my conscience over the issue. By the time the sun came up in the morning, I knew what I must do. I would confront Sedgwick Burns again, but this time head-on, and I would give him only one alternative, he was to stop his thieving or be reported by me to the police. When that meeting took place, he promised that he would end stealing items from the dead bodies. I hate to admit it to you, but I was a damn fool for having taken his word for it, or for having ever trusted him again.

"The following morning shortly after I arrived at the funeral home, I checked to see if the box of stolen items was still in his cabinet drawer--it wasn't! Apparently, Burns hid it somewhere probably thinking that if I were to report his thefts to the police, they'd search and find the items where he'd hidden them. Instead of reporting him like I should have, I decided to give him another chance to discontinue his thefts.

"It couldn't have been more than six months later when I discovered his original petty thefts had grown to the point where he was now double-billing many of our clients for goods and services. Where all that extra stolen money was going, or how much money he'd taken thru his thefts, I didn't have any idea because he was also doctoring our books. He finally went too far when I got a complaint from the husband of one of our client's. That gentleman was convinced the burial costs had included two separate charges for the same service. The indications were quite clear to me that he was correct in his disturbing accusation, so I arranged a surprise audit of our books by an independent auditing service which confirmed my suspicions and revealed just how extensive Burns' clandestine operations were.

"This time I had more than enough of what he was doing to our business, and there was no longer any way for our partnership to continue. I then decided that I would buy him out, primarily because he said he didn't have the money to buy me out. Well, after a further investigation of him, I learned that the reason he'd been stealing from our clients and our company was that he was in debt up to his eyeballs to a group of local gamblers. It seems that he had been a habitual gambler for many years, which was something that I never suspected of him, and that had been the primary reason he'd lost five of his original six funeral parlors over the years. It was entirely out of character for that man who, otherwise was well known to be a tightwad and a skinflint. I was extremely angry with him, and it was highly distressing when he finally decided to tell me about his destructive gambling sickness.

"Had Sedgwick Burns only confided in me about his serious gambling earlier, we possibly could have worked something out, but he decided to handle it in his way. That was what destroyed him, and that was what darned near took our funeral home down the drain as well. Soon after he left the business, I began to uncover a lot more of his dirty, underhanded work, but I don't want to go into that with you as it serves no further purpose talking about it. I have already told you a heck of a lot more than I had planned to talk about, but I felt it was necessary for me to go into this detail for you to understand why Sedgwick Burns and I ended our business partnership."

After he made that last statements to me, Cranshaw momentarily stopped talking while he leaned far forward in his chair and looked straight into my eyes. After a somewhat uncomfortable delay, he finally spoke.

"Now, what I'm about to disclose to you is highly confidential, and I must caution you that you are not to breathe a word of this to anyone. Outside of the police department and myself, no one knows about it, and if it ever leaked out to the public, it could very possibly ruin my business. Strictly due to what you found inside your cellar and your garage loft, I feel that you have the right to know this. Do I have your promise to keep this information confidential, Mr. Braden?" Cranshaw spoke in hushed tones as he continued looking squarely into my eyes.

Cranshaw had been telling me some highly personal and upsetting revelations about his ex-partner, and he was now about to disclose something to me that is even more bizarre, something that I really did not want to hear from him. I was now beginning to feel very uncomfortable over this while I sat there listening to his disclosures and cautions. What could he possibly tell me now that was so terrible it could destroy his business? Much of what he had already confided to me was shocking to me almost beyond belief, so what more could he possibly relate that could further astonish me? I did not hesitate to answer him because I knew that I would keep my word to him in the matter, whatever it might be. Still, I would very much rather he did not tell me anything more and just stop talking and let me leave here and go home.

"You have my word on it, Mr. Cranshaw, whatever it is," I said in a firm and clear voice, "and just out of curiosity, can you tell me what your reason was to get the police involved?"

Before Cranshaw answered my question, he gulped down the last mouthful of his Scotch and then he lit another cigarette. "The police became involved after his disappearance, and I had to tell them about his gambling, and as much as I hated to do it, about those other disgusting things that he was performing. None of it gave me any pleasure having to admit to them that I was in partnership for several years with a thief, and something even more reprehensible to me. Do you understand?" Cranshaw said quietly with a flushed and embarrassed look on his face.

"Yes, I can certainly understand your feelings, Mr. Cranshaw, but again I ask, what is it that you are referring to that is even more reprehensible than his thieving from your clients and from the business? I do not have a clue to what you might now be talking about from all you have already told me. Please go on with the story if you will, Mr. Cranshaw."

"In addition to Burns being a thief and a man with an uncontrollable and destructive gambling addiction, Cranshaw said, the man was a practicing necrophiliac." His face went noticeably pale as he made that last statement to me.

"What does that word mean?" I asked because I had never heard the word ever used before.

After a short hesitation, he said, "It means that he had an erotic fascination with corpses. Or more clearly stated, he had a perversion or sexual attraction to dead women, and it was something he acted upon. I'm sure you know what it is that I'm saying to you."

"Oh, my dear God, you must be joking with me!" I respond.

"How do you know that he was like that?" I asked the question with a feeling of total revulsion for the statement I had just heard him say to me.

"I knew about it because I once caught him at it!"

It took almost a full minute for me to be able to comprehend precisely what it was he was telling me, and then all I could do was to glare at him with my mouth open in disbelief. As he sat looking at me while he waited for my response, I felt a little sick to my stomach, and I became unable to so speak. Finally, after several seconds had passed, I was able to control myself again, and I asked, "Did that happen before or after you discovered that he was stealing items from your clients and money from your firm?"

"As a matter-of-fact, It was a short time after he and I had formed our partnership," he responded.

"Then," I asked, "why in the world did you stay with him so long? Why did you not break away from him and start your own funeral business?"

I observed Mr. Cranshaw as his face suddenly reddened as he answered me.

"I'm ashamed to tell you this, Mister Braden, but I was young at that time, and I was overly impressed with the man and all that he and the Burns family had accomplished. Even though I had discovered what he was, I convinced myself that his disgusting sexual perversion was none of my business, so I said nothing to him about it, at least not in the beginning, but I did later."

"And just when was that?" I asked with just a hint of sarcasm. "After I found out about his stealing from our clients and from our company and his falsifying our books."

" Did he confess to his having done all those things?"

"Yes, because he had to confess it to me since I had already caught him at it, but I have told you about the surprise audit of our books which uncovered his whole rotten theft scheme."

"Now, getting back to what you had said about Burns' disgusting act of sexual perversion you had witnessed when you first became his partner, when were those other instances that you caught him at it?" I asked wanting a straight answer from him.

"No, I never caught him doing that again, but I was reasonably sure it was continually going on. It had a lot to do with those clients he would invariably select for himself for the embalming and preparation procedure. Almost without exception, he would choose the younger and prettier women to work on, and he'd leave the rest to the other morticians who worked for us. I suppose that I always had a suspicion about what he was up to, but I never could bring myself to say anything more to him about it. I just figured it was his hang-up and he wasn't hurting anyone. Oh, I know, Mr. Braden, you probably think it was a rather callous attitude, and you're right. I realized later how wrong I was to allow it to continue but I didn't think about it that way at that time."

"No, not when you thought it was not affecting your business, but the minute you discovered he was also stealing from you, it became concerning to you. What kind of attitude is that anyway?" At almost the instant I said that I was sorry because I realized that I was way out of line with my remarks, and so I stopped. I knew that I had better get a hold on myself before I angered him to the point where he would refuse to help me.

"Anyway, Mr. Cranshaw, what has all of this got to do with those items that are stored at my house and the fact that Sedgwick Burns had disappeared many years ago?" I asked, trying to quickly steer the conversation entirely in another direction.

"Those items, as you wish to refer to them, which you discovered on your property, are just a few of the things Burns stole from our business. As for his sudden disappearance almost nine years ago, no one is certain that he didn't go into hiding after everything hit the fan over his gambling. If you will remember, I told you about his serious gambling problems, and I happen to know that he was scared to death about the money he owed to those dangerous men. Even after I bought out his share of our business, he was still hurting for more money. I know that because it's what he told me. He even tried to borrow more money from me, but I flatly refused to give it to him. I had my problem trying to repay the loan I made from my bank to enable me to buy his share of the business. Besides, he was a gambler, and I wouldn't be able to trust him to repay the money even if I had it to lend to him."

"What possible use would Burns have for stealing all that embalming fluid and that other item I found hidden in my cellar? I asked. Another thought that occurred is why in the world did he hide six old coffins in the garage loft? It seems to me that none of those things are of any significant value. It is reasonable to assume it wasn't enough to settle up with the gamblers. If he owed debts to them, it must have been a considerable amount of money involved for him to disappear over, and it does not seem likely that he stole those things to sell them. What other possible reason did he have for taking them?"

"You have a lot of questions for me to try to answer for you, Mr. Braden, but I have no plausible answers to any of them. There is only one thing I know for sure, and that's that Sedgwick Burns never did anything without giving it plenty of thought. Whatever his reasons might have been for taking those things from our business only he knows, and he is not around for us to ask."

Glancing at my wristwatch, I saw that it was 10:15 P.M. We had been talking for more than two hours, and Elaine was probably worried sick about me being gone so long, and she is probably having a fit over it. I knew I had to cut our conversation short and leave immediately. "I am very sorry, Mr. Cranshaw, but I just noticed the time. I am afraid I have to go now because my wife will begin to wonder what happened to me. Thank you very much for taking so much of your valuable time to talk to me this evening. I promise you that what we have talked about here tonight will not be discussed by me beyond this room. Now may I ask, what arrangements can we make to have those items removed from the loft in my garage?"

"Can you call me sometime tomorrow during the day?" Mr. Cranshaw asked as he stood up from his desk and extended his hand to me.

"I will do that, Mr. Cranshaw," I said as I shook his hand. "Thank you again for your time. Good night!"

"Good night, Mr. Braden, and please be careful driving home."

Walking through the dimly-lit corridor, I noticed all of the chapels were now dark, and only a row of tiny lights illuminated the way to the front door. Behind me, I could hear Blake Cranshaw as he closed and locked his office door. I will have a lot of explaining to do to Elaine about where I have been for so long when I arrive home, and the thought of it was not very comforting to me.

~Chapter Ten ~

MORE DISCOVERIES

I was definitely in the doghouse with Elaine over my late night meeting with Blake Cranshaw. Later that evening when I finally arrived home and she confronted me, I tried to cover up my activities with another of my lies. I told her that I had decided to finish the report in my office rather than bring it home--just as I told her earlier that I would do. She knew that was not the truth because she told me she had called my office several times during my absence and received no answer. Although she did not say it to me, I felt confident she thought I might be playing around on her with another woman. Well, the way I had been acting lately I could not say that I blamed her for thinking that way. The situation had become so severe I began to think it would be easier to tell her the truth about everything rather than to continue trying to cover up the disturbing facts just to protect her. I surely did not want to risk a breach in our marriage over a house, but I would have to pick the right time to tell her the truth, and then I would have to hope that she would be able to handle it. Those six coffins in the garage loft and those utterly disgusting and astonishing facts about Burns which Cranshaw had revealed to me would indeed be too much for Elaine to handle, so I would not mention those things to her. As it was, it was difficult enough for me to control some of Cranshaw's gruesome revelations myself.

The following morning while we were sitting at our breakfast table, there was barely a word that was spoken between Elaine and me. After all the years we have lived together as husband and wife, it was not difficult for me to read the signs of mistrust and disappointment Elaine was feeling. When we finished our meal, I asked her to sit with me in the living room because I had something important to tell her. By the anxious look on her face, I sensed she thought I was about to say to her that I was involved with another woman. As much as I hated to tell her what had really been going on, I knew that it was not nearly as bad as what she was probably imagining.

It took me a long time to relate the upsetting details to her because I had to carefully leave out those parts of the story which I felt she could not possibly be able to handle, as well as those revelations which I had promised Blake I would keep entirely to myself. Several times during my drawn-out, craftily edited, and profoundly disturbing narration, I could precisely detect the fear and anguish she was feeling. When I finally finished telling her the major parts of the story, Elaine came into my arms and sobbed uncontrollably. I held her for a long time feeling helpless to do anything more than keep her close to me and reassure her of my unending love for her.

Eventually, when Elaine appeared to be somewhat back in control of her emotions and was finally able to speak, she asked me if I thought we should put the house up for sale. I told her that it was a bit premature to make that decision, and I further reasoned that, after all, it was only a matter of clearing out some additional unwanted junk from our property and with that done, everything should return to normal. Reluctantly, Elaine agreed with me, but I could only wonder how long that would last. Now that she knew most of what had been happening, I began to experience a welcome relief from all the sneaking around and lying to her that I had been doing.

Sometime later that same afternoon, I finally was able to place a call from my office to Blake Cranshaw, and within a few seconds, his receptionist answered it. "Burns Funeral Home, May I help you?"

"I Would like to speak to Mr. Cranshaw."

"Can I ask who's calling?"

"My name is Rick Braden, and Mr. Cranshaw is expecting this call from me."

"Mr. Cranshaw is on another phone at the moment, Mister Braden. Do you mind waiting for a minute or two, or shall I have him call you back when he's through with his call?"

"I will wait," I said softly. I then heard the phone being put on hold and a familiar hymn began playing in my ear. After a minute or so the music stopped, and I heard Cranshaw's voice on the other end of the line.

"Good afternoon, Mr. Braden, I'm sorry to have kept you waiting. Are you at your home now?"

"No, I am still at my office, but I will be leaving for home shortly. What time will it be convenient for you to stop by my house?"

"Well, I have a few things I still have to take care of before I'll be able to leave here. Let me see, does six o'clock sound agreeable to you?"

"Six o'clock is fine with me, and please do not forget to bring some clothes with you that you will not mind getting dirty. That garage loft is covered with dust and cobwebs, and I do not know what else we will get ourselves into up there."

"I already have those things in the trunk of my car," he responded. "I'll be there at six o'clock sharp."

He was just about to hang the phone up when I said, "Wait, you have forgotten to get the address of my house. Let me give that to you."

"That's not necessary, Mr. Braden, I've been to that house several times in the past years. Have you forgotten that Sedgwick Burns was my business partner?" Cranshaw said that in a teasing voice.

"Of course," I answered simply. "I will see you at six."

During my drive home from my office, I reviewed some of the events that had taken place since that first day we moved into our property, and I decided to try to rationalize each of the incidents in my mind. Except for my finding some very unusual and upsetting articles, and hearing some very bizarre stories about the previous owner of the house from Dave Farrell, from Hector Bates, and Blake Cranshaw, nothing much has happened. Now that I had decided to level with Elaine, and she now knows almost as much as I do about the situation, what is it that was still so disturbing to me? I did not know that answer to my question. Sure, there have been a few illegal acts that had been committed by me, at least according to what Blake Cranshaw said, but they were only done to protect my wife's fragile mental state. There were those stolen items from Cranshaw's business still stored in my garage loft, and the overdraft thefts that were committed by Burns, but they were past history and they were also never any of my concern. It now seemed a matter of my clearing the garage loft of the six coffins and dozens of cartons of chemicals, and then Elaine and I could continue to carry on with our lives--just as we had done before we bought the damn old house. Going through those concerns in my mind calmly and rationally seemed to relieve some of the anxiety I had been feeling.

My most significant remaining problem was to try to convince Elaine to continue living in our house. When I told her about the additional cartons of embalming fluid I found stacked in the garage's loft earlier this morning, she appeared to have taken it a lot better than I had expected that she would. Since then, I could only imagine she has thought about nothing else, and she may well have worked herself into a frenzy by the time I arrive home. I could only hope and pray that would not be the case. I also hoped that Blake and I do not uncover any additional surprises that could alter the course of my present thinking.

Upon my arrival at my home, I saw Elaine standing in the yard next to the fence, and she was talking to Shirley Farrell who was hanging wet clothes on her line. The minute Elaine saw my car drive up, she waved to me and gave me a big, toothy smile. That was an excellent sign! She must have come to grips with her fears while I was at work. Hopefully, that should make it a lot more comfortable for me with Blake Cranshaw since I will not have to hedge around in front of the two of them.

I wondered if Elaine said anything to Shirley about our difficult conversation this morning. I will have to ask her about that later when we are alone. I also do not want Dave Farrell hanging around here while Cranshaw and I are looking around in the garage loft. I wonder if Cranshaw ever met Dave Farrell. I seem to recall that I mentioned his name to Cranshaw a couple of times in our long conversation last evening.

I wanted to talk to Elaine when the two of us were at home, and then I asked her about her visit with Shirley. According to Elaine, she never mentioned anything to Shirley about our problems in the house, or even mentioned Sedgwick Burns in their conversation. Elaine then told me that Shirley was chewing her ear off about Dave consuming a full case of beer every three or four days, and saying she was sick and tired of his lounging around the house every weekend. It was just a lot of back-fence gossip that they had engaged in, and it was not at all like Elaine to have involved herself in that kind of conversation. Well, if it took Elaine's mind away from the other problems she and I had talked about after our breakfast, it served a very beneficial purpose.

When I tactfully tried to question Elaine further about it, I sensed that she was still quite disturbed by all that I had told her earlier, but she was putting on a brave front for my sake. After rationalizing everything that had happened, she agreed that our answer was to clear all of those problem items out of our home and out of our lives, and then go on from there. The fact that our two boys were involved with helping me to dispose of unwanted things was something she said that gave her new courage. When I was satisfied that I had said all that I could to help further relieve her of her anxiety, we both sat down at the dining room table and ate the dinner Elaine had earlier prepared for the two of us.

The time was about five minutes before six that evening while I was standing in the front of my yard looking over a patch of flowers alongside the driveway, when a large black sedan pulled into the drive and parked. I could see Blake Cranshaw behind the steering wheel, and as I began walking up to the car to greet him, he opened the car door and stepped outside.

"Good evening, Mr. Cranshaw" said to me before I could speak.

"Yes, it is a fine evening, Mr. Cranshaw." I responded. "I see that you had no trouble finding my house after all," I chuckled. "By the way, that's a nice looking vehicle you are driving, is it a new model?"

"It's eight years old, but this particular type of limousine never changes very much from one year to another." After walking away from the car, he walked over to the side of the driveway and for a minute he stood looking up at the house before he came over to where I was standing.

"From what I can see of the house," Blake said, "there's nothing much that has changed except for the yard. It looks like someone's done a bit of landscaping since I last saw it." "How long has it been since you were last here?" I asked casually.

He thought for a moment and said, "That was about ten or possibly twelve years ago, but I'm not certain of that. It was just before things between Burns and I started to go sour, and we still were on a reasonably friendly basis. We weren't friends, but we were business associates. I just never could warm up to Burns primarily because he wasn't a very personable man, and just my knowledge about his perversion made me feel uncomfortable around him. It never bothered me during our business dealings, but it was something I felt on a social level. I knew from the very beginning that Sedgwick Burns never dated, and for quite some time I had the idea that he might be a homosexual. In truth, he wasn't a very attractive looking man, with his being so heavy, and always wearing dark, drab, outmoded clothes. He was nearly bald, and he wore a cheap, red wig to cover up that fact. The man had no conception whatsoever of good grooming, and I was sometimes embarrassed by the way he looked when he attended the funeral services. He even wore red suspenders under his waistcoat. Although I always wanted to talk to him about his unusual choice of the clothing which he wore around our parlor, I never did it. In fact, the first time I ever saw them I couldn't help but laugh, and I was sorry I did that because I could tell that it had hurt his feelings."

"Before we go inside the house to meet my wife, Mr. Cranshaw, I want you to know that I told her almost everything this morning about why I was so late getting some last evening, so I think it would be an excellent idea if we both refrain from mentioning any of those things in her presence."

"My God!" Blake immediately shot back at me. "Are you telling me you told her about those things I told you about last evening?" Blake's face had reddened noticeably as he loudly responded with alarm. I told you all of that stuff in the strictest of confidence, and you promised you'd not repeat any of it to another soul.

"Of course I had enough sense not to say anything about the coffins to her, or to mention the highly personal facts you revealed to me about Burns and his perversion. I kept my word to you about all of that just as I said I would. I had to tell her something though, as much as I hated to do it because of the way I have been acting lately, and then getting home as late as I did last night. I was in a terrible spot that was causing real problems between my wife and me because Elaine was beginning to have some serious doubts about me and about our marriage. If you are a married man, Mr. Cranshaw, you should be able to understand that?"

"I am a married man, and I know that kind of problem only too well. In my line of work, I'm rarely able to be on time for anything, and my wife Marge has had many sleepless nights worrying about what I might be doing late at night. We've had a lot of heated arguments and disagreements over her worrying over that. Do you think your wife is now able to come to grips with those discoveries you've told her about now that you had a serious talk to her about it? Do you think she's now able to cope with her anxiety and fears?" "I would have to say no to your question, Mr. Cranshaw, but at least she is now working on the problem the best she can. I do think, However, we should soft-pedal whatever additional surprises we may uncover today. Her mental attitude is still quite fragile at the moment, so with that thought in my mind, and at the risk of being redundant, let me caution you to be very careful about what you say in front of her. Is that okay with you?"

"Certainly! But would you mind, Mr. Braden, if we call one another by our first names? With all the time you and I are spending together, being so stiff and formal gets to be a bit tedious for me." "That's a change that would be perfectly fine with me, Blake. I believe that is your correct first name?"

"Yes Rick, it's Blake, but shouldn't I be calling you Richard?" "No, my name is Rick. It was a name that my mother chose for me before I was born. My dad objected to it, but she won out--as the women usually do. I must say though, most people think it is only my nickname--just as you have, and that has sometimes caused me some minor complications. Anyway, let us go into the house, and I will introduce you to my wife, Elaine."

The minute Blake and I entered the front door; I sensed Blake's surprise at the vast number of improvements that were underway inside.

"By God! This place looks great! I wouldn't have recognized it as the same house, Rick."

"I believe I may have told you that Elaine was a student of architecture and interior design when she was in college, I remarked proudly. Although she never actually worked in that profession before, Elaine has retained all of the knowledge and skills she acquired while she was a student in college. Completely renovating this old monstrosity of a house has been her first major project, and as far as I am concerned, she has been doing an amazing job of it."

"When she finishes here with this project, do you think that she'd consider doing over our house for my wife and me?" Blake asked earnestly.

"You will have to ask her that question yourself, Blake. Here she comes now."

Elaine approached us as she came into the foyer from out of the side hall. She was wearing a blue silk blouse and a pair of white slacks, and she looked very striking as she put out her hand to Blake and said, "Good evening, Mr. Cranshaw, I am so happy to meet you.

Rick has told me a little about you, and your reason for your visiting our home this evening."

"I'm delighted to meet you, Mrs. Braden, and Rick's told me about you as well. I was just remarking to him about the wonderful changes you've made so far in this house. The last time I stood here in this foyer, which I seem to remember was ten or eleven years ago, I was overcome with a feeling of dark gloom and utter depression from the gloominess of the rooms and it melancholy appearance. I would have to say you've certainly accomplished wonders with what I've seen so far. Would it be possible for me to see what the rest of the house looks like?"

"By all means, Mr. Cranshaw," Elaine quickly answered agreeably.

"Before I show it to you, you should know that the remodeling is still a long way from being completed, so I ask you to please is understanding of that fact. Now, I would like you to follow me." With that she quickly turned and strode toward the door to the kitchen while Blake and I followed closely behind her.

About half of an hour or so later, and after having completed a fast tour of our house, Blake asked Elaine if she would consider acting as a decorating advisor to his wife. When he first mentioned that to me in the front hall, I was not sure he was earnest about it, but apparently, he was. I had the idea he said it only to be complimentary, but apparently I was wrong about that. Blake went on to explain that he and his wife had no understanding of colors or design, and because of that, his house was uninteresting and bland. Since Blake and his wife were planning to redecorate their place before the Christmas holidays, the timing seemed to be just perfect. Elaine told him that as soon as she finished with her present remodeling plans for our house, she would be calling him and making arrangements to preview his home. She guessed it would take her about another three to five months to complete all that still needed to be done within our house before she would be able to take on another project.

Looking up at the wall clock, I saw it was 7:15 P.M., and Blake and I still had a whole lot of work to do. I remembered I was unable to open the garage door before because I did not have the key to that lock, and I did not intend for us to climb that ladder and enter the loft through the trapdoor in the ceiling--as I had done. I especially did not want Blake to have to do that.

Just before we left the house, I picked up two flashlights, a hammer, and a large screwdriver from the cellar. The latter two items were to be used to open the locked side door. For us to get into the stairway leading up to the loft, I would have to break open that old lock. After inserting the tip of the screwdriver between the bolt and the door jam, I slammed the handle of the screwdriver with the hammer. Then by using the combination of my muscle and leverage, I was able to get enough of a bite on it to pry the two elements, apart and the lock quickly snapped.

When the door to the stairwell opened, the foul smell of mildew seemed to cascade down the stairway from above, and it quickly engulfed the two of us. It was almost a little too strong for me to endure, and looking at Blake, I could see a look of revulsion upon his face.

After each of us had taken a minute or two which we used to clear our lungs, we both started climbing up the narrow stairs to the loft. It was quite dark when we arrived at the top of the stairwell, so I handed Blake a flashlight, and then the two of us began beaming our lights around the interior of the loft. We could see that it was loaded with a variety of junk, just as I had seen it the last time I was up there. For Blake and me to be able to get to where the coffins were laying on the floor behind the file cabinets, it was necessary for us to climb over a virtual mountain of boxes, cartons, furniture and even an old brass bed. Once we overcame those obstacles, we stopped to catch our breath, and that was when Blake finally spoke to me.

"What in the name of heaven is all of this stuff in here?" "Except for the row of coffins, the old file cabinets, some office furniture, and the cartons of embalming fluid, I do not have any idea about whatever else is up here," I answered.

With both of our flashlights beamed on the tarp which was covering the coffins, Blake edged closer, and he then slowly and carefully slid the tarp away to fully reveal the covers to each of the coffin's. As I stood close by and watched, Blake played his light low onto the first nameplate which read Augustus M. Weedan. I had an immediate flash of recognition when I heard him read the man's name aloud from the nameplate. That was the name of a former governor of the state, the one who Pat Driscoll told Elaine and me about. I remembered that she had pointed out his house the first time we came here. Governor Weedan's old mansion is only within a block or two away from my house.

Blake continued reading names from the other nameplates: "Ferdinand T. Boyer," that name meant nothing to me. "Elmer S. Bates," that name had a very familiar ring to it. There's a Hector Bates who lives next door to this house, but that could not be any of his family, I thought. Blake continued reading: "Solomon Morley III, James P. Dupont, and Harry P. Whitaker." He had finished reading all the names from the brass plates on the six coffins, and I had recognized the one name, the ex-governor named Weedan. But that man had been dead long before either Blake or I had been born! It was more than crazy that we were now looking at his coffin lying here in my garage loft. By the appearance of the other five coffins, they looked to be equally as old as this one, and I concluded they were all from the same period, probably very early in the nineteen hundreds. As I was about to comment to Blake on the governor's coffin, he reached down and began unlatching the lock from its cover. I was utterly dumbfounded to see him do that, and I spoke out in a loud and nervous voice.

"I sincerely hope you are not going to open it up, Blake."

"I have to open it!" He quickly answered, "If there are any remains still inside these old coffins we'll have some additional problems we'll be having to deal with." Upon completing his statement, he slowly lifted the cover of the coffin, and then he very quickly jerked his head back from it. His face immediately became a mask of shocked horror, for lying inside the coffin where the partially mummified mortal remains of Augustus M. Weedan.Blake stood motionless for several minutes as he stood over the coffin and stared at the corpse.

He continued to stay there transfixed as I approached the coffin to make fast look inside. Just as Blake had done, I quickly jerked my body back from the sight of it, and then I let forth with a low and painful sounding bellow, "Oh my dear God! What in the world are we going to do now over this shocking turn of events?"

For what seemed like a long time, neither of us could utter a sound, we could only stare down at the dead and dried, blackened and shriveled remains that lying inside the coffin. It was hard for me to visualize that what I was now seeing had once been a living and breathing human being. I began to feel nauseous and I thought I might throw up, but that feeling quickly passed. Before I could again collect my senses, Blake was already unlatching another coffin lid, and within that one was the same gruesome sight, a dried-up corpse. Blake did the same thing to the next coffin, and the next, until all six of them were laying on the floor of the loft with their lids fully open and exposing the petrified and frightening remains occupying each of them.

"Finding these ancient cadavers hidden here in this loft," Blake said in a painful sounding voice, "is something I might have expected of Burns. We've now found ourselves mired in a very deadly serious problem for us to deal with, Rick. If the news about this discovery ever gets out, it will undoubtedly destroy my funeral business. Despite the fact that I had nothing whatsoever to do with this, it will adversely affect me and could easily ruin me." When Blake finished with his remarks, he dropped down on a wooden crate, and despite the dim light in the room, I could see the dark cloud of gloom and despair that had settled into his eyes.

"How can that possibly be?" I asked. "You just said that you had nothing to do with it, so how can it negatively affect your business?" Blake seemed so terribly distraught; I was just attempting my best to console and reassure him.

"Because of the name Burns, or have you forgotten, Rick? The name of my establishment is Burns Funeral Home, and I was Sedgwick Burns' business partner for many years."

"No, Blake, I have not forgotten about that, but how will that fact destroy your business?"

"Because Sedgwick Burns is, without any question in my mind, the person, who had hidden these dried-out corpses here in this loft. And by the looks of them, and the ages of the coffins, this happened many years ago, very possibly long before the time he and I were business partners. It's probable that one would ever believe that I didn't have something to do with it, or at least that I had knowledge about it."

"But none of that can be true!" I said excitedly.

"Why is that?" Blake asked.

"Because one coffin contains the remains of Governor Augustus Weedan, and that man has been dead for seventy-five years or more. That happened long before you and Burns were even born, Blake, so how could your ex-partner Sedgwick Burns have had anything to do with it?"

"What the heck has that got to do with anything? Blake shot back at me impatiently. You must understand, Rick, it matters little whether or not Sedgwick Burns Jr. or Sedgwick Burns Sr. was the guilty party. It's enough that one of them was the culprit. All the public will hear is that these bodies were found in the garage loft of a house that had belonged to the Burns family, and they'll then draw their conclusions. Even if I were to change the name of my funeral parlor to Cranshaw Funeral Home, it would never work because everyone knows who I am, and they all know that I had been Sedgwick Burns' partner for many years. In my business, we rely almost entirely on referrals, and those referrals are earned through the quality of our services and our good reputations. Cast the slightest aspersion upon our moral character, or our business conduct, and we're through. If I were to rate the seriousness of our discovery here as it relates to my chances of survival in the funeral business, I would have to say that I can think of no worse problem for my company to survive. Do you now understand, Rick?"

"Yes, now that you have explained it to me I understand why you are so concerned. But tell me this, Blake, what other choice do we have but to bring this to the attention of the authorities? I have an anxious and nervous wife whose waiting for me inside my house, and whose on the edge of a complete nervous breakdown over this property now. If I tell her about this new horror which we have uncovered in this loft, she will end up in a mental institution for certain. We have also plunked down a lot of hard-earned cash to fix this old joint up to where it is now, but once this news leaks out, all of that money will all but evaporate if we are forced to put it on the market. Who in the world would be willing to buy a house after six old dried up dead bodies were discovered in its garage's loft? The answer is to that question is no one!"

"You're right, Rick," Blake said as he got up from his seat and came over to where I stood. Putting his hand on my shoulder he said, "It's apparent that we both have a heck of a lot to lose, Rick, and for that reason alone we have to develop a plan to dispose of what's hidden in here so we don't have those disastrous things happen to either of us and to our families."

"What kind of a plan might you are suggesting Blake? You are not telling me that we should remove these coffins and bodies from here and then hide them somewhere else, are you?"

"That's exactly what I'm saying to you, Rick. You apparently forget that I'm in the undertaking business, and I handle dead bodies all the time as a matter of routine. If we can get these coffins out of here, you and I can load them into a truck and dispose of them elsewhere, and with that done no one will ever be the wiser. Then we both can relax and go on with our lives just like none of it had ever happened."

"By your use of the words dispose of them, just what are you suggesting we are to do with them?"

"First of all, Rick, let me tell you that I recognize all of the people who are in those old coffins lying here on the floor. No, I don't mean that I ever met any of them because as you said, they lived long before our time. I do, however, know all of those names on the coffin's nameplates because those same names are engraved on the stone fronts of their mausoleums, and each one of those entombments is located in the same place, which is Oak Hill Cemetery. That old cemetery is located within a mile or so from here."

"Just as a matter of interest, all six of these gentlemen were very prominent in politics in this state. I wonder why they were selected to become part of this collection, other than the fact their tombs were easily accessed. And, while I'm mentioning it, that's where we can return their bodies since they belong there anyway. I seem to remember there was something other than politics about all six of them, but I can't seem to put my finger on it at the moment. I believe I'll eventually remember what it is about them."

"I do not have a single clue as to why they were selected, Blake," I responded, "and as for your comments about returning the bodies to their crypts, well, I guess we now have to decide on our doing exactly that, or about our reporting this find to the authorities."

"I'm all for our doing what I had just suggested we do, Rick, unless you have a better idea to tell me about."

"Do I have any other choice in the matter?" I asked.

"Of course you have a choice, but you'll have to be ready for the consequences if we call the police and report what's stored in here, and I don't believe you're ready for our doing that, or do you possibly think that you are?"

"Well . . . no!" I answered after a short hesitation. "I think we should do just as you have suggested and get rid of these bodies before someone else finds out about them. When do you want us to do it?"

"What's wrong with tonight?" Blake quickly responded. "We can load and haul them out of here right after it's fully dark."

"That will not work!" I answered firmly. "That neighbor next door by the name of Dave Farrell, is a very light sleeper, and he told me that he sleeps with his bedroom windows open. Dave is a rather likable fellow, but he is inclined to be very nosey, and he talks a lot. Besides that, he hated Burns with a passion, and if he thought for one minute that Burns had stashed bodies in this garage loft, well, you can only imagine where that will lead to."

"Yeah, I see your point, Rick. It Probably would be better if we did it during the daylight hours when we could see what we're doing.

In that way, no one will become suspicious of what we were doing. What do you think about our doing it tomorrow afternoon?" "I have to work tomorrow, so that idea is no good for me," I said. "Anyway, I think it would be better if we wait until Saturday morning. Then we will have the whole day to do whatever needs to be done."

"That idea sounds all right to me," Blake responded, "but we don't want to delay things a day longer than that because every day the coffins are here they are at risk of being discovered. That's ironic in a way since they've probably been hidden in this loft for a good many years, but who knows for certain? Well, whatever we do tonight we had better make sure that broken lock on the stairway door is fixed; otherwise, someone is likely to wander into this place."

"I will nail the darn entrance door shut! I said, but I will leave the nail heads protruding so that I can easily remove them with a pinch bar when we are ready to get back inside. Incidentally, you know something that seems rather odd to me Blake?"

"What's that?"

"It is about that grandnephew of Burns named Clayton Matthews. I'm now wondering why he never cleared this loft out? Dave Farrell told me that Matthews spent a good deal of time here on the property and that he sold off a lot of the furnishings from inside the house. It seems only logical to me that he would have checked the contents of this loft for anything that might have been saleable. I would have done that."

"I agree, Blake said, but what if he did poke around up here in this loft and he found these coffins. He could have called the police to report it, but I don't think he'd have done that. I rather think he would leave everything just exactly as he found it."

"Why would he decide not to call the police, Blake? Again, that's just what I would have done if I were in his shoes."

"You are forgetting that Clayton Matthews was Burns' grandnephew, and blood is thicker than water. Also, he may have theorized that his reporting such a find would adversely affect his status as the heir to his uncle's estate. At the very least, it could have delayed the sale of the property, or it could even cause it to be revoked. Who knows what his thinking was? I'd have to say that it's safe to believe that he just never took the time or the energy to look in the loft and that he knew nothing whatsoever about what had been hidden here."

Before Blake and I left the loft, we closed and locked all six of the coffins and covered them over again them with the tarp. After we shook hands to seal our agreement, we left the garage and I nailed the loft's entrance door shut.

Blake briefly stopped back in my house only long enough to bid farewell to Elaine and make mention to her that he would see us again on Saturday when he returned to pick up the items stored in the loft. Of course, Blake was referring to those cartons of embalming fluid which Elaine already knew about, and not the six coffins and their grisly contents which she knew nothing at all about. I was thankful she did not suspect for a moment that Blake and I had discovered those gruesome corpses, and I was probably not about to tell her anything about them.

Just before I dropped into my lounge chair in our living room, I poured myself a stiff drink of scotch and water. It was a double, but I certainly needed it. I still had some time ahead of me to think and worry about what Blake and I had planned for Saturday. My God! I thought, How did I ever get myself entangled in this horrible mess?

~ Chapter Eleven ~

SECOND THOUGHTS

While I was at work in my office on Friday afternoon, I decided to make a phone call to Blake Cranshaw before I left for the day. I wanted to talk to him about our plans for removing the coffins from the garage loft on Saturday morning. Because of that profoundly disturbing discovery of the corpses in our garage's loft and after Blake Cranshaw had left, I spent a restless night tossing and turning in my bed until it was almost daylight. I just could not stop thinking about those old coffins and what was in them, and those frightening thoughts were extremely upsetting to me. It also had occurred to me that Blake Cranshaw and I could not handle moving all of the heavy coffins and the boxes of embalming fluid all by ourselves and that we would need some outside help. Cranshaw told me he would be driving a truck large enough to handle all of it, but that was not going to be the problem, as far as I was concerned. The problem would be getting the coffins down those narrow stairs and then onto the bed of the truck. That would be a difficult job for only the two of us. I was not a very physical specimen of a man because I have spent most of my working life in an office, and by Cranshaw's appearance, he could have even more difficulty doing physical work than I would. But, then again, one can never be certain about what people are capable of from appearances.

As I was busily commiserating in my mind over my latest set of problems, a thought hit me almost like a thunderbolt. I surmised that Sedgwick Burns was the man who was responsible for those coffins being stored up in the loft, but he could no have done it all by himself. He had to have had at least one more accomplice who helped him carry them into the loft where we found them. Then I remembered that in my recent conversation with Hector Bates, he told me he had seen Sedgwick Burns and another man carrying things up the stairway to the loft, including a coffin. Because we found six coffins in the attic, Burns must have brought the other five at times when Bates was not watching. It was evident that Hector never considered that there might be a body inside the coffin he had seen, or I am sure he would have mentioned that to me during our conversation. I now wondered who Burns' accomplice was. Could that person have been that same man that Dave Farrell had seen in Burns' yard on another occasion?

The mystery surrounding Sedgwick Burns has grown more profound and more disturbing with each new revelation. I also wondered how many more grotesque discoveries I might discover hidden on our property before it is all over with. Maybe I should go straight to the police after all, and tell them about what was hidden in the loft. I knew my doing that could very well cost me plenty, but I was beginning to believe it was the right thing to do. On the other side of it, there was Elaine's mental state to think about, and additionally, we would suffer a severe monetary loss on the sale of the house. Also to be considered was what Blake Cranshaw and I would be doing on Saturday morning. By our not reporting those bodies to the police we would most certainly be breaking the law, and in the long run, the costs could be much higher for the two of us if we were caught. There was even a possibility I could end up in prison for withholding vital information on a case that was still pending--the disappearance of Sedgwick Burns. That missing person case apparently being still open after more than eight years had passed.

With the full realization that Blake and I could not possibly handle those coffins without outside help, I knew that I would have to involve my two boys on Saturday. The whole miserable affair just kept expanding with each passing day, and I was almost sure that much of what has already transpired was enough to get me in deep trouble with the law. The very fact that I had not reported what I found in the loft kept nagging at me, and it was becoming harder and harder for me to believe that we could continue to get away with withholding that information from the authorities. If we move the coffins from out of the loft on Saturday, the desecration of six dead bodies would probably more than guarantee Blake and me twin bunks in a cell, but only if we are caught in the process of doing it! Blake Cranshaw and I had met and talked together, then we found the bodies and still had not reported any of those things to the authorities. All of those actions would conceivably be viewed as a criminal conspiracy, and it could be the basis for an additional charge against us. Not being the least bit familiar with that aspect of the law, I did not know the answers to any of those things, but they troubled me very much. Aside from what it could do to my family and me, I had to consider the impact on Blake. I did not want to see him lose his funeral business. When I added up all of the pluses and minuses, I knew that I had no other choice than to go along with Cranshaw's worrisome idea. Those coffins had to be removed from my garage's loft on Saturday--just as we planned. As much as I hated to do it, I knew that I had to enlist the aid of my two boys to help me again. I felt sure that I could depend on their complete discretion in this highly important matter.

After all of my hours of endless soul-searching and lost sleep, my decision was finally indelibly settled in my mind. Blake Cranshaw and I would handle this problem ourselves and we would keep the authorities completely out of it. Besides, what good would my telling them about the coffins do to help them locate Burns? It seemed quite apparent to me that my discoveries had no relationship to his disappearance so many years earlier. His welching on gambling debts was, more than likely, the entire reason for his fast departure. Once I had painfully turned everything over in my mind and made that hard decision, I called Glenn first, and then I called Ron. Since I could not discuss the details over the phone, I insisted that both boys meet me somewhere away from our homes to talk. Several places were suggested, but we finally settled on Belamy's Family Restaurant. We scheduled our meeting for seven o'clock in the evening. Since that time would interfere with their usual dinner hour, I suggested that we have our dinner at the restaurant. Both Ron and Glenn readily agreed.

Hanging up the phone after I had finished talking to my two sons, I immediately called Blake Cranshaw at his office to tell him what I had decided to do. I already knew that he would not be too happy about what I had done, but for the reasons I had painfully worked out in my mind, I knew that it is what I had to do, and if Blake did not like it, he would just have to accept it!

I was able to make that Call to Blake right after arriving at my office, and Just as I had expected would happen, Cranshaw erupted into a minor rage on the phone when I told him that I had asked my boys to help us on Saturday. It had taken a while for him to cool down, which he did after I explained my concern about our physical inability to handle the coffins all by ourselves. Blake eventually agreed that we needed the help as long as my sons would keep what they saw entirely to themselves. His prime concern was for us to restrict the number of people who knew about it to limit the possibility of any information leaking back to the authorities. My concern was more about what we would do with the coffins once we had them loaded into the truck. Cranshaw said he would explain that to me when he saw me on Saturday morning. We both agreed that he would arrive at my house at eight o'clock, and that he would be driving a two-and-a-half-ton truck which he still had to rent. That was where we left it when we finally said our good-byes.

I knew that I would have to arrange some kind of a plan to get Elaine out of the house on Saturday. It was not necessary for me to tell her about Cranshaw and me removing things from our garage because she already knew about that. The only things she did not know about were the coffins we had found in the loft and what was inside them. That was why I did not want her anywhere near the house while we were removing things from the loft and then loading them into the truck.

Because both of my son's wives and my grandson would be left alone while Ron and Glenn would be helping Blake Cranshaw and me, I would have to get the three women together to do something to keep them away from our house for a few hours. While I was skimming through the morning newspaper, I spotted an advertisement for a traveling circus that was in town, and there was a Saturday matinee. That seemed to be the perfect answer to my problem, I would buy them all tickets for the circus. Little Henry had never been to a circus, and although he just turned four years old, he should still be able to enjoy it. Before leaving my office, I called Elaine, and I told her about my circus idea, and although I was not there to see it, I could almost visualize her face light up with joy and anticipation.

"Since Glenn and Ron will be helping you and Mr. Cranshaw remove those things stacked in the garage's loft," Elaine said to me, "what better way could there be for us ladies and little Henry to pass the time until after it's over and we'd return to our house."

Just the prospect of Elaine watching her grandson having such a good time looking at the animals and the clowns at the circus was enough for me. I told her that I did not want her to mention anything about the cartons of embalming fluid I had found in our garage's loft to either of our daughters-in-law, and she readily agreed. She did say, however, that they probably already knew because she was thinking was their husbands had told them. I did not agree with her about that, and I said to her that both of our boys had given me their word, and I knew that I could depend on them not to say anything to anyone, including their spouses.

On my way home from my office after I finished work, I made a fast stop at Ticket Master where I purchased three adult tickets and one child's ticket for the circus matinee on Saturday. That vital chore out of the way, I immediately headed home, and as I pulled my car into my driveway, Dave Farrell spotted me, he came over to the fence to chat.

"Hey, Rick," he said, "I haven't seen you around for a few days. How have things been going with you?" Dave asked me that in a slightly tipsy sounding voice.

"I'm doing very well, Dave, I said. I have been tied up at the office a few nights, and by the time I get home I am dead tired. What have you been up to?" I asked in a disinterested manner trying to brush him off politely. With everything else that was distracting me, I was not a bit anxious to engage in any of Dave's small talk

"It's the same old thing," Dave answered. "Say, Rick, I saw you and Sedgwick Burns' former business partner in your yard the other evening and he was talking to you. I know it had to have been that Cranshaw fellow because I immediately recognized his limousine parked in your driveway."

Good, God, I thought. Does anything ever get by this man? The last thing in the world I wanted him to know about was Blake Cranshaw and my connection to him. Now I would have to fabricate another pack of lies to cover that up. When would I ever be able to tell anyone the truth again? Just because Dave is so darn nosey, he is liable to see what we would be doing on Saturday. Now we would have to take extra measures to so that he does not discover what we will be Hauling out of the garage loft. Still, I do not know how it would be possible for us to hide those activities from nosey Dave's eyes without him seeing those coffins.

"Mr. Cranshaw stopped by my house to retrieve a few of his business papers that had been left here in the house before Burns disappeared," I lied. "They were some of Burns' business files and other papers that had been left upstairs in our attic."

"He stayed a long time for only doing that, Rick," Dave replied. "By any chance did you two empty a few bottles of beer in the meantime?" He asked with a knowing grin.

"No! Once he saw the interior of the house, and he noted all the changes that Elaine had made, he asked me if he could look around the place. Knowing how Elaine is, she was more than happy to take him around inside and show him all of the improvements she's made in the place."

"Yeah, I understand what you're saying. Maybe Shirley and I will be available to tour your house whenever it's convenient, Rick. Anyway, what was it that Cranshaw came to your home for again?" "As I said, Dave, it was a batch of old files that related to his funeral business. He did not explain what they were all about and I did not ask him."

"Did he say anything about Burns to you? What I mean to ask is, have they ever gotten a line on him and where he'd been?"

"He said nothing about Burns to me at all, Dave. All he told me was that he had once been Burns' partner in the funeral business, but I already knew that because you told me as much."

"Everyone in Forest Oak knows that," he responded, "and they know it was that Cranshaw fellow who made the place into the success that it is today. When Old Man Burns had the parlor, it was a reasonably run-down operation. I've been told that at one time Burns had a whole string of funeral parlors, but I later heard that he had lost all but the one on Franklin Street. The only reason he still did any business was due to his name, although I wouldn't have used his parlor to bury my dog."

"I thought his funeral parlor was located on Clinton Street, and not on Franklin Street." I made that remark to Dave out of curiosity because that was where I had gone to meet with Blake Cranshaw.

"That parlor on Clinton Street had never belonged to Burns," Dave responded. "I've been told that it was built by Cranshaw after they broke up their business partnership. The place is less than ten years old."

"May I ask what became of Burns' old funeral parlor, the one you just mentioned on Franklin Street?"

"Oh, it's still there, but it's being run by someone else. The fellow who owns it now was once one of Burns' embalmers, or so they tell me. Apparently, he had been with the Burns family for many years-- all the way back to the time Burns' dad was still around. I saw him a couple of times here in the yard, but that was a long time ago. He was helping Burns with something around his house and in his garage, and I seem to remember thinking he was fixing one of the cars, but

I'm not sure about that. I even had a chance to speak to him one day, but all he did was stand and glare at me, and then he turned his back to me and walked away. He was a really creepy-looking character who walked with a slight limp. He reminded me of that old time movie star Peter Lorre. Do you remember him, Rick?"

"Yes, I remember him! Anyway, Dave, did you ever see that creepy guy hanging around here after that?"

"Nope, I can't say that I ever did. Say, Rick, before I forget to ask, did you ever get to meet our neighbor Hector Bates?"

"Yes, I did meet him when I stopped by his house a short time back. He's a nice old gentleman. I even had a cup of tea with him while sitting in his parlor. By the looks of it, he does not get out of his house much anymore. Who is the one who does his grocery shopping for him? I asked."

"Oh, that would be Betty Maloney, she's his neighbor from across the street. Betty takes care of his shopping and other things that Hector can't do for himself. She's a widow lady who's hoping to change her status, but why she'd want that old fossil Hector, I can't possibly imagine. Still, it may be only his company she's interested in because being all alone can't be much fun for anyone. Did Bates have anything to say to you about Sedgwick Burns?"

"Only that he blamed Burns for several missing tools from his yard--the same as you did. Other than that, he did not have too much to talk about, so my visit lasted only about half-an-hour. That was when the old man told me he was tired and he had to get to bed. I am afraid it is not too much of a life for Hector. Maybe sometime before the snow flies, Elaine and I will have a barbecue out here in our yard, and we will invite Hector and that Mrs. Maloney, along with you and Shirley."

"That sounds good to me," Dave said. "What are your plans for this weekend, Rick?"

Before I could answer him, Dave quickly spoke.

"Me and my better half are going to be visiting our daughter Lydia in Carlingville. That's a small town located about seventy-five miles north of here on County Road B. She and her husband Bernie have a nice little truck farm they've been running. They have only ten acres of ground, but it's very productive. Shirley and I will be bringing back some tender and delicious asparagus for you and your wife when we return home late on Sunday. Those kids grow the best asparagus I've ever tasted."

"Both Elaine and I will appreciate that, Dave. I like asparagus, and I know it will please Elaine as well." Thank God, I thought, they were going away for the weekend. I tried hard to mask my feelings of relief. Now we will not have to worry about Old Nosey getting an eyeful of what we are planning to be doing on Saturday. "When are you and Shirley leaving for your visit, Dave?" I asked.

"Oh, we'll probably be cutting out of here at first light in the morning, about six I would guess. It takes us only two hours at most to make the drive, but Shirley and I like to stop on the road for breakfast. We found ourselves a heck of a good place to eat in Bradenton right on the highway next to the canning factory. Do you know the place?"

"I cannot say that I do, Dave. Well, I see that it is about time for me to get inside since I still have to get washed up before we eat. Both you and Shirley take care of yourselves and be careful driving. Say hello to Shirley for me and Elaine, and the two of you have a good time this weekend, and please do not forget about that asparagus you promised to bring back here for us."

"Have a nice evening," Dave said as he turned and walked back into his yard. "You'll have that asparagus on Sunday evening, and that's a promise."

Elaine was very pleased and she seemed quite happy when I handed her the four tickets for the circus. She told me she had called each of the girls, and they had made arrangements to meet at our house for breakfast before driving to the circus grounds. At first, Paula thought little Henry was too young to be able to enjoy the circus, but Elaine soon convinced her that she was wrong. My Goodness, she told her, I was just about his age the first time my father took me to a circus, and I can still remember it. Now that their plans were finally made, the three women were all excited about their day out.

Elaine wanted to know how much time it would take to complete all that we had to do in our garage, and I guessed about three to four hours, but I said I did know for sure. She cautioned me about us stopping long enough to eat something for lunch, and to be sure I did not strain myself while lifting and carrying, and not to put too much strain on our boys. The last thing she told me was that she had been making some sandwiches and leaving the food in the refrigerator so we could stop what we would be doing and have a lunch break.

"Before you start making something for our dinner tonight, Elaine, I am not eating at home," I said as I watched her trying to decide on a meal from her stock in the pantry. With that said, she turned to me and asked, "How come? Are you going back to see Blake Cranshaw at his funeral parlor again tonight?"

"No Honey," I responded. "I am meeting with our boys at Belamy's, and I already told them that we would be eating our supper there. I do not want their wives around while we discuss our plans for tomorrow; besides, it gives me a chance to visit alone with them, and that is something that I rarely get an opportunity to do anymore. I will be meeting them at seven tonight, so I do not have a lot of time to get ready. I still have to take my shower and change my clothes before I leave."

"That sounds like a good idea to me, Rick. I didn't have any thought about what to cook for our dinner tonight anyway, and I was just about to suggest canned tuna fish on toast. See what a delicious gourmet meal you'll be missing, she said with a smile and a gentle thump on my arm." I could tell that Elaine was feeling in a good mood. Her light-hearted feeling was apparently due to the circus tickets I bought, and her plans to be with her grandson and her daughters-in-laws tomorrow. Her good mood was a welcomed change from the gloom and depression she had been experiencing ever since I had told her about my grim discoveries of the embalming fluid in the cellar and our garage loft.

At 6:30 that evening, I was already in my car and driving in the direction of Belamy's Restaurant. Just as I pulled up in front of the place, I saw Glenn's car roll in next to mine. I also saw Ron's car which was parked in front a few spaces away, so I guessed he must already be inside waiting for us. Glenn and I left our vehicles and entered the restaurant together, and we immediately spotted Ron seated in the back booth with a menu already in his hands. He was carefully scrutinizing the bill of fare to make his choice for the meal he would be ordering for is dinner.

Ron is a good eater, and his size and his weight shows it. At six-foot-two and 210 pounds, he is as solid as a football player, which is what he was in high school. When he graduated and started college, he tried out for the football team, but because he had a bone chip in one knee that disqualified him from playing. Being cut from the team did not upset him too much because he was determined to concentrate his efforts on his studies.

When Ron had announced his engagement to Paula, both Elaine and I were very pleased because we liked her the very minute we had been introduced to her. Ron had met her on campus in the beginning of his second year at college, and they started going steady before the end of that quarter. Almost immediately after Paula and Ron graduated, they were married, and they set up their housekeeping in a rather small, rented, two-bedroom apartment close to our house.

It was about two years after Ron and Paula were married when their son Ronald Henry Braden was born, Elaine felt that all of her dreams had been answered because she had a grandson who she quickly began calling Little Henry. The name Henry, being my son Ron's middle name had been decided upon as a memorial to Elaine's late father, Henry Jackson. I admit that I enjoy having a grandson in our family just as much as Elaine does.

My younger son Glenn is quite a bit different from his older brother Ron in a several ways. In addition to being two years younger, and a bit shorter and lighter, Glenn's interests are a lot different from Ron's. He selected art as his major for his four years in college, which was something I was not in agreement with. I thought that after he graduated he would have a tough time making a decent living as an artist, but it turned out I was dead wrong about that! All through high school and college Glenn carried a straight 'A' average in all his art classes. After he graduated, he immediately landed a good-paying job with one of the top advertising agencies in the state and he has been with them ever since.

Glenn met his wife Martha, who is also a commercial artist, at the studio where they both were employed. The two of them dated for about a year before Glenn proposed to Martha and his proposal was accepted. Soon after they married, Martha was forced to leave her job since the company would not permit both of them to continue working in the same studio. Since Glenn was making more money than Martha, she agreed to leave the company and find another place for employment. Within two weeks, Martha was happily established in another advertising agency close to Glenn's office. Occasionally, the two of them even managed to have lunch together.

When Glenn and I joined Ron in his booth in the restaurant, and had finished with our greetings, we ordered our meals. Ron chose the New England roast duckling with dumplings and rice, and Glenn selected the roast pork with mashed potatoes and dressing, with a dish of apple sauce on the side. I ordered the same. Our meals were superb, and after we finished eating, we ordered our coffee.

After I had determined we had enough privacy for us not to be overheard in our conversations, I proceeded to tell the boys about everything that had happened since I last saw them. When I got to the part of the story about finding the six dried-up dead bodies in the coffins, they noticeably cringed because hey both had a lot of trouble dealing with that unexpected development.

Upon our finishing our meals and coffee, it was time for us to leave the restaurant. I told them both I would be expecting them at my house at eight o'clock sharp in the morning, and for them to be sure to wear their work clothes. Having said our goodbyes in the parking lot, we headed to our cars to return to our homes.

Elaine had patiently been waiting for me at the door when I arrived home, and she had a scotch on the rocks and water for me in her hand. She passed the drink to me with a smile on her face as she asked, "How are our two boys?"

"They are both fine and dandy, Elaine," I said. "The two of them and their wives and Little Henry will all be here at eight in the morning. I think it will be nice for all of to have our breakfast together--just like we used to. Maybe we can still do a little shopping for something extra-special to eat."

"I'm way out ahead of you," Elaine, said. "I have a smoked ham that I took out of the freezer, and we'll even have some grits with our scrambled eggs."

"That sounds good to me, Honey. Now I am heading right to bed because I am as tired as the devil, and I still have a whole lot to do in the morning. Do not forget to set a place at the table for Blake Cranshaw. He will be arriving at the same time as the boys. Oh, before I forget to mention it to you, Dave and Shirley will be leaving early in the morning. They are heading to their daughter's house for the weekend. Dave also said he would be bringing you some asparagus from his daughter's truck farm when they return home on Sunday evening."

"Dave and Shirley are both nice people, but they are so darn nosey it sometimes makes me sick," Elaine said. "I don't tell her anything that I don't want broadcast all around the neighborhood. It isn't Shirley as much as it is Dave. If the man had a hobby of some kind or other, he wouldn't have so much free time on his hands to worry about other people's business. Shirley told me recently that she's about fed up with his drinking. All they have is their daughter Lydia, and she lives pretty far away from Forest Oak. I'm happy to hear that they're spending the weekend with their daughter. Shirley also told me that Lydia wants to have a child before it's too late for her, but her husband won't hear of it. Some people can be so selfish and self-centered, can't they?"

"I suppose you are right," I responded, "but it sounds to me like A lot of backyard gossip, Elaine, and you know I do not care much for that. But getting back to your plans for tomorrow, do you think you will be back home with the girls and Little Henry before six in the evening?"

"Oh, I would think we'd be home a lot sooner than that since Glenn and Ron will be here working with you, and their wives and Henry will be stopping back here with me."

"That sounds good! How was your dinner tonight, Elaine?" "It was just dandy!" She said with a little laugh in her voice. "I ate almost a whole can of tuna fish over rye toast, and it was delicious. Good night Dear. See you early in the morning."

"Good night Elaine."

~Chapter Twelve ~

THE REMOVAL

At eight o'clock on Saturday morning, a large yellow truck bearing the name Rentway began slowly backing into our driveway. Blake Cranshaw was behind the steering wheel, and he nodded at me as he carefully moved the heavy vehicle toward the north end of the garage where he expertly angled the truck so that its back end of it was facing the front corner of the garage nearest to the side door. Turning off the ignition, Blake got out of the cab and walked over to where I was standing. He had a brown, paper bag in one hand, which I guessed contained his change of clothes because he was now wearing a crisp, blue sports shirt and navy-blue dress slacks.

"Good morning!" Blake said to me with a light and friendly air. "I see neither of your sons has arrived yet. What time are you expecting them?"

"They should both be arriving here any minute now," I said. "By the way, Blake, that truck you are driving looks to me like it is a bit too large for our needs."

"I don't think it's too big for our purposes Rick, he responded. We'll be placing those six coffins side-by-side, on the bed of the truck, and they'll take up most of the forward section. We can then stack the cartons of embalming fluid, along with whatever else we might discover, behind them so the coffins can't be seen from the street while I'm driving."

"You told me you would be filling me in on all the details of your plan before we began the project this morning, Blake. Are you ready now to start discussing that with me?"

"I think it would be a better idea if we wait until your two boys are present, and in that way I won't have to go through it all over again if that's okay with you?"

"That's perfectly fine with me, Blake, but I have a very disturbing feeling that this may end up being a day we will just as soon forget. Also, Blake, Elaine is expecting that when Glenn and Ron and their wives get here, we are all going to have some breakfast in her new dining room before we start our work."

"I've already had something before I left home, but I could use another cup of coffee," Blake answered.

"Elaine will be disappointed if you do not eat something, Blake, since she made a big breakfast for us thinking we will need the energy for what we have that is facing us. By the way, she and our two daughters-in-law, and our grandson will be leaving us right after we finish our breakfast. They will be spending most of the afternoon at the circus in town. I bought them their tickets yesterday so that we can have this place to ourselves for the better part of the day."
"By your buying tickets for that circus matinee was certainly good thinking on your part, Rick, but what about that nosey fellow next door?" Blake asked as he pointed a finger toward Farrell's house. "You said that he sees everything that goes on around here?"

"I saved the best news for last, Blake. My neighbor and his wife have already left this morning for the weekend. They are visiting their daughter out of town, and they will not return here until sometime late tomorrow. How is that for having some unexpected good luck?"

"I'd say that is definitely a stroke of luck for us, Rick," he said with a look of relief on his face."Is there any chance that your other neighbor will be snooping around outside?"

"If you are referring to Hector Bates, I rather doubt it. He is quite old, and he stays inside his house most of the time. In fact, I can never remember seeing him outside since I have been living here. The only time I had ever seen the man was that day I went over to his house and introduced myself to him. Besides, he has very poor eyesight even if he should be watching what we might be doing."

"Let's hope that our good fortune holds out until we finish things up here later this morning," Blake said rather wearily.

"There is one thing I feel I have to remind you of before we go into the house, Blake. Please do not say anything in front of Elaine about those coffins we will be moving from the loft. As I said to you earlier, I never told her about them, and certainly nothing about their contents. If I told her the truth she absolutely would not be able to handle it, but you already know all about that."

"Yes, I know, Rick. You've already told me about that several times," he answered rather sarcastically. "I understand your concern, and as I had promised you several times before, I won't say a thing about it. Looking beyond me, he said, I believe this could be one of your sons arriving because a car just pulled into your driveway."

I looked toward the front of the house and I saw that it was Glenn and Martha, and they were driving slowly toward the back of the drive toward us. He stopped a few feet away from where Blake and I were standing, and when he got out of his car, I noticed that he was already dressed in his work clothes.

"Good morning, Glenn, I see that you are already dressed for action this morning. Good morning Martha. I want the two you to meet someone."

As the three of them shook hands, I said, "Blake Cranshaw, this is my younger son Glenn and his wife, Martha. Glenn's a commercial artist working for Flanders, Fielding, and Katz. Glen, Mr. Cranshaw here is the owner and director of the Burns Funeral Parlor, and he is the gentleman I told you and your brother about at our dinner last evening."

Our greetings over with, we all started walking toward the side door of the house. Just as we approached the door, Ron's car pulled into the driveway. He waved to us as he continued driving to the back of the drive to park near Glenn's car.

"Do not block the driveway, Ron!" I hollered over to him. "Park on the grass. We will need room to drive the truck out after we have it loaded."

Having heard my request, Ron backed his car behind Glenn's station wagon, and as he then got out, I noticed that he also was properly dressed for work.

"Good morning, everyone!" Ron said in a loud and cheerful voice. "I see that we're all here this morning on time and ready for action. I'm sorry we arrived a bit late, but it took us longer than I anticipated for the drive this morning. Traffic is rather heavy."

As Ron and Paula and Henry approached us and spotted Blake, Ron said, "I don't think we know this gentleman." Putting his hand out to Blake he said, "I'm Ronald Braden, and this is my wife Paula and our son Henry. We are all happy to meet you, Sir."

"Ron, this is Blake Cranshaw, he is the man I spoke to you and Glenn about last night at dinner. After breakfast, Mr. Cranshaw is going to tell us what his plans are for taking care of those cartons and other things that are in the loft, I said as I pointed my finger in that direction. At the moment, your mother is in her newly remodeled kitchen waiting for us to come inside and eat our breakfast, so let us now all go inside and move into the kitchen."

While allowing the others to get ahead of us, I gently steered my two boys a few feet away from them while I spoke to them quietly. "Let me caution the two of you again not to breathe a word in front of your mother or to the rest of them, about what is hidden in that garage loft. It is just better that we refrain from discussing anything at all about what we will be doing today. Your mother already knows what is in those cartons since I told her that much, but as for those coffins, well, that is entirely another matter, and she is a lot better off not knowing about it." I looked closely at both of them as I awaited their responses.

"You know we won't say anything about that, Dad," Ron answered as he turned toward Glenn who nodded in agreement.

When we entered the house, Elaine was standing inside the door, and she greeted us with a cheerful voice and a friendly smile. After all the comments were over with praising Elaine for how nice the new kitchen turned out, we were all seated around the table in the kitchen. Elaine began pouring our coffees and Paula started bringing in the food from the stove and placing it in front of us on the table. At first, Blake was going to have only a cup of coffee, but he ended up eating a couple of slices of rye toast with strawberry jam and a strip or two of ham.

"I'm not a big breakfast eater," Blake remarked.

"Well, I am Ron said as he helped himself to a large plateful of the scrambled eggs and ham."

During the time we were eating our meal, we talked about the weather, our son's work, Henry's various amusing antics, and about everything else except about what we were there to do. When the table had been cleared of everything except the pot of coffee and our cups, Elaine, Martha and Paula excused themselves and left the table with Henry. They would be visiting together in the living room. Now that we were alone and away from the others, the four of us men to talk freely.

"Do any of you mind if I smoke a cigarette?" Blake asked with a look of embarrassment.

"Go right ahead," I said as I handed him an ashtray which I took down from a kitchen cabinet. He then offered a cigarette he had taken from the pack to each of my sons, but he learned that they, like their father and mother, never use tobacco.

Leaning back comfortably in his chair, Blake lit his cigarette with a loud snap of a cigarette lighter which broke the silence in the room. After he took a deep drag on the cigarette, he turned his gaze toward the three of us with a searching look on his face.

"I don't know how much information your dad has conveyed to you two men about what's been going on here in this house, but there is something that you both should know before we all get started inside the garage's loft," he said as he pointed his finger toward the back of the house.

"Our Dad has already told us everything and, we are both well aware of the risk," Ron said as he looked at Glenn.

"That's good!" Blake responded. "Now here's the plan that I've worked out to dispose of those items. The first thing that we'll have to do is get that stairway door open. That should be easy enough because your dad left the nail heads exposed to allow for a pinch bar to pull them out. With that done, we have to clear a path through that accumulation of junk inside the loft. That path will have to be large enough for us to carry the coffins down the stairs and outside to the tailgate of the waiting truck. Since both of you fellows look healthy and strong, you should be the ones who carry them down the stairs while your dad and I can handle their being loaded inside the truck from the tailgate. Now you'll need a light so you can see what you're doing up there. Do you have an extension cord and a light, Rick?"

"Yes, I have one that will have to be plugged into the electrical outlet in the lower level of the garage. We will have to get it from the cellar before we leave the house."

"That's good! We must be certain we do all of our loading of everything as quietly and as quickly as possible. We don't want any of your neighbors hearing a commotion and checking to see what we're up to. I even thought about covering up the coffins with a tarp as each one is carried down to the truck, but that would only cause someone who might be watching us becoming suspicious. It's best that we do the job fast and openly and in that way, we should get it all done in two hours or less. Are you all with me so far?"

"We completely understand what you've just said, Mr. Cranshaw, and we're with you all the way," Glenn answered as he looked at Ron who quickly nodded in agreement.

"Once we have all six of the coffins securely nose-loaded onto the back of the truck, we will be loading something behind them. The cartons of formaldehyde are to be carried down the stairs after all six of the coffins get loaded. They are the items we'll use to block the outside view from the back of the truck. There may also be a few other items that you may run across when you're moving things around in the loft. If you don't know what they are, please let me know, and I'll decide if they are to go along with the rest of the stuff, or if they are to remain just where they are."

"Items like what?" Glenn asked.

"Well, let me put it this way to you. If you see something you can't recognize, let me know about it and I'll decide if it's something we should take along with us on the truck." Having finished with detailing his plan, Blake briefly looked at each of us for our concurrence. There were no questions, and no one objected to the job we each had to do.

"I know you're all probably wondering where we'll take those coffins once we have them loaded. That was a real problem for me to wrestle with for awhile, but I finally worked it out. All six of those bodies had been removed from their crypts in the Oak Hill Cemetery. Who did it, when it was done, and why it was done is anyone's guess, but that's not important at the moment. The thing that is important, and I'm sure your dad stressed this point to both of you, is our getting those coffins and their contents out of here.

"If your dad and I were to arrive in the cemetery with a loaded truck, and we begin unloading the coffins from it, we could end up behind bars. I know that. Even though I'm in the funeral business, and I'm well known to the gate tender at Oak Hill Cemetery, that'll cut no ice with him, nor will it matter to the police. There's one way, however, where I can get the coffins inside the cemetery without arousing anyone's suspicion, and that is to bring them through the gate one at a time and over a period of time. That'll be done sometime later when I use my truck to deliver a concrete burial vault with a coffin and its cadaver safely loaded inside."

"Will you explain that to us in some more detail, Mr. Cranshaw?" Ron asked in a somewhat bewildered voice.

"First let me tell you this," Blake said. "All in-ground burials at Oak Hill Cemetery require that coffins and their contents must be contained within a burial vault. These vaults are made of poured concrete, and they are fitted with a heavy matching lid. The inside dimensions are more than sufficient to accommodate almost any size casket or coffin that has ever been made.

"Now, here's my idea: When we leave here, all six coffins will be brought to my funeral parlor where we will off-load them at the garage entrance located at the back of the building. Today is a perfect day to do it because my embalmer is not working. I have only one wake in progress, and that parlor won't be open for viewing until six o'clock tonight. The only person working there today is my receptionist, and she stays at her desk at the front of the building taking care of walk-ins and answering the telephones. For all intents and purposes, we'll have a good two hours or more in which to do what we have to do while we're here, but it shouldn't take us much more than an hour and a half, or possibly the two hours to finish it."

At that point, Blake stopped talking while he lit another cigarette, and after his having taken a couple off fast drags on it, he continued telling us of his plan:

"As each coffin is carried inside the building through the delivery entrance, we'll shuttle it right into the back storeroom. That room is large enough to contain all six of the coffins without any problem, as well as all the cartons of embalming fluid. Once they are secreted in that room, there is no chance they'll be discovered because I have the only key to its door. After that, each time I schedule a burial at Oak Hill Cemetery, I'll have the manufacturer deliver the burial vault to my funeral parlor--rather than deliver it directly to the Oak Hill cemetery lot, which is their usual custom. I'll concoct some kind of plausible story for the vault people to satisfy the change in my normal routine. At that time, I'll need some help to load the coffin into the vault, and we can then use my utility truck with its electric hoist to make the delivery to the cemetery. I'll have to rely on your dad to help me with that chore. Once we enter the cemetery grounds, we'll locate the proper mausoleum where we'll return the coffin containing the body to its intended resting place. When that's all done, we'll drop off the empty vault at its proper grave site in the cemetery and no one will ever be the wiser."

"How do you propose to gain access to each one of those old mausoleums?" Ron asked.

"Being in the funeral business, I have a master key which fits most of them. Although those mausoleums are quite old, I see no problems there."

"But what about those other locks where your key doesn't fit, how do you plan to get into them?" Ron again asked.

"That's a good question, and I have already worked that one out. Since those crypts are very old, their locks are mostly of the same type and manufacture. I'm certain I can get my hands on a skeleton key, lost keys for crypts are always a problem we have to handle for our clients. I'll make it a point to visit the cemetery beforehand and try the key on all six of the crypt's locks before I do anything else. Are there any other questions you want to ask me before we get started?"

"Not at the moment," I said, "but I am sure we will think of some more questions before we are through today. Let us get started, gentlemen." That said, I got up from my chair and headed toward the door to the cellar. "I will meet you at the truck. I have to get the light cord, the flashlights and the pinch bar."

"Is there some place where I can change into my work clothes?" Blake asked.

"Why not change your clothes in the bathroom? It's just around the corner to your right." With that said, I headed for the cellar.

Just as I was about to go down the stairs to the cellar, Elaine saw me at the basement door and told me that the women and Little Henry were ready to leave for the circus. With that, she quickly left and returned to the living room where the ladies all gathered up their things before they said their goodbyes to us and reminded us not to overstress ourselves. "We'll be back home here just as soon as the show is over with, Elaine remarked, and I don't want you to forget to eat the lunches in the refrigerator I had prepared for all you fellows."

Arriving at the truck several minutes after we all waved our goodbyes to the ladies, I saw that Blake had already opened up the chain gate at the back end of the truck. The four of us stood there for a minute or two while we surveyed the emptiness of its interior.

Handing the extension cord and light to Ron, I began using the pinch bar to pull the nails from the stairway door. That done, I yanked it open, and that familiar foul gust of dampness and decay engulfed us.

"Good Lord!" Glenn said, "it smells like that door hasn't been opened for ages. What the heck is that foul odor from?"

"Well, it's not from the bodies in the loft, if that's what you are thinking," Blake responded, "it's most likely from all the other junk that's stored up there and from the heat that builds up under the roof."

"Where do I plug this thing in?" Ron asked referring to the electric light cord?

"The electric outlet is inside the garage," I said, "Open the first overhead door, and you will see another door at the far wall where the outlet is. You had better have Glenn go with you because you will have to use the ladder to hand the light up to us through the trapdoor. The ladder is hanging on the side wall to the right on hooks. It is heavy, so do not try to handle it all by yourself, so have Glenn help you with it." I then handed Blake one of the flashlights, and we started climbing the stairway up to the loft.

When Blake and I stood at the top landing, we could hear the scraping sounds of the ladder moving into position. A minute or so later we could hear the trapdoor opening and the noise of it dropping back on its hinges and hitting the floor. A few more seconds passed before the light illuminated the darkness of the loft in the area of the trapdoor, and then we heard Ron's voice.

"Okay, Dad. I'm ready for you with the light." Then in a louder voice we heard him say, "Holy smokes! What in the world's being stored up here? What a pile of junk to have to wade through! I'm coming on up."

"No! I shouted to him. Put the light where I can reach it and be careful that you play out enough electrical cord. I want you to go back down the ladder and be careful when you close the trapdoor that you do not cut the extension cord. After you are down, replace the ladder on the wall hooks and close the garage door behind you. You and Glenn can come up here using the stairway after those things are done. Oh, one last thing, look around before you come up here to see if any of my neighbors are watching what we are doing."

"I hear you, Dad, and understand. We'll be there in a minute."

After doing what I had asked them to do, both boys joined Blake and me in the loft at the top of the stairway. There were so many things blocking our way to the coffins and the trapdoor we had to spend the next several Minutes moving a virtual mountain of stuff to make a wide access to the trapdoor where the light was. After bringing the light to a spot to where the coffins were lying on the floor, I hung it over a low ceiling rafter. Next, we slowly removed the tarp, and all six of the dark wooden coffins were then openly bathed in light. Glenn and Ron stood next to Blake and me, and it was rather obvious they both became visibly shaken at the very sight of them.

"Are you going to open one of them up?" Glenn asked anxiously.

"I don't think that's a very good idea!" Blake quickly answered him. "It's best that you don't see what's inside. All those corpses have been dead for about seventy-five years, and they're not pretty to look at. That's especially true after having been baked in the summer heat of this loft for God only knows how long. If you don't believe me, just ask your dad because he saw them and he knows what I'm saying is true," he said as he turned to me for my confirmation.

"He is absolutely right about that!" I said. "Now, let us get busy because we have a lot to do and the day is getting shorter by the minute."

'The two of you husky and healthy looking fellows should be able to handle the coffins without too much trouble," Blake remarked as he looked at Glenn and Ron. "Those bodies inside the coffins are so completely dried out, I'd guess they may have maybe 60 percent of their original weight. What remains are the coffins themselves, and since they are all made of solid oak, they'll still be rather heavy to lift. To be on the safe side, you each should pick one of them up and see if you can handle it without the help of your dad and me. Each one of you is to take hold of the handles and give the coffin a short lift." With that, Blake walked over to the first coffin and showed Ron how it was to be done. Glenn walked around to the other side of it and grasped its handles, and with a huff, he helped his brother hoist the coffin from the floor, and Blake and I noted that neither one of them showed much strain in their faces.

"It's not too heavy," Glenn remarked. "We can handle it without your help." Then looking at his brother, he asked, "What do you think about it, Ron?"

"You must be kidding me, my little brother, I can take two of them at a time," he answered with a grin.

"That's great! Blake answered. Set it back down, and your dad and I will go down to the truck where we will be waiting for you. Give us a few minutes to get there, then bring the first one down the stairs to us and we'll take it from you at the tailgate. We will both be waiting inside the back of the truck so you two will have to hoist it up to the level of the bed of the truck. Is that understood, fellows?"

"It's understood!" Both boys answered him almost in unison.

Blake and I left the loft, went down the stairs, and climbed up into the back of the truck. Once there, we waited for the first coffin to be brought down to us from the loft. Within a few minutes we heard the sound of a coffin being carried down the stairway as it bumped against the walls. Finally, the first of the six coffins was placed on the truck bed, and Glenn and Ron quickly returned to the loft for coffin number two. Blake and I immediately grabbed the handles of the coffin and scooted it to the front of the truck. Several minutes later, the second coffin was brought down the stairs and we handled that one just as we had the first.

It took another forty-five minutes for all of the coffins to be brought down from the loft and loaded aboard the truck. When that part of the job was done, we all rested for about fifteen minutes before we tackled our next project, which was to bring down all the cartons of embalming fluid. Those would be loaded on the back of the truck to block the outside view of the coffins. We did not want anyone nosing around, so I asked Glenn to stand guard while Ron, Blake, and I went back into the loft. I specifically chose Glenn to do that since I had noticed how flushed his face had become from all the lifting and carrying of the coffins. Looking intently at Ron, I saw that he did not have that same problem.

When Blake and I were back inside the loft, I began opening one of the cartons close to the trapdoor. This stack of cardboard cartons looked similar to those from the cellar which we had previously disposed of, but I could now see that they had different color labeling on the outside. Pulling one of the bottles from inside, I shined my flashlight on its label. As I did that, Blake walked over to see what it said. Like the earlier cartons from the cellar, it read: Egyptian Chemical Company, Aromatic Embalming Fluid.

"God-darn that Sedgewick Burns," Blake bellowed angrily, "this is some of the stock he'd stolen from our business--part of that double billing and pilfering I told you about, Rick. I can't imagine what Burns had in his mind when he took all of this embalming fluid. I also can't imagine what possible use Burns might have wanted it for. Well, it's formaldehyde, so it's still good, and I can use it in my parlor. Now, let's get it out of here and down to the truck," he said as he lifted the first carton up to his shoulder. Ron and I followed his lead, and before too much longer we had all of it loaded aboard the back end of the truck practically filling up the existing space.

All four of us working together carefully examined the remaining contents of the loft, looking for items which we could take along with us, but we found nothing more that had to be removed from the garage's loft. Blake took a few minutes to scan a few of the documents in the file cabinets and file boxes and declared them all to be records from the funeral home's far distant past. When all the cartons at the back of the truck were braced correctly, we closed and locked the chain gate. While the other three waited nervously, I returned to the loft to turn the light off and used my flashlight to see my way out, nailing the stairway door shut before I left.

As Blake climbed into the cab of the truck and started the engine, he instructed us to meet him at his funeral parlor. Glenn, Ron, and I then climbed into Glenn's car while we waited for Blake to pull the truck out of my driveway. We decided to follow closely behind him just in case he had any kind of a problem. After a forty-five minute drive, we arrived at his place of business. Glenn parked his car in the lot close to the rear of the building, while Blake maneuvered the big truck up to the garage entrance, the one with the sign that read Deliveries.

With the touch of a wireless controller, Blake opened a big double overhead door and then motioned for us to follow him. He then opened an inside door containing a small stack of cartons similar to those we had taken from my garage's loft. I visually determined there would be more than enough room to accommodate the cartons of embalming fluid, so all four of us immediately began removing them from the back end of the truck. Once we had all of them neatly stacked along one wall in the storeroom, Glenn and Ron carried the coffins inside one-by-one, and carefully positioned them in the center of the room--just as Blake had directed them to do.

When the boys finished with their job of unloading and stacking, Blake locked the door of the storage room behind us as he said, "That was done quickly and efficiently men. Now I think it's time for a beer if anyone's interested in snapping of the lid on a cold one with me?"

"That sounds great!" Ron answered without hesitation.

"I can also go for a cold beer," Glenn responded.

"Come along with me, gentlemen," Blake beckoned, as he pointed us in the direction of another room. "There are some chairs we can sit on when we get inside," he said. We then entered the windowless room with walls painted with a high-gloss white enamel. The room contained little more than a stainless steel table with a large overhead light, several chairs, a glassed-front cabinet, and more of those same cartons of embalming fluid stacked against one wall. On a wheeled pedestal, I saw what appeared to be an apparatus similar to that which I had found in my cellar and had thrown away at the dump. This place has to be the room where they prepare the bodies, I thought to myself as I watched Glenn and Ron taking visual note of everything in their sight. Each of them had a somber look on his face.

"I'll get us some cold cans of beer," Blake said as he opened a door and quickly exited the room. A minute or two later he returned carrying four cans. With the beer in our hands, the four of us talked about the events of the day, and about the plans for the future handling of the coffins. Blake told the boys, as delicately as possible, a little of what went on inside that room, confirming that it was used for body preparation--just as I had thought it to be.

By the time we were ready to leave it was almost one o'clock in the afternoon. Blake still had the truck he had rented which was to be returned to the rental lot where he would retrieve his car parked outside the office.

After thanking Blake for all of his help, and bidding him our goodbyes, we left the funeral parlor in Glen's car and headed it directly back to my house. Upon our arrival, the three of us men joined our spouses and Henry. They were sitting in the parlor talking about their experiences at the circus. Apparently, they left earlier than they had planned to leave because Henry became cranky and hard to manage. It seems that he was just a little too young to enjoy the circus. When we walked into the living room, he was sleeping soundly on the couch cradled up next to his mother.

"It looks like the three of you had a good workout today disposing of that useless junk in our garage," Elaine said as I dropped down on the couch next to her. "Did you get to finish your entire project, Rick?"

"Everything has been taken care of, thanks to the hard work of our two sons," I said as I hugged her and planted a quick kiss on her cheek. "How did your day go in the circus?"

"Well, the girls and I had a great time, but all that Henry wanted to do was sleep. The only time he showed any interest at all was when a big red-nosed clown came by him and tickled him on his tummy and woke him up. The clown had scared the little fellow, and he began crying, and it took a while for us to quiet him down again. I guess we'll take him to the circus again, but he'll have to be a little older before that happens."

Right after my son's wives each came up to me and had given me a fast peck on my cheek, they went back to their seats and their conversations with their husbands. Excusing ourselves, Elaine and me left the living room and walked out into the kitchen. When we were seated at the table, she asked me about our activities, and I gave her a brief description of what we had done, leaving out everything that had to do with the coffins. I told her only about the cartons of embalming fluid, and I said we had to stop at Cranshaw's funeral parlor to drop them off.

When Elaine asked me what else of interest we had found hidden in the loft, I told her we did not have the time to look much beyond those items of embalming fluid, but I would check it out again someday very soon. I also made mention of the brass bed that I had seen there, and she immediately told me that she wanted me to get it down so she could look it over. If it's in decent shape, it might fit right into the decor of the third bedroom, Elaine said a bit excitedly. We ended our conversation with my promise that I would bring it down from the loft for her, but she would have to wait a while until I gathered up my energy to go back up there again. I still had the difficult job awaiting me to remove those old file cabinets and file boxes containing ancient files, and then haul them to the county dump. That would be the ideal time for me to mention that I will be needing help from Ron and Glenn again, and to make my time frame for doing it as indefinite as possible. "They are both good workers, Elaine, and I certainly cannot lift all those cabinets and boxes by myself," I remarked.

Just as Elaine and I were about to leave the kitchen to again join the family in the living room, I said, "Im expecting to hear from Blake Cranshaw again, Elaine. Please be sure to let me know whenever he calls." She assured me that she would do that, and after a few seconds of thought, she asked me what possible reason would he have to contact me again. Once more, I had to concoct another lie and tell her that he wanted to discuss some of his business accounting problems with me. Temporarily satisfied with my explanation, she returned to the living room, while I half-heartedly followed close behind her.

"Well, folks, what will it be? I asked loudly to everyone as I entered the room Belamy's Restaurant or Red Lobster? Take your pick."

"Red Lobster!" Everyone said.

"We will leave just as soon as the boys, and I get washed up and change into some fresh clothes. The three of us are so hungry we could eat a couple of horses."

"I'm sorry, all they serve at that restaurant is seafood," Elaine chimed in. We'll have to go somewhere else if you have a taste for horse meat. Elaine made that last remark with a chuckle, and everyone laughed.

I thought that kind of humor was just what was needed for my sons and me to banish the gloom of an otherwise gruesome and tiring day. I also felt that getting those bodies out of my garage had lifted a thousand pounds off of my shoulders. For the first time in days, I felt as if I could breathe again, and I was determined to have a good time tonight with my family.

~*Chapter Thirteen* ~

THE PLOT BEGINS TO THICKEN

It had been two weeks to the day since we had removed the coffins and secreted them in the storeroom at the Burns' Funeral Parlor. I was working in my yard on the flower beds that Saturday afternoon when Elaine told me I had received a telephone call from Blake Cranshaw. Responding to the call, I was immediately aware that Blake sounded very excited and somewhat mysterious when he asked me if I could meet him at his parlor, while also stressing that I should get there as quickly as possible. I told him I was wearing my gardening clothes, and that I would have to wash up and change before I left, but Blake said for me to leave my house immediately, and to come just as I was. I tried to get him to explain the problem he was having, but he told me that he could not talk about it on the phone, and I was just to get there in a hurry and not lose any more time. I agreed to do it, but after hanging up the phone, I became a bit concerned and started to question in my mind what his motives might have been for calling me in such a rush.

When I explained the strange phone call to Elaine, I quickly got into my car and headed directly to the Burns Funeral Home. Just as I approached the back of the building, I saw Blake standing at the end of his parking lot motioning for me to drive to where he was.

Parking my car in an open slot, I got out and walked quickly to where he was waiting for me.

"What is it that is so darned urgent, Blake, that you could not wait for me to clean up and change into something decent to wear?" I asked, and I did not even try to mask my irritability.

"Come with me, Rick! I want to show you something" Blake said excitedly as he quickly turned and walked toward the open entrance door to the garage. When we were both inside, I could see the utility truck he had previously mentioned to my sons and me earlier. It is parked inside one of the large open stalls. I followed close behind him as he entered the storeroom where I immediately saw that one of the coffin's lids was wide open, and it was obvious that the cadaver had been rudely disturbed. The dead man's suit jacket, his shirt, and tie, which I had previously neatly seen, were now pushed roughly aside, and a black looking corpse was openly exhibited. As I glared at the sight of it, I could easily count every single one of his ribs.

"Who in Hell did this terrible thing to this corpse," I asked Blake quite loudly and in a feeling of deep Disgust.

"I did," Blake replied. "Yesterday I was thinking about why Burns had selected these particular six bodies to be removed from their crypts, and I knew there had to be a better reason for him doing that than the fact that Oak Hill Cemetery was conveniently located to his house. I just couldn't understand what possible use he would have for these old and dried-up cadavers, and then it came to me in a flash, all six of these men were killed at the same time and in the same manner."

"What?" I responded incredulously. "Sedgwick Burns was not even born when that event occurred. How could he have had anything to do with it?"

"Hold on now for a minute, Rick," Blake said. "I didn't mean to imply that Burns had anything to do with that murder. I believe the man was not involved in those ancient killings. What I'm saying to you is that all six of those men had been brutally murdered at the same time, and all of their bodies were sealed into their respective mausoleums on-or-about the same day. The dead and mutilated bodies had been taken to the Burns' Mortuary for preparation just before their final internment in their crypts. It seems evident to me, the reason the Burns Mortuary was selected to do those procedures was because of their reputation for being able to reconstruct the worst cases of cranial disfigurement. Since all of those men were killed in some explosion inside their office, the condition of those bodies must have looked really awful."

"How do you know all this your telling me?" I asked.

"Merely because I carefully examined each of the six cadavers, and by doing that I could see the extent of reconstruction that had taken place on them. A good percentage of what is contained in those coffins turned out to be plaster, wax, and other compounds which are holding together what little remained of the original skulls and bones and flesh. The heat in the loft where they eventually were stored had caused practically all of the original wax to melt away, and that's what I first noticed when I examined the bodies. After finding that, I immediately wondered why they all suffered similar wounds. That was when I decided to check at our local library for some answers, and I learned that they all were killed from the ravages of a deadly bomb blast.

"I took the energy to view the rolls of microfilm covering the newspaper accounts of the time, and there were all the answers I was looking for. If I had the inclination to do so, I could probably find the actual written records of their reconstructive procedures and interments. Those records are probably still hidden inside some of those old file cabinets that are stored in your garage's loft.

"I would have to say that Sedgwick Burns Senior had done a masterful job on them. Do you remember I told you that difficult or extensive body reconstructions were the things that man had excelled at?

"Now keep this straight in your mind, Rick, we're not talking about Sedgwick Burns Jr., whose the man who previously owned your house, we are now talking about his father Sedgwick Burns Sr., and possibly his grandfather Solomon, who was the man who founded the Burns Mortuary. Just for the record, my partner's skills in the reconstruction of severely damaged bodies had significantly diminished over the years through his heavy drinking. Most of those clients he worked on with massive cranial damage had to be redone by someone else because of Burns' pronounced loss of his of ability, and because of his sloppy work. Eventually, Burns and I came to an understanding that he wasn't to touch that kind of client, and I can tell you that it greatly distressed him. He insisted that he still possessed those same skills he learned while working with his father, but it just wasn't true! His drinking, his gambling, and carousing around, most assuredly, had a lot to do with the deterioration of his past skills. But who's to say for sure why it eventually happened?"

"Well, now that we know all of that, Blake, what possible difference does it make to us, and why all the excitement? When you called me this afternoon, I thought someone had discovered those bodies we had stashed in your back storage room, and I darn near had a heart attack! I said rather angrily."

"I am very sorry that my call upset you, Rick, I was pretty upset myself over what I had discovered about the bodies. Anyway, the primary reason you are here now is that I have a concrete burial vault to be delivered to Oak Hill Cemetery this afternoon, and I'll need your help to load one of the coffins into the vault and make that delivery. That was the reason why I told you on the phone not to bother to change from your work clothes. I already had the manufacturer deliver the vault here to my garage," he said, as he pointed in that direction. The gray concrete box I saw lying on the floor was much larger than I had imagined it would be.

Immediately after Blake and I had removed the heavy lid from the concrete vault using the electric power winch from Blake's truck, we gently placed one of the now closed and locked coffins inside of it. That was the same one that Blake had showed me when I first walked into the storeroom--the coffin containing the remains of Ferdinand Boyer. When that was done, Blake started up the truck and deftly repositioned it closer to the concrete burial box. I quickly attached the cable hooks--as Blake instructed me to do before he started the winch. The vault lifted slowly off the floor, and when it was in the proper position, Blake swung it over the bed of the truck and lowered it down and it came to rest on top of a couple of thick wooden planks.

"Let's get a move on, Rick," Blake said. "I want to get this delivery over with as soon as possible. I have another service that's scheduled for four this afternoon, and we don't have a lot of time. I think it's best for you to ride with me to the cemetery, and I'll return you here to your car when we are done." He then slid behind the steering wheel and turned the key in the ignition. I climbed into the truck's cab next to him, and as he drove out of the garage, he pressed the remote control button for the electric garage door. In a few seconds, I heard it close behind us with a loud bang.

"You said all of those men had been killed in an explosion?" I said. "It's funny though, I do not seem to remember ever having read anything at all about that incident in any part of our state's history. When exactly did that happen, Blake?"

"The date of the incident was August 3, 1912." He responded. "As I may also have said to you earlier, they were all state politicians, and that fellow Weedan was the governor. The other five men were some of his political hacks. All were a part of the same ruling party in the state, and I would imagine they had their hands pretty deep into the pie. What I mean is, they were getting kickbacks and other perks for their political favors. But again, that was the way things were usually done back in those early days. For that matter, it still works the same way today, only on a much larger scale. It seems that Weedan's political enemies, and from what I read in that article, he had plenty of them, decided to change things. Their way of doing that was to plant a bomb in the governor's meeting room. You know the rest!"

"One of the men who was severely injured by the blast had a younger brother whose name was. . . are you ready for this Rick?" He hesitated for an instant as he turned to see my response to his question and then said, "His name was Hector Bates. I seem to recall your telling me that this is the man whose living next door to you? If that is where the man is now living, I have to wonder if it's just a coincidence, or should that bring up a very intriguing question for us to think about."

"That is a pretty darn good coincidence if that is what it is, but my neighbor Hector Bates cannot be more than 85 or possibly 90 years old, and the one you are talking about would have to be about a hundred and twenty."

"Yeah, that's true, Rick, but he may have had a son who now lives in the house next to yours. How many people are there in this state with the name Hector Bates? Think about that, Rick. For my money, he's that dead man's son, or at least he's a relation of his, and that question gives us some more to think about."

"That does indeed seem to be more than an odd coincidence, if that is what it is. I talked to that old man, and he never mentioned a single word about what you have just told me. In my mind, there is little doubt that Bates dislikes Burns, but his feelings toward him are for entirely unrelated reasons. He said to me that Burns was stealing from him and that he was a very unfriendly neighbor who would not even talk to him. From all reports, Sedgwick Burns was a terrible man to have as a neighbor. Other than the fact that Burns' father may have been the man who had taken care of the six bodies after the explosion, what does that have to do with my next-door neighbor Hector Bates' father--if that is who the man was?"

"Let's not forget all of that happened more than seventy-five years ago, and neither of us even knew there had been a governor by the name of Weedan. I certainly didn't know that. Did you ever hear of him before, Rick?"

"Yes, at the time Elaine and me first visited our house with the Realtor, she mentioned that name to us as she pointed his home out to us, and the next time I heard that man's name spoken was when you read his name from his coffin's brass nameplate. It seems that there is a connection here with that name Bates, and just because we are not able to make that connection now, does not mean that it does not exist. Sometimes certain deep wounds that are suffered by families fester for a long, long time before they are finally able to be forgotten."

Just as I finished my last statement, Blake drove through the front gate of Oak Hill Cemetery. At the gatehouse, Blake slowed the truck as we passed the guard who waved us right through as soon as he recognized Blake behind the wheel of the truck.

Driving through neat rows of granite monuments, I read many of the names carved upon them: Jones; Flannegan; Morley; Delaver, and O'Brien. I read the dates engraved in some of the mossy old stones, and I noted that many were from the last century. Here and there, I glimpsed ugly and grotesque winged angels and large hideous looking vultures perched menacingly atop granite monuments. On top of one particularly large monument, there loomed a darkly-hooded, stone figure in a frightening posture hovering over a grave. The effect of all that I was seeing was quite depressing to me.

When we entered the end row of especially grim looking marble mausoleums, I again began reading the names that were Imbedded in the marble above their doors as we slowly drove past them: Vandyke; Rigeretto, Baines; Rudolpho; Eldridge, and then finally, I saw the name Boyer.

Blake stopped the truck in front of that one because it was the place where we would be replacing the coffin inside. Before I left the vehicle, I carefully studied the mausoleum through the truck's side window. It was a hideous-looking, dark brown marble, boxlike structure, and over its heavy bronze door was a barred window. The door had become heavily tarnished by moisture and age to a dirty green color, and to either side stood large, marble flower pots. To me, they looked more like blackened, polluted birdbaths than they did flowerpots. At each corner of the crypt's roof there stood a marble vulture with bulging eyes and drooping wings. I had never seen anything that was more suggestive of gloom and death than that mausoleum, and I wanted only to get the job over with, and Blake and I get the heck out of there!

Leaving the cab of the truck, we both walked over to the door of the mausoleum where I watched as Blake inserted a key into its ancient lock. With a few slow twists and a hard shove against it, the door swung back on its hinges while it emanated a low moaning sound.

I quickly followed Blake inside and was surprised to see a room measuring no more than eight or ten feet wide by twelve feet deep. There was barely enough space for the two of us to walk between its drab, yellow, marble walls which were narrowed because on either side of the room stood covered marble vaults stacked three high. A plaque on the lower bottom of one stack read Ferdinand T. Boyer, September 17, 1871--August 3, 1912. Above that one, I read: Catherine L. Boyer, November 23, 1879--May 28, 1934. That last one was probably his wife, and he had preceded her in death by twenty-two years. Apparently, the woman never married again. Glancing at the names engraved on the other marble vaults, I guessed them to be for their children or other family members since most of them had the same last name.

Located under a small leaded-glass window at the back end of the narrow crypt there was a low marble bench. That back window had been installed with iron bars on the outside to protect the colorful, stained glass interior. A diffusion of soft colors shown through its dirty window and softly illuminated a soft hue of color inside the crypt. I was about to comment on that pleasant effect to Blake when he began to unscrew the cover from the vault engraved with Ferdinand Boyer's name. With both of us working together, we removed the cover and discovered that the vault was empty--just as we both expected it to be.

Before attempting to remove the coffin that was resting inside the concrete vault on the bed of the truck, we looked in all directions to see if we were being watched by anyone outside. Other than an old man in the distance who was planting flowers on a grave, we saw no one. As quickly as we could, we removed the cover from the concrete vault, then the two of us gently lifted the coffin and slid it off the truck, placing one end of it on the ground. After climbing down from the truck, we each took a handle and carried it briskly inside the mausoleum. Taking a minute or two to rest ourselves after our exertion, we carefully placed the coffin into its empty niche and replaced the vault's cover before Blake screwed it tightly closed. As we left the mausoleum, Blake closed the door and twisted the old key in the lock a few times.

"That's number one," Blake said. "Let's hope the rest of them go as quickly and as smoothly as this one did. Now we'll have to deliver the concrete vault to the place where it will be used tomorrow for an arranged burial." We took care of that task in record time, and we were now heading out of the Oak Hill Cemetery and heading the truck back to Blake's funeral home where my car was parked.

When Blake drove the truck out of the cemetery's back gate, I asked him where he had found the key to Boyer's crypt, and he said it was an old-standard which he had found in a desk drawer in his office. "I've already tried it on the other five crypts," Blake noted, "and it fits all but one of them, the door to Governor Weedan's mausoleum. When I checked it out, I learned it has a substantial padlock and chain fixed through its door handles. I'll just have to use a bolt cutter on it when it's the Governor's turn for his delivery."

"What a day this has been!" I said with a heavy sigh. "No one would ever believe what you and I had been up to today. That is if I was crazy enough to tell them about it--which I am not. Do you ever get used to seeing these kinds of things in your line of work Blake?"

"What kinds of things are you referring to?" Blake asked as he turned to look at me.

"Oh, you know, the morbid stuff like that gloomy old mausoleum we just left. What an awful depressing monstrosity that thing was. Are there many more like that one around?"

"That old crypt that we had just visited looked downright cheerful to me compared to some of those I've seen, Rick. You've got to remember, in the distant past many people viewed death as a dark and mysterious happening. In the days before so-called enlightenment many people looked upon death and dead bodies as the work of the Devil. Most of those scary looking monstrosities that you saw adorning some of those older monuments perched on top of many of the grave's sights were put there for a reason."

"What could possibly be the reason for anyone wanting something as ghastly as that?" I asked.

"Those ugly things were placed there to scare away evil spirits," Blake said while squarely looking at me and sounding very serious and matter-of-fact.

"But, that kind of thinking is just pagan and silly," I said with a rather nervous laugh because I was thinking that Blake was just joking with me. "There is no such thing as an evil spirit! Well, not as far as I knew anyway."

"Those things may be silly to you and me, but as I said, we are now living in a time of enlightenment where we don't hold to that bazaar and morbid thinking anymore. However, all the way back in time to the early centuries and even earlier, people were backward in their ideas about death. All they knew about it was what they had been told by their parents and by their grandparents.

"The majority of people were also extremely superstitious in those early days, and many of the scarier haunted house tales originated during that time. If you'd been around then to be able to look at many of those older mausoleums and monuments, you would immediately have discovered that the gruesome-looking ones had originated during that period. It was somewhat after that time when most people were beginning to have a much better understanding and a more realistic attitude toward death. Oh, there were still some of those ugly mausoleums that exist which used the monsters to chase away the evil spirits, but they'd become fewer and fewer with time.

"Can you believe it, Rick, there are some people who insist on their being buried above ground, like in that mausoleum where we had just left, because they expect to wake up after they die? And, as a matter of actual fact, there are still a few of those crypts around that have a bell installed inside that's to be loudly rung from inside of the crypt if the dead person wakes up and finds himself locked inside."

"I have a hard time swallowing that one," Blake, I said in an amused voice.

"It's the honest truth, Rick, and the fact that we have been embalming dead bodies for decades, that doesn't always deter that kind of illogical thinking. The fact of the matter is, even if they aren't dead when they bring them in our funeral parlors, they are undoubtedly stone-cold dead when they leave there. No human being can survive having all of his blood drained from every part of their body, and having it replaced with embalming fluid. It's no more than pagan thinking to believe that it matters what happens to one's body after he or she dies. Take it from me, dead is dead, and there's no way for anyone to change it. I don't publicly express my feelings on this particular subject because of my being in the funeral business it wouldn't be smart for me to do so, but I think cremation is the most sensible way to go. It's what I have decided I want to be done with my body after I die."

"This entire conversation is giving me the willies, Blake. I would rather that we talk about something else now." Even as I said that to him I felt a slight shiver engulf me.

"I'm sorry that I forgot, Rick, that you are not conversant with this subject. In my line of business my associates and I talk about these things the same way you might talk about your lunch or dinner, or the weather, so please forgive my lack of consideration," Blake said.

"How long do you think it might be before we have the next delivery of a casket for the cemetery?"

"There's no telling about that. It could happen tomorrow, and then again it may be a month from now. It all depends on when I have the next ground burial scheduled at Oak Hill Cemetery. As I may have told you, I've already informed the vault people that I'll want all future deliveries of burial vaults to my parlor instead of directly to Oak Hill Cemetery, and they are to continue to do that until I tell them otherwise. Don't forget Rick, I'm the one who places the order with them for the client, and that gives me control of where it's to be shipped. I also know in advance of the day that I'll be receiving it, and that's when I'll call you. In that way, you'll usually have at least a day's notice in advance of when I'll be in need of your help again. This time was different because I spent too much time examining the six bodies, and the burial arrangement at Oak Hill is scheduled for tomorrow morning."

"That all sounds okay to me, I said. Would there ever be a possibility that we would be making a delivery to the cemetery sometime in the evening?"

"It's possible, and would that be any kind of a problem for you?"

"That would be no problem whatsoever," I assured him. "I was just wondering about it. Oh, before I forget to mention it to you, Blake, there is something that I have been told by one of my neighbors and I need to ask you about it."

"Then, go ahead and ask me, Rick."

"My nosey neighbor Dave Farrell told me that Sedgwick Burns' ex-embalmer now owns and operates Burns' old parlor, the one on Franklin Street. He also told me that he had seen him hanging around Burns' house on a few occasions in the past when Burns was still living there. I just wondered if he was the man who was Burns' accomplice in what we found in my garage's loft. I say that because Hector Bates also told me he had seen Burns and another man carrying a coffin into the garage, but I believe I have already told you about that. If Dave Farrell saw him doing that he would have recognized him. In fact, Farrell told me that he spoke to the man who was Burns' embalmer, but the man ignored him. Seems rather strange, huh?"

"That parlor on Franklin Street was where I began my partnership with Burns. It was one of those that had been built by his father in 1908. Incidentally, it was the last remaining funeral parlor the Burns family owned. At one time there were six of them around the state, but they had all fallen by the wayside after his father died and Sedgwick took over and started his gambling. Of course, I knew nothing about his gambling and drinking problem at the time I became his partner because he told me only that those parlors had become unprofitable, and that was why he closed them. That was just another lie that he said to me. His father never knew about the closings and business failures because by that time he was dead and in his grave.

"Soon after Burns and I broke up our partnership, I sold the funeral parlor on Franklin Street to Bruno Stenn, who had been one of our embalmers for many years, and he opened the business there under his name. I never could understand how he was able to do that because as a backroom employee he was adequate, but as a funeral director, he just wasn't qualified. Before I transferred the parlor to Stenn, I had taken most of my existing business along with me. I'd later heard that his business never grew beyond a small number of those clients who lived close to the Franklin Street Parlor.

"Bruno Stenn had worked for Old Man Burns for a time before his son Sedgwick took over the business. Personally, I never liked the man, and he didn't much like me either, so we both shied away from each other. Stenn took most of his orders directly from Burns, and I didn't much care for that arrangement, but he had been a fixture around the funeral parlor for so long I didn't complain too much about him to Sedgwick. Once, however, I fired Stenn for his conduct despite Sedgwick's strong objections over me having done that without first consulting with him!"

"What was that all about?" I asked Blake, sensing his agitation.

"It was just before the time I caught Burns with his hand deeply jammed into the cookie jar--so to speak. But I already told you all about that. As it was, I had already called for the audit of our books and financial ledgers, and I was sitting behind my desk in my office going over some of those accounts. It was rather late in the evening, and I was the only one still in the building, or so I thought. There should have been no one else there, except for one client who was laid out in the front parlor. Everything inside the building was quiet when all at once I heard a loud bang that seemed to be coming from somewhere in the back room. Thinking that something had fallen from a shelf, I quickly got up from my desk and walked down the hallway to see what had happened. As I entered the body preparation room, I noticed that there was a corpse laid out on the table and he was a gruesome mess to look at. The entire upper half of the man's skull had been badly crushed and one of its eyes was hanging from its socket. The right jaw had a compound fracture with part of the jawbone protruding right through his cheek. The face of the victim was black as coal from the trauma, and even one of the ears was half ripped away from the side of his head. It would be an impossible task for that body to be put in any condition for viewing because it was strictly a case for a closed casket!"

"The first thing that came to my mind was what is this corpse doing there? I knew that the only client we had was laid out in the front parlor, and it couldn't be one that was brought into the building without my knowledge. That was when I saw Bruno Stenn; he was hiding deep in the shadows in a corner behind a file cabinet. He nearly scared me out of my wits. When I questioned him about the man on the table, he told me that it was a friend of his and that he promised the man's wife that he would take care of the body for her. He also told me that she didn't have the money for a standard embalming and funeral service. I was very angry with him, and I said to him he should have told me about it and I would have taken care of it without charge to the man's wife. We do that service on occasion for those who are destitute.

Before he continued with his narration, Blake took a cigarette from his pack and lit it. After a few deep drags, he flipped it out the open window of the truck. "I have to give these God-darn things up one of these days because they're beginning to get to me." "Now, where did I leave off?' He asked me."Oh, I remember now, I was standing in that room giving Stenn all kinds of flack about the body lying on the table when I happened to notice something else lying next to it. There was a bag of plaster of Paris and a pan on a counter. As if that wasn't enough, there were several blocks of wax lying next to the plaster. Like a bolt from the blue, I knew what he was up to, Stenn was going to try to reconstruct the man's face and head! That was something that he had absolutely no business doing, and I made that point to him in a very intense manner! Suddenly, and without any warning, he lashed out and struck me in the face with his open hand. Luckily for me, it was a glancing blow, and I wasn't seriously injured, but later my jaw swelled slightly, and the bruise turned dark, so I had to mask it with makeup for the services that evening."

"What happened after Stenn hit you?" I asked.

"After that, he ran out of the building, and I wasn't to see him again until the following morning when I walked into the body preparation room. He there sweeping up the area with a broom, and the body that had been there the night before was gone. The first thing I did was to ask him what had become of the dead man's body, and Stenn acted like he didn't know what I was talking about. Can you believe that the son-of-a-bitch tried to bluff his way out of it, even though he and I both knew the truth? I got so angry I told him that he was fired and to get out of the building. He did leave, but later that day Sedgwick cornered me in my office and pleaded with me to give the man another chance. Sedgwick said that Stenn had been with his father for more than twenty years, and he felt that he deserved another chance. Being the big softy that I am, I relented, and I allowed Stenn to stay. I never had any more trouble with him, but I never again trusted him after that incident.

"Soon after Sedgwick Burns and I ended our business partnership, I decided to build my new funeral parlor at a more modern location on Clinton Street, and when it was finished, I put the old Franklin Street parlor on the market. Bruno Stenn heard about it and told me that he would like to make me an offer for the building. I was a bit reluctant to do business with him, but he was so persistent we finally struck a deal and he took the place over. I think he had the idea that he was going to take over my entire clientele, but that wasn't going to happen. I'd warned him in advance that he was not to count on any of my existing business since I would be taking that with me to my new parlor when the building was completed. He went ahead with the deal anyway, and after the closing, I moved into my new building. Later I heard that he wasn't doing very well with his parlor and that his building on Franklin Street was deteriorating badly. Since I'd already sold the building, I felt it was none of my business, but I still felt sorry for the damned old fool."

"Did Stenn have any more contact with Sedgwick Burns after that, or do you know anything about that?"

"Not to my knowledge, but, what has that got to do with anything?" He asked.

"Oh, I don't know exactly, I responded. It just seems that those two had probably kept in touch with each other. Hector Bates' reference to the man who helped with the coffin sounds like it could have been Bruno Stenn. Also, Dave Farrell told me a little about him being there a time or two at Burns' house. I remember he described the man as looking like that old spooky looking movie actor named Peter Lorre. Is that what Stenn looks like?"

"That description fits him right down to his nasally sounding voice. When he worked for us, I always made sure that he stayed in the back room away from our clients because I didn't want him to scare them away. Well, here we are back to my parlor, Rick. I'll drop you off next to your car. It was an exciting day for us to say the least, and the next time you hear from me I'll be calling for your help for another delivery--just as I told you earlier. Be sure to say hello to your lovely wife for me. Good night, Rick!"

On my drive back to my home from there, my mind was tormented with all sorts of sinister plots, and I wanted to know a lot more about Sedgwick Burns--the man who had owned my house. I also wanted to gather more information about Bruno Stenn, and part of the puzzle my next-door neighbor Hector Bates may have paid a part in.

My body and my mind were tired, and I was also quite hungry for not having eaten anything all day. As busy as Blake and I were, we had both completely forgotten about eating. I then wondered if Elaine prepared something good for our dinner. I should know that answer soon enough, I thought, as I pulled my car into our driveway. It began to rain, and I wished I had finished with my flower garden project before I left the house today. Oh well. Tomorrow is another day.

~ *Chapter Fourteen* ~

AN UNWELCOME VISITOR

Early on a warm and sunny afternoon in July, Elaine was sitting at the kitchen table trying to decide upon a suitable wallpaper for our master bedroom. She had just opened up a book from a pile of samples stacked on the table when the front doorbell rang. Upon her opening the door, she saw a stranger standing on the threshold.

"Good afternoon, Madam," the man said with a pronounced German accent. "Is this the residence of Sedgwick Burns?" The man asked as he attempted to look past her and into the house. He appeared to be middle-aged, of average weight and height, with a bushy gray mustache over a ruddy face, and had thinning gray hair. His black pin-striped suit was rumpled and shabby looking, and he wore a white shirt with a frayed and yellowed collar open at the neck. Elaine immediately thought the man seemed to be entirely out of character for the neighborhood.

"I'm sorry, sir, but Sedgwick Burns no longer lives in this house. My husband and I bought it from his estate early this past spring."

"What I meant to ask is this the house that once belonged to Sedgwick Burns?" the man quickly said. "But I guess you've just answered that question for me."

"And, just what is it I can do for you, Mr. . . . ?"

"My name is Stenn, Bruno Stenn."

Elaine thought the name had a slightly familiar ring to it, but she couldn't quite remember where she'd heard it before. "Precisely what is it that you're after, Mr. Stenn?"

The man hesitated for several seconds before he answered her and then he said, "is your husband home, I would like to talk to him. I'm sorry, Madam, but I don't think I caught your name."

"The name is Mrs. Braden, and yes, my husband's home but he's in the back bedroom reading his morning newspaper." Elaine knew that I wasn't there because I was at work, but she knew better than to tell that to a stranger at our door. She felt very uncomfortable standing there talking to him because there was something about his appearance and his demeanor that made her quite nervous. Within only a minute or two, Elaine became very anxious to terminate the conversation and to close and lock the door.

"My reason for coming here," the man went on to say, "is to retrieve something that was left here in the house that belongs to me."

"May I ask what that might be, Mr. Stenn?"

"It's a book, or rather it's a ledger, that I had left with the previous owner of your house, Sedgwick Burns. That was quite some time ago, many years ago, and before he disappeared. I had only left that book with him, and it's something I would like to have returned to me because I now need it in my business."

"My husband and I have been through this house from top to bottom, Mr. Stenn, and we found no book or ledger such as you've described." Elaine was starting to become more and more anxious, and even a bit fearful as she stood there in the open doorway talking to this strange man.

"But it's in your house, it's just not in a place where you would expect to run across it," he insisted.

"I'm sorry, Mr. Stenn, but I can't help you," Elaine said as she started to close the door, but the man's face suddenly changed into a menacing scowl, and he quickly forced his foot in the door. With his foot firmly wedged between the frame and the door, he abruptly ordered Elaine to Call your husband to the door and let me talk to him!

Suddenly, and without any further comment, Elaine stomped down hard on his foot causing him to withdraw it immediately from between the door and the jam. Then she quickly slammed the door and locked it, leaving Stenn standing outside of the house cursing her loudly while pressing the doorbell.

When Elaine didn't respond to any of his demands, the man started loudly banging on the door with his bare knuckles. When Elaine ignored all of his efforts to get her to answer the door a second time, he finally gave up and left.

Elaine watched him through the leaded-glass door panels until his silhouette disappeared from her sight. A minute or two later, she heard a car start its engine, and just as she looked out the front window, she saw an old, black Ford sedan driving of our driveway and into the street. Elaine watched the car until it disappeared from her sight in a cloud of white exhaust smoke. Feeling an immediate sense of relief, she quickly called my office to report the disturbing incident to me and I was outraged and disturbed after hearing all that Elaine had to tell me. By the sound of her voice, she was still very excited and quite nervous thinking that Stenn might decide to come back to the house and cause her further trouble. As much as I wanted to leave the office to get home to console her, I was unable to break away at that time because I had a significant project I was in the middle of, and it just was not possible for me to leave. Before Elaine and I ended our conversation, I warned her to be sure that all the doors and windows to the house were locked and bolted, and for her to call the police if he dared to come back to our house to bother her further.

For the balance of that afternoon, it was sheer misery for me knowing that Elaine was home alone and that she was in such a distressing state of mind. The hours passed slowly for me until it was finally time for me to leave my office, and I made a beeline for my car in the parking lot and shot out into the flow of traffic almost recklessly. Cars were moving at their usual snail's pace during the homebound rush hour, and it took me the better part of an hour before I finally arrived at the house and pulled into our driveway.

Before I got out of my car, I tapped the horn a few times to signal Elaine to look out the window and know that I had arrived. I did not plan to use my key to let myself into the house because I knew that Elaine had double-locked both outside doors--just as I had instructed her to do.

Upon reaching the side door of our house, I loudly knocked so Elaine would be able to hear me, and when the door opened, I found

Elaine standing just inside the room with both her arms open and waiting to embrace me. Wrapping her arms tightly around my neck, she pulled me against her and said, "Thank God you're home, Rick. I was so frightened when that man started to get belligerent with me, I thought for sure he would charge right past me into the house. I even lied when I told him you were in another room reading a newspaper, but I'm sure that he didn't believe me." "Exactly what did he say he was after, Elaine?' I asked as we slowly disengaged from our embrace. I looked into her eyes, and I could still sense some of the fear she was still feeling as a result of her earlier unexpected and disturbing experience.

'The name the man gave me was Bruno Stenn, and he said that he was here for something that belonged to him, something he said that he'd left with the previous owner, and he described it as a book or a ledger."

"What did he say it contained, Elaine?"

"All he said was that he needed it for his business, whatever that is, and that he had left it with Mr. Burns sometime before Burns had disappeared. It doesn't seem reasonable to me that he came looking for that book so many years later. Our entire conversation at our door couldn't have lasted much more than a minute or two, but it was the way the man looked and talked that frightened me. When I refused to let him in, he quickly became very demanding while trying to force himself through the door and into the house. I have to say again, Rick, it wasn't as much what he said as it was the way he said it. Can you understand why I was so frightened?"

"I understand your feelings completely, Honey. Now let us go into the kitchen, and we can talk more about it over a hot cup of tea." I was speaking softly to Elaine while trying to bring her down from her present plateau of emotional distress.

As soon as the two of us were both comfortably seated at the kitchen table and Elaine had our two cups of tea poured, I noticed that she seemed to have become a bit calmer than when I first met her at the side door. For the next several minutes she repeated everything that had happened from her memory of the incident almost word for word.

I was now becoming extremely interested in knowing more about that mysterious book or ledger that Stenn was looking for, and I made up my mind that I would immediately try to find out about it. I even thought about calling the police and reporting the incident because I was thinking this man Stenn might know something about Burns' disappearance years ago, and maybe that ledger played some part in that mystery. Before I would take that kind of action, however, I decided to pay a visit to Bruno Stenn at his place of business on Franklin Street, and I decided I would do that just as soon as our dinner is over. If I am not satisfied with the answers he gives me, I could then to go to the police if I feel it is necessary.

Elaine thought that my going to his funeral parlor to talk to him would only provoke the man, and then he could show up at our house again.

"But that is my prime reason for going there this evening and confronting the man," l protested. "I want to find out where that darn book is hidden so that I can bring it to him later. That will make it unnecessary for him to ever come back to our house again and bother us." That statement seemed to help dispel some of her fear and anxiety.

The immediate members in family had long ago recognized that Elaine is a very high-strung and sensitive individual, and many of the things that upset her are those same things which are overlooked by me and our two sons. Her sensitivity may have had a lot to do with Elaine's home life before we were married. Her father was a dentist who had a thriving practice in Bradenton, and her mother was his dental hygienist. According to what Elaine told me about them, there had been a lot of disharmony in their home, and Elaine had been a witness to most of it from the time she was a young child. Elaine felt some of their marital problems were due to their spending too much of their time together, both on the job and in their home. As an only child, she never had a chance to interact with a brother or sister, and she had no one to confide in to help her cope with her parents constant arguments.

In an attempt to escape her unhappy situation at home, Elaine enrolled in a college located in a distant city. She did that almost immediately after she graduated from high school. Elaine told me it was more to get away from home than it was for her to get a higher education. As for her interest in architecture and interior design, those were desires she had developed in her early teens while reading dozens of books and magazines on that subject. Both of Elaine's parents are no longer living, which had left deep sadness in her life because she was never able to bring some peace and happiness into their troubled marriage before they died. Whenever their names were brought up in a conversation, I could see the tears begin to cloud her eyes. Except for an aunt, who is her mother's younger sister, and a first cousin of hers who lives in Philadelphia, Elaine has no one but our two boys and me.

As soon as our dinner was over with, Elaine and I cleared the table and loaded the dirty dishes into the dishwasher. Then I lost no time in changing into a pair of light slacks and a polo shirt before I told Elaine I was going to see Bruno Stenn at his funeral parlor, and I expected to return home within an hour or so. She accompanied me to the side door, kissed me lightly on my cheek, and then closed the door and locked it tightly. I could also hear the chain lock securely snapped into place behind me.

During my drive to Stenn's Mortuary, I rolled a lot of troubling thoughts around in my mind. It seemed strange to me that I had only recently heard that man's name, and today he was at my front door and upsetting my wife. I wondered what was so important to him about a book that he would do that, and just why he thought it was still somewhere in our house after almost nine years had transpired since Burns went missing.

I now remembered that Dave Farrell told me that Stenn had been there at the Burns house before, but that was a long time ago while Burns was still living in the house. Since those earlier visits by Stenn, most of the contents of the house had been disposed of by Clayton Matthews. Wait a minute! Most of it except for what we removed from the cellar and the loft over the garage! Could it be those dead bodies or chemicals he was looking to see, and he was just using a lost ledger as an excuse to get into the house? Oh, no! That thought was too darn farfetched for me to even consider. For him to even suggest that he knew anything at all about those things would reveal his involvement, and he could not possibly be that stupid.

His unexpected and unwelcome visit had to be over a book that was extremely important to him, and he believed that it was still somewhere in our house, but what exactly could it be that important? I also wondered why he had waited all these years to come to the house wanting to retrieve it. None of what I was thinking seemed to be logical to me. Now that I had arrived at his funeral parlor, it may not be too much longer before I learn a few of the answers to those disturbing questions that are festering in my mind.

Bruno Stenn's Mortuary looked to be a run-down and drab looking building located in a seedy looking section of town. Many of the older and larger houses in the immediate area had long-ago been converted into rooming houses, with For Rent signs hung in their dirty windows. Junk cars, trash, and other signs of human debris appeared to be everywhere. Stenn's Mortuary, aside from its overall dreary appearance, had a sad look of neglect. On the side of one wall, I could see a mass of graffiti where angry, and frustrated street artists had spray-painted their turf signs and other vulgarities.

It was not difficult for me to imagine that Bruno Stenn's clients were forced to use his services only because they had no other choice. Turning my car from the street into the parking lot adjacent to Stenn's funeral parlor, I noticed only two automobiles occupying its cracked and broken-asphalt parking spaces. I immediately saw that one of the cars in the lot was an old, black Ford sedan which fit the description of Burns' old 'clunker Ford' that Dave Farrell, and more recently the car Elaine had described to me. It was beginning to get dark, so I parked at the front of the lot to take advantage of the light from the street lamp in front. I did not want to return to my car in total darkness--not in this neighborhood!

Upon my entering the front door of Stenn's establishment, I first noticed the decidedly outmoded appearance of the interior of his parlor. It was much as I expected it to be, very dark and dismal looking, and the ornately hand-carved lamp tables and chairs reminded me of something right out of the Rue Morgue. The main parlor's floor was masked by Persian carpeting which had been worn thin by the feet of countless mourners, and stained by the tears of all those melancholy souls who had trod upon its surface over the years. Peeling paint hung precariously in patches from the baroque cathedral ceiling, while several, large, wrought-iron candelabra stood mute guard at the entrance to each dark chapel. A tall grandfather clock provided the only movement in the room, with its big brass pendulum swaying back and forth, back and forth as a reminder of the ever-constant passage of time. While I silently stood there, my mood was becoming dark and morose, reflecting the aura of that depressing place. I was about to walk out the door and escape from that morbid room when I heard footsteps coming toward me from the back of the hallway.

"May I possibly be of service to you, Sir?" I heard a man from behind me say.

"Ye . . . yes," I stammered as I quickly turned around to face him. "I would like to speak to Mr. Bruno Stenn."

"I am Bruno Stenn," he said in a soft, nasally voice. "What is it I can do for you?"

Before answering him, I took several seconds to study his appearance. The description Elaine had given me earlier of him perfectly fit Stenn, except for the missing tie. This evening Mr. Stenn was wearing a solid black one.

"Is there some place where we can sit down and talk, Mr. Stenn?" I asked after I had shaken his hand and introduced myself. "We can talk right here," Stenn said as he pointed to two nearby heavily-carved and darkly upholstered chairs. When we were both seated and facing each other, he said, "You must be the husband of the woman I talked to earlier this afternoon, the new owner of Sedgwick Burns' house."

"You are correct, Mr. Stenn, and that is the reason I have come here tonight to see you. I want you to tell me exactly what property of yours you feel is still in my house." I spoke to him very deliberately while I looked directly into his eyes.

Stenn must have sensed my lightly-veiled anger, and he immediately said, "I'm very sorry if my visit this afternoon upset your wife, Mr. Braden. I never intended to do that. Sometimes my abrupt manners are unintentionally offensive. I'll have to work to correct that problem."

I sensed that he was looking to me for acceptance of his lame explanation, but it was not forthcoming.

"May I again inquire, Mr. Stenn, what exactly is it that you are after? Is it a book or a ledger or is it something else?"

After several seconds of indecision, he finally answered me. "As I told your wife, it's a ledger book that belongs to me."

"What makes you think that it is still in my house, Mr. Stenn? After all, the house has been emptied of practically everything that had belonged to Sedgwick Burns. That was done long before I ever bought the place, and I can tell you I never saw any ledger or log book lying around anywhere."

"You just said that the house had been practically emptied," he responded. "Does that mean there are still things there that may have belonged to Mr. Burns?"

"Well, yes, there still are some things that were left there," I answered. "There is a heap of cardboard cartons still lying up in our attic room, but they appear to be full of worthless items and trash. It is entirely possible that your so-called ledger book is inside one of those cartons. I suppose I can look around for it when I find some free time, and if I locate it, I will give you a call. By the way, what does your book look like? Is there a name, or any other kind of identification on it which will help me to locate it?"

"No! You wouldn't be able to find it. I'll have to look for it myself."

"That is not possible!" I spoke forth forcefully. "You are not to come back to our house again for any reason whatsoever! Do you understand?" I heard my voice beginning to grow louder and angrier.

After several seconds of hesitation, Stenn spoke almost inaudibly. "I said I was sorry for having frightened your wife earlier today, Mr. Braden. Maybe if you are at home when I arrive, it will make a difference."

"Definitely not!" I quickly shot back at him.

"Then what can I do?" He asked meekly.

"You will just have to rely on my being able to find your precious log book. Now tell me what the heck it looks like so that I can leave here and go home! I am exhausted, and I do not have the time to sit here and argue with you over it!"

"You will never be able to find the log, Mister Braden." "And why is that," I bellowed. "Is it hidden?"

"In a manner of speaking, yes."

"Look, either your damn book is hidden or it is not! I snapped," growing weary of his cat-and-mouse tactics.

When Stenn finally realized that he was not getting anywhere with me, he stood up from his chair and extended his hand to me. "Thank you anyway, Mr. Braden. I guess I'll just have to forget about the ledger. If you happen to run across it, please call me because I'm still interested in recovering it." He then abruptly turned his back to me and strolled down the dimly-lit hallway toward the end of the building.

Taking a last look around the room, I left the building and returned to my car.

On my way home, I tried again to put what had happened to Elaine and what was said to me by Stenn, entirely out of my thoughts, but it did not work. If there had been a mystery before my visit with Bruno Stenn, it has now only been compounded. What in the heck kind of ledger was Stenn looking for? What could it possibly contain that makes it so important to him. Why did he wait those many years to attempt to retrieve it? And why did he insist on coming to our house looking to find it? The way he talked about the ledger, I had the distinct impression that he knew exactly where to put his hands on it inside our house, but there was a reason he did not want me to know that. I could not understand why he would not tell me where his book was so I could retrieve it for him. What dark and mysterious motives could he possibly have? I just could not develop any kind of a logical explanation for any of it. It was fairly evident that only Bruno Stenn knew the answers to my many questions, and he was not talking.

When I arrived home, I knew that I would have to tell Elaine what had happened at Stenn's Mortuary even though I realize that information might further upset her. I wanted her to understand that the man still seemed very determined to get his hands on that book, and he might very well be dangerous. Again, I could not make up my mind about calling the police and telling them about what had transpired with Elaine at the front door, and then ask them for advice. Since Sedgwick Burns was still officially listed as a missing person, and there might be some ongoing investigation in the works despite the passage of so much time. Stenn's inquiries and his strange behavior might be of particular interest to the police. Another thing I had to consider was that Stenn might decide to return to our house at a time when I am not at home, and that is all Elaine would need to hear from me. She would never want to be left alone in the house again if I told her that. Still, if I do not warn her, and later he shows up again at our door, then what? I knew that I would have some really tough decisions to make, and I decided not to discuss any of it with Elaine until I do.

I began to think that maybe I could get Paula to stay with Elaine for a couple of days until her nerves cooled down and she returned to normal. I knew that Elaine would enjoy having Little Henry around the house because she was always telling me that she never got to spend enough time with her grandson. It almost seemed as if she blamed me for that situation. In truth, about the only time I get to see him, or the other family members, are the few occasions we have a Sunday cookouts in the yard. Since we bought the cursed house, those cookouts had become quite rare. When we were still living in our other house, it used to be almost a family ritual for us to have the family over every Sunday. Sure, we get to go to their homes occasionally for visits or holiday dinners, but for me, that is just not the same.

~ Chapter Fifteen ~

THE BURGLARY

We were going to have a family picnic, and I was almost as excited about it as Elaine. Originally, it was to be a backyard barbecue at our house, but we all got together and agreed it would be a welcome change to have a picnic somewhere out in the fresh air and sunshine of the countryside. Ron suggested that we have it at a picnic grove he knew of located on the edge of a small spring-fed lake. In that way, we could have something else to do after we finished eating--like us getting some use out of Glenn's aluminum canoe. Maybe we could even squeeze-in a bit of fishing.

When Ron called Glenn and Martha to tell them about his idea about a family picnic, they said they would be happy to bring their canoe along with them, and we could all take turns paddling it around the lake. Ron and Paula could sit with Henry on the floor of the canoe and give him his very first boat ride. At first, Elaine was against the idea saying Henry could fall from the boat, but I assured her that he would be wearing a life preserver vest--just like the rest of us would be using. Both Ron and Glenn are sticklers for safety. The idea for our family picnic had surfaced only last Wednesday evening when I called Ron and invited him and his family to come to our house for a Sunday afternoon barbecue. He told me that he and Glenn had already discussed the possibility of us having a family picnic, and had planned to call us about it later. When I mentioned it to Elaine, she was all for it. After I finished talking to Ron, I handed the phone to Elaine, and the ladies agreed upon the different foods they would bring along. Almost immediately, Elaine had to rush right down to the supermarket to purchase those food items she'd selected for us to bring to the picnic.

Since it was not too far out of our way, it was decided that we were to meet at Glenn's house early on Sunday morning, and Just as Elaine and I pulled up in front of their house, we saw Glenn and Martha hoisting Glenn's canoe on top of his station wagon. While the ladies visited in Martha's kitchen, I helped Glenn securely fasten down his canoe using straps and thick rubber bungee cords.

That done, we retired to the shade of the patio where we plopped ourselves down on a couple of lounge chairs. We were soon joined by the two ladies who were chattering with excitement just like a couple of magpies.

I realized this family picnic could be the right opportunity for me to talk to Glenn or to Ron about Bruno Stenn's unexpected visit to our house, or anything about my later visit to his funeral parlor. I had already told both of them about my experience at Oak Hill Cemetery on the day that Blake Cranshaw and I made the first body delivery. Both boys said they were willing to help Cranshaw with the next delivery of a burial vault, but I told them I did not want them to become further involved in the matter, and that I could handle it very well by myself.

Because Ron and Paula had not yet arrived, and Elaine and Martha were still within listening distance, I took a few minutes to tell Glenn I would be filling him in on the latest events involving Stenn just as soon as I could get him and Ron alone. The perfect time, I said, would be while the three of us would be in the canoe while the ladies are involved with other matters connected with the picnic. Glenn immediately sensed that something serious must have happened when Bruno Stenn made his unwelcome visit to our house and had badly frightened his mother, and later when I confronted Stenn at his mortuary.

It was not very much longer before Ron and Paula arrived, and we all compared notes to be sure that we brought along all of the things we had decided to bring along with us for the picnic. That was when Martha agreed to show off the cake she had baked. Henry's eyes lit up when she lifted the cover of the cake carrier and displayed it for us. He was all for reaching out and grabbing himself a big fistful of the chocolate, but he had to settle for a finger full of the dark sweet frosting.

Since we needed only one car for our trip from Glenn's house to the picnic grounds, it was decided that Glenn would drive using his station wagon since it was the largest of the three cars. It was also the car with his canoe already strapped on top of its roof. With everyone and everything loaded inside the car, including life jackets, canoe paddles, food, ice chests, etc., we were just barely able to close the back of the car, but we managed.

During our forty-five minutes of driving to the picnic grove, Henry slept in Paula's lap while the rest of us prattled on about the everyday events in our lives. Glenn said that he had been given an assignment by his boss to develop the advertising displays for one of the firms top accounts, and we all congratulated him on his success. Ron told us about his involvement in revamping his company's accounting systems and procedures, an area of the business that he particularly enjoyed. Elaine and I were very proud of our two sons. As usual, there were a few comical stories about Henry's antics which we all always enjoyed hearing about.

"That boy's a chip off the old block," Elaine said. "By the way he's growing, it won't be too long and before we may be having another football player in the family." She was, of course, referring to Ron's playing football for a time when he was in high school and later as a freshman in college.

Upon our reaching the picnic grove, Glenn maneuvered his car into a parking space, and we all got out and stretched our legs. Before we unloaded the car, we decided to scout around for a shaded picnic bench, so we asked the ladies to remain with the car while we three men went off scouting. Fanning out in different directions, we would be looking to find the best spot we could to have our picnic. Ron was the first one back to the car, followed by me, and then by Glenn. After comparing notes, we decided that Glenn's picnic spot sounded the best, so we proceeded to unload the car. Each of us began carrying what we could handle, while Paula looked after Henry. With our arms fully loaded, we all fell in line behind Glenn who headed toward that great picnic spot with a very large table, as Glen described it.

Just as we topped a small hill, we could see the shoreline of the lake and the picnic bench which was about twenty feet from the edge of the water under a giant willow tree. "What a perfect setting for us to enjoy our picnic," I heard Elaine exclaim, "but all of us had better keep our eyes carefully pinned on Henry because he may decide to head straight for the water."

As quickly as we finished piling everything we had carried with us on the picnic bench seats, the ladies covered the tabletop with a colorful plastic tablecloth, and they began to place the dishes on the table. Since Ron had the foresight to stop at a convenience store for ice before he arrived at Glenn's house, we had an ice chest that was filled to the top with cubes. We placed that in the shade next to the trunk of the nearby willow tree. We planned to engage in our other activities for a couple of hours and then eat our picnic dinner after we all had worked up a good appetite.

While the women visited together and talked about their everyday events, Glenn, Ron, and I returned to the car to retrieve the canoe, the paddles, and the life preserver vests. There was even a tiny vest for Henry which Paula bought after she heard about the canoeing adventure we planned for him. Ron and Glenn braced the canoe over their heads while I led the way with my arms loaded with the paddles and the vests. Upon our returning to the women, we unloaded everything on the bank of the lake only a short distance from our picnic table.

It ended up being a wonderful day for all of us because everything that occurred during the balance of that happy day went just as we had planned. Henry got to have his ride in the canoe with Paula and Ron, and he enjoyed it so much we could hear him squealing halfway across the lake. When it was my turn to paddle the canoe around the lake with Ron and Glenn, I took that opportunity to tell them all about Stenn's surprise visit to our house, and my later visit with Bruno Stenn at his mortuary. Both boys wanted to go back with me to confront Stenn with a demand for answers from Stenn, but I told them I would handle it by myself. Glenn suggested that he and Ron spend next Sunday at our house helping to search for that mysterious book, or whatever it was, that Stenn was after. I told them I would think about it and I would let them both know later in the week. That was just the place where we left it.

Shortly before dusk, we packed up Glenn's canoe and some other things and headed back to the parking lot and Glenn's car. This time it took us two trips to get all of it brought there and loaded into the car, including the paddles and life vests, and then the task of again strapping down the canoe. We were all pretty tired out after our full day of activities at the grove, and no one had much energy left to carry on much in the way conversation during our drive back to Glenn's house. When we got there, we unloaded his car, and Ron and I switched our things back to our respective automobiles. That done, we helped Glenn hang his canoe back inside his garage. Paula wanted to make us a pot of fresh coffee, but none of us was interested in her doing that, all we wanted to do was get back to our own homes and call it a day. For a short time I followed behind Ron's car, but he made a right turn at the intersection leading to his house, while I continued driving on ahead toward our house.

As we arrived at the house, and I was about to turn into our driveway, I saw a light that was on upstairs in the attic window. Rather than continue into the driveway as I would normally do, I parked my car at the curb, and I turned off the headlights. I could plainly see the light in the window was just below the turret room.

"Did you leave that light on in our attic, Elaine?" I asked as I pointed a finger toward the window.

"No, I did not!" Elaine responded. "I haven't been up there for several days. Are you sure it wasn't you who left the light on, Rick? When was the last time you were up there?"

"The last time I was in the attic was about two weeks ago, but I never turned a light on while I was in inside. I used a flashlight to check for a leak in the roof. That was right after we had that rainstorm, and I saw a trickle of water on the ceiling of the downstairs bathroom. I was able to trace it to one of the chimneys where it turned out to be a leaky flashing around the base. I will have to get to that place one of these days and fix it. But I had already told you all of that!" I responded a bit impatiently.

"If you didn't leave that light on, Rick, and I didn't leave it on either, then who did?" Elaine asked.

When I slowly got out of the car, I went around to the passenger side and opened the door for Elaine. After I helped her to get out, we both stood at the curb looking up at the light in the window while trying to puzzle out what it meant. Finally, I decided I would go into the house and check it out instead of standing there in the growing darkness and speculating over it.

Not knowing what I might find when I got there, I insisted that Elaine get back into the car and lock all the doors and then wait for me until I returned. She wanted to look for a telephone booth and use it to call the police, but I told her that it would be embarrassing if they sent an officer out and then they found everything in the house in good order. I felt I had to check it out myself, and if I discover a problem--that would be the time for us to call the police. She reluctantly agreed with me as I started walking fast toward the side door of our house. By this time it was dark outside, but the street lamp in front of our house illuminated the side yard enough for me to see.

When I arrived at the side door, I immediately noticed that one of the glass door panels had been broken, and pieces of it crunched under my shoes when I stepped on the porch. Taking a firm hold of the door's handle and giving it a twist I discovered it was open. I had no doubt in my mind that the door had been securely locked before we left the house because I had locked it myself. I had even hooked the chain lock on the door before we left the house through the front door. Entering the hall, I found the chain had been snapped and part of it was dangling on the door jamb.

"We have had a break-in here," I said aloud. "Of all the things to happen to us, and in this nice neighborhood!" I was both shocked and angry.

I hesitated to go any farther inside the house for fear that the intruder might still be somewhere inside, so I returned to my car where Elaine was nervously waiting for me. As I quickly slipped into the driver's seat, I started the car at the same time I began explaining to Elaine what I had found. Her face was pinched and anxious as she asked me what I was going to do. I told her that I was doing what she had first suggested we do, and that was to look for a telephone so I could call the police.

Within only a few minutes, I spotted a phone booth in front of a convenience store about two blocks away, and I quickly pulled the car into an open slot. As I fumbled in my pocket for a quarter for the telephone, Elaine handed me one she had already taken from her purse. After I dialed 9-1-1, I waited several seconds before a voice came on the other end of the line. Meanwhile, Elaine waited for me in the car with her eyes pinned on me and with a worried look on her face.

"Good evening. You have reached the Forest Oak Police Department, Desk Sargent Haines speaking."

"I want to report a house break-in!" I said nervously.

"May I ask your name, Sir, and what is your address?"

"My name is Rick Braden, and my address is 1110 Cobblestone Lane, Forest Oak." I said. "How long will it take to get someone over here?" I spoke in a loud and anxious voice.

"I'll dispatch a patrol car to your home immediately," the officer said. "Are you calling me from inside the residence, Sir?"

"No, I am calling you from a nearby pay phone. The burglar may still be inside my house so I did not want to use the telephone there."

"That was good thinking, Sir. Please give me your name again." "The name is Braden, Rick Braden. I am with my wife, and we will be waiting in our car which will be parked at the curb in front of the house when your officers get there, and please tell them to hurry!"

"A patrol car has already been dispatched and it's already on its way. Please be calm, Mr. Braden, and continue to wait for them outside. Whatever you do, don't go inside the house until the officers arrive and they tell you that it's safe for you to go inside."

"I understood!" I answered and then I hung up the phone.

As soon as I got back in my car, Elaine asked me what the police had said on the phone, and I repeated our brief conversation to her. Driving out of the lot, we arrived back in front of our house in a matter of only minutes and I again parked my car at the curb. By this time it was completely dark outside, and the light in the attic window was still on. While we waited for the police patrol car to arrive, we speculated about why our house was selected for the break-in. It was at that moment when Elaine suggested it may have been that man Bruno Stenn who was the one who broke into our house.

"That's rather funny," Elaine, I said, "because that same thought had occurred to me. When I met Stenn at his funeral parlor, he seemed determined to get his hands on that ledger book, still, when I insisted that he would have to rely on my finding it, and I told him he was not allowed to be there with me to look for it, he backed down pretty darn fast. Perhaps it was at that moment he hatched a plan to break into our house and steal the book. I would say that the conclusions are that it was Bruno Stenn who was the man who broke into our house!"

I suppose I could tell the police about Bruno Stenn and our suspicions of his being the man who broke into our house, but that might bring about other matters that were better left alone. I was now thinking about what we had removed from our garage's loft. No, I would leave Bruno Stenn's name out of it when I am talking to the police, and that was what I told Elaine to do as well. She agreed to go along with me, but she was having a little difficulty understanding what my motives were. In her mind, just as in mine, Stenn was definitely the prime suspect in the burglary, but again, Elaine knew nothing at all about the dead bodies that had been removed from the loft, and I still had no intention of telling her about them.

Two police patrol cars responded to my call to my telephone call, and the total elapsed time since I reported the burglary until their arrival in front of our house was probably no more than five minutes. Neither one of the arriving cars made use of their sirens and their flashing lights. When I got out of my car to talk to the officers, I asked them about that, and they said it was because they hoped to catch someone inside the house and they did not want to scare away whoever was there. I told them about the broken window in the side door, and they asked me for my front door key which I handed to one of them. As the four officers started walking toward the house, they waved me back to my car where Elaine was waiting for me.

"We'll let you know when you can come back inside your house, Sir," an officer cautioned. Elaine and I watched intently as one officer went around to the back of the house, and the two officers went to the side door. As the officers searched around outside our house, we noticed none of them used a flashlight. That was probably for the same reason they did not arrive on the scene with their flashing blue lights and screaming sirens on, I suggested to Elaine. They do not want to alert the burglar of their presence at the house.

When several minutes had elapsed, two of the officers at the side door were joined by the one who came from the rear of the house. Elaine and I watched as they drew their pistols from their holsters at the same instant they pushed the side door open and entered. Immediately, the lights in that part of the house went on, and we followed their advance through the first level by watching the lights being turned on. Meanwhile, we saw the policeman who had been at the front door enter the house. The lights on the second level of the house began to turn on starting in the master bedroom and ending at another back bedroom. Several minutes later we saw a second light turn on in the attic room.

Elaine and I waited patiently in our car for a good ten or more minutes before one of the officers came outside and asked us to come back inside the house with him.

"We searched everywhere inside and outside the house," the officer said, "but we were not able to locate the burglar, but there's no doubt you've had a burglary. That side door's glass panel had been broken and the safety chain was busted. We don't have a lot of these kinds of problems occurring here in Forest Oak, but they do happen occasionally, he remarked apologetically. Most of the home invasions are committed by young punks who are looking for something to steal to sell for money to buy drugs. It's our biggest headache, and it only seems to be getting worse with each passing year."

Upon our returning to our house, we went into the kitchen where we were joined by the officer who had been stationed outside in the back of the property. "Not a thing back there," he said to his partner. "I even took a look behind the garage. Nothing there! Did you find any sign of him inside the house?"

"We found no one in the house, was the officer's response, but it was obvious to me that the place had been hit. It's funny though, none of the drawers were pulled out, and from what we observed throughout the house nothing seems to have been touched. If it was not for that broken window pane and busted safety chain, I'd say that no one's been in here. It may be that they were scared away by the sound of a car driving up outside before they had a chance to take anything." Turning his eyes toward me, he asked me if after I saw the light upstairs, "Mister, Ah, I'm sorry, I never got your name. "Rick Braden," I answered, "and my wife's name is Elaine."

"How long was it, Mr. Braden, after you saw that light upstairs in your attic before you left to make your call and when you returned to the house? He produced a small notepad and pen from his pocket, and he looked at me as he awaited my answer.

"I would say that it could not have been more than five or six minutes," I answered.

"Did you see anything besides that light in your attic?"

I noticed nothing else except for the broken glass in the side door and the door being open. I had enough sense not to go inside--not knowing if the burglar was still there."

"That was the right thing for you to have done, Mister Braden. Now how about you, Mrs. Braden, did you see anything that you want to talk about?" he asked as he turned his attention to Elaine and awaited her reply.

"I didn't see anything more than that light in the attic," Elaine replied.

"Did either you or your wife happen to notice if there was a strange car parked nearby, or at the curb in front of your house?"

"If there was a car there, neither of us paid any attention to it," I answered. "but to tell you the truth, Officer, we did not take any notice of anything more than that light in our attic. There was no car parked at the curb in front of our place, though. I know that for certain because that is where I parked my car rather than driving it directly it into my driveway, which is what I would ordinarily have done."

At that minute, the two officers who had been searching upstairs joined the rest of us in the kitchen, and the burly, red-haired man spoke first. "I think the burglar was scared away before he could start to loot the place," he said. "The only thing that appears to have been disturbed in your house is in your attic, the place where you said the light was on. By any chance, did one of you happen to knock down a pile of cartons from a stack of them up there and scatter them onto on the floor?"

Elaine and I both answered no.

"That's pretty darn strange," he said as he placed his fingertips to his chin in an act of concentration. "I can't imagine why anyone would bother with a lot of cartons in an attic room when you have so many valuable things lying around inside your house. It just doesn't make a bit of sense to me. What do you think, Lacey?" he asked as he turned his eyes toward one of his fellow officers.

Before Officer Lacy answered the question for him, he looked at me, and then at Elaine, and he asked, "Was there something that you had stored there in your attic that may have had some special value to the burglar. Could there possibly have been something like a chest of silver service, or a coin collection, or possibly something else that's valuable like that?"

"There was nothing like that stored up in our attic," I said. "Everything there was left when the previous owner of the house moved out, and most of it is probably just worthless junk that I have not yet gotten around to dispose of in the county dump."

"Say," Officer Lacy asked, "Isn't this the same house that used to belong to that funeral home guy who disappeared many years ago? What was his name?" he asked as he looked at his partner for help?

"The name of the man you are talking about is Sedgwick Burns," I responded, "and this is the same house he used to own, but we bought it from his estate last spring."

"That's right! Sedgwick Burns was the name of the man who disappeared about eight years ago," Officer Lacey said. "I suppose you and your wife know all about that, Mr. Braden. That missing person file is still active, as far as I know anyway. Did anyone from our department ever contact you about any of that?"

"Why would they?" I asked.

"Oh, no reason, I guess. I was just curious," Lacey responded. "Well, I guess we've done about all we can do around here tonight," the redheaded officer said" So we'll all be leaving you now, but I suggest you use something to block that broken pane of glass in the side door before you go to bed tonight. I'm not suggesting the burglar will return. That's highly unlikely, it's the night flying bugs that you may want to keep out of the house. Also, before I forget, Mr. Braden, I want to return your front door key which I'd borrowed from you." He then handed me my key, and I dropped it into my pocket.

"Officer Lacey, may I ask you just one last question before you leave?" I asked.

"Go right ahead," he responded.

"Why did you refer to whoever broke in here as burglars, rather than a single burglar? Is it not possible that a lone burglar broke into our house tonight?" I asked.

"Yes, that's entirely possible, but it's rather unlikely. Most burglaries are usually committed by two or more culprits. One of the two acts as a lockout while the other guy ransacks the premises. If we're dealing with dopers, which we more than likely are, you can be almost certain there were at least two of them who were involved. Anyway, that's what our experience has been."

After I escorted the officers to the front door, we thanked them for responding so quickly to my distress call, and for checking our house for uninvited guests. Officer Lacey told us that we should expect to hear from a police investigator in the morning and that a fingerpaint team would be arriving at our house later in the day. He cautioned us about touching too many of the surfaces, especially at the side door and up stairs in the attic because we could disturb the burglar's prints.

Elaine and I stood on the front porch as we watched the police cars drive away, and we then stayed for a few more minutes while we breathed in the fresh nighttime air.

"Thank Goodness, Dave and Shirley Farrell are in Las Vegas," Elaine said. "If they had been here when the police arrived, we'd never hear the end of this."

"You may be right about that, Elaine, but on the other hand, the burglary may not have happened if they were home and their lights were on in their house. Besides, you know how nosey Dave Farrell is, so anyone breaking our door's side window would have been heard or seen by him. Think about that one."

Both Elaine and I began to feel the same sense of uncertainty about the safety of our own home because of this disturbing incident. After a while, I put my arm gently around her waist, and I led her back inside the house as I securely locked the front door behind us.

"If it was not so late, I would like to call Glenn and Ron, and tell them what happened," Elaine said with an anguished look.

"You can do that in the morning, Dear," I answered. "Right now I want to take a look at the attic room and see what it was in our attic the police officer had been talking about. Do you want to come upstairs with me to the attic to see what things there now look like, Elaine?"

"No!" Elaine quickly answered. "Please don't forget Rick. You still have to put something over that broken glass in the side door as the policeman suggested. There should be a piece of heavy cardboard down in the cellar you can use for that purpose."

"I will take care of that project before I go to bed," I said as I headed for the stairway. "After I get back down from the attic, how about a cup of hot tea or cocoa before we retire for the night?" She did not answer me. Elaine had her mind in another direction, and I think I knew where that was.

The attic room was just as the officer had described it to us. There were about a dozen cardboard cartons that were scattered around with some the contents spilled out on the floor. From what I could see, they contained a variety of clothing, knick-knacks, and other seemingly useless articles. As I surveyed the mess, a thought suddenly occurred to me. Could it be that the burglar was not after something that is hidden in one of those boxes, but maybe he was after something that was hidden under or behind them?

With the pile of cartons now pulled down from where they had been stacked next to the wall, I was just able to see the faint outline of a flush door. It was centered on the back wall, and I became convinced that the door had been purposely blocked with that pile of cartons to hide it from view. While I stood there staring at the door, I became even further convinced that what had been hidden behind that door was the reason our break-in had taken place. In my mind, there was no doubt that it was Bruno Stenn who had broken into our house, and his sole purpose was to take that so-called ledger he was so set on retrieving. What could it possibly contain that was so important for him to risk doing what he did tonight? Chances are I might never have the answer to that question, but for the moment, I would satisfy my curiosity and see what there is hiding behind that flush door!

Before I could reach the door, I had first to walk over some scattered junk from the opened cartons. I wondered if the policeman had done the same thing and if he opened the door to check if a burglar was hiding there. When I grasped the door handle, I gave it a hard twist, but it was locked. I was determined to get the door open and take a look inside, but to do so I would need some tools like a hammer and a screwdriver and a flashlight in case there was no light inside the room.

Having gone downstairs to the cellar to retrieve the needed tools from the cellar, I was just about to return to the attic when Elaine stopped me in the back hallway and asked me what I was doing. I told her that I was merely trying to put the scattered things back into some semblance of order, and I asked her if she would like to come along with me, while knowing full well she would decline my invitation. She did decline, but she also cautioned me about messing up any fingerprints, as the police officer had cautioned us about. I assured her I was careful while handling the cartons, and that it looked like they had only been shoved aside, and not opened up and handled by the burglar.

Returning to the attic room, I attacked the door lock with the hammer and the screwdriver, and in short order I quickly sprang the lock and then pushed the door slowly open. It was dark inside, and with my flashlight I projected the beam of light in all directions. I saw that it was a large room, and off to one side was a metal table, which was quite similar to the table I had seen in Blake Cranshaw's back room in his funeral parlor. Continuing to look around the room, I was startled when I realized just what this room was used for because I did not doubt in my mind that it is a body preparation room! Even a familiar looking bloodletting device was standing in one corner, along with several gallon bottles of the same brand of embalming fluid as those bottles I had found in the cellar and in the garage loft.

Having finally overcome the terrible shock of my highly disturbing discovery and when I partially regained my senses, I quickly exited the room and pulled the door closed behind me. I then began stacking up several of the fallen cartons to hide the door. There was no reason for Elaine to know anything about this latest find because I would have to do something about it as fast as I could. I decided I would contact Blake Cranshaw after I got to my office in the morning, and maybe he would be able to help me with this latest unexpected and totally intolerable situation.

~ *Chapter Sixteen* ~

TRYING TO SOLVE THE PUZZLE

The morning after the burglary, Elaine received a telephone call from a police investigator asking her if we had discovered anything that was found missing after the officers had left the house the evening. Elaine thought about telling the investigator about Bruno Stenn, and how determined he was to get hold of that journal, but she thought better about doing it so she said nothing.

The police investigator told Elaine she would have a brief visit from the evidence division with a burglary instance follow-up by noontime, and he asked her if she would give the investigator any information that she could. I was already at work, and Elaine had just hung up the phone after telling Paula all about the events of the burglary when she placed her telephone call to me.

Since Elaine had already spoken to Paula and filled her in, I knew Paula would tell Ron about the burglary. When I finished my call from Elaine, I called Glenn's office, but he was not in, so I left a message for him to call me at my office. Finally, I called Blake's funeral parlor, but his receptionist told me he was conducting a funeral and she did not expect him back before noon. I asked her to have him call me at my office when he returned. It seemed to me that

I was already batting zero in getting things done this morning, and it did not seem to be a right way for me to start out my day.

Shortly before noon, Glenn called me in response to my message to him earlier, and I told him about what had happened the previous evening at our house. He was shocked and upset when he heard my suspicions about Bruno Stenn being the one who broke into our house, and he was even more upset when I rather briefly told him about the hidden room I had discovered in our attic. His reaction was that he wanted to come over to my house that very evening to help me examine the room. I told him that I first wanted to talk to Blake Cranshaw when I got through with work because I needed to get his advice. Before I hung up the phone, Glenn said that he would call me back later to find out what Cranshaw had to say about it.

It was sometime after one o'clock that afternoon, when Blake returned my earlier call to him. Since he was busy with another funeral service he did not have time to talk with me for very long, but he asked if he could see me after I finished work. Blake readily agreed to meet me at a cocktail lounge close to his funeral home at 5:30. He thought it would be a right place for us to talk without being disturbed, and he seemed quite anxious to hear all that I had to tell him.

I received Glenn's phone call in my office at three that afternoon, and he wanted to know all the details about my conversation with Blake Cranshaw. I told him I had not yet had a chance to discuss anything with Cranshaw, but I would be seeing him sometime around 5:30 in the evening. Glenn then made me promise to call him when I got back home. In the sound of his voice I could detect the deep concern Glenn felt for his mother and me. His reaction to our problem is consistent with his loving and caring attitude. In that regard, Ron is much like Glenn, although he lacked some of Glenn's sensitivity.

I placed a telephone call to Elaine just before I would be leaving my office because I wanted to explain to her that I would be late getting home tonight. I told her about the meeting I had arranged with Blake Cranshaw to tell him all the details of the burglary and to ask him for his advice and assistance in the matter. I also mentioned to her that it was possible I would be returning to our house with Cranshaw after our meeting was over with; therefore, she should plan on the possibility of having a guest for dinner. Elaine was having a difficult time of it while trying to understand why Blake Cranshaw's visit was necessary, but she knew nothing about the secret room in our attic which I wanted Cranshaw to examine. I had to tell her yet another lie by saying that I had found some papers in one of the boxes in the attic and I wanted Cranshaw to examine them because they might shed some light on the contents of that so-called logbook that Bruno Stenn was after. I hated to be so deceitful about the book, but I was still trying my best to protect Elaine from any of those upsetting facts which I knew she would not be able to handle.

Before we finished our conversation and I hung up my phone, Elaine told me about the police investigation at the house. She said two men had arrived a few minutes past noon in a panel truck with Crime Scene Investigators lettered on the side. They brought several pieces of equipment into the house, including cameras and a fingerprint kit. While the technician was busy dusting everything within sight of our side entry door, she was telling one of the investigators about every detail of what had transpired at the house from the instant we first saw the light in the attic until the four officers later left the house.

At 4:25 that evening, I left my office and headed directly to my car in the parking lot. It was just 5:30 when I arrived at Donovan's Pub, which was the cocktail lounge where I agreed to meet with Blake Cranshaw. As I walked into the bar, I saw Blake sitting at the back end of the bar chatting with a husky, red-faced bartender, while Blake sipped on a mixed drink. When he spotted me walking in, he motioned for me to take the stool next to his, and he asked me what I was drinking. I told him I would have a small glass of light beer. Not having eaten any lunch, I was not about to have anything stronger than that before my evening meal. As soon as the bartender placed my glass on the counter, we picked up our drinks, and we walked to the booth nearest to the back of the lounge. There were only a couple of patrons sitting on stools at the bar, and I could see several more seated in booths. What I had to tell Blake Cranshaw was for his ears only, and I did not want to be overheard by anyone else.

It took me quite sometime to tell Blake all about the burglary and about my discovery of the secret room in my attic. When I finished talking, Blake seemed to stare at me for a long moment before he spoke in the most solemn voice I had heard him use before.

"Well, Rick, it looks like you and I will just have to pay a visit to Bruno Stenn's funeral parlor." At that moment, I saw a look of apprehension in the eyes of a man who had previously seemed almost totally in control of himself, and a cold chill ran all the way down thru the center of my spine.

"What have I gotten myself into?" I said to Blake. "Will I ever be able to get these terrible events over with and living my life back to normal again?" I asked that because I was feeling utterly helpless and discouraged.

"I honestly wish I could answer your question for you, Rick, but to be completely honest with you, I don't know anything at all about that log book Stenn was after, and I'm just as curious as you are about its contents. The very fact that the man broke into your house to steal it tells me that he was desperate to get his hands on it, and I agree with your suspicion that it was Bruno Stenn who was your burglar. But the thing that bothers me the most is why he waited all these years to go after that book? Just think about it for a minute, Rick, your house was vacant for probably eight years or more, and during that time he could have easily gained access to it and taken the book. Why did he decide to do it now after the house had been sold and occupied by your wife and you? It just doesn't make a bit of sense to me. Does it to you?"

"No sense whatsoever!" I replied.

"Do you have any suggestions as to what we should do, Rick?"

"I have none!" I replied. "That is the reason I am here talking to you now, Blake, I wanted to pose that same question to you hoping that you would have some of the answers. Anyway, I would like you to have dinner with my wife Elaine and me tonight at our house. After dinner's over, you and I can examine that secret room in our attic. There is a good chance that we may be able to find something there that could shed some light on this ongoing mystery. Will that work into your plans for this evening, Blake?"

"I'll first have to call my wife and talk to her before I accept your kind invitation for dinner, Rick. As for my examining that secret room, even if I can't make it for dinner tonight, I can probably stop by your house later this evening and examine it. I'll call Marge now and see if she's already started preparing our meal. If she hasn't started her cooking yet, I'll tell her that I have an appointment and I'll be home late. Will that be okay?"

"That is perfectly okay with me, Blake," I answered. I then watched him get up from the booth and walk over to the wall phone to make his call. When he returned to our table a minute or two later, he seemed pleased and he was smiling.

"It's all set, Rick; Marge hadn't yet started cooking our dinner, so I told her I hoped to be home sometime after ten tonight. Do you think that will allow us enough time to do all that we'll have to do?"

"I would have to say it will depend entirely on what we might find," I answered. "Before we leave here, I want to call Elaine to confirm that you are coming for dinner with us this evening. When I talked to her earlier, I mentioned that we might be having a guest for dinner, but then I was not sure when I asked you could make it."

Blake and I arrived at my home at about 7:00 that evening, and as we pulled into the driveway, I could see Glenn's station wagon parked there. I guess I should have anticipated his being here after our conversation earlier. Glenn must be a lot more worried about the situation than I had thought. Well, his being here should not complicate things. I was sure he would not be foolish enough to bring Martha with him because when I talked to him, I asked him to say nothing to her about the hidden room I had discovered in my attic. As far as I knew, Martha knew nothing at all about what has been happening in our house, and I wanted to keep it that way.

When Cranshaw saw Glenn's station wagon, he asked me if it belonged to Glenn. He recognized it because it had been parked in my driveway the day we removed the coffins from the loft. I told Cranshaw it was Glenn's car, and that he was deeply concerned over the recent break-in, and that he was not aware that I had set up this meeting tonight. We both agreed that since Glenn already knew most of what has been going on, he could be helpful to us in our quest for answers. I also sensed Blake liked Glenn, and he would probably enjoy his company.

When we walked into the house, we got the greetings out of the way, then the three of us men settled ourselves comfortably in the living room and waited for Elaine to call us for dinner. I took that opportunity to satisfy Glenn's burning curiosity by giving him most of the details relating to the burglary, as well as a quick description of the secret room I had discovered in the attic. He said that he had been unable to do any work after he talked to me about it earlier, and that was the reason he had decided to come to my house tonight, rather than call me later as he said he would. I could tell that he was embarrassed by showing up, but I assured him that both Blake and I felt he could be helpful to us in our search for answers to the riddle surrounding the mysterious ledger book. After I said that to him, I saw Glenn's face immediately brighten up.

Once Elaine had our evening dinner cooked, out of the oven and on the table, she called the three of us into the dining room to eat. It was a meal that she was able to prepare on rather short notice, but Elaine seemed to be unconcerned about her ability to do it. I was always proud and happy over Elaine's superb cooking skills which she daily demonstrated for me, for our children, and our dinner guests. Tonight she outdid herself with a special meal of roast pork, stuffed mushrooms, string beans, roasted potatoes, a tossed salad, and hot French bread. Everything she served was extra delicious, and Blake was most complimentary of the meal, which probably made the rest of Elaine's day for her.

With our delightful dinner over, Glenn helped his mother clear the table while Blake and I went into the living room to talk while we waited for him to join us. Blake asked me if I minded if he smoked a cigarette, and I told him that it was okay. I then handed him an ashtray while he lit his cigarette as he said, "I have to give these darn things up one of these days, but it's a hard habit for me to break."

"May I ask you a question, Blake?" I asked.

"Ask away," he answered

"Just how many years has it been since you been smoking cigarettes?" I asked him that question strictly out curiosity.

"Maybe forty years," he answered with a pained look on his face.

"I never got started smoking," I responded, "nor had Elaine or either of our boys ever picked up the habit. Someday I may sit down and add up all the money we have saved in this family by our not being smokers."

Just as Blake was about to respond to my last comment, Glenn entered the room. He took a seat across from us and looked at me and then at Blake as he asked, "Are we going to look at that room in the attic now?"

"Yes, Son," I answered. "Did you say anything to your mother about it while you were in the kitchen?"

"Of course not, Dad," Glenn immediately replied. "I told her that I was going to help you and Mr. Cranshaw look for that log book in case it was still hidden somewhere in the attic. Isn't that just what you wanted that I should to tell her if she asked?"

"That is right, Glenn. Now let us go upstairs to the attic and take a look around, but before we go, we had better grab three flashlights. I did not get a chance to see if there is a light switch in that secret room because I was in and out of there so fast."

"Where do you keep them, Dad?"

"In the cellar at the bottom of the stairway," I replied.

Blake and I left the living room and started walking toward the stairs leading to the attic. Once we were up there, we waited for

Glenn while we stood and surveyed the pile of cartons and other things that cluttered up the attic. I then described how the boxes had been piled up in front of the back wall to hide the view of the door, which was quite similar to the way it was now. I also explained that I had replaced them so that neither Elaine nor the police investigators could see the secret door when they arrived to take fingerprints. Because I had broken the lock when I first gained entry to that room, they could have accessed it and concluded it had been an embalming laboratory. That frightening discovery would have opened up a whole can of worms for us about the coffins and the bodies. Blake agreed with my logic and said it was the only thing I could have done.

In several minutes, Glenn joined us in the attic, and he had the three flashlights in his hands. I asked him to remove the piled-up boxes from in front of the door, and without any hesitation he jumped right to the task.

I would have felt some apprehension worrying that Elaine might come up the attic steps while we were inside that room, but she had told us that she had her laundry to do in the cellar, which meant she would be down there for an hour or more and away from any noise that we might make. She seemed disinterested in our tedious ritual of formally searching through a lot of cartons and other stuff while looking for a book that she was convinced had already been taken in the burglary, and she thought what we were doing was nothing more than a study in futility. It was quite apparent that Elaine did not know what we were really up to, which was examining a secret embalming laboratory that I had discovered hidden in our attic.

Just as soon as Glenn had our pathway through the cartons to the door cleared, Blake and I joined him at the front at the door. Before I opened it, I looked first at Blake and then at Glenn, and I said, "I think I know what this place is, or was, but Blake will have to be the one to determine if my conclusions are correct. Remember what we are looking for is a logbook or a ledger of some description being the only reference that was made to it by Stenn when he confronted Elaine so it may be as small as a pocket notebook, or it may be a large canvas bound ledger. Now let us all go inside and check the place out."

It took me but a minute to open the door, and the three of us then entered the dark room. With our flashlights turned on, Blake quickly found a light switch at a side of the door and pressed. A bank of bright lights recessed above a frosted glass panel in the ceiling lit up the room with almost daylight brilliance.

If we thought for even an instant that we would have any chance of finding that stolen ledger, we immediately discovered otherwise because on top of one of the dusty filing cabinets we could see a dust-free rectangular area where something had recently been removed. The three of us had no doubt whatsoever what that something had been.

Almost as soon as Blake examined the equipment in the room, he arrived at my earlier conclusion that it was, indeed, an embalmer's workplace! Apparently, all those things we found stored in the cellar and in the loft were the supplies which were probably used in this room. Sedgwick Burns must have been using this room in the house for embalming dead people, and possibly body reconstruction purposes. If it was being done in conducting legitimate business, which is highly doubtful, then he must have been performing surreptitious procedures.

"Good Lord!" I exclaimed, "If my wife hears about this turn of events, our house will be put on the market the first thing in the morning! As it is, I think that is exactly what I want to do myself. There is no way I can continue living in a house that has been used to embalm dead bodies." I was excited and highly agitated by this discovery, and although I suspected as much when I saw the room before, and now that Blake has confirmed my suspicions, I nearly went over the edge in shock.

"It will all be okay, Dad," Glenn said as he put his arm around my shoulder. "Sooner or later Mom has to know what's been happening around this house, and I think you must realize that. I know both of you have put a lot of hope and sweat into this property, but, Dad, it's only a house. There are a lot of others out there on the market from which you can choose. Sure, Mom's going to be very unhappy and disappointed because she has worked so hard to fix the place up, but she can do that with the next house. As for your yard, you have barely gotten started on it. I think the best thing to do is to tell Mom the truth about everything, and then contact the police and also tell them everything."

"I cannot do that," I said. "As much as I would like to do it after seeing this room, I no longer have that option available to me. It is much too late, and too much has happened for us to report any of it to the police."

"Why is that?" Glenn asked looking confused over my last statement.

Before I could answer Glenn's question, Blake, quickly spoke up as he looked at Glenn. "It's because your dad and I would both go to jail, Glenn," he said in a low and anguished voice.

"But, why is that?" Glenn asked as he squarely turned to face Blake.

In a slow and detailed manner, Blake began explaining to Glenn. "When your Dad and I removed those dead bodies from the garage's loft, we committed a felony. The fact that they were there in the first place was a crime, but by removing them without first contacting the authorities about them being found there compounded the crime. Then we compounded it again when your dad and I returned that first body to its crypt in Oak Hill Cemetery. That was one of the reasons why we didn't want you or your brother to become involved in any of this. He thought it was bad enough to have already involved the two of you in the removal of the cartons of embalming fluid from the cellar, and later those coffins in the loft. Now get one thing straight in your mind, Glenn! No matter what transpires after this, you and your brother are to be entirely kept out of this thing, and you are never to breathe a word of this to anyone! Both your dad and I have a rock-solid agreement regarding this matter. Do you now understand the serious implications to all of this?"

"I think I do now, Mr. Cranshaw, but aren't you jumping to conclusions? None of us had anything to do with any of the things that are found here. All that we've done is to remove those items from the property. Anyone coming across such things in their home would probably have done the same thing."

"There are a couple of other significant things you should know about, Glenn," Blake said. "The first is that it would ruin me and my funeral home business for which I had worked so long and so hard to build. I don't want to burden you with the details of why that's true, but your dad knows all about it. Primarily, it has a lot to do with business ethics, my reputation, and the negative reaction to the news. Then there's the reason's which you just touched upon, your parents hard work and the time they invested in renovating this house. It will also not be as easy as you may think to sell a house where six dead bodies were uncovered in the garage's loft, as well as revealing that a secret room containing a fully functional embalming laboratory was discovered in the attic. There will be a very substantial financial loss which your parents will have to suffer. Have you given these things any thought? Blake asked as he looked squarely at Glenn."

"No, I'm sorry to say that I simply thought it was the only way out. I've always been taught by my parents to do the right thing and to always be truthful, but I'm now beginning to realize that those ideals don't always apply in real life situations, especially in a situation like this one."

"I am truly sorry, Son," I said. "I should never have involved either you or Ron in any aspect of this nightmare venture. I can see that now but it is a little late for me to cry over my mistake. We will just have to see this thing through to the bitter end and hope that when it is finally over and done with, we will be able to keep it from your mother. Somehow, I will try to convince her to sell the house, and in that way we may be able to save all of us a lot more pain. Are you with me on this, Glenn?"

"I'm with you, Dad, and also with you, Mr. Cranshaw. But where do we go from here?"

"I think that we had better decide that question right here and now," Blake responded. "First, I would like to leave this room and find a more comfortable place where we can sit and continue with our conversation."

Upon leaving the secret room, Glenn flipped the light off and closed the door behind us. Blake and I went downstairs to the living room while Glenn stayed in the attic and stacked the cartons to again block the view of the door to the secret room. When that was done, he rejoined us in the living room. Elaine was still in the cellar washing clothes, which gave us another chance to talk openly without her hearing us.

Blake spoke first, "There is no question that all of that equipment and supplies we discovered in that upstairs room will have to be removed at some time, and hopefully we should be able to do that very soon." He looked at me while he awaited my reply.

"I agree with you, Blake," I said, "but do you really feel there is no need for us to do it immediately?"

"Not unless you're concerned that your wife will somehow discover the hidden door in the attic and then venture inside."

"That is always a possibility," I responded, "but I have already told her that the cartons blocking the door contain nothing but a lot of useless junk, and that seemed to satisfy her curiosity, at least for the time being. Still, at some point, she's going to want to start going through those cartons to see what's inside them. Hopefully, it will be after she completes those projects she is presently working on which need to be done. I seem to remember that awhile back she told me she had intentions of sorting through that stuff to get ready for a big neighborhood garage sale, but that will not happen before next spring. I think it will be safe for the time being, or at least I hope it will be. What else Blake?"

"Is there anything else stored in your cellar that I should know about, Rick?"

"I know of nothing that we have not already discovered." I then looked at Blake quizzically. "Just what are you driving at, Blake?"

"Does your cellar have a concrete floor or a dirt floor?"

"You are not being serious and only kidding with me! Are you suggesting that Burns may have buried dead bodies in the cellar?"

"It's certainly within the realm of possibility," he answered with a steady gaze. I then knew Blake wasn't kidding with me.

"Just what kind of man was that Sedgwick Burns?" As I asked that question of Blake, I looked over at Glenn who was hanging onto our every word we had spoken.

"I've already told you all about him in great detail the first night you visited with me at my funeral home."

"That is not what I am asking you now, Blake. What I mean is he capable of doing something like that?"

"Doing what?"

"You know, burying bodies in the cellar. I believe that is what your question about the cellar floor implied?"

"Yes, you're right, Rick, I did imply that. I would have to say that Sedgwick Burns was easily capable of burying bodies in his cellar. After all, the man was a full-blown necrophiliac, but I've already told you about that utterly loathsome and disgusting other side of Burns."

At that point in our conversation, Glenn, who had been listening carefully to our discussion, interrupted us with a question. "What in the world is a necrophiliac, Mr. Cranshaw, does that have something to do with the funeral business?"

Blake did not laugh at Glenn's statement, but Glenn had such a severe look on his face I had to hold myself back from doing so myself. After a short hesitation, and with a grin on his face, Blake decided to gently explain the meaning of the word to Glenn.

"Necrophilia, or more properly, a necrophiliac is a man who has an abnormal sexual fascination with corpses," Blake answered in a very abbreviated and matter-of-fact sentence.

As Blake explained the meaning of the word to Glenn, I carefully watched Glenn's face, and I could see an immediate look of deep disgust and repulsion come over it.

"Oh, you're just joking with me, aren't you, Mr. Cranshaw?"

"No, Glenn, I'm not joking about it!" Blake answered tersely. Glenn pushed himself deeper into his seat and said no more.

"Well, to answer your first question, Blake, our cellar has a solid concrete floor, and from my observations down there, there's been no new concrete poured there for a long, long time. The only thought that I have in my mind is that both of my neighbors have complained about missing their gardening tools--things like shovels and spades and other thing s like that. Do you think there is a possibility that he was using those tools to bury bodies in his backyard?" As I asked Blake that I began to feel a bit nauseous.

"I wouldn't rule that possibility out entirely," Rick, Blake answered.

"Then where do we go from here," I asked? I looked first at Blake and then at Glenn for the answer to my question.

"Well, we don't start by digging up your yard and your garden," Blake quickly responded, "if that's what your hinting at, Rick. That's not to say we won't get around to doing that before it's all over and done with. However, I think our best approach is for you and me to pay a visit to Bruno Stenn's Mortuary. I've been feeling lately that there have been just a few too many connections between Bruno Stenn and Sedgwick Burns for us to overlook. Now Stenn's gone so far that he's broken into your house for a mysterious log book which he claims belongs to him. That's something that's a heck of a lot more than sheer coincidence. For the life of me, Rick, I can't understand what the connection might be between that book and the six corpses we've pulled out of your garage's loft, that's if it turns out that there is a connection there. As far as anyone knows, Sedgwick Burns is out of the picture. After his having been missing for almost nine years, there is more than a good chance he's dead. Still, there's a possibility the mystery of his disappearance may somehow be tied into all that's been going on in this house since you bought it, but I rather doubt it."

"As I already told you, Blake, I had talked to Stenn at his funeral home, and he told me absolutely nothing. What makes you think that another visit there at that place will produce any new answers for us?"

"Because you and I will be visiting his establishment when he's not there," he said that just above a whisper, which caused Glenn's eyes to open wider, and also enough to create a wave of apprehension in me.

"Now it seems we are talking about our breaking and entering a property to add to our growing list of felonies, Blake. Oh, what the heck, it will just add a few more felonies for us to deal with if we are caught."

"And, just when do you suggest we do this thing, Blake?"

"What do you think about our going there tomorrow night?" Blake answered. "I happen to know that Stenn will be attending a statewide mortician's seminar at the Jamison Hotel in Bradenton. That affair is scheduled to start at six, and it won't be over until sometime after ten. That should give us more than enough time to get inside his place, look around for the stolen ledger, and get back out of there before he returns."

"How do you know that for sure--about the seminar I mean?"

"Because I was also invited to attend that affair, Rick. It's one of those yearly functions that's practically a requirement for people in my business to attend. From my knowledge, Bruno Stenn has never missed a single one of those affairs since he bought the business from me. Although I've seen him there over the years, I always managed to avoid him like the plague. He has his group of cronies whom he associates with, and they appear to me to be nothing more than a pack of ghouls, as far as I'm concerned anyway."

"I am willing to go with you tomorrow evening, Blake, but my son stays home," I said that as I looked straight at Glenn, who started to object. I put my hand palm forward which he knew was my signal for him to cease. He knew from the past that any further argument by him would be fruitless.

I had no sooner agreed with Blake's time for us to meet at his parlor the following evening when Elaine walked into the room. Her arms were loaded with a pile of clean and dry laundry. I could smell the fresh, pleasant odor from clear across the living room.

"What did you fellows find in the attic?" Elaine asked as she began sorting the clothes on a nearby table.

"Just as you had guessed, Honey, there was not a log book anywhere in the attic. We carefully searched in every nook and cranny, and there was not a sign of it. We have finally concluded that Stenn must have found the book and taken it with him. Well, it was not ours to keep anyway. I said in a flippant manner."

Since I had driven Blake in my car to my house, I was now ready to drive him back to Donovan's Pub where he had left his car outside at the curb. Glenn offered to drop him off there since it was not too far out of his way, and both Blake and I agreed for him doing it.

Once the two of them left, Elaine told me she still felt that I should tell the police about Bruno Stenn being the one who broke into our house, but I again I tried to dismiss that idea from her mind. Unknown to Elaine, Blake Cranshaw and I had other ideas on how to deal with him. My only hope was that Stenn would not catch us in his mortuary where he could deal with the two of us.

~ *Chapter Seventeen* ~

A FEW MORE PIECES OF THE PUZZLE

It was another work day for me, but when my alarm clock went off at six that morning, I decided to skip work and sleep late. The fact that I had not taken any time off this year, and the thought of what Blake and I were facing tonight, did not put me in any mood to go to work today.

A little after seven, Elaine came into my room and was surprised to see me still lying in bed. I explained my decision to stay home, and she said that would give the two of us a chance to enjoy a nice leisurely breakfast for a change.

After showering and changing into fresh clothes, I had Elaine make a call to my office and say that I would not be in today because I had some stomach problems, but I hoped to be well enough to be back in the office tomorrow morning. My taking the day off was not a problem since most of my work was at a point where there was nothing that was particularly pressing for me to complete.

Having finished eating a relaxed and enjoyable breakfast, Elaine and I sat in the living room and casually read the morning newspaper. Later that morning, Elaine reminded me that she had a hair dresser's appointment scheduled for one o'clock that afternoon, and she wanted to do some shopping afterward that. She said she had also made arrangements for Alma Hutchins, her lady friend who had worked with her at the mall, to stop by the house and pick her up about 12:45.

Elaine finally told me she would like to stay home to keep me company, but since she had already made both appointments, she did not want to break them at the last minute. I assured her that I would amuse myself around the house while she was gone, although I would certainly miss being with her.

For the rest of that morning, I fussed around the cellar and the yard doing a variety of small jobs. Since the weather would soon be coming into the early fall season, I had to think about what I was going to do about planting a small vegetable garden next spring. A few years back, and while we were still living in our other house, I purchased a small gasoline-powered plow for use in my garden. It was one of those hand controlled and self-propelled implements, which is like holding onto a bucking bronco when you are using it. I sometimes felt it was much easier when I dug up the sod with my reliable four-pronged pitchfork. For one brief moment I thought about dragging that plow out of the garage and trying it out at the back of the yard, then remembering what Blake had said to me about the possibility of bodies being buried in my yard, I decided against it. I really did not believe that it was possible, but after having reckoned with everything else that I had found on the property, I was not absolutely sure it was not possible.

Shortly before one o'clock that afternoon, Alma's car pulled into our driveway and she honked the horn. Looking up from my patio chair where I had parked myself, I saw Alma wave and smile in my direction just as Elaine emerged from the side door of the house. While she was getting into Alma's car, Elaine looked over at me and called out, "Don't work so hard that you'll wear yourself out this afternoon, Dear. I should be home about five or so. If you get hungry, you'll find some leftover tuna salad in the refrigerator. Good Bye!" Alma's car then slowly backed out of the drive and the two ladies were on their way.

A short time later, while I was raking up dead leaves that had fallen from our big oak trees, a wild thought occurred to me. That first time I visited this house with Elaine and Pat Driscoll, Pat told me about the Forest Oak Historical Society. She said if I ever wanted any information about the town, or about any of its more important people, that would be the best place to go to find the answers. I wondered why I had not thought about that before because I might just find some answers there that could possibly be helpful to me?

As soon as I finished raking up the last of the fallen leaves, I stuffed them into a half dozen large plastic bags and placed them at the curbside for the weekly trash pickup. With that project out of the way, I returned to the house where I scouted out a telephone book to find the listing for the Forest Oak Historical Society. It was in a building located at the intersection of Lincoln and 34th Streets, and that was close enough to our house for me to walk, so that was what I decided to do since I felt invigorated after raking the leaves. Having showered and changed into some fresh clothes, I locked up the house and headed toward 34th Street. After a rather brisk fifteen-minute walk, I arrived at the building and in large gilded letters, I read high above the old wooden structure's entrance: Forest Oak Historical Society.

I opened the door and walked inside where I saw a rather elderly, silver-haired lady with a pleasant smile who spoke to me from behind a desk inside the door.

"Good afternoon, Sir, have you been to visit us before? I don't think I ever saw you here before."

"This will be my first visit," I answered.

"Then, you're in for a treat. May I ask, are you a resident of our lovely town of Forest Oak?"

"Yes, I am. I bought a home here just this past spring." "Welcome to our community. May I now ask your name?" "My name is Rick Braden, and I live here with my wife Elaine, but she was not able to be with me this morning because she had another appointment."

"Oh, that's too bad Mr. Braden. Perhaps she will be able to make it the next time you visit us. My name is Annabelle Merriweather, she said as she offered her tiny hand to me to shake. When we had dispensed with our greetings, Miss Merriweather handed me a pen for me to sign the register book. Taking the pen from her delicately manicured hand, I scribbled my name and address in the book and returned the pen to her. "Is there an entrance fee?" I asked.

"No, but you may care to contribute something, Mr. Braden. Most people drop a dollar in the box, but it's entirely voluntary." Retrieving my wallet from my hip pocket, I removed two one-dollar bills and dropped them into the box.

Having observed what I had done, she said "Thank you very much, sir, we can use every dime we take in because it takes quite a lot of money to maintain this large old house. I'm just a volunteer, you understand. Our Historical Society provides something of the history of our community," Miss Merriweather said, as she then turned her attention away from me and in another direction.

The interior of the large living room was that of a typical Mid-Victorian house not unlike the one Elaine, and I recently had bought and moved into, except that this one was almost filled with a variety of china cabinets, display cases, and bulletin boards covered over with copies of old photographs. All of the antique furniture that was lying around the room was tagged and dated. My eyes quickly fell upon an ugly, brown leather and dark wood, couch tagged: Circa 1885, contributed by Mr. Jacob Finch. I could not imagine why anyone would want a piece of furniture in their home that looked that bad, and also from the looks of it, a very uncomfortable thing to sit on. Tastes change, I thought, and I thank God for that change or we would still be sitting on relics much like that couch.

For more than an hour, I wandered from one display board to another while peering intently at hundreds of old photos of Forest Oak during its early days. In all the photographs I saw, there had been only one of them which showed the front of Sedgwick Burns' Mortuary, and that one dated back to 1896. There was not a single photo of Sedgwick Burns himself or his father, although there were dozens upon dozens of photos of other prominent Forest Oak businessmen. There was also a large photograph of Governor Weedan, who was one of the dried-up corpses we had removed from the garage loft. I finished looking at all the photographs which were displayed, but I still saw no photos of my house or any pictures of any of the Burns' family members.

Having seen all that was of any interest to me, I was about to leave the building, when I thought I would ask Miss Merriweather if there were any other photographs for her display boards. She was now sitting at a roll-top desk reading through a batch of old, yellowed letters which were held together by a faded pink ribbon. I could see tears that had welled up in the old woman's eyes as she silently read through one of the letters. I wanted to talk to her, but I hesitated to interrupt her from her train of thought. When she saw me looking her way, she quickly wiped her eyes with a little lace hankie Miss Merriweather held in the palm of her hand, and she spoke to me.

"I know that you must think the letter I was reading was written to me, Mr. Braden, but it wasn't. It's part of a small packet of love letters which I discovered hidden away under a drawer from this old writing desk which had been donated by a resident to the society. I discovered it earlier while I was checking through the drawers. You would be surprised at the things people forget to remove before they deliver these pieces of furniture to us, and quite often we run across important documents which had been secreted under and behind the drawers. Whenever it's possible, we return those things to their owners, however; in this situation, the owner of the letters I was reading died a long, long time ago."

Miss Merriweather looked at me intently while she tried to gauge what my reaction had been to her brief dialogue. Perhaps she was thinking that she owed me some explanation for her tears. "It is none of my business, Miss Merriweather, to whom those old letters may have been written," I said softly. "I just assumed they had been written to you when I saw how deeply you were moved as you read one of them."

"I would like you to stay for a moment or so if you will, Mr. Braden, while I tell you the story about that letter. Can you possibly spare me that moment of your time?"

"Why of course," I said. "As it turns out, Miss Merriweather, I was just about to ask you that same question, but you go ahead and tell me what it is you want to say to me first."

"Thank you very much," she responded as she held the letter in her delicate and exquisitely frail fingers she said, "this is a letter that was written to a young lady by her lover and it is dated in the year1864, which was during the time of the Civil War. I won't mention any names because some of the distant descendants of the lady may still be living here in Forest Oak. The writer was a soldier in the service of the Union Forces, and he was billeted at a house in Georgia close to the enemy. The letter tells about the hardships that he and his fellow soldiers had to endure, but mostly it tells of his love for the young lady to whom he had written the letter. It was his last evening before he was to go join a battle against the enemy forces, and that was the last letter she received because shortly after writing that letter he was killed, and I have no doubt that had occurred in the same battle he wrote about in his letter. The lady he had written the letter to was never to marry, and she lived to be 98 years old. It was a friend of her great, great grand nephew who contributed the writing desk to our society, and it was secreted inside that desk where I found the packet of letters. You now know the sad story behind that writing desk," she said softly, "and now, Mr. Braden, what is it that I do for you?"

"There is something that you may be able to tell me, Miss Merriweather. Are those old photographs that are on the display boards the only photographs you have?"

"Heavens no, we have hundreds more, but we simply don't have the room to display all of them--the board space is so limited, you see. Are there some special photographs you're looking for, Mr. Braden? Perhaps I can find them for you."

"Well, perhaps you can, Miss Merriweather. I have already told you that my wife and I live in Forest Oak. What I did not tell you, is that we bought the old Burns' house over on Cobblestone Lane. Do you know the place?"

"Why, of course, I know that house! Everyone in town knows of the Burns' mansion and the Burns' family. They were one of the most prominent families to settle in Forest Oak. Incidentally, my late husband Melvin was waked at their parlor on Franklin Street, and he was buried in Oak Hill Cemetery more than twenty-six years ago, God rest his soul! The old Burns house is a lovely old house, a true Mid-Victorian masterpiece, but I must admit it's been many years since I saw it. Is it still looking as stately as ever?"

"I cannot really answer your question since I had never set my eyes on the place before last spring when we bought it. Actually, the house is in good shape structurally, but we have had to do a lot of renovation to the inside. As for its exterior, it could use a good coat of paint and some landscaping."

"I'll have to make it a point to stop and see it when I'm in that section of town, she said. Do you think your wife would mind if I did that, Mr. Braden?"

"Oh, I am certain you will be more than welcome to visit our house at whatever time you care to stop by, Miss Merriweather. A minute ago you said that you have hundreds of photographs that are not being displayed on your boards. Is there any possibility you might have a few photos of the Burns' house during its heyday?" "It's a possibility, but I can't tell you that for certain. Are you interested in only pictures of the house, or would you like to see photographs of Mr. Burns, as well?"

"Anything that you may find like that would be appreciated, Miss Merriweather. You see, although we now own the house, we have never seen what the previous owner looks like."

"Oh my dear man, she responded in a gentle voice. Don't you know anything about his disappearance many years ago?"

"Oh, yes I know about it because I learned it about it at the time I bought the house. It was more than eight years ago according to what I was told. Some people intimated that he may even be dead." I looked at her as I awaited her reaction.

"Well, yes, I have also heard that same rumor, but there are a couple of people in town who say that they have seen him since he disappeared."

"Maybe it was just someone who looked like Sedgwick Burns," I suggested.

"Sedgwick Burns was not a man whose appearance could easily be mistaken for someone else, young man."

"Why is that?" I asked trying to hide my curiosity.

"First of all, he was quite a large man. Obese would be a more descriptive word for him. He had a very ruddy face covered with a thick, red, Vandyke-style beard and a funny looking handlebar mustache which he kept waxed and twirled. He had a full head of flaming red hair, which may or may not have been his own. He looked more like Red Beard the Pirate than he did a prominent funeral director, and I must say without meaning to be disrespectful, Mr. Burns himself was a very funny-looking man. Another thing about him was that he always drove around town in that dirty-looking old automobile. It was disgraceful to see a man of his position in the community driving that old car. Other times he was behind the wheel of a big funeral car, and that was the car, the black limousine, that he has been seen in driving in and around town."

"About two or three months ago, my lady friend Mary Ledbetter told me she had also seen him driving that black car down the avenue, and he had a man sitting next to him in the passenger seat. Mary said that the instant she saw the car she knew it was Mr. Burns' funeral limousine. She said that when she tried to get a better look at him, he quickly turned away from her in an obvious attempt to shield his face. It's just what she said it looked like he had done." "Did your lady friend Mrs. Ledbetter, see what the man sitting next to Mr. Burns in the car looked like?" I asked her that question while chasing after a long shot.

"Yes, I do remember her telling me that. She said that she had gotten a good look at that man sitting in the passenger seat. He was a small-appearing ruddy-faced man, with pop-eyes. It was funny at the time she told me about him she said he reminded her of some old and spooky movie actor whose name escapes me for the moment." "Could she have possibly said Peter Lorre, Miss Merriweather?" A look of instant recognition came onto her face as she answered me. "Oh, you are right! That's the name she said, Peter Lorre! I knew that it was one of those spooky character actors from the 1930s."

Miss Merriweather smiled and seemed to be very pleased with herself for what she just told me.

So, I thought, it now seems that Burns is not dead after all! He is still very much alive, and probably still kicking, or at least he was still breathing a few months ago! As soon as I meet with Blake tonight, I had better tell him about this because it could change our plans to visit Bruno Stenn's mortuary tonight. If Burns is here and he is in hiding, he could very well be spending time in Stenn's funeral parlor, and we sure as heck do-not want to run into any more surprises.

"To your knowledge, Miss Merriweather, did your lady friend, Mrs. Ledbetter, ever tell that story to the police about her seeing Burns?"

"Not to my knowledge. Do you think she should have done that?"

"Perhaps," I answered simply.

Before I left the building, I gave her my telephone number and asked Miss Merriweather if she would call me if she had any success in locating the photographs I asked her about. As an afterthought, I dropped five dollars into the collection box. "The money is because you were helpful to me, Miss Merriweather," I said as I waved goodbye to her.

During my casual walk back to my home from the Forest Oak Historical Society, I rolled the latest events around my mind. Could it be true that Sedgwick Burns is alive after all? It could be true because no one ever said that he was dead for certain, and if the man Mrs. Ledbetter saw was Sedgwick Burns, why in the world would he be hiding out here in this town? That seems a very dumb and dangerous thing for him to do. Better yet, what in the world was he doing driving around in his black limousine in Forest Oak where he could be easily seen and recognized? If he still owes those gamblers money, which seems apparent, he has become very careless. It seems that Burns just walked away from all of his property and took off, and rational people do not do those kinds of things. Burns' house and property would have been left to rot if it were not for his grandnephew Clayton Matthews from California. As it happened, Burns had been legally declared dead after seven years had passed and he never showed up. After that, Matthews got the house and whatever else the old fool left him.

It had to be a sheer coincidence that the man Mrs. Ledbetter saw driving around in town looked like Sedgwick Burns, and that the passenger in his car looked like Stenn, and that the car. . . . wait a darn minute, those are just too many coincidences! I think Burns is probably still alive, and he is hiding somewhere nearby in town. Maybe he is staying in Stenn's mortuary as I had given a thought about earlier, or perhaps he is living in Stenn's house--wherever that is. Well, as usual, I will have to talk to Blake Cranshaw about all of this and ask him what he thinks. Maybe he will be able to tie things together and make something of this crazy jigsaw puzzle. Now it seems that I have a whole lot more to worry about before I meet with Cranshaw later this afternoon. For the first time in my life, I began to experience a profound sense of fear.

~ Chapter Eighteen ~

A STARTLING DISCOVERY

I walked into Blake Cranshaw's office at precisely 5:15 that afternoon, and I saw him sitting behind his desk reading a newspaper. The minute he saw me, he quickly lowered the paper and peered at me over the top of it. I noticed that he and I were both wearing the proper attire for house-breaking, which was blue jeans and a dark polo shirt. Since his feet were hidden under his desk, I could only guess that was wearing sneakers--just as I was wearing. Before I could say a word to him, he spoke to me.

"Good afternoon Rick. I see that you're right on time as usual. Are you ever late for anything?" Blake asked with a big grin on his face.

"I am never late when it comes to breaking and entering," I said to him jokingly as I returned his grin. He quickly laid the newspaper on top of his desk, and when he stood up from his chair, he reached across the top of the desk to shake my hand.

"Now, are you still game, Rick, or have you since had a change of heart over what we're planning to do this evening?" He asked, referring to our plan to check out Bruno Stenn's funeral parlor. "I am raring to go, I lied, but there have been a few interesting developments that I have to talk with you about before we leave here because it may change our decision to do as we had planned on doing."

Returning to his seat, he motioned for me to take the chair across from him. As I sat on the edge of the chair, I leaned forward and asked if we could be overheard since his office door was open. Blake said that there were no services at the moment, which was what I noticed when I entered the building. The only other person in the building, Blake assured me, was his receptionist, and as he had mentioned to me before, she always occupied a small desk at the front of the building.

Once I felt that I had Blake's full and complete attention, and was satisfied we were alone, I told him all that had happened at the Forest Oak Historical Society earlier in the day. When I got to the part about a lady having seen Sedgwick Burns driving down the street in a big, black limousine, Blake said it must surely have been a case of mistaken identity. When I related the woman's highly detailed description of the car, its driver, and especially the driver's passenger, he quickly changed his mind.

"So, it now seems as though that darned old fool Sedgwick Burns isn't dead after all!" Blake responded as he stared up at the ceiling. "You know something, Rick, what you just told me doesn't surprise me too much. Oh, I guess I accepted the fact that he may have been dead like many others in Forest Oak believed, especially after the lapse of more than eight years of his being missing. Still, this news that he's still alive doesn't come as too much of a shock to me. Part of my doubt had to do with those debts he owed to the gamblers. They're not the kind to let deadbeats off the hook. Do you know what I mean? I can see a man like Burns being unable to face up to that kind of a problem and going deep into hiding. With what you're telling me about his resurfacing here in this town, and being casual about driving around for everyone to see, well, that defies any reasonable explanation."

"I had much the same idea as you about his being dead until I started thinking about all that he had left behind when he disappeared. Take my house as an example. I paid two hundred and five thousand dollars for that place, and all that money, as far as I know, had been directly handed over to his grandnephew from California, a man by the name of Clayton Matthews. I know Burns had no more financial interest in your partnership since you had already told me that, but there certainly must have been other things of value he owned when he just walked away. Why, for instance, did Burns not sell the house at that time. Could he possibly have used that money to pay off his gambling debts? That would have been the smart way to handle it, and not leave town and stay in hiding for all those years, if that is what he had done! None of it seems right to me! But then again, practically everything that has happened in connection with Sedgwick Burns has not been right for me." I said in a puzzled voice. "Does any of it make any sense or logic to you, Blake?"

Before Blake answered my questions, he opened his desk drawer and took out a fresh pack of cigarettes, peeled the cellophane band from it, opened one end of it, and knocked the new cigarette pack against his hand to start the cigarettes poking out of the container. Next, he took one cigarette and gently placed it between his lips. I was getting used to this sort of ritual which he went through before he answered any serious questions.

"I have to agree with most of what you just said to me, Rick, but have you ever considered the possibility that he may have been hiding out in California with his grandnephew during the time he was supposed to be missing?" Blake then looked straight into my eyes gauging my reaction to what he had just said. Finally, he snapped his lighter open and ignited the end of his cigarette, took a quick puff from it, and then inhaled deeply before he puffed out a large cloud of white smoke. When he saw me observing the mechanics of his smoking so intently, his face flushed slightly, and through another puff of the cigarette smoke he repeated some very familiar words to me, "I have to give up these God-darn things one of these days."

"That is just about what you always say to me, Blake, about the smoking, I mean. Now, as for what you said about Burns being in hiding in California with his grandnephew, I must say that I had never given much thought to that possibility."

"Well, I've thought a lot about it, Rick. In fact, I've given a whole lot of thought to about everything connected with Sedgwick Burns since you first contacted me about those items you found in your cellar.

"Just for the heck of it, Rick, think about this scenario. Sedgwick Burns finds himself heavily in debt to the gamblers, and he doesn't have the cash to pay them off. They give him a certain amount of time to make good on his notes, but Burns defaults. Those dangerous people offer you only a couple options if you welsh, You can immediately pay off the debt to them with exceptionally high interest, or you can have your knee-caps and your arms broken, or possibly even get yourself killed. To them it's just a simple business transaction, you pay, or you suffer a lot, or you die! Now consider a man like Sedgwick Burns facing those options.

"You don't know this fact about Burns, but I do. He couldn't stand much pain. He wasn't squeamish at the sight of blood or anything like that, but he simply couldn't tolerate pain. I remember the time he was in the process of embalming a client and his probe slipped, and it jabbed him in the back of his hand. I could hear his screams all the way into my office, and when I got to him, he was doubled over in pain with tears in his eyes. It was little more than a mere pin-prick from the probe, something which required nothing more than a small Band-Aid to cover the tiny wound. You see, Rick, just the thought of his being beaten up would be enough to send him deep into hiding, let alone the threat of having his kneecaps smashed with a baseball bat, or his being killed."

"Was it possible he could have sold his house and used that money to satisfy the debt to those gamblers?" I asked.

"Maybe there wasn't enough equity left in Burns' property to cover the gambling debt," Blake responded. "Anyway, as the buyer of his house, you should be the one to know the answer to the question."

"Just as you said, Blake, I guess I should have known the answer to that question, but I never paid any attention to that aspect of the real estate closing. I relied entirely on my attorney to take care of details like that."

"Well," Blake began, "let us assume that what I just suggested was the situation with Burns, the man didn't have enough equity left in the property if he'd sold his house to be able to pay off his gambling debts to those gamblers. He knows that if he doesn't pay them all that he owes them he's going to be very sorry. I would guess that he decided it was time for him to leave town and go into hiding. Where does he go? He has no living relatives other than a grandnephew named Clayton Matthews, a man who's living in California. The nephew is not only his only living relative, but he's also his sole heir who stands to inherit everything after Burns dies.

"Now if he's smart, and I can tell you that Burns was a very shrewd and cunning man, he'll lie to his nephew! He'll tell him that he got into some kind of a jam with the law, maybe because of his business conduct and that he needs to disappear from town for a while. For the grandnephew to give him a place to stay, Burns may have promised him the title to his house, while neglecting to tell him that it was already heavily mortgaged. Then there's that beautiful and valuable antique convertible car he owned that he had hidden away in his garage--the car you had described to me. What a strong incentive that would be to induce a young fellow to cooperate! That car may very well have been the frosting on the cake which Burns used to convince Matthews to take him in and cover for him. I seem to remember that you told me the car was disposed of shortly before Burns had disappeared?"

"That is what my next door neighbor Dave Farrell had told me."

"Okay, let's just guess that the car had been turned over to Matthews at that time and that it acted as Burns' down payment to Matthews for providing him a safe hiding place in California. Has any of what I've been saying to you beginning to make any sense at all to you so far, Rick?"

"Go on with it!" I asked him eagerly.

"Now Burns still has the problem with his house and how he can resurface long enough to sell it, and at the same time avoid retribution from the gamblers? He quickly realizes that he can't, but he knows that he still has to keep a promise he'd made to his grandnephew for keeping him hidden! What does he do? He stays away for seven years, and after that time he is declared legally dead. Soon after that, the property goes to Matthews, but the clinker in the coal pile is that Matthews discovers he'd been duped because of the heavy mortgage that remained on Burns house. He eventually kicks Burns out off his house, and Burns resurfaces here in Forest Oak.

"It seems that gamblers have very long memories, and if they discover Burns is still alive, they'll kill him for sure! That's why he had to stay in hiding for as many years. Just why it is that he is now back here in town and apparently no longer in fear of the repercussions from the gamblers is anyone's guess. Anyway, Rick, To my way of thinking, my scenario seems to fit together almost like a jigsaw puzzle."

"I have to tell you it does not entirely fit neatly together for me, Blake. For instance, who was the person who kept up the mortgage payments to the bank for all the time when Burns was somewhere in hiding? Then there are the monthly expenses incurred by the management company, and none of those things came cheaply. Also, sometime after Burns disappeared, it was probably his Grandnephew who spent a considerable amount of money having a new furnace installed, along with central air conditioning, and all new electrical work in the house. It would have made a lot more sense for the house to have been rented or sold during that time, rather than leaving it unoccupied. Finally, if Burns was so worried that the gamblers were still after him to maim or kill him, why would the man now be openly driving about town with Stenn, of all people, and in his livery car which everyone here recognizes on sight. A lot of those things do not comfortably connect in my mind."

"It could have been Matthews who was paying all of those bills for Burns, Blake responded. He could have done that on the promise of the final reward after seven years when Burns would be declared dead. Then there's that beautiful antique Cord automobile I'd just mentioned. It's possible the car was sold using some of the proceeds to cover the upkeep of the mortgage payments, as well as those expensive improvements you just summarized. A rare and well-maintained classic car such as that old Cord automobile could conceivably be worth hundreds of thousands of dollars. They're extremely rare and are sought after by serious collectors. Clayton Matthews could have taken care of selling that rare car without having to reveal the fact to anyone that Burns was still alive.

"There's also another important fact you seem to have forgotten about, Rick. I am now referring to those old coffins filled with bodies that were hidden inside your garage's loft. If Matthews had rented the house, as you suggested, the tenants quite possibly could have discovered them--just as you discovered them. And, as for your last statement, if the man that lady said she saw driving around town with Stenn was truly Sedgwick Burns and not just someone who looked like Burns, he must be completely off his rocker showing himself around town and taking the risk of being murdered by those gamblers. It's a good bet they're probably still after him even after he's been missing for more than eight years." Blake took another long drag on his cigarette and then looked to me for my responses to all that he just said.

"I do not think that Matthews would have been dumb enough to carry that heavy a financial burden for so long a time, I said. Could it be possible that Burns was working in California, and he was paying all of his bills through his grandnephew--as you suggested? As for those six bodies he had hidden in the loft, he probably didn't know anything about them being there, or if he did know, he could have had them removed just as we did?"

"Possibly, Blake responded, but maybe he didn't have time to dispose of those bodies. From our own experience in your garage loft, you saw how difficult it was to do even for the four of us working, and with that nosey neighbor of yours always watching, it would have meant taking a terrible risk of discovery.

"Sedgwick Burns was a licensed mortician and funeral director in this state, but I doubt that he'd be able to practice either trade in California. They'd soon discover who he was if he tried to get references, and they'd quickly learn that he was listed as a missing person. No, if Burns did any work while in hiding in California, it had to be something other than what he was trained to do, perhaps something like a livery chauffeur, or doing some other job around a parlor that wouldn't require licensing. In that way, it would have been possible that he could have earned enough to cover those expenses you just mentioned.

"There is one thing is certain in my mind anyway," Blake continued, "Burns had to keep a low profile or risk being found out. If those gamblers had an inkling that he was still alive and in hiding somewhere in California, Burns was as good as a dead man. Of course, everything I have just said to you is pure speculation on my part since neither one of us has any real idea where Sedgwick Burns has been for the last eight years. The only thing we knew, or think that we knew, is that Burns is probably still very much alive and that he's now hiding somewhere near here, and very possibly hiding out with his old employee named Bruno Stenn. Anyway, we had better get moving, Rick, We have just enough time to get to Stenn's mortuary before dark!" Blake said as he wearily hoisted himself from his chair and headed for the door. I followed close behind him as we left the building.

Upon our reaching the parking lot, we decided to use my car since Blake said Stenn would know his vehicle by sight. That made a lot of sense to me. My present hope was that Stenn was not within ten miles of his building while we were unlawfully visiting the place.

The last thing in the world we now need is to have Stenn walk in on us while we were in the process of searching for that missing journal."

Before Blake and I left the parking lot, Blake went to the trunk of his car and removed a jimmy bar, a hammer, and two flashlights and then dropped them on the floor of my car near his feet. "We'll be needing these things, he said as he slammed the door shut. It's time for us to leave here and get the dirty deed over and done with!"

During the forty minutes it took Blake and me drive to Stenn's Funeral Home, we talked about the circumstances that had brought us to this unlawful and possibly dangerous action we were about to undertake. The two of us were now preparing to break into a man's place of business, a funeral home owned by a man Blake said could be a very dangerous and unpredictable individual as evidenced by the time Stenn had struck Blake in the face. Our sole purpose was to look around to try and find that mysterious book that Stenn had stolen from my attic. Blake thought we should be able to get into the building and search the premises and be out of there in less than twenty minutes. Since the mortician's seminar normally lasted for about four hours, he felt we would have plenty of time in our search to find it and then leave.

One thing Blake cautioned me about was for me not to shine my flashlight near the windows when we are inside the building. Blake said any light that might that be observed from the street could be seen, and someone passing by the building might call the police. When I inquired about a possible burglar alarm system within the premises, Blake laughed and said, "Have you ever heard of anyone breaking into a funeral home? What would they steal from there, other than a dead body?"

Just as soon as we got within sight of Stenn's Mortuary, I slowed the car down while Blake and I peered out at the parking lot. The entire area was dark except for the light that shone from the street lamp at the front of the building. The lot was also empty except for the same old black car that I had seen there during my earlier visit with Stenn. As I drove past the lot, Blake said, "Do you see that car parked there in the lot, Rick? That's Burns' old black Ford; I can't believe Stenn has it!"

"How could Stenn have attended the seminar if his car's still here?" I asked nervously.

"It's more than likely he drove his Cadillac limousine to the seminar. Then again, maybe one of his cronies picked him up in another car. If you are guessing that he's here just because that old Ford is in the lot, Rick, you're wrong. Stenn wouldn't miss that meeting for anything, and that's a fact."

"Oh, I am not worried about him being here now," I said, "I am only worried that he may drop in on us when we are inside his building. As for that old Ford parked in his lot, I think it probably had been sold to Stenn by Clayton Matthews. Anyway, that is what Dave Farrell had told me. Maybe he bought Burns' old Cadillac hearse as well as his Ford."

"I didn't know that Matthews knew Stenn, Blake said. There just seems to me to be too darn many coincidences to suit me. It's entirely possible that Stenn was in on the disappearance plot right along with Burns and Matthews. Now that I'm thinking a bit more about it, I have to say that idea makes a whole lot of sense to me." "Can you please explain that to me, Blake?" I asked.

"Okay. We've already guessed that Stenn was the one who helped Burns with those bodies you found in your loft. You recently learned that Burns was seen driving his old hearse around town, and who's his passenger? Bruno Stenn! Stenn pays a visit to your house where he scares the wits out of your wife, so that evening you pay him an unfriendly visit here at his parlor and he begs you to allow him to search your house. He's seeking a mysterious ledger or book, which now appears had been hidden somewhere in your house. When you suggested to him that you'll help him find it, he quickly declined your offer. Within a few days of your visit with him, your house is burglarized and the ledger is taken from a secret embalming room you discovered in your attic. Is there any doubt in your mind, Rick, that it was Stenn who did that?"

"Your theory sounds to me, Blake, that your thoughts are right on target! Can you tell me if there was more of a connection between Burns and Stenn than an employer-employee relationship?"

"There was!" Blake responded with some intensity. "I had always had the suspicion that Bruno Stenn shared Burns' loathsome, abnormal attraction to the dead female clients because I had more than an inkling that they were both necrophiliacs. Because of what they were, there was no limit to what they would do to cover for each other. Yes, as I look more clearly at it now, I have to say that Bruno Stenn is surely a co-conspirator in Burns' disappearance. There isn't a shadow of a doubt in my mind about that. It's no wonder Stenn was able to carry on as a functioning funeral director because he probably had Burns coaching him from the sidelines all the while. That may even be the price Burns had to pay to get Stenn to cooperate with him."

"The whole idea of what you just said sickens me in my stomach, Blake," I said as I screwed my face into a look of deep disgust.

"Are you ready for us to go into the building now?" Blake asked.

"Let us get it over with quick and then get the heck out of here," I responded. "I only hope my tires are still on the car when we return to it."

"This neighborhood has deteriorated badly since I sold the business to Stenn," Blake remarked. "The building looks like an inner-city tenement now. It makes me wonder how Stenn had been able to pay his bills."

Parking my car in the street at the curb, we both hurriedly stepped from the car, and at the same time Blake picked up the flashlights and tools from the floor. After I had locked the car doors, we started walking briskly toward the building, and when we were parallel with the entrance to the parking lot, Blake stopped. Before we go further into the lot let us look around to be certain that we are not being observed.

Having looked in all directions while trying to appear casual, we were convinced that we were not being watched by anyone before we entered the lot. As we passed by the old Ford, Blake whispered, "That's Burns' Ford all right! There's no mistaking it."

Blake told me the best place to enter the building was through the side delivery door, but upon our reaching it we saw that it had a heavy chain with a padlock looped through its two handles. As I stood there and watched, Blake inserted the end of the jimmy bar between the lock and the steel door, and then pulled hard against it. The lock was no match for the combination of the bar and Blake's strength, and the chain quickly snapped open.

That done, I slowly opened one side of the double door and we both slipped inside the building. Then, quickly and quietly I closed the door behind us. Blake clicked his flashlight on and played its bright beam around the room. Since there were no windows in that room, he apparently was not concerned about any light being seen from the outside.

Looking inside the room I saw that it was a mess of cartons, boxes, filing cabinets, and even a casket that was set up on two sawhorses. With all the clutter inside that place, I could not imagine how Stenn had any room to work.

Sensing my question, Blake decided to answer it for me. "Oh, it's just what it appears to be, a storeroom," Blake said. "The embalming room is through that other door," he then pointed at it by using the light beam from his flashlight.

"Where do we start looking for the log book, Blake?" I asked just above a whisper.

"Well, you can be certain it won't be in this storeroom. Most likely it's somewhere in his back office. That's next to the embalming room through that same door." Again he flashed his light on it to indicate the right door.

Blake began walking slowly and carefully toward the door with me right at his heels behind him. Before he opened the door, he again reminded me to keep my light facing down toward the floor because there were several, large frosted-glass windows in the room that would allow the light to be seen from the outside.

Once we were both inside the room, the first thing that caught my eye was a stainless steel preparation table at the center of the room with a pull-down light hanging above it. I was momentarily startled when I saw a body lying on the table covered over with a white sheet. When I beamed my light fully on it, I could see a vague image of the dead body through the thin cloth covering it. It appeared to be the torso of a large man with a heavy dark beard. I could easily see the apparatus for removing blood and for pumping in the embalming fluid. The tubes appeared to still be connected to the body. Turning my light and my eyes away, I then saw the door that led to Stenn's office. I was just about to go there when I saw Blake pull back the sheet from the table and then emit a loud howl.

"What is it Blake? Have we been discovered? Did you hear someone coming?"

"No, that isn't it! The reason I just stopped you is because I know who that man is who had been lying under that sheet on the table!"

"Who is it?" I asked incredulously, my eyes betraying my fear.

"I should know who he is" Blake continued, "because I worked with that man for many years. The body we're seeing lying on that embalming table is my ex-partner, and the previous owner of your house, that dead man is Sedgwick Burns!"

~ *Chapter Nineteen* ~

FRAMING THE PUZZLE

When the initial shock of our discovery of Sedgwick Burns' dead body began to pass, Blake pulled the sheet entirely away from the body, and he then held his flashlight steadily onto the ashen face of the corpse. In a loud voice he said, "Come over to the table here by me, Rick, I want to show you something I find to be very interesting."

Reluctant to move closer to Blake and the body, I hesitated. "Come over here!" Blake repeated, although this time it was more of a command than it was a request. "What I am looking at here is very important. For God's sakes, Rick, the man's dead! So there's nothing for you to be afraid of from him."

After spending several more seconds building up my courage, I finally walked to the side of the table directly across from Blake before I looked at the corpse in the bright glare of Blake's flashlight. What I was looking at was a man who appeared to be in his middle to late sixties, with a thick mixed gray and red beard, a thin crop of flaming red hair, and a silly looking mustache, that was curled up at both ends. That face perfectly fits the physical description I had been given for Sedgwick Burns by Miss Annabelle Merriweather!

"What am I supposed to be looking at, Blake?" I asked nervously, as I was trying to fathom what there was for me to see, other than the stiff body of a dead man lying on an embalming table. Blake placed the beam of the flashlight full onto the dead man's face while he pointed at his forehead and the bridge of his nose. "See that Rick!" Blake inquired excitedly.

"See what?" I asked. "All I can see is the pasty face of a dead man. What else is there for me to see, Blake?" I was now becoming a little agitated. All I wanted to do was get on with our search for the log book, and then get the heck out of this morbid and depressing place.

Blake looked up at me with a scowl, and said, "That's not his skin you're looking at, Rick! It's wax and some other compound which I'm not familiar with. When Burns was killed, his head was severely mangled, probably with a blunt instrument of some kind. What you are seeing here is an extremely skilled job of cosmetic reconstruction."

"How do you know that?" I asked in disbelief. "It looks just like the man's flesh to me."

"Of course, it does," he answered. "You're not skilled in the art of cosmetic reconstruction, and that's exactly what you're supposed to think, but it's not his flesh, it's soft wax and some newer compound. I've never seen a better job than what I'm looking at now, and I simply can't believe that Bruno Stenn did this. The man was nothing more than a reasonably adequate embalmer, a man who didn't possess the skill or the knowledge to do work of this quality. No! Someone other than Bruno Stenn did this highly professional job of facial reconstruction on Burns' body. I can't begin to imagine who it might be."

"What you're telling me, Blake, is all very interesting, but I am more concerned about why he is lying dead on that table than I am about his so-called reconstructive facial surgery. What kind of a weapon would have killed Burns that would have required the kind of reconstruction that you are talking about, if that is what it is?" Immediately following my last comment, Blake began an even closer examination of the corpse's head and skull. I watched him closely as he gently ran the tips of his fingers very slowly down and across those areas of his face, and where his fingers had probed, I could see a slight smearing of the makeup that had been used to tone the flesh-like compound. When he was finished with his examination, Blake turned his attention to me and said, 'He apparently was killed from a massive blow to the skull, but it wasn't from a blunt instrument as I first thought. From what I've now been able to determine from my rather cursory examination, it looks like it was something heavy and sharp, perhaps a hatchet or a meat cleaver. Without question, Sedgwick Burns had been brutally murdered." Upon hearing that, my eyes locked into a stare with Blake's! I was unable to respond to what he had just said, and I began to have some difficulty swallowing! Next came a feeling of panic, and I felt that I had to get out of that place as quickly as my legs could carry me. In spite of it, I was unable to make my body do as my mind commanded! Blake must have sensed the dread and the feeling of panic that had engulfed me, so he quickly walked to my side of the table and put his hand on my arm.

"It will all be okay, Rick," Blake said. "There's no need for us to worry. Bruno Stenn's at that conference, and he won't be back here for hours. Sedgwick Burns is stone-cold dead, and there's nothing that we can do about that situation, so let's just get busy and finish what we came here to do tonight, and get busy and search to find that log book that Stenn had stolen from your house! As for the murder, we'll have to think of some way to notify the police about it before Stenn has a chance to dispose of the body. But that task will have to wait until we're finished here, and then we can decide how best to handle it. How are you feeling now? Do you feel well enough to help me look for that book?"

Things were happening much too fast for my mind to be able to function properly. I knew that I wanted to leave, but something deep inside me told me that Blake is much more in control of things than I am, and his decisions are a lot more rational than mine as well. "I am okay now," I answered, "it was just the surprise and shock of it that rattled me so badly. Let us get it done and then get the heck out of this bleak tomb, Blake," I said as I started walking toward the door leading to Stenn's office.

Once we entered the office, Blake immediately began rummaging through the file cabinets while I concentrated my search inside Stenn's desk. I had just gone through one row of drawers and started on another drawer when I heard Blake say, "I think this is probably the thing we're here to find."

Turning to face him squarely, I saw that Blake held a gray leather-bound book in his hands. It didn't look like a ledger book to me. It looked more like an ordinary diary.

"That is not it," I said. "Stenn told me that he was after a ledger book. He said the same thing about it when he talked to Elaine."

"That may be how he referred to it," Blake said, "but what I'm reading on the cover of this diary in block letters says otherwise."

Blake then handed the book to me, and using my flashlight I read its cover which was boldly hand-printed in large black letters: CONFIDENTIAL FILE OF SEDGWICK BURNS SR.

That would be Sedgwick Burns' father, and it seemed we had found what we were looking here to locate. Now it is time for us to get out of here, and Blake and I wasted no time as he headed toward the office door and then out of the building.

Before we left the premises, we linked the broken chain through the handles of the door so that it appeared just as we had found it. Once we were safely in my car and we were heading back to Blake's funeral parlor, I finally began to relax. While I was driving, Blake's attention was absorbed in the diary we had taken from Stenn's office, and he was struggling to read it while using the car's small overhead dome light.

Not a word had been exchanged between us until I was nearing Blake's funeral home and Blake finally spoke, "Do not drive to my office just yet, Rick. Instead of that I'd like you to drive over to Donovan's Pub where we'll have a drink or two, which is something I feel that I need, and then we should be able to talk. There's something I find to be very interesting that I've been reading in that book, Rick, and it may be the very key to everything that has been happening." Blake appeared now to be more perplexed now than before we found the diary.

Once Blake and I were inside the Pub and were seated comfortably in a back booth, Blake ordered our drinks from a slim blond barmaid.

I noted that when we walked in the door, she had smiled at him and called him by his first name. By her flirtatious manner, I suspected there might be a relationship between them other than his just being a regular patron of Donovan's, but it was none of my business.

When our drinks were delivered to the table, Blake lifted his glass and tossed about half of his down before he began to tell me about what he'd read in the journal that had excited him so much. He talked in a shallow voice so that no one sitting in the adjoining booths could overhear him. In fact, he spoke so quietly it was difficult for me to hear his words, so I had to lean halfway across the table and slightly tilt my head to one side.

"First of all," Blake began, "let me say that it's a personal journal and not a so-called ledger. The first portion of the text was written by Sedgwick Burns' father whose name originally was Solomon Burnstein, and the balance of the journal was written by his son Sedgwick Jr. The journal dates to the very first part of the nineteenth century, or from the time when Sedgwick Jr. was still a young man. In those days the Burns family owned and operated six funeral parlors in the county, and they commanded a position of power and respect. If you will recall, Rick, when we first talked about this in my office, I told you that when Solomon Burnstein came to this country from Germany where he'd been a fish merchant, but he became a mortician after robbers had murdered his oldest son Aaron. I won't go over that again, but what I want to remind you of is the fact that he built his reputation because he'd become exceptionally skilled at body reconstruction.

"After Solomon Burnstein's son Sedgwick became a partner in the family business, he learned much from his father, but eventually, he developed even greater skills on his own. The journal is an outline of everything his father had taught him, and those many additional techniques Sedgwick had developed on his own. It's a veritable goldmine of information. The diary is so thorough and so detailed it should be published as a guide for every Funeral Director and Mortician in the trade."

When Blake finished telling me a few more details from the book, he sat down slowly in his seat and this time he took a long drink from his glass. As I struggled to somehow respond to his statements, I watched him take a cigarette from his pack, light it, and then took a deep puff of the smoke as he scrutinized my eyes to try and determine what my reaction had been to what he had just told me about the journal.

Following an uneasy pause, I finally said, "That is all very interesting, Blake, but I cannot see why that journal was so crucial to Bruno Stenn that he would risk breaking into my house to steal it. He could more easily have told me what the darn thing was all about and where it was hidden in that attic room. Why all the mystery? And another thing, why did he wait all those years to come looking there for the book? I have asked myself this question before, and you and I have discussed this as well. Still, I would have to say that none of it makes any sense or reason to me."

"The answer to your first question is that he probably had already killed Burns, and he didn't want to have to answer a lot of questions. I don't know what the man had in his mind exactly, Rick. As for your second question, why did he wait so long? It could be that he only recently learned of the Journal's existence, and, as for Stenn telling you where the journal was hidden in our house, naturally, he couldn't do that with you being there with him and discovering that hidden room and what it probably had been used for.

"Let me create another scenario for you, Rick, and see how it plays out for you." He again gave me a careful look trying to determine if I was open to yet another of those many theories which he liked to throw at me in that fashion.

"Go right ahead, Blake," I said, "I'm listening."

"Before I do, I'd like to order us a couple more drinks;" he said as he motioned for the little blond barmaid to send us two more of the same. When the drinks arrived, Blake quickly gulped his down and pushed his empty glass to the end of the table.

"To better understand all that I have to say, Rick, you must comprehend the depravity in the mind of Bruno Stenn. I've already told you much about him, and you've also had the displeasure of meeting the man, so I'm sure those things have helped you to form your own negative opinion of him. Now let's first review what we already know: Bruno Stenn is a loner. He probably chose his profession because it afforded him two opportunities. One was to distance himself from intimate contact with other people, and another was his embalming profession gave him the chance to occasionally indulge in his perverted necrophilia pleasures. Stenn probably also had visions of grandeur within the limits of his trade. I had seen that evidence at the time I caught him trying to reconstruct a severely broken corpse. I told you that when I chastised him for his reaction was to strike me in the face, clearly showing that he has a violent temper.

"To my knowledge, the only man who had ever shown Bruno Stenn any friendship or compassion of any kind was my ex-partner Sedgwick Burns. Do you remember me telling you that after I fired Stenn for hitting me, it was Burns who saved his butt by convincing me to give him another chance? Outside of the parlor, I don't believe that either of them had any social contact. I did sense, however, that they probably shared their perversion together at some time or another."

Blake called the barmaid over to our table to order another round of drinks for us, but I asked her to make it only one drink for Blake and nothing for me. In a few minutes, she brought Blake his glass and placed it on the table next to him. Gulping the drink, Blake continued with his comments. "Although Sedgwick Burns had been prohibited from doing any further reconstructive procedures on our clients, I always knew that he strongly resented that restriction. Stenn was Burns' protégé, and Stenn never lost his intense, and probably, obsessive interest in his mentor's advanced techniques and procedures.

"With all of that in my mind," Blake said, "it seems only logical to conclude that Stenn would want to get his hands on that detailed instruction journal once he learned of its existence either before or after he'd killed Burns."

As the barmaid picked up Blake's empty glass, she smiled at him and whispered something to him before she left and returned to the bar.

"I just do not buy it, Blake!" I said.

"Why not?" He shot back at me as he lifted his glass to his lips and took a drink. I could tell by the way he was talking that he had become a bit more than tipsy over his drinks.

"If as you say, Stenn was Burns' protégé, I would think he should have learned most of those procedures during the time he was working alongside him, wouldn't you think?"

"But you're forgetting, Rick, until recently, possibly up until the last year or less than that, we are pretty much in concurrence that Burns was hiding out in California with his grandnephew Clayton Matthews. We have to assume, therefore, that there wasn't any opportunity for Burns and Stenn to have worked together. It also happens that there aren't that many clients who would require that particular procedure to be done. It is used mainly on those who were involved in horrific traffic or industrial accidents, that sort of thing. So even if Burns returned from California more than a year ago, it's probable that he had only a very limited opportunity to perform that type of reconstruction. Perhaps a few of Stenn's clients required it, but then who knows?"

"Okay, that certainly makes good sense to me now, Blake, but if Stenn had any knowledge of where that diary was hidden, how come he did not attempt to get it, or at least make an effort to get it? Why would it remain hidden in that secret room in the attic for all those years, and then why would Stenn suddenly come looking for it and take the risk to break into my house and steal it?"

"Again, Rick, it seems more than likely that Stenn only learned about the existence of the book recently--as I just said to you a minute ago. Let us try another theory on for size, Rick. Maybe the reason Burns didn't have the book with him when he disappeared was that he had to get out of his house in a big hurry. I seem to remember you telling me that practically everything he owned had been left in the house?"

"No, Blake, What I said to you was that a few pieces of his furniture remained in the house along with a bunch of other junk in cardboard cartons he left in the attic room. If he left anything else there of value, I never saw it. Well, now that I think about it, Dave

Farrell did tell me that Clayton Matthews had sold off a lot of the furniture and some other things after he acquired the place, so maybe you are right."

"Perhaps it was something I read in the newspaper at the time it was still news," Blake responded. "I seem to recall that it said the house was just as if he had walked out of it to go to the corner store even leaving food sitting on the kitchen table. That sounds to me like he was in an awful big hurry to leave, doesn't it seem that way to you, Rick? I guess that he left so fast he didn't have time to take anything, much less the time to uncover that old journal from behind all that junk hidden in the secret room in your attic."

"Why would he have been in that much a hurry to leave?" I asked that question mostly to express my disagreement with Blake's theory.

"Again, Rick, it seems you might have forgotten what his reasons were for hiding out in California? He was trying to get away from those gamblers to whom he owed a lot of money. He even may have been tipped off by someone that they were on their way to his house to get him! They might have been banging on his front door, and he had no time to take anything with him!"

"All right! Your theory is starting to make more sense to me, but the biggest question that remains for me is who killed Burns and why? Do you have any opinions on that matter, Blake?"

"Without any question whatsoever in my mind, Rick, it was Bruno Stenn who murdered Burns," Blake responded with total certainty in his voice as he lifted his glass from the table and took another hefty swallow of his drink.

"But why did Stenn kill Burns?" I asked as I looked at Blake with an expression almost approaching skepticism.

"It could have been because of a falling out between the two of them, but who can say why? Keep in mind that when you are dealing with two bizarre people like Sedgewick Burns and Bruno Stenn, anything at all is possible. The only thing that I know now is that we will positively have to inform the police about what we found lying on the embalming table in Stenn's back room!" His voice had become lower and solemn. He picked up his glass again and stared straight ahead at me with an anguished look on his face. After another fast gulp of his drink, he set his drink back down on the table.

"I already know that, Blake," I said, "but how do you propose we report it to the police without revealing the way we discovered the body was by our breaking into Stenn's funeral parlor this evening?"

"When the time comes, we'll have to figure out how to accomplish that, but there is one other thing that will be a bigger problem for us, unless we tell the authorities the identity of the dead man on the table, how will they know who he is? The fact that he's had facial reconstruction would not be apparent to them. The changes that had been made to his face were not noticeable to you, so how in the heck would they even suspect he's been murdered? To the police, the body will appear to be nothing more than a regular corpse which is there in the parlor being embalmed. They will think the body was being prepared for a wake and a funeral. Then again, they may even think the caller was a crackpot. I suspect they get calls like that more often than we may think. Anyway, if they believe the call is legitimate, they may decide to investigate it.

"It seems reasonable that they won't go through the bother of a search warrant before they enter the building. At the very least, they'll seek out Stenn for his permission to enter his building. If they do that, you can bet your last dollar that Stenn will lie to them, and tell them it's just a regular undertaking job, and that will be an end to it. Bruno Stenn, sure as the devil, will never admit to them that the dead man is Sedgwick Burns. He'll then get away with cold-blooded murder, and there's not a thing we can do to stop it. The way I see it, Rick, the only option available to us as decent human beings, is to call the police and do our very best to convince them the call is not a joke. We need to convince them that the dead body lying on the embalming table is Sedgwick Burns, a man who has been missing for more than eight years, and who is still listed as a missing person who's been brutally murdered."

"You are right, Blake, and I agree with everything you have just said. I will be the one to make the telephone call to the police, and I will do it from a phone booth. We should try to find a phone some distance from this area so they cannot trace it back here. Now, when I make that call, I will just tell the police that the body is that of Sedgwick Burns, who has been missing for more than eight years, and that it appears he died under very suspicious circumstances. Without a doubt, they will perform an autopsy on the body, and they will discover that he had been murdered. I will not say anything else about it, and I will immediately hang up the phone! As far as the police will know, I could be an enemy of Stenn's who is ratting on him, or I could be a burglar who discovered the body when I broke into the place. One thing is for certain, they will find the broken lock on the door's chain when they arrive at the building to investigate the call, and they will immediately know there had been a burglary. How does it sound to you Blake?"

"The story sounds reasonable enough to me, Rick, but what about Stenn when the police arrest him for the crime? Do you think our names will be brought into it? Not mine necessarily, because I have had no contact with him for many years, but your name could be mentioned. After all, you were the one he'd stolen the journal from, and there's a good chance that the burglary part of it will become known. We know for sure there's a police report of that burglary at your house on file that could pop up sometime during any investigation, so there's more than a good chance they'll contact you for some answers sooner or later."

"I guess I will just have to take that chance," I said woefully, feeling somewhat like a martyr.

After what seemed to be a long silence, Blake suddenly appeared perplexed, and with an almost apologetic tone he said, "You know, Rick, the more I think about this telephone call we're planning, the more I realize we aren't fully thinking this thing through carefully enough and, we're forgetting something that could end up backfiring."

"What is that?" I asked in amazement.

"We have no choice but to go to the police and tell them the truth about the body and, about everything else that we know. That'll include the fact that we removed those six corpses from your garage loft."

Just wait a God darn minute, Blake!" I spoke out in anger. "I thought we finally had it all mapped out. Why is it that all of a sudden you now feel we have to change our plans? I was feeling miffed at Blake, and I began to feel apprehensive about the whole idea of our calling the police."

"Because, Rick, it will all come out in the police's investigation that's why," Blake responded. "We both have been suffering under a wishful delusion while thinking that we could, somehow, cover everything up. Do you think for one minute that any of what's happened won't be brought to light after they nail Stenn for Burns' murder? I think now it's better if we go to the police and tell them everything. Maybe if we make a clean breast of it we will still be able to walk away from this wretched and cursed problem we've found ourselves engrossed in. I can honestly think of no other way to handle it, Rick. My so-called great plan of deception a few moments ago was nothing more than an attempt to delude myself and you into believing that if we're careful and smart we could pull it off. The police in this area may be slow, but they are by no means stupid!" Having made his point to me, he sat back in his seat and gulped down the last of his drink. Once more he placed his empty glass on the table as he motioned for the barmaid.

"Well then, I guess that's it, Blake. I still wish we could report the body and say nothing about the possibility of a murder having been committed, but as you said, it probably will not work. Apparently, there is no way we can beat this thing, and if you are convinced that it is what we have to do we may as well get it over with." I said that in a dejected and beaten voice. "Are you ready now for us to leave for the police station?"

"In just a minute or two we can leave, Rick," he answered. "I just ordered two more drinks, and I don't know about you, but I feel that we will need another drink before this night's over with."

As it turned out for me, more accurate words had never been spoken.

~ *Chapter Twenty* ~

A VENGEFUL REACTION

When Blake and I left Donovan's Pub, we were all set to drive directly to the nearest police station and tell them everything, but within a minute or two after I started my car, Blake reached over and turned the ignition key off.

"Maybe we're being little too hasty, Rick," Blake, he remarked. "Let's talk about it some more and see if we can possibly think of a different way to handle this thing, a way that won't be quite for bad for us. I just got a case of cold feet thinking about what the consequences could be. I guess I'm not as forthright and honest as I fooled myself into believing I was," he said with more than a tinge of embarrassment in his voice.

"For Heaven's sake! Blake," I bellowed, "just how many times will we continue change our plans?" I was beginning to become quite disturbed over it, but in all honesty I was relieved to hear him do it again because his thoughts now closely mirrored my own. From the beginning, I was less than anxious to face the law and have to deal with the resulting repercussions we would be facing for our illegal actions.

Trying again to formulate a plan that would be agreeable to both of us, we sat in my car for a long time while we were trying to think of a more acceptable approach to what I considered to be a self-destructive one. With Blake's backing down, we were again back to square one, and I wondered if we could ever come to grips with this difficult problem that was facing us and then make a firm decision. We could go directly to the local police station and tell them about Burns' body lying on an embalming table in Stenn's Funeral Parlor. That would be one way to start things moving, but it would require us to tell about our breaking into the building and stealing back the journal. Immediately, we would both be charged with a felony. Another way to handle it would be to make that anonymous phone call we talked about earlier. Again, that would be my preferred method to handle it, and the more I thought about it the better I liked it. Getting us both implicated in the break-in was a chance we would simply have to take. As a result of the investigation, which would surely follow, we could be charged with the removal of those six corpses from my garage loft, but we would just have to accept the consequences for that act. One thing that I asked of Blake, and he again agreed to it without hesitation, was to keep Ron and Glenn's names entirely out of any of it.

When we both reached the point where we had finally, and with much frustration and soul searching, eliminated every other acceptable option, we drove a few miles from Donovan's Pub where we located an isolated phone booth near a closed super market. I pulled my car into the lot, turned off the headlights, and then mumbled, "I guess this is it, Blake. Once we make this telephone call, we will have to be ready to accept whatever comes our way. Are you absolutely certain it's what you want to do?"

"You and I have gone over that ground a half a dozen times. Rick, and neither of us has been able to come up with a better alternative to making this call. We have looked at this dilemma from every angle, and it's pretty much cut and dried, we can call the police an alert them to the fact of the murder or we keep quite about it and allow a cold-blooded murderer to go free. Sure, we can always reason that Burns was thought to be dead anyway because he was missing for so many years, so what does it really matter? No one but you and me and

Bruno Stenn would ever know the truth, but I know that I wouldn't be able to live with that on my conscience, and I'm quite certain you wouldn't be able to live with it either, Rick.

"The action that we are about to take by calling the police may even cost both of us our freedom, and perhaps much more than that, and you and I should fully realize that. There is more than a good chance that I'll lose my business before the smoke clears, but that's also a chance I'm willing to take. You have a lot to lose as well, Rick, your job and your house and all, so ours is certainly not an easy decision for either of us. Now, let's get the call over with before I change my mind again," he said as he climbed out of the car and headed for the dark phone booth. I slipped out from behind the steering wheel and joined him. Just as I reached for the phone to make the call, Blake took my arm and gently steered me aside.

"I know that we'd decided earlier that you would be the one to do the talking, Rick, but if you don't mind, I'll do the talking. I have a particular knack for being able to change my way of speaking and my voice, and I think I can make myself sound like a bum or a vagrant. That would be more in line with someone who might have broken into Stenn's funeral parlor. It may be as silly as it can be, but if I can cover my identity by doing it, what the heck! What do you think, Rick?"

"It sounds okay to me," I responded. "I wasn't too keen about making that phone call anyway. Do you have a quarter?"

"Yes," he answered as he dropped the coin into the phone slot. After a short hesitation, he began dialing the number. Several seconds elapsed and then I heard Blake began speaking in an uneducated voice and pattern.

"Hello, is dis da Police Department?

I wanna report a murder.... No, my name ain't important, but you can find da dead body in da back room of Bruno Stenn's Mortuary over on Franklin Street. No! No! It ain't no damn joke! Da man's been murdered! Listen to me will ya? There's a man lying in da back room on a table. Yes, have your coroner guy check da body out. Dat's right! He'll find out dat da guy's been murdered! How da hell do I know who did it? Okay, da dead guys name is Sedgwick Burns. Dat's right, Sedgwick Burns. Who yam I ya ask? I yam just a citizen doin' his duty, officer. Hell no! I done wanna leave my name. No, I done wanna get involved. Good-bye!"

While I was listening to Blake on the phone taking in that strange dialect, I found it hard for me to keep from laughing out loud, and if it were not for the extreme seriousness of our situation, I believe I would have given into that impulse. I couldn't hear what was being said on the other end of the line, but I was able to follow the conversation fairly well by listening to Blake's statements and responses

Having completed his totally-out-of-character, and to me, rather hilarious call, Blake slammed the phone back on the receiver as he took my arm to guide me back to my car.

"Dumb jerk! Blake then mumbled as he climbed into the car. When I told the officer about the body he asked me if it was a prank. I had a bit of difficulty convincing him it was real–you heard what I said to him, but after I mentioned Sedgwick Burns' name to him his tone changed rather quickly, and he finally said he would dispatch a squad car there immediately. He was very anxious to have me give him my name, but again as you heard, I wasn't about to be that dumb. I'm sure he was attempting to have the call traced, but then again, I think they now have that system for recording origins of inbound calls the minute they are received. Hey! Let's get out of here in case he dispatched a squad car to this phone booth." We then took off from there in a big hurry and made a couple of fast left-hand turns.

Upon our arrival back at Donovan's Pub, Blake asked me if I cared to join him for a last drink of the evening, but I politely declined his offer. After our earlier drinking bout, I was still feeling a bit light-headed since I normally don't drink anything at all when I drive. This night was a rare exception for me. Blake and I finally parted company in front of Donovan's, and I watched as he entered the bar. His last words to me before he left were, "Give me a call tomorrow at my office." He could be certain that I will.

It was quite late in the evening by the time I finally arrived home, and I was fairly sure that Elaine would be waiting up for me, and she would be worried about where I had been. The minute I entered the house, she came running toward me and then clamped me in a tight embrace. She was trembling, and I could see a look of fright in her eyes. When she was finally able to speak, she said, "That man called here just a few minutes ago and he said some terrible things to me on the phone, Rick." She was extremely upset and her words came spilling out in a mishmash of syllables.

"Who called you, Elaine, and what did he say?" I asked in a bewildered voice.

"The. . . . That man who came to the house before, that Bruno Stenn!" Elaine stammered.

"Just what did he say to you?" I asked as I tried to speak calmly and quietly.

"He said he wanted that ledger book back or we will both be very sorry. It was horrible, Rick. He was using some of the worst profanity I have ever heard, and I was so frightened I even thought of calling Glen to get him to stay here with me until you arrived home." As Elaine looked at me, I could see that her eyes were still open wide with fear.

"I hope you didn't call Glen, did you Elaine?"

"No, Rick, but I was just about to call the police when I heard your car pull into our driveway. What in the world is going on, Rick, and for what reason is that man calling our home and making those horrible threats? Just what were you and Blake Cranshaw up to this evening?" Elaine asked in an emotion-charged and very irritated voice.

I was more than reluctant to tell Elaine about the events of the evening, but I knew that the truth would soon come out, and I also felt I had done enough lying and covering up over this situation for a lifetime. The next hour was filled with wrenching pain and a good deal of embarrassment for me as I attempted to relate most of the details to Elaine, beginning with my first discovery of the embalming fluid in the cellar. That was one of the few things I had already told her about. I remembered how upsetting that had been to her, but when I told her about the six coffins filled with corpses that Blake and I and our two boys had removed from the garage's loft, she broke down crying hysterically. It took me several minutes to calm her before I was able to continue with my story.

After having related each of the events in as close to chronological order as I possibly could remember them, I talked to Elaine about the events of today, and to the part where we found the dead body of Sedgwick Burns, and about the telephone call Blake and I made to the police. That was when she completely fell apart, and this time there was virtually no way for me to calm her down. That was when I realized just how terribly traumatic these gruesome revelations were to her.

Some time later that evening, and at a point when she seemed to finally be able to gain a vestige of her composure, I helped her upstairs to her bed and I tucked her in. Before I left her room, I explained to her that I had some things I had to work out in my mind, and that I would join her there shortly. I left her while feeling a sense of deep shame and remorse for what I had put her through.

I also felt like such a total fool for what I'd gotten myself, my wife, and my family into. All of it was for no other reason than that I was trying to protect Elaine from the unpleasant news of my first discovery, and that had escalated into a seething monster of lies and deception. The situation which I had unknowingly created had morphed into a classic study in the fact that a lie feeds upon itself. Well, it was much too late for me to cry about the many dumb and foolish mistakes I had made. I knew, without a single doubt in my mind, that I would just have to accept the repercussions whatever they might be.

Now that Bruno Stenn has begun to make phone calls to my home with his threats, I cannot visualize how I could possibly avoid any further involvement with the police. Then, just as I was about to reach for the phone to call the police to report Stenn's threats to

Elaine, I heard a loud commotion in the front hallway that sounded like the shattering of glass at the side door. Quickly jumping up from my chair, I raced toward that area of the house to investigate.

As I reached the doorway to the dining room, I saw him come bounding out of the back hall and he was clutching a rusty looking hatchet in his hand. It was Bruno Stenn, and his eyes were glaring with a fiery rage, with flecks of spittle dripping from the corners of his mouth. He looked to me more like a mad dog in the throes of a rabies attack rather than he did a man. As he stopped for a few seconds while he hatefully glared at me with the hatchet held high over his head, Stenn spoke, but it was more like the low growl of a wild beast than it was the sound of a human being.

"Where in hell is my God-damn ledger?" Stenn demanded of me in a loud and menacing voice. "I know it was you who stole it from my office tonight, and I won't leave here until I get it back! If you don't give it to back me, I'll kill you, you bastard, so help me!"

"What makes you think I was the one who took your book, Mr. Stenn?" Although I was filled with terror, I tried to appear unshaken by his loud and deadly threat.

You were the only one who knew that I was after it, and you must have discovered that I took it from your house. Now, either I get that ledger back from you right now or I'll split your wretched head open with this hatchet! He continued advancing slowly toward me the hatchet still poised over him ready to strike out at me.

Having now evolved into a state of visible terror, I started backing away from him, but at that precise moment, and from the corner of my eye, I saw Elaine's head appear near the top of the stairway. She'd apparently been awakened by the noise of the glass door breaking and by Stenn's loud shouting. I prayed that she'd regained enough of her wits to use the upstairs phone to call the police.

As I continued slowly backing away from Stenn, I saw that Elaine had disappeared from the upstairs hallway where I had last seen her. I prayed that she'd get to the bedroom phone and call the police. In the meantime, I would try to defuse this crazy man's raging anger while I delayed him long enough for the police to arrive.

"Why is that book so important to you, Mr. Stenn?" I asked as I tried to speak to him as respectfully, and as appeasing as possible. For a moment or two he stopped his advance toward me as he thought about what I had asked him. Then, as I continued slowly backing out of the room, he again began to pace me as he said, "It belongs to me, and I only want to get back from you what is mine!"

"But it has Sedgwick Burns' name on its cover." I said. "How can you think that it belongs to you?"

"I more than earned that book after all the years I worked like a damn dog for that man, I covered up for him, and I even committed hideous acts to please him. As my reward for my sacrifice and devotion to him, he turned on me like I wasn't even a person. He told me I would never possess his skills, and I would never be capable of doing the work I wanted to do. He said that I would never be anything more than a lowly errand boy who was meant to clean up his clutter after him. But I fixed him! Oh, brothers, did I ever fix him! Yes, I was finally able to prove to him just how great my skills were. Now, you had better give me my God-damn ledger or you will also die, you son-of-a-bitch!" As he bellowed, he made a fast lunge at me with the hatchet flailing wildly at my head.

Somehow, I was just able to duck from Stenn's vicious charge at me just in the nick of time, and was barely able to escape from his murderous attack. I prayed that Elaine wouldn't be foolish enough to come down those stairs and get in the middle of this nightmare because if she did, I would not be able to protect her. As it was, I was trying desperately to save myself from this raving maniac who seemed dead set to murder me.

I was finally able to run into the living room where I grabbed the first thing I could lay my hands on to try to defend myself. It was one of our floor lamps, and I used it like a pike pole to keep him away from me. Unexpectedly, Stenn made a vicious swing with the hatchet catching the shade on the lamp and it shredded into pieces. I tried to batter his face with the broken glass of the light bulbs which remained in the socket, but he easily pushed it aside with his hatchet.

The fury of our battle created a thunderous disturbance inside our house, and I guessed the sounds were being carried to the outside where I saw some of my neighbor's lights had gone on. I was beginning to lose my strength, but Stenn seemed to grow all the stronger as the rage he was directing at me increased. Finally, with a mighty swing of his hatchet, he knocked the lamp pole from my hands and I fell backward over the ottoman and onto the floor. He was standing over me in seconds, his eyes glaring with sheer rage and insanity. As I watched helplessly, he lifted the hatchet to deliver the deadly blow to my head. Suddenly, and without any warning, a heavy vase came crashing down upon his head, showering his face and arms with hundreds of shards of broken glass. Stenn's limp body fell heavily across mine, and we both laid there on the floor in a pile of broken glass and splinters.

When someone lifted Stenn's unconscious body from on top of me, I was just able to slowly get to my feet. I then saw who it was who came to my rescue and save my life the last second before I would have lost it. My rescuer was my nosey neighbor Dave Farrell! I immediately embraced him in a big bear hug while I became overcome with a feeling of gratitude to him from the very bottom of my heart, I was also feeling terribly ashamed that I had so often spoken badly of him because he was always poking around for news. I then vowed that I would never feel that was about him, or criticize him again for merely being nosey. In fact, I was grateful that he was nosey enough to be concerned about what was going on inside my house because and as a result of it he saved my life.

"Who in the heck is that madman lying there on the floor who was trying to kill you, Rick? If I'd gotten here just one second later, you'd be lying there dead on the floor with your brains spilling out on the carpet!" Dave said excitedly as he steered me over to the couch and sat me down.

"God! Dave! How can I ever begin to thank you for coming to my rescue like you did? Do you recognize that man lying there?" I asked as I pointed at Stenn's prostrate body. I was now feeling deep and extreme exhaustion as I turned my eyes away from Stenn.

"Am I supposed to know him?" Dave asked in a bewildered voice as he looked closer at the face of the unconscious man lying on the floor.

"That man is Bruno Stenn," I said loudly just as Elaine came into the room. She was in a terrible state of fright and turmoil, and when she saw Stenn lying on the floor, her eyes opened wide in amazement.

"Are you all right Rick?" Elaine quickly asked as she saw me sitting there with Dave Farrell standing next to me. "I was so terribly frightened when I saw that man with the hatchet in his hand, and he was threatening you with it. How were you able to defend yourself?" As she spoke, she turned and looked at Dave and said, "Of, course, it was you, Dave! It had to be you because Rick didn't have any kind of a weapon to use to stop him. Thank you from the bottom of my heart for saving my husband's life. How can we ever thank you enough for what you've done for us?" She then ran to Dave and wrapped her arms around his neck in an expression of profound appreciation.

"Did you call the police as I had asked you to do, Elaine?"

"Yes I called them from the bedroom phone, and they said they would get here immediately."

"Well, if we had waited for them to arrive to help me, I'd be dead now," I said wistfully. "I am thankful that Dave must have heard all the commotion here and came over to our house to investigate what was happening here." There just were no words for me to express how I now felt about my next door neighbor Dave Farrell.

"It is Bruno Stenn!" Dave said in a shocked voice. "Why was he going after you with that hatchet while trying to kill you? Rick?"

"It's a very long story, Dave, and I'll tell you all about it sometime, but not tonight! There's still too much excitement going on now for me to even be able to think straight. I am now thinking that we had better keep a tight eye on Stenn to make certain he doesn't wake up and go completely crazy again, I said as I got up from the couch and walked over to where Stenn was lying sprawled on the floor. Reaching down close to him, I removed the hatchet from his limp hand and I carried it to a nearby coffee table where I laid it until the police could take it away. I assumed it was the murder weapon he had used on Sedgwick Burns, and that would be a piece of evidence they would be needing at Stenn's murder trial."

I had just returned to my seat on the couch when I heard the scream of police car sirens. In a few seconds they were in our driveway, and we could see the blue lights flashing through the translucent window shades. Seconds later, we heard a number of car doors slamming, and then the sounds of running feet, as they came bursting into the house. There were three officers followed by two more. All five of them had their revolvers drawn as they began looking around in all directions.

"Where's he at?" An officer shouted to us.

Elaine pointed at Stenn lying on the floor and said "that's him."

"Is that the man who attacked your husband?" An officer asked Elaine.

"Yes, that's the man lying there unconscious on the floor!"

As the first officer kneeled down next to Stenn to feel his pulse, he turned Stenn over on his back and then snapped a pair of handcuffs on the still unconscious man's wrists. Turning to Dave and me, he asked, "Which of you Gentlemen is the lady's husband?" His eyes quickly switched from Dave to me while awaiting an answer.

"I am her husband," I said in a low voice while being almost sure that those words would end up implicating me in some very serious trouble.

"Is he alone, or is there an accomplice still somewhere in your house?" This time he looked directly at me when he asked his question.

"I am certain he was alone," I answered. When I said that, the officer turned to the other officers who were standing in the room, and he instructed them to go through the house anyway, just to make sure there was no one else hiding inside. He then turned his attention back to me.

"Are you able to tell us what happened here tonight, Mr. Braden? I'm sorry, do I have your name right?"

"Yes that is correct, Officer. My name is Rick Braden, and this is my home." Pointing my finger toward Elaine, "and that lady is my wife Elaine. She is the one who called you on the phone."

"Now, may I ask who this gentleman is?" the officer asked as he turned his gaze toward Dave.

Before Dave could respond to the officer's question, I spoke out, "He's our neighbor from the house next door. His name is Dave Farrell, and he's the man who saved my life tonight." I then turned toward Dave with a grateful look.

Okay, the officer said as he continued to jot down in his notebook all that I told him. "I'll be needing statements from all three of you before we leave, so please wait around for a while, Mr. Farrell." At that moment he was joined by two of the other officers who reported that they had searched the house from the cellar to the attic.

"The house is completely empty," the officer loudly said as he kneeled down to look at Stenn's face. "We'd better call for an ambulance, Pat. This guy's out like a light, and I don't think we should attempt to transport him from here by squad car." He then showed another officer the area on Stenn's head where a trickle of blood was oozing from under his hairline. "I think he may have a brain concussion, so we had better just wait for the paramedics to arrive before he can be moved."

Elaine, Dave, and I, along with two of the police officers, gathered around the dining room table while we were required to give full statements to the officer. Those statements concerned every single detail of the disturbing events that had occurred in my house tonight. Since Dave came into the picture only at the last minute, he was questioned first. Dave told the officers about hearing the sound of the glass door breaking, the loud hollering, and then the sound of things being smashed inside my house. He said he knew it wasn't a domestic argument because we were a lovely couple who never even raised our voices.

Dave further recalled that when he got to the side door of the house he heard me being bodily threatened by a man, and that was when he came inside to see what was happening. When he saw that I was about to have my head split open with a hatchet by Stenn, he hit the man on the head with a heavy vase to stop his attack. He knew it was something he felt he had to do to stop the assailant from killing me with the hatchet which he had raised above my head. When the officer asked him if he knew the man who had attacked me and who was now lying unconscious on the parlor floor, Dave told him that he recognized him, and that he believed his name was Bruno Stenn.

The minute he mentioned Stenn's name, the officer who was doing the questioning turned to his associates and said, "This is the guy we've got the all-points bulletin out on. He's that funeral director they want for questioning about a homicide. We had better keep a close watch on that mug until the paramedics get here. If they don't decide to take him to the hospital emergency room, we'll have them take him from here to the County Jail's infirmary."

It wasn't but a few minutes later when an ambulance came screeching into our driveway, sirens blaring and red lights flashing. Two men in white jackets and trousers came quickly into the house, and after a cursory examination of Stenn, they lifted him from the floor and onto a canvas stretcher. After another hurried conversation with the policeman called Pat, they removed Stenn from the house and loaded him into their ambulance. Then, just as quickly as the ambulance had arrived, it left for the hospital.

When Officer Pat was finished questioning Dave Farrell, he told him Dave he was free to leave, but he should expect to hear from someone from the Police Department sometime tomorrow. As Dave prepared to leave our house, I shook Dave's hand and gave him a bear-hug, while I again thanked him for saving my life. Walking along with him to the side door, our shoes crunched loudly on the broken glass from the door that had been shattered for the second time. "Good night Dave," I called as I watched him walk away in the semi-darkness heading toward his house next door.

Although it was quite late in the evening, there was a small group of people standing on the sidewalk in front of our house. They were looking at the police cars and at our house while they talked in whispers and stood around in their night clothes. Just as Dave got to our gate, several of them came up to him in an attempt to engage him in conversation, but Dave just ignored them and he continued walking toward his home.

Before I returned to my house, I noticed that there were flashes of lightening in the dark sky to the west. "It looks like we will be having some rain before morning," I mused. "Oh well, my grass can certainly use a good soaking." As I stood there in the semi-darkness, I prayed that would never see another day like this one had been, and I shuddered as I realized that I had a lot of rough days that were still facing me.

It was much later, or earlier, depending on which side of midnight I'm talking about, when the last of the police officers left our property. Elaine and I had finally completed our statements relating to the events of that evening, and I had told them only what had occurred from the time I arrived at home in the evening until they showed up on the scene. In any event, I figured that the authorities would want to talk to me again before very long.

I felt tired to the bone and very weary. The experience I had been through had drained almost everything from my mind and my body, and I had a hard time falling asleep after Elaine and I went to bed. I couldn't believe that I had dug such a deep hole for myself, and in such a short period of time! Just before I finally was able to fall asleep, I thought about Blake Cranshaw, and I wondered what his reaction would be tomorrow when he would hear about what had happened. I felt that with everything else for me to think about, I was in no hurry to that find out.

~ *Chapter Twenty-One* ~

THE FINAL PIECES OF THE PUZZLE

It seemed to me as though I had barely nodded off to sleep when I heard the loud hammering of my alarm clock signaling that it was time for me to wake up and get ready for work. I was so fatigued I could barely reach my arm across the bed to push the button on the alarm clock to turn it off. As I continued lying there in my bed, my mind was a clutter of confusion from a variety of tormented dreams, and I could not seem to orient myself to exactly where I was. Slowly I began drifting back to sleep, but just before that happened I made a glance at the alarm clock. It was seven o'clock, and if I planned on going to my office today, I knew I had better get out of my bed and get a move on. As nearly as I could determine in my disoriented state, I had only about an hour or two of sleep since I had fallen into my bed. It was going to be a miserable day for me while trying hard keep myself awake, and also trying to keep my mind on business.

Swinging my legs out from under the covers, I sat on the edge of my bed while I widely stretched my arms and yawned loudly. After rubbing the cobwebs of sleep from my eyes, I went into the bathroom, stripped my pajamas off and then climbed into the shower. While I stood there under the warm water and lathered myself, I thought about the disturbing events of the previous evening, and I wondered how long it would be before I would be expected to answer for my criminal actions and my many stupid errors in judgment. Until those things happen, all I could do is to go on with my life one day at a time while I try to deal with any new disturbing developments. The thought of how all the recent trauma would ultimately affect Elaine, Ron, and Glenn, was uppermost in my mind, and as for how it would affect me, I knew that I would have to stand up and face the consequences, whatever they may be.

Having gulped down a quick cup of bitter tasting instant coffee, I quickly scribbled a note for Elaine and left it on the kitchen table. It said that I had already left for my office, and I would call her sometime later that afternoon when I find a free moment.

As I walked out of my side door I stepped onto some pieces of glass from the broken window, and I immediately became aware of how quiet it was outside. It was in stark contrast to the chaos and excitement of the previous night. There were no longer spectators loitering on the front walk, and my driveway was clear of police cars. It was just as if none of it had ever happened, as though it had only been a crazy dream of mine.

While I backed my car out of the driveway and into the street, I thought about Dave Farrell, and I quickly glanced over at his bedroom window. What a guy! It took a heck of a lot of guts for Dave to have taken the immediate action that was required of him to stop Stenn from murdering me. If he was a different kind of a man without the courage to act as he did, I might not be leaving my house for work this morning. At that moment, I felt another sharp surge of guilt for the way I had often maligned him for being nosey. I then thought that I would have to do something, like deliver him a case of his favorite beer; that might do for a start. But, on second thought, my doing that could get me in hot water with Shirley because she has been telling Elaine that Dave's drinking is getting totally out of hand. I could talk to Elaine about it later, and maybe she will have some good ideas about it.

This workday morning turned out to be rather busy for me at my office, for which I was feeling grateful. A few essential things had piled up while I was gone, so I charged right into them which helped to turn my mind away from my other troubles. At my morning coffee break, several of my coworkers wanted to talk to me about the article they had read in the morning newspaper detailing the attack on me at my house the previous night. Since I had not bothered buying a morning paper, that news coverage came as a surprise to me. Anyway, I was in no mood to discuss any of those disturbing events with them. When I said I would have to tell them all about it at a later time, it was apparent to me they were disappointed. At my noontime lunch break, I made a beeline to the newspaper stand at the corner and pumped a quarter into the slot. As I pulled the paper from the box, my eyes immediately caught a large banner headline:

SEDGWICK BURNS FOUND MURDERED IN MORTUARY

~Forest Oak, September 29 1998~

The dead and mutilated body of Sedgwick Burns, respected businessman and longtime resident of Forest Oak, was discovered late last night in the back room of Stenn's Mortuary, located on Franklin Street. The police received a tip about the body from an anonymous telephone caller who directed them to the mortuary. Mr. Burns had disappeared more than eight years ago and it had been revealed that he had incurred massive gambling debts which had been his reason for leaving town.

It now appears that the owner of the establishment where the body was found, Bruno V. Stenn, had been an employee of the Burns Funeral Home until the time of Burns' disappearance. Stenn's Mortuary had previously been known as Burns Funeral Home until it was purchased by Stenn sometime earlier. At this time, Mr. Stenn is the prime suspect in Burns' death, although no motive for the killing has yet been established.

~ ~ ~

When I finished reading that newspaper report, my eyes then focused on another front page article which read:

LOCAL FOREST OAK RESIDENT ATTACKED BY HOME INVADER ~Forest Oak September 29 1998~

Homeowner Rick Braden, a recent home buyer in Forest Oak, was brutally attacked in his home on Cobblestone Lane last evening by a man wielding a hatchet. The assailant, Bruno V. Stenn, 65, had earlier been sought by the police as a suspect in the brutal slaying of Sedgwick Burns, the man whose mutilated body was discovered earlier in the evening lying on a back room table in Stenn's mortuary.

Mr. Braden, although badly shaken by his experience, wasn't injured. A neighbor, David T. Farrell, came to his aid and was able to subdue the assailant and then hold Stenn until the police arrived to arrest him.

Mr. Stenn, who was seriously injured in the melee, was immediately taken by the police to the County Hospital where he is presently undergoing observation and treatment. At this time there has been no further word from the hospital about his condition.

Details about the reason for the attack are not yet available, said Police Detective Patrick Reilly, who is the officer in charge of the investigation.

~ ~ ~

Shortly after returning to my office from my break, my telephone began to ring. The calls were from local newspaper reporters who were asking me about what had happened. Apparently, they already talked to Dave Farrell, who had given them his version of the story, and they now wanted to talk to me. Of those reporters who called my office, they all asked me two questions in common, why did that man come to your home and attack you, and did that attack on you have anything to do with the murder of Sedgwick Burns? I told all the callers the same thing, I cannot talk about to you about any of it until I first discuss it with my lawyer. I also said that at this time it was strictly a matter for the Police Department. Their calls to my office finally became so annoying to me that I asked our switchboard operator to stop putting any outside calls through to my office phone.

At about three o'clock that same afternoon, I found the time to make my telephone call to Elaine. When she answered the phone, she sounded extremely irritable.

"Those blasted reporters have been hanging around here all day, Rick. I can't get a thing accomplished with them harassing me. I had to tape a piece of cardboard over that broken glass in the side door because they were trying to come into the house through there! I have the place locked up tight now, but that doesn't seem to dampen their determination to talk to me. It's a regular zoo around here! Another thing, there's a crowd of spectators hanging around the front of our house, and I can't imagine why they're there. It isn't as though there's anything for them to see."

"I have a good idea of what you're going through, Elaine. My office phone has not stopped ringing all morning. By the way, have you seen this morning newspaper yet?"

"Yes, I have read it, Rick, Shirley Farrell brought one over with her. She's here now while keeping me company until you get home. She told me the reporters cornered Dave in their driveway this morning as he was leaving for work. Dave gave them a brief description of what went on here last night, but then he had to leave. Oh, Rick, will this horrible nightmare ever end for us? I just don't know what we're going to do."

"I am sorry, Elaine, I do not know the answer to that question. I suppose I will have to meet with someone in the District Attorney's office before it's all done and over with. Dave Farrell and I have already given our initial statements to the police about what happened at our house last night, but we have to remember that I am also deeply involved in a murder investigation. That is not something that will simply blow over, so we will have to be prepared for the worst of it that's still to come. Now, have you heard anything from Ron or Glenn this morning?"

"Yes, Ron was the first to call me very early this morning. He'd heard the news on the radio, and he was very upset about it. He called because he wanted to ask if we were both okay. I told him that it had been a terrible ordeal, especially for you, but that we were both doing fine now. He wanted to come right over to the house, but I told him that it would be better for him to go to work today. He then said that he and Paula and Henry would stop by our house sometime this evening to visit with us. I asked him not to bother, but he insisted. I had no sooner finished my conversation with Ron and hung up the phone when Glenn called. It was the same story from him, except he'd read about it in the morning newspaper. He said that he and Martha will be at our house tonight to see how we're making out. I told Glenn that should be okay. I hope their visit won't interfere with anything you may have already planned, Rick."

"Their visits should be okay, Elaine, as a matter of fact, it will give me an opportunity to tell the boys exactly what happened, rather than have them speculate about it by listening to it on the radio and reading the newspaper reports. It will also allow me to tell them how important it is for them to keep quiet about their involvement with the removal of those old coffins from our garage loft. I do not want them involved in any aspect of it, Elaine, so be extremely careful what you might say to anyone, especially to Shirley and Dave Farrell, and also those pushy newspaper reporters." My tone was solemn and very firm, and I added, "I am probably in enough trouble as it is without someone creating additional problems for me. It is not that I am not grateful to Dave Farrell for what he did last night, but we still have to be realistic, Elaine."

"But, Rick, I haven't said a word to the reporters, and as for Shirley, all we talked about was what had happened in this house last night. If you could only see her, Rick. She's so proud of Dave for what he did that she can hardly stand it. It wasn't that long ago that she was talking to me about leaving him, and now he's a big hero to her. At least something good is coming out of it."

"Well, that is something I suppose, but I still have a lot of questions I will have to answer for to the authorities, and I still do not have the foggiest idea of how I am going to handle those questions that they will be putting to me."

"Rick, you still haven't told me about what happened to you and Blake Cranshaw's last night, or don't you intend to tell me about it?" She seemed not only curious but quite agitated when she asked me that question.

"You will get the unabridged details from me after I get home this evening. I am sorry, Elaine, but I have to go now. Please try to remain calm, and whatever you do, do not talk to those reporters. If any one of them unduly pressures you, call the police to have him removed from our property. Goodbye, Honey."

"Goodbye, Rick. I'll be seeing you when you get home, and please be careful."

After I hung up the phone with Elaine, I looked at the wall clock and saw that it was 3:45 P.M. I still had time to call Blake Cranshaw to find out how he was handling the situation. I dialed his number, and within a minute his receptionist answered the phone and put my call straight to Blake in his office.

"Good afternoon, Blake Cranshaw speaking, how may I help you?" Blake answered in a pleasant and unexpectedly calm voice. "Hello, Blake, Have you heard the news yet?"

"Are you kidding me?" Blake shot back at me. "That's all I've heard on the radio or read about in the newspapers all morning. What in the heck happened last night anyway? I was going to wait to call you at home this evening and ask you all about it."

"You should have read all about it in those articles in the newspaper!" I said, "Stenn attacked me with a hatchet right inside of my living room, and can you guess what it was he was after?"

"My guess is that it had to be that diary that we took from his office, but how in the world did he know that it was you who'd taken it?"

"Well, just before Stenn attacked me, he told me that no one else knew he had it, and since it was stolen by him from my house and I had visited him shortly before that, he had to put two and two together. His deductions were similar to mine when that book was taken from my house by him in the burglary. Not to change the subject, Blake, but has anyone contacted you yet about Burns?"

"Yeah, several newspaper reporters called me the first thing this morning. They were wanting some background information about Sedgwick Burns and our business dealings years ago in the funeral business. I brushed them off because I didn't want to say anything to them. They're nothing more than a pack of hounds, and they can only make trouble for us. Now tell me about what happened to you."

It took me about twenty minutes to tell Blake all that had occurred at my house after I had returned home last evening. Once he was satisfied that he knew everything that had transpired, we discussed our situation as it related to our involvement in the case, and what we might expect from the authorities. Blake was in favor of the two of us going to the District Attorney's office, and telling him all that we knew about the case, and then just let the chips fall where they may. I also felt that was now the smartest thing for us to do, so the two of us agreed to meet at the District Attorney's office at six o'clock. Blake told me he would make the call and set up the appointment for us. Before doing that, however, he would call his wife and fill her in on all that had occurred up to this point.

I was shocked at his last statement, and I lashed out at him. "Do you mean to tell me that your wife has not been told anything at all about what has been going on? I thought that I had a good reason for not telling Elaine about it because of her sensitivity problem, but eventually it all came out in the wash. What could possible be your reason to withhold that information from your wife, Blake?"

"Well, I know I never discussed it with you, Rick, but my wife and I are not exactly on the best of terms, we haven't been for several years. Due to a few of my past, shall I say indiscretions, she's been looking for any excuse to begin a divorce action against me. I didn't tell her anything because I didn't feel it was the smart thing to do to give her any more ammunition to use in a divorce settlement. Do you get the picture?"

"I.... I'm sorry Blake," I stammered, "I never had any idea about any of that and I did not intend to pry into your personal life."

"Don't let it bother you, Rick. The most important thing we both have to do now is to keep our wits about us and try to work our way out of the difficult situation the two of us are now facing."

Hanging up the phone after we said our goodbyes, I again called Elaine and I told her what Blake and I had decided. She still sounded upset and agitated, but she said she realized that difficult decision had to be made. When our upsetting conversation ended, I sat for a long time and fretted over my seemingly hopeless situation. One thing was for certain, I had no one to blame for my foolish and reckless behavior other than myself. For perhaps the hundredth time, I silently cursed myself for having agreed with Elaine to buy what had turned out to be a house right out of the very pits of Hell.

~ *Chapter Twenty-Two* ~

CLOSING THE CASE

At 5:45 P.M., I grabbed my briefcase from my desk, walked out of the door of my office, and then headed straight for my car in the parking lot. While sliding behind the steering wheel, I casually glanced into the back seat of the car and I saw the diary which we had stolen back from Bruno Stenn's mortuary laying there. I suddenly remembered that Blake had left it there after he had glanced through it, and then he must have forgotten to take it with him. Reaching for the book, I placed it on the passenger's seat next to me so I would remember to bring it with me to the district attorney's office.

Upon arriving at the Municipal building, I parked my car in the visitor's lot, retrieved the book, and then walked briskly toward the front entrance door of the building. Before I reached the door, I noticed Blake's Cadillac limousine parked in a slot next to the building; apparently he had already arrived for our meeting.

Reaching the office of the District Attorney, I took notice of the name on the glass entry door which read Elmer P. McDonald. I wondered if he would be the man Blake and I would be talking to, or if it would be one of his assistants. As it developed, we ended up being assigned to an Assistant District Attorney by the name of

Woodward Burrows. When I entered his office, I saw that Blake was already seated in a chair in front of Burrows' desk. Once the formalities were exchanged, I laid the diary on his desk, and I told Burrows it was something he would probably be in need of in the course of our inquiry.

Woodward Burrows was a large framed, silver-haired and ruddy-faced man with a friendly air and a broad winning smile, and I have to say that his appearance had the immediate effect of making me feel calm and comfortable. When Burrows shook my hand as he greeted me, I detected an Irish, or perhaps it was a Scottish accent. Before the three of us began our talk, Burrows asked if either of us would care for a cup of coffee, which we both politely declined. He slowly poured a cup for himself from a carafe with empty cups that was set up on a small table next to his desk. When he had taken a sip of his coffee, Burrows leaned back in his swivel chair and hesitated for a moment while he turned his attention to look first at Blake and then at me before he spoke.

"I certainly know who you are Mr. Braden. You're the man who was attacked last night in your home by Bruno Stenn. Is that correct?" He continued looking intently at me for my answer.

"That is correct, Mr. Burrows," I answered softly.

His attention was then directed to Blake as he said, "You, Mr. Cranshaw, were at one time the late Sedgwick Burns' partner in the Burns Funeral Home. Am I correct on that score?"

"That's also correct, Sir," Blake responded.

"Now, Gentlemen, I want to confirm that your presence here, each of you, is of your own choosing, and you had not been coerced to appear here by anyone from this office. Is that correct?" "Yes, Sir," I said. I was now beginning to feel it necessary for me to be cautious about any further answers I might give to Burrows.

"I initiated the telephone call to your office, Mr. Burrows," Blake quickly answered. "I did that after Mr. Braden, and I decided it was the right thing for us to do, so my answer to your last question which you had directed to me is another yes."

"Do both of you gentlemen understand that you are entitled to be represented by legal counsel before you begin to talk to me?" Burrows paused for a few seconds to hear our answers

"We both understand that" I said as I looked at Blake for his concurrence. "Having a lawyer was something we had discussed on the phone, but we decided to forgo hiring one. We thought we would take our chances and hope to escape any criminal repercussions for our actions, if we presented those activities as irresponsible, rather than as illegal or criminal behavior. Perhaps we are both being foolhardy, but here we both are talking to you, and without the benefit of any legal counsel."

"Then, gentlemen," Burrows stated, "do you both understand that anything that you may say to me here will be duly recorded and can be used against you in a court of law if it comes down to that?"

"Yes, we both understand that." Blake and I answered the question almost in unison.

"All right, then, Gentlemen, I'm now going to call in a stenographer who will take down your statements as we talk. Are you both ready for me to do that or do you have any thing you might want to ask me first?"

Both Blake and I answered him in the affirmative.

When the male stenographer took a seat and started adjusting his stenotype machine, Burrows wasted no time in asking us a barrage of questions. After we both gave our names, addresses and our present occupations, he asked a few things about our families, and then he got into the heart of the matter, the reason we both were there to talk to him.

Between Blake and me, we told him everything, from the time I had first discovered the cartons of embalming fluid in my cellar, right up to the attack on me in my home by Stenn. I made sure to emphasize my fear and grave concern for my wife's fragile mental state at the time we did those things.

During the time we all sat there talking, almost three hours had passed, but it took that much time to complete the interviews. Burrows intently listened as he watched the two of us carefully. The stenographer tapped away at his machine while recording every word in the room that was spoken. Occasionally, Burrows would ask us a question to clarify a point; other than that, he sat in his chair as he watched our eyes and mostly listened. When we finished relating everything that we could possibly remember, he sat for a time in his chair while he contemplated his response to us. When we had finished with the interviews, Blake and I told Burrows we hoped we had not done anything much more than having used very poor judgement, and that we were hoping for vindication from any really serious infractions of the law that could cause us to be prosecuted.

After a short period of time had passed, we were informed by Burrows, that if the murder case against Bruno Stenn came to trial, he would be the one who would be prosecuting the case. As it looked at the moment, his office expected to present the evidence for Sedgwick Burn's murder to the grand jury in a few days, and they were waiting to secure an indictment against Bruno Stenn on first degree murder charges. Since Stenn had not yet been officially charged with a crime, no legal proceedings could be started. Meanwhile, the police were testing the hatchet that he had threatened me with because it was believed to be the same weapon that Stenn used to murder Burns.

I asked Mr. Burrows if Stenn was still in the hospital with a fracture to his skull. He said he was, and that he could not predict when he would be transferred from the County Hospital to the Central Jail's hospital building where he could continue his medical treatment.

With some hesitancy, Blake asked Burrows what we might expect to happen to us. Burrows said that we had, indeed, broken the laws, some of them quite serious. He then said if we both continued to cooperate with his office, it might work out all right for the two of us. With that said, he smiled and told us to stick around town since they may be needing both of our testimonies at the criminal hearing for Stenn.

With the first of our ordeals over for the time being, Blake and I left Burrows' office, both of us feeling like a million pounds had been lifted off our shoulders. Even though we were not home free, so to speak, we felt that what Burrows had said to us gave us some reason to hope for the best. When we reached the parking lot, we said our farewells and agreed not to contact each other until we were called to testify at the criminal proceeding. We would do that unless something of significant importance came up before that event which required us to meet with Burrows in is office again.

When I arrived at my home, I saw both Glenn's car and Ron's car parked in our driveway, and the minute I walked into the house they were all over me with their questions. I had to repeat a lot of what I had earlier said to Burrows, along with what his responses were to me. When I told them that Burrows said to me and Blake Cranshaw that there was a good possibility of our avoiding any serious criminal charges, they were ecstatic. Usually, I am not much of a drinking man, but that news called for something a lot stronger than coffee for me. I went to the kitchen where I located a bottle of gin I had stored in a base cabinet for special occasions, and I proceeded to mix myself a stiff martini. "Tonight," I said to everyone, "I am going to forget all of my troubles and woes and try to have a good time for a change. Does anyone care to join in with me for a martini," I asked? No one declined my offer.

It was a week later when I received a telephone call from Mr. Burrows' office, and I was asked if I could meet him in his office that same afternoon at two o'clock. I also was told that Blake Cranshaw had already been notified and that he would be there to attend the meeting with me. Burrows also told me that there had been some rather startling developments in the case that could possibly have an effect on the two of us. Hearing that, I immediately became downhearted, and my voice quickly betrayed that downhearted feelings to Burrows. He quickly responded that the investigation was going well and that the new evidence should not especially complicate anything that he had said to Blake and me about our legal situation, but there were some important points that still required clarification from the two of us.

At 1:45 in the afternoon on Tuesday, I walked into Burrows' office, and I took a seat in front of his desk. Shortly after that, Blake Cranshaw entered the room and he occupied a chair next to mine. After finishing with the pleasantries, Burrows got right down to business with the two us.

Most of the information he told us about relating to Burns' disappearance Blake, and I had already figured out some time back. That included the fact that Burns had been hiding out for several years in California with his grandnephew Clayton Matthews. The reason he had left Forest Oak so quickly was that the men he owed gambling debts to were closing in on him. That essentially substantiated what Blake had already guessed, but then Burrows dropped a bombshell on us! Stenn was not going to trial because he had already signed a full confession for the hatchet murder of Sedgwick Burns. Both Blake and I were overwhelmed with relief when we heard that bit of good news because that meant neither one of us would have to testify at a trial. To verify my thinking on that score, I asked Burrows that meant that neither of us will have to testify?

"It looks that way, Burrows said cautiously, but we'll still require your complete cooperation to clear up any remaining questions that might arise."

"Looking toward Blake," Burrows said, "As for those five remaining dead bodies you're holding in that storage room in your funeral home, Mr. Cranshaw, I strongly suggest you immediately get all of them back to where they belong, and I don't mean back into Mr. Braden's garage loft. Each body is to be replaced and properly sealed by you in its mausoleum after the surviving families have been adequately notified. Now, I know Mr. Cranshaw that may eventually cause you some public relations difficulties--as you had indicated to me earlier, but taking care of that is entirely your responsibility. If you do that in a prompt and dignified manner, you'll hear no more about it from this office."

He then turned his attention to me, and with an intense look, he said, "Mr. Braden, I am afraid I have some very bad news for you." After hearing that, my heart nearly dropped from out of my chest, and fear gripped my throat. I could already see myself looking out from behind the steel bars of a prison cell. Before I could ask him what the bad news was, he spoke to me again.

"The last time you and Mr. Cranshaw were here in my office you both told me every single detail of what had transpired, right up until that very first moment you were sitting before my desk, is that correct?"

I could not even begin to imagine what he was driving at asking me that, and the tension continued to mount in me.

"That seems to be correct, Mr. Burrows," I said. Beads of cold sweat were beginning to form on my brow, and my throat started to further tighten up. I kept trying to review in my mind what we had talked about at our last meeting that I may have missed telling him about, but I could not remember leaving out a single detail. What could he possibly have found out that I had not already said to him? I was sitting there in my chair feeling thoroughly confused and dumbfounded.

After a few seconds of delay, Burrows continued on reviewing what I had earlier said to him.

"During our initial conference, you told me how all of your difficulties had started when you first discovered those cartons containing gallon bottles of embalming chemicals stacked in your cellar. You said that you disposed of those items to shield your wife from the fact that Burns may have performed some of his embalming procedures inside the house. Then you told me that your wife was extremely squeamish about those kinds of things and that she would not want to live in the house if she ever found out about those macabre discoveries."

I merely continued looking straight ahead at him almost like in a trance, and completely bewildered at whatever his reasons might be for reviewing my previous answers. Before he spoke again, his expression became even more severe, and I had finally reached a point where I just wished he would get whatever it was all about finished and done with. As it was, he was torturing me with this rehash of what was said at our meeting last week.

"Then, Mr. Braden, I would strongly suggest that you and your wife make arrangements immediately to find another house to live in. In fact, it is my strongest recommendation that you arrange to move from that place you are living in just as early as possible, perhaps even as soon as tomorrow morning."

When he delivered that statement, its effect was like a sledgehammer thundering in my ears. "Will you please explain that to me, Sir?" I said in a feeble and shaky voice.

"I will, Mr. Braden, but I suggest you take a tight hold on both arms of your chair before I do. When Bruno Stenn confessed to the murder of Sedgwick Burns, he also admitted to his having committed a multitude of other heinous and despicable crimes along with Sedgwick Burns. Those crimes included grave robbing and body mutilation, and most of these acts occurred before Burns had left the state and disappeared, and at the time he was still living in his house on Cobblestone Lane, the house your wife and you own and are now occupying.

"In Stenn's statement to us, he told us how the two of them dissected dead bodies in a secret room located somewhere in your attic, and he described how they buried the body parts at different locations, both in and around Forest Oak, including in your backyard. According to what we learned from him, there could be as many as twenty corpses and parts of bodies buried there under your flower gardens. Stenn told us the reason for what they had done was Burns' insatiable desire to perfect his reconstructive body procedures. Apparently, he had visions of one day being able to apply his techniques to living tissue, and they were close to trying that experiment when Burns was forced to leave town in a big hurry. That occurred almost nine years ago when he began receiving death threats over his unpaid gambling debts.

"When Bruno Stenn killed Sedgwick Burns, it was sometime after Burns returned here from his hideout in California, and they decided to begin those same kinds of experiments again. This time it would be with live people rather than using dead bodies they had dug up from graveyards, including Oak Hill Cemetery. Many of the dead bodies that they had more recently used were those patients they planned to procure bodies to test the book's detailed procedure, and Stenn had taken bodies from his funeral home to use for this purpose. Apparently, many of the caskets that were buried did not contain bodies at all but were mostly failed experiments that Burns and Stenn had conducted. The original bodies in those particular coffins had been replaced with sandbags before the caskets were sealed in the ground just before burial." It just happened that his last victim was his mentor, Sedgwick Burns. It is a story with an actual irony, when through his selfishness and cruelty, Burns had created his personal assassin--Bruno Stenn.

"Sedgwick Burns and Bruno Stenn both was nothing more than a couple of fiendish ghouls and monsters, and if they didn't have a falling out that caused Burns murder, it is entirely possible they would have begun their plan to kidnap people to supply their demand for experimental subjects. At least, that is what was told to us when we talked to Stenn.

"Within a couple of days, we will have crews of men who will begin digging up your lawn and your garden and unearthing the bodies and body parts that are buried there, Mr. Braden, and as I said, I think it would be a lot better if you and your wife leave that house before that gruesome process begins."

I had all but lapsed into a state of total shock over Burrows revelations, and I looked at Blake who appeared to be just as stunned as I was. Before I could collect my senses, Blake turned to Burrows and asked, "What did Stenn tell you had been their purpose for hiding those six coffins in Rick's garage loft?"

"Stenn told us that it was Burns' doing, and that all he did was help to bring them into the house from their crypts in Oak Hill Cemetery. He said that Burns wanted to carefully study the reconstruction that his father had performed on those bodies. He also felt that those individuals were the best work his father had ever done and that the cadavers should have been enshrined." Now the big question I'd like to ask of you Mr. Burrows, what was Stenn's reason for killing Burns?" Blake asked.

Blake and I both looked intently at Burrows to see what his answer to that question might be.

"Stenn claimed that Burns had made promises to him for many years that he would teach him the art of body reconstruction. Stenn had been allowed to do most of the preliminary work on the bodies, but when it came to the complex finishing touches, Burns always insisted on doing that himself without allowing Stenn to even be present in the room. Stenn said he had been put off one time too many by Burns, and in a fit of uncontrollable rage, he split his skull with a hatchet.

"Stenn said that Burns had only recently confided to him about the diary which his father had written, giving incredibly detailed instructions for his reconstruction procedures, and as long as Burns was in the picture he knew he would never have an opportunity to attempt any of the reconstructions by himself. He said that as long as he and Burns working together, he had pressing need to get the book, but after he had killed Burns he had a consuming compulsion to get his hands on it. That is why he broke into Mr. Braden's house to steal it, and the irony of it was that his very first patient for the book's detailed procedure just happened to be his victim and his mentor, Sedgwick Burns. It is a story with an actual irony, when through his selfishness and cruelty, Burns had created his personal assassin--Bruno Stenn.

"We do not believe that Stenn will ever spend time in prison for his crimes," Burrows said. "The man is apparently as mad as hell, and he will no doubt live out his remaining years at the State Asylum for the Criminally Insane in Unionville."

"Why is it that no one had ever reported any of that activity to the authorities?" Blake asked. "I'm talking about Burns digging up his backyard and planting all those corpses there? It seems almost inconceivable to me that he could have done that without being observed by one of his neighbors. From what Rick's told me, he has a nosey neighbor who sees and hears everything. How did these things possibly escape his notice?"

We both looked intently at Burrows while anticipating his response.

"Well, the police did receive a call about someone digging in the garden very late one night. That report was made a year or so before Burns' disappeared and began hiding in California, but they dismissed it as a crank call. It seems it happened sometime late in October, and it was thought to be nothing more than a Halloween prank phoned in by some neighborhood kids."

"Oh, then it seems that Dave Farrell did report it," I remarked.

"No, it wasn't that name you're saying," Burrows answered. He then quickly skimmed through a sheaf of papers on his desk and after locating what he was after he looked up at us and said, "The police report said the caller's name was Bates, Hector Bates."

"That would be my neighbor to the north," I said. "Now that I think about it, my large flower garden area is viewable only from Bate's house, and not even Dave Farrell has a view of that area. Hector Bates is the only neighbor who was able to see what was going on there, and since he has very poor eyesight, and he also wears a hearing aid, it's no wonder there was only one report in spite of all the late-night activity that must have occurred there." "Well, that clears up the last question I had in my mind," Blake said. "I want to take this opportunity to thank you for all you have done for me, Mr. Burrows, and I know that goes for Rick as well." Blake turned to me for my concurrence, and I nodded my head in the affirmative while thinking that a simple thanks seemed so trivial for what he had done by keeping the two of us out of jail. "I was happy that I was able to do what I did for the two of you, Burrows said. But it is not yet entirely over with because you gentlemen will still have to appear at that court hearing." Turning toward Blake, he continued, "I know Mr. Cranshaw that you feel that diary or ledger is an essential tool in your profession, and I will see that it is turned over to you after we are through with it."

"I will appreciate that, Mr. Burrows. You can be certain that I'll put that book to the best use possible, not only for myself but everyone in my trade. I had a chance to take a quick look through its pages, and I was fascinated with the valuable information it contained. I plan to have it published and make it available to anyone in our business who wants to have a copy."

Burrows next turned to face me and said, "have you thought any more about you and your wife immediately vacating your house--as I told you to do?"

"Yes! I have, Sir, and my wife and I will be out of our house in a day or two at the latest. Just where we will be moving to from there, I have no idea, but we will work that out. We have two married children who will temporarily put us up until we can work things out permanently. It is a rotten shame that we have pumped so much time and money into that old house only to have it all end up this way, but at least I am not sitting in jail for all my mistakes, and that means more than anything else to me."

When I left Burrows' office with Blake, I felt that everything had worked out for the best in spite of the financial loss Elaine and I would still have to suffer. After all, we still had our health our two wonderful sons, two exceptional daughters-in-law, and my sweet little grandson, and if Blake handles his end of the agreement with Burrows, he would be able to keep his business with no bad publicity appearing in the newspapers.

When we said our goodbyes, Blake and I headed for our cars, and as I climbed behind the wheel, I waved one last farewell to him. No doubt we would meet again at that hearing that Burrows mentioned, but after it was all over and done with, I doubt that our paths would ever cross again.

My future finally looked brighter since I no longer had to deal with the specter of spending time in jail, and my life once again seemed worth living. "Whoopee!" I shouted out the window of my car as I started the engine and headed toward my home on Cobblestone Lane. I just could not wait to tell Elaine the good news that I would not be spending time in jail for all my stupid decisions I had made. The bad news about the many bodies and parts of bodies that are still buried in our yard, and about the need for us to immediately leave our house before the police begin digging up our yard, and our need to quickly find another place for to live, well those terrible developments will just have to wait until tomorrow morning before I am able to work up enough nerve to tell her about them.

~ The End ~

About the Author

After his retirement about forty years ago, author Richard J. Johnson began his hobby writing poetry, and from that beginning he drifted into a literary career writing short stories, which eventually morphed into his authoring a variety of full-length novels. In addition to his poetry and fiction novels, he has written several country-western songs, children's fables, and three biographies, including his own autobiography, which is currently a work in progress which he titled Looking Backward.

Richard was born and educated in Chicago, Illinois, during the midst of the difficult years of the Great Depression. After his Honorable Discharge from the United States army at the end of the Korean War, he spent thirty years in Chicago as an executive in the Commodities Trading, marketing and Export business. Since then, he has been living in Largo, Florida, with his wife Alice, a nonfiction book writer, who until her death in the year 2018 she had been Richard's personal editor. Richard has two children, and four grandchildren who are living in Illinois.

~ *Mortuary Mansion* ~

In this entirely different background story for of novel, author Richard J. Johnson weaves a terrifying mystery involving a 1880s mansion hiding a painful and unsettled past.

When Rick Braden and his wife Elaine buy an old, Victorian mansion, they have no idea that they were buying more than just an old house. Once having been owned by an eccentric mortician who mysteriously disappeared eight years earlier, the house hid a number of dark secrets and mysteries that slowly bubbled to the surface. As Rick continued to learn more about the mortician and the properties unhappy past history, he became caught up in a disturbing maze of frightening and macabre discoveries that threatened to destroy his marriage and ruin his life unless he could solve it.

If one has ever hesitated to delve into the history of an old house before buying it, he'd do well to read about the horrendous events that had transpired within Rick and Elaine Braden's Mortuary Mansion before committing to a purchase.

www.ingramcontent.com/pod-product-compliance
Lightning Source LLC
Chambersburg PA
CBHW061557100726
47898CB00002B/418